COMETH THE HOUR

ALSO BY JEFFREY ARCHER

THE CLIFTON CHRONICLES

Only Time Will Tell   The Sins of the Father
Best Kept Secret   Be Careful What You Wish For
Mightier than the Sword

NOVELS

Not a Penny More, Not a Penny Less
Shall We Tell the President?   Kane and Abel
The Prodigal Daughter   First Among Equals
A Matter of Honour   As the Crow Flies   Honour Among Thieves
The Fourth Estate   The Eleventh Commandment
Sons of Fortune   False Impression
The Gospel According to Judas
(with the assistance of Professor Francis J. Moloney)
A Prisoner of Birth   Paths of Glory

SHORT STORIES

A Quiver Full of Arrows   A Twist in the Tale
Twelve Red Herrings   The Collected Short Stories
To Cut a Long Story Short   Cat O' Nine Tails
And Thereby Hangs a Tale

PLAYS

Beyond Reasonable Doubt   Exclusive   The Accused

PRISON DIARIES

Volume One – Belmarsh: Hell
Volume Two – Wayland: Purgatory
Volume Three – North Sea Camp: Heaven

SCREENPLAYS

Mallory: Walking Off the Map   False Impression

JEFFREY ARCHER

THE CLIFTON CHRONICLES

VOLUME SIX

COMETH THE HOUR

MACMILLAN

First published 2016 by Macmillan
an imprint of Pan Macmillan
20 New Wharf Road, London N1 9RR
Associated companies throughout the world
www.panmacmillan.com

ISBN 978-1-4472-5219-1 HB
ISBN 978-1-4472-5220-7 TPB

1 3 5 7 9 8 6 4 2

A CIP catalogue record for this book is available from the British Library.

Typeset by Ellipsis Digital Limited, Glasgow
Printed and bound by CPI Group (UK) Ltd, Croydon, CR0 4YY

TO UMBERTO
AND
MARIA TERESA

My many thanks to the following people for their invaluable advice and research:

Simon Bainbridge, Alison Prince, Catherine Richards, Mari Roberts, Dr Nick Robins, Natasha Shekar, Susan Watt and Peter Watts.

THE BARRINGTONS

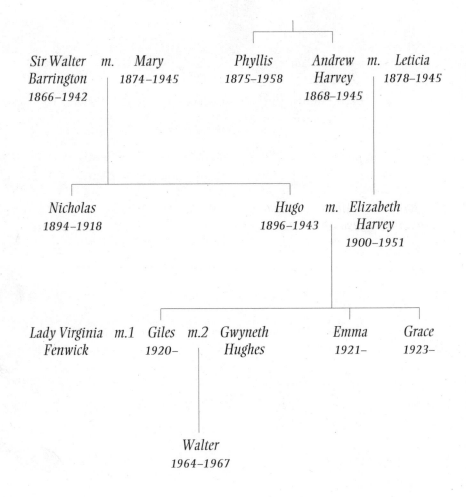

Sir Walter   m.   Mary   Phyllis   Andrew   m.   Leticia
Barrington   1874–1945   1875–1958   Harvey   1878–1945
1866–1942   1868–1945

Nicholas   Hugo   m.   Elizabeth
1894–1918   1896–1943   Harvey
                                                     1900–1951

Lady Virginia   m.1   Giles   m.2   Gwyneth   Emma   Grace
Fenwick   1920–   Hughes   1921–   1923–

Walter
1964–1967

THE CLIFTONS

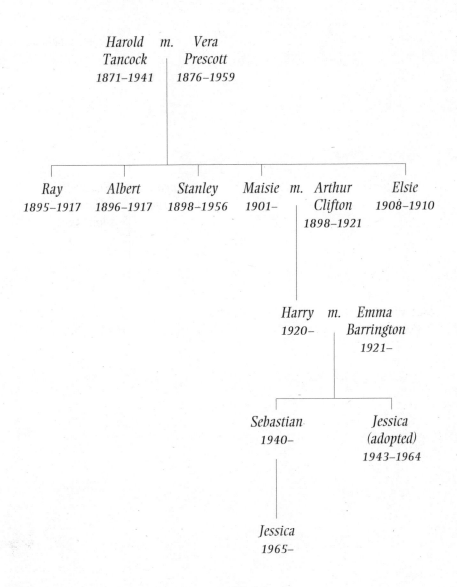

Harold *m.* Vera
Tancock   Prescott
1871–1941   1876–1959

Ray   Albert   Stanley   Maisie *m.* Arthur   Elsie
1895–1917   1896–1917   1898–1956   1901–   Clifton   1908–1910
                                           1898–1921

Harry *m.* Emma
1920–   Barrington
           1921–

Sebastian   Jessica
1940–   (adopted)
                   1943–1964

Jessica
1965–

PROLOGUE

The PA system crackled. 'Would all those involved in the Lady Virginia Fenwick versus Mrs Emma Clifton . . .'

'The jury must have reached a decision,' Trelford said, already on the move. He looked round to check that they were all following him, and bumped into someone. He apologized, but the young man didn't look back. Sebastian held open the door to court number fourteen so his mother and her silk could resume their places in the front row.

Emma was too nervous to speak and, fearing the worst, kept glancing anxiously over her shoulder at Harry, who sat in the row behind her as they waited for the jury to appear.

When Mrs Justice Lane entered the courtroom, everyone stood. She bowed before resuming her place in the high-backed red leather chair on the dais. Emma transferred her attention to the closed door beside the jury box. She didn't have to wait long before it swung open, and the bailiff reappeared followed by his twelve disciples. They took their time finding their places, treading on each other's toes like late-arriving theatregoers. The bailiff waited for them to settle before he banged his rod three times on the floor and shouted, 'Will the foreman please rise.'

The foreman rose to his full five feet four inches and looked up at the judge. Mrs Justice Lane leant forward and said, 'Have you reached a verdict on which you are all agreed?'

Emma thought her heart would stop beating as she waited for his reply.

'No, my lady.'

'Then have you reached a verdict on which you are agreed by a majority of at least ten to two?'

'We did, my lady,' said the foreman, 'but unfortunately, at the last moment one of our number changed his mind, and we have been stuck on nine votes to three for the past hour. I am not convinced that will change, so once again I am seeking your guidance as to what we should do next.'

'Do you believe you could reach a majority of ten to two, if I gave you a little more time?'

'I do, my lady, because on one particular matter, all twelve of us are in agreement.'

'And what is that?'

'If we were allowed to know the contents of the letter Major Fisher wrote to Mr Trelford before he committed suicide, we might well be able to come to a decision fairly quickly.'

Everybody's eyes were fixed on the judge, except for Lady Virginia's advocate, Sir Edward Makepeace, who was looking closely at Donald Trelford, Emma's defence counsel. Either he was a formidable poker player or he simply didn't want the jury to know what was in that letter.

Trelford rose from his place and reached into his inside pocket, only to find that the letter was no longer there. He looked across to the far side of the court, to see that Lady Virginia was smiling.

He returned her smile.

HARRY AND EMMA CLIFTON

1970–1971

1

THE JURY WAS OUT.

The judge had asked the seven men and five women to make one final effort to reach a verdict. Mrs Justice Lane instructed them to return the following morning. She was beginning to think a hung jury was the most likely outcome. The moment she stood up, everyone in the well of the court rose and bowed. The judge returned the compliment, but it wasn't until she had left the court that a babble of chatter erupted.

'Would you be kind enough to accompany me back to my chambers, Mrs Clifton,' said Donald Trelford, 'so we can discuss the contents of Major Fisher's letter, and whether they should be made public.'

Emma nodded. 'I'd like my husband and brother to join us, if that's possible, as I know Sebastian has to get back to work.'

'Of course,' said Trelford, who gathered up his papers and, without another word, led them out of the courtroom and down the wide marble staircase to the ground floor. As they stepped out on to the Strand, a pack of baying journalists, accompanied by flashing cameras, once again surrounded them, and dogged their steps as they made their way slowly across to the QC's chambers.

They were finally left alone once they'd arrived at Lincoln's Inn, an ancient square full of neat-looking town houses that were in fact chambers occupied by barristers and their clerks. Mr Trelford led them up a creaky wooden staircase to the top floor of

No.11, passing rows of names printed neatly in black on the snow-white walls.

When Emma entered Mr Trelford's office, she was surprised to see how small it was, but then there are no large offices in Lincoln's Inn, even if you are the head of chambers.

Once they were all seated, Mr Trelford looked across at the woman who sat opposite him. Mrs Clifton appeared calm and composed, even stoical, which was rare for someone who was facing the possibility of defeat and humiliation, unless . . . He unlocked the top drawer of his desk, extracted a file and handed copies of Major Fisher's letter to Mr and Mrs Clifton and Sir Giles Barrington. The original remained locked in his safe, although he was in no doubt that Lady Virginia had somehow got hold of the copy he had with him in court.

Once they had all read the letter, hand-written on House of Commons paper, Trelford said firmly, 'If you will allow me to present this as evidence in open court, Mrs Clifton, I am confident we can win the case.'

'That is out of the question,' said Emma, handing her copy back to Trelford. 'I could never allow that,' she added with the dignity of a woman who knew that the decision might not only destroy her but also hand victory to her adversary.

'Will you at least allow your husband and Sir Giles to offer their opinion?'

Giles didn't wait for Emma's permission. 'Of course it must be seen by the jury, because once it has, they'll come down unanimously in your favour and, more importantly, Virginia will never be able to show her face in public again.'

'Possibly,' said Emma calmly, 'but at the same time, you would have to withdraw your candidacy for the by-election, and this time the Prime Minister won't be offering you a seat in the House of Lords as compensation. And you can be sure of one thing,' she added. 'Your ex-wife will consider destroying your political career a far greater prize than defeating me. No, Mr Trelford,' she continued, not looking at her brother, 'this letter will remain a family secret, and we will all have to live with the consequences.'

'That's pig-headed of you, sis,' said Giles, swinging round. 'Perhaps I don't want to spend the rest of my life feeling responsible for you losing the case and having to stand down as chairman of Barrington's. And don't forget, you'll also have to pay Virginia's legal costs, not to mention whatever compensation the jury decide to award her.'

'It's a price worth paying,' said Emma.

'Pig-headed,' repeated Giles, a decibel louder. 'And I'll bet Harry agrees with me.'

They all turned towards Harry, who didn't need to read the letter a second time, as he could have repeated it word for word. However, he was torn between wishing to support his oldest friend and not wanting his wife to lose her libel case. What John Buchan once described as being 'between a rock and a hard place'.

'It's not my decision to make,' said Harry. 'But if it were my future that was hanging by a thread, I'd want Fisher's letter to be read out in court.'

'Two to one,' said Giles.

'My future isn't hanging by a thread,' said Emma. 'And you're right, my darling, the final decision is mine.' Without another word, she rose from her place, shook hands with her counsel and said, 'Thank you, Mr Trelford. We'll see you in court tomorrow morning, when the jury will decide our fate.'

Trelford bowed, and waited for the door to close behind them before he murmured to himself, 'She should have been christened Portia.'

◄○►

'How did you get hold of this?' asked Sir Edward.

Virginia smiled. Sir Edward had taught her that when facing cross-examination, if an answer doesn't help your cause, you should say nothing.

Sir Edward didn't smile. 'If the judge were to allow Mr Trelford to present this as evidence,' he said, waving the letter, 'I would no longer be confident that we will win the case. In fact I'm certain we'd lose.'

'Mrs Clifton will never allow it to be presented as evidence,' said Virginia confidently.

'How can you be sure?'

'Her brother intends to fight the by-election in Bristol Docklands caused by Major Fisher's death. If this letter were to be made public, he'd have to withdraw. It would end his political career.'

Lawyers are meant to have opinions on everything, except their clients. Not in this case. Sir Edward knew exactly how he felt about Lady Virginia, and it didn't bear repeating, in or out of court.

'If you're right, Lady Virginia,' said the elderly QC, 'and they don't offer the letter as evidence, the jury will assume it's because it doesn't assist Mrs Clifton's cause. That would undoubtedly tip the balance in your favour.'

Virginia tore up the letter and dropped the little pieces into the waste-paper basket. 'I agree with you, Sir Edward.'

◄o►

Once again, Desmond Mellor had booked a small conference room in an unfashionable hotel, where no one would recognize them.

'Lady Virginia is the odds-on favourite to win a two-horse race,' said Mellor from his place at the head of the table. 'It seems Alex Fisher ended up doing something worthwhile for a change.'

'Fisher's timing couldn't have been better,' said Adrian Sloane. 'But we'll still need to have everything in place if there's to be a smooth takeover of Barrington's Shipping.'

'Couldn't agree with you more,' said Mellor, 'which is why I've already drafted a press statement that I want you to release as soon as the verdict has been announced.'

'But all that could change if Mrs Clifton allows Fisher's letter to be read out in court.'

'I can assure you,' said Mellor, 'that letter will never see the light of day.'

'You know what's in that letter, don't you?' said Jim Knowles.

'Let's just say I'm confident that Mrs Clifton will not want the jury to see it. Which will only convince them that our beloved chairman has something to hide. Then they will surely come down in Lady Virginia's favour, and that will be an end of the matter.'

'As they're likely to reach a verdict some time tomorrow,' said Knowles, 'I've called an emergency board meeting for Monday morning at ten o'clock. There will only be two items on the agenda. The first will be to accept Mrs Clifton's resignation, followed by the appointment of Desmond as chairman of the new company.'

'And my first decision as chairman will be to appoint Jim as my deputy.' Sloane frowned. 'Then I'll ask Adrian to join the board, which will leave the City and the shareholders in no doubt that Barrington's is under new management.'

'Once the other board members have read this,' said Knowles, waving the press statement as if it were an order paper, 'it shouldn't be long before the admiral and his cronies decide they have no choice but to hand in their resignations.'

'Which I will reluctantly accept,' said Mellor, before adding, 'with a heavy heart.'

'I'm not convinced Sebastian Clifton will fall in with our plans quite that easily,' said Sloane. 'If he decides to remain on the board, it might not be quite the smooth transition you have in mind, Desmond.'

'I can't imagine Clifton will want to be a director of the Mellor Shipping Company after his mother has been publicly humiliated by Lady Virginia, not only in court, but in every national newspaper.'

'You must know what's in that letter,' repeated Knowles.

◄○►

Giles made no attempt to change his sister's mind, because he realized it would be pointless.

Among Emma's many qualities was a fierce loyalty to her family, her friends, and any cause she believed in. But the other side of that coin was a stubbornness that sometimes allowed her personal feelings to override her common sense, even if her decision could result in losing the libel case, and even having to resign as chairman of Barrington's. Giles knew, because he could be just as obstinate. It must be a family trait, he decided. Harry, on the other hand, was far more pragmatic. He would have weighed up the options and considered the alternatives long before he came to a decision. However, Giles suspected Harry was torn between supporting his wife and loyalty to his oldest friend.

As the three of them stepped back out on to Lincoln's Inn Fields, the first gas lights were being lit by the lamplighter.

'I'll see you both back at the house for dinner,' said Giles. 'I've got a couple of errands to run. And by the way, sis, thank you.'

Harry hailed a taxi, and he and his wife climbed into the back. Giles didn't move until the cab had turned the corner and was out of sight. He then headed off at a brisk pace in the direction of Fleet Street.

2

SEBASTIAN ROSE EARLY the following morning and after reading the *Financial Times* and the *Daily Telegraph* he just couldn't see how his mother could hope to win her libel trial.

The *Telegraph* pointed out to its readers that if the contents of Major Fisher's letter remained a secret, it wouldn't help Mrs Clifton's cause. The *FT* concentrated on the problems Barrington's Shipping would face should its chairman lose the case and have to resign. The company's shares had already fallen by a shilling, as many of its shareholders had clearly decided that Lady Virginia was going to be the victor. Seb felt the best his mother could hope for was a hung jury. Like everyone else, he couldn't stop wondering what was in the letter Mr Trelford wouldn't allow him to read, and which side it was more likely to help. When he had phoned his mother after returning from work, she hadn't been forthcoming on the subject. He didn't bother to ask his father.

Sebastian turned up at the bank even earlier than usual but once he'd sat down at his desk and begun trying to work his way through the morning mail, he found he couldn't concentrate. After his secretary Rachel had asked him several questions which remained unanswered, she gave up and suggested he go to court, and not return until the jury had delivered its verdict. He reluctantly agreed.

As his taxi drove out of the City and into Fleet Street, Seb spotted the bold headline on a *Daily Mail* placard and shouted 'Stop!' The cabbie swung into the kerb and threw on his brakes. Seb jumped out and ran across to the paperboy. He handed him fourpence and grabbed a copy of the paper. As he stood on the pavement reading the front page he felt conflicting emotions: delight for his mother, who would now surely win her case and be vindicated, and sadness for his uncle Giles, who had clearly sacrificed his political career to do what he considered the honourable thing, because Seb knew his mother would never have allowed that letter to be seen by anyone outside the family.

He climbed back into the cab and wondered, as he stared out of the window, how he would have reacted had he been faced with the same dilemma. Was the pre-war generation guided by a different moral compass? He wasn't in any doubt what his father would have done, or how angry his mother would be with Giles. His thoughts turned to Samantha, who had returned to America when he'd let her down. What would she have done in similar circumstances? If only she would give him a second chance, he wouldn't make the same mistake again.

Seb checked his watch. Most God-fearing people in Washington would still be asleep, so he realized he couldn't phone his daughter Jessica's headmistress, Dr Wolfe, to find out why she wanted to speak to him urgently. Was it just possible . . . ?

The taxi pulled up outside the Royal Courts of Justice in the Strand. 'That'll be four and six, gov'nor,' said the cabbie, interrupting his thoughts. Seb handed him two half-crowns.

As he stepped out of the cab, the cameras immediately began to flash. The first words he could make out above the melee of hollering hacks was, 'Have you read Major Fisher's letter?'

◄○►

When Mrs Justice Lane entered court fourteen and took her place in the high-backed chair on the raised dais, she didn't look pleased. The judge wasn't in any doubt that although she had firmly instructed the jury not to read any newspapers while the trial was taking place, the only subject they would be discussing in the jury room that morning would be the front page of the *Daily Mail*. She had no idea who was responsible for leaking Major Fisher's letter, but that didn't stop her, like everyone else in that courtroom, from having an opinion.

Although the letter had been sent to Mr Trelford, she was certain it couldn't have been him. He would never involve himself in such underhand tactics. She knew some barristers who would have turned a blind eye, even condoned such behaviour, but not Donald Trelford. He would rather lose a case than swim in such murky waters. She was equally confident that it couldn't have been Lady Virginia Fenwick, because it would only have harmed her cause. Had leaking the letter assisted her, she would have been the judge's first suspect.

Mrs Justice Lane looked down at Mrs Clifton, whose head was bowed. During the past week she'd come to admire the defendant and felt she would like to get to know her better once the trial was over. But that would not be possible. In fact, she would never speak to the woman again. If she were to do so, it would unquestionably be grounds for a retrial.

If the judge had to guess who had been responsible for leaking the letter, she would have placed a small wager on Sir Giles Barrington. But she never guessed, and never gambled. She only considered the evidence. However, the fact that Sir Giles was not in court that morning might have been considered as evidence, even if it was circumstantial.

The judge turned her attention to Sir Edward Makepeace, who never gave anything away. The eminent silk had conducted his brief quite brilliantly and his eloquent advocacy had undoubtedly assisted Lady Virginia's case. But that was before Mr Trelford had brought Major Fisher's letter to the court's attention. The judge understood why neither Emma Clifton nor Lady Virginia would want the letter to be disclosed in open court, although she was sure Mr Trelford would have pressed his client to allow him to enter it in evidence. After all, he represented Mrs Clifton, not her brother. Mrs Justice Lane assumed it wouldn't be long before the jury returned and delivered their verdict.

◄○►

When Giles phoned his constituency headquarters in Bristol that morning, he and his agent Griff Haskins didn't need to hold a long conversation. Having read the front page of the *Mail*, Griff

13

reluctantly accepted that Giles would have to withdraw his name as the Labour candidate for the forthcoming by-election in Bristol Docklands.

'It's typical Fisher,' said Giles. 'Full of half-truths, exaggeration and innuendo.'

'That doesn't surprise me,' said Griff. 'But can you prove it before polling day? Because one thing's for certain, the Tories' eve-of-poll message will be Fisher's letter, and they'll push it through every letterbox in the constituency.'

'We'd do the same, given half a chance,' admitted Giles.

'But if you could prove it was a pack of lies . . .' said Griff, refusing to give up.

'I don't have time to do that, and even if I did, I'm not sure anyone would believe me. Dead men's words are so much more powerful than those of the living.'

'Then there's only one thing left for us to do,' said Griff. 'Let's go on a bender and drown our sorrows.'

'I did that last night,' admitted Giles. 'And God knows what else.'

'Once we've chosen a new candidate,' said Griff, quickly slipping back into election mode, 'I'd like you to brief him or her, because whoever we pick will need your support and, more important, your experience.'

'That might not turn out to be an advantage in the circumstances,' Giles suggested.

'Stop being so pathetic,' said Griff. 'I've got a feeling we won't get rid of you quite that easily. The Labour Party is in your blood. And wasn't it Harold Wilson who said a week is a long time in politics?'

◄o►

When the inconspicuous door swung open, everyone in the courtroom stopped talking and turned to watch as the bailiff stood aside to allow the seven men and five women to enter the court and take their places in the jury box.

The judge waited for them to settle before she leant forward and asked the foreman, 'Have you been able to reach a verdict?'

The foreman rose slowly from his place, adjusted his spectacles, looked up at the judge and said, 'Yes, we have, my lady.'

'And is your decision unanimous?'

'It is, my lady.'

'Have you found in favour of the plaintiff, Lady Virginia Fenwick, or the defendant, Mrs Emma Clifton?'

'We have found in favour of the defendant,' said the foreman, who, having completed his task, sat back down.

Sebastian leapt to his feet and was about to cheer when he noticed that both his mother and the judge were scowling at him. He quickly resumed his seat and looked across at his father, who winked at him.

On the other side of the court sat a woman who was glaring at the jury, unable to hide her displeasure, while her counsel sat impassively with his arms folded. Once Sir Edward had read the front page of the *Daily Mail* that morning, he'd realized that his client had no chance of winning the case. He could have demanded a retrial, but in truth Sir Edward wouldn't have advised his client to put herself through a second trial with the odds tipped so heavily against her.

◄o►

Giles sat alone at the breakfast table at his home in Smith Square, his usual routine abandoned. No bowl of cornflakes, no orange juice, no boiled egg, no *Times*, no *Guardian*, just a copy of the *Daily Mail* laid out on the table in front of him.

HOUSE OF COMMONS

LONDON SW1A 0AA

12th November 1970

Dear Mr Trelford,

You will be curious to know why I have chosen to write to you, and not Sir Edward Makepeace. The answer is, quite simply, I have no doubt that both of you will act in the best interests of your clients.

Allow me to begin with Sir Edward's client, Lady Virginia Fenwick, and her fatuous claim that I was nothing more than her professional advisor, who always worked at arm's length. Nothing could be further from the truth. I have never known a client who was more hands-on, and when it came to the buying and selling of Barrington's shares, she only had one purpose in mind, namely to destroy the company, whatever the cost, along with the reputation of its chairman, Mrs Clifton.

A few days before the trial was due to open, Lady Virginia offered me a substantial sum of money to claim that she had given me carte blanche to act on her behalf, in order to leave the jury with the impression that she didn't really understand how the stock market worked. Let me assure you that in reply to Lady Virginia's question to Mrs Clifton at the AGM, 'Is it true that one of your directors sold his vast shareholding in an attempt to bring the company down?' the fact is, that is exactly what Lady Virginia herself did on no fewer than three occasions, and she nearly succeeded in bringing Barrington's down. I cannot go to my grave with that injustice on my conscience.

However, there is another injustice that is equally unpalatable, and that I am also unable to ignore. My death will cause a by-election in the constituency of Bristol Docklands, and I know that the Labour Party will consider re-selecting the former Member of Parliament, Sir Giles Barrington, as its candidate. But, like Lady Virginia, Sir Giles is hiding a secret he does not wish to share, even with his own family.

When Sir Giles recently visited East Berlin as a representative of Her Majesty's Government, he had what he later described in a press statement as a one-night stand with a Miss Karin Pengelly, his official interpreter. Later, he gave this as the reason his wife had left him. Although this was Sir Giles's second divorce on the grounds of adultery, I *do not consider that that alone should be sufficient reason for a man to withdraw from public life. But in this case, his callous treatment of the lady in question makes it impossible for me to remain silent.*

Having spoken to Miss Pengelly's father, I know for a fact that his daughter has written to Sir Giles on several occasions to let him know that not only did she lose her job as a result of their liaison, but she is now pregnant with his child. Despite this, Sir Giles has not even paid Miss Pengelly the courtesy of replying to her letters, or showing the slightest concern for her predicament. She does not complain. However, I do so on her behalf, and I am bound to ask, is this the kind of person who should be representing his constituents in the House of Commons? No doubt the citizens of Bristol will express their opinion at the ballot box.

I apologize, sir, for placing the burden of responsibility on your shoulders, but I felt I had been left with no choice.

Yours sincerely,

Alexander Fisher, Major (Rtd)

Giles stared down at his political obituary.

3

'Welcome back, chairman,' said Jim Knowles as Emma walked into the boardroom. 'Not that I doubted for a moment that you would return in triumph.'

'Hear, hear,' said Clive Anscott, pulling back Emma's chair so she could take her place at the head of the table.

'Thank you,' said Emma as she sat down. She looked around the boardroom table and smiled at her fellow directors. They all returned her smile. 'Item number one.' Emma looked down at the agenda as if nothing untoward had taken place during the past month. 'As Mr Knowles convened this meeting at short notice, the company secretary hasn't had time to distribute the minutes of the last board meeting, so I'll ask him to read them to us now.'

'Will that be necessary, given the circumstances?' asked Knowles.

'I'm not sure I'm fully aware of the circumstances, Mr Knowles,' said Emma, 'but I suspect we're about to find out.'

Philip Webster, the company secretary, rose from his place, gave a nervous cough – some things never change, thought Emma – and began to read out the minutes as if he were announcing what train was due to arrive on platform four.

'A board meeting was held at Barrington House on Tuesday 10 November 1970. All the directors were present, with the exception of Mrs Emma Clifton and Mr Sebastian Clifton, who both sent their apologies, explaining that they were otherwise engaged. Following the resignation of the deputy chairman, Mr

Desmond Mellor, and in the absence of Mrs Clifton, it was agreed by common consent that Mr Jim Knowles should take the chair. There then followed a long discussion on the future of the company and what action should be taken if Lady Virginia Fenwick were to win her libel case against Mrs Clifton. Admiral Summers placed on record that he considered nothing should be done until the outcome of the trial was known, as he was confident that the chairman would be vindicated.'

Emma smiled at the old seadog. If the ship had sunk, he would have been the last to leave the bridge.

'Mr Knowles, however, did not share the admiral's confidence, and informed the board that he had been following the case closely and had come to the reluctant conclusion that Mrs Clifton didn't have "a snowball's chance in hell", and that not only would Lady Virginia win, but the jury would award her substantial damages. Mr Knowles then reminded the board that Mrs Clifton had made it clear she would resign as chairman if that was the outcome. He went on to say that he considered it was nothing more than the board's duty to consider the company's future in that eventuality, and in particular who should replace Mrs Clifton as chairman. Mr Clive Anscott agreed with the acting chairman and proposed the name of Mr Desmond Mellor, who had recently written to him explaining why he felt he had to resign from the board. In particular, he had stated that he could not consider remaining on the board while "that woman" was in charge. There then followed a long discussion in the course of which it became clear that the directors were evenly divided on the issue of how to handle the problem. Mr Knowles, in his summing-up, concluded that two statements should be prepared, and once the result of the trial was known, the appropriate one should be released to the press.

'Admiral Summers stated that there would be no need for a press statement, because once Mrs Clifton had been exonerated, it would be business as usual. Mr Knowles pressed Admiral Summers on what he would do if Lady Virginia won the case. The admiral replied that he would resign as a member of the board, as there were no circumstances in which he would be willing to serve under Mr Mellor. Mr Knowles asked for the admiral's words to be recorded in the minutes. He then went on to outline his strategy for the company's future, should the worst happen.'

'And what was your strategy, Mr Knowles?' asked Emma innocently.

Mr Webster turned to the next page of the minutes.

'It's no longer relevant,' said Knowles, giving the chairman a warm smile. 'After all, the admiral has been proved right. But I did consider it no more than my duty to prepare the board for every eventuality.'

'The only eventuality you should have prepared for,' snorted Admiral Summers, 'was handing in your resignation before this meeting took place.'

'Don't you think that's a little rough?' chipped in Andy Dobbs. 'After all, Jim was placed in an unenviable position.'

'Loyalty is never unenviable,' said the admiral, 'unless of course you're a cad.'

Sebastian suppressed a smile. He couldn't believe anyone still used the word 'cad' in the second half of the twentieth century. He personally felt 'fucking hypocrite' would have been more appropriate, although, in truth, it wouldn't have been any more effective.

'Perhaps the company secretary should read out Mr Knowles's statement,' said Emma. 'The one that would have been released to the press, had I lost the case.'

Mr Webster extracted a single sheet of paper from his file, but before he had the chance to utter a word, Knowles rose from his place, gathered up his papers and said, 'That won't be necessary, chairman, because I tender my resignation.'

Without another word, he turned to leave, but not before Admiral Summers muttered, 'Not a moment too soon.' He then fixed his gimlet eye on the two other directors who had backed Knowles.

After a moment's hesitation, Clive Anscott and Andy Dobbs also stood up, and quietly left the room.

Emma waited for the door to close before she spoke again. 'From time to time, I may have appeared impatient with the company secretary's fastidious recording of the board's minutes. I now concede that Mr Webster has proved me wrong, and I apologize unreservedly.'

'Do you wish me to record your sentiments in the minutes, madam chairman?' asked Webster, without a hint of irony.

This time Sebastian did allow himself a smile.

4

ONCE HARRY HAD EDITED the fourth draft of Anatoly Babakov's remarkable memoirs of Stalin's Russia, all he wanted to do was take the first available flight to New York and hand the manuscript of *Uncle Joe* to his publisher, Harold Guinzburg. But there was something even more important that prevented him from leaving. An event he had no intention of missing, under any circumstances. His mother's seventieth birthday party.

Maisie had lived in a cottage on the Manor House estate since her second husband's death three years before. She remained actively involved with several local charities, and although she rarely missed her daily three-mile constitutional, it was now taking her over an hour. Harry would never forget the personal sacrifices his mother had made to ensure he won a choral scholarship to St Bede's, and with it the chance to compete with anyone, whatever their background, including his oldest friend, Giles Barrington.

Harry and Giles had first met at St Bede's over forty years ago, and seemed an unlikely pair to end up as best friends. One born in the back streets of the docks, the other in a private ward of the Bristol Royal Infirmary. One a scholar, the other a sportsman. One shy, the other extrovert. And certainly no one would have predicted that Harry would fall in love with Giles's sister, except Emma herself, who claimed she had planned the whole thing after they'd first met at Giles's twelfth birthday party.

All Harry could remember of that occasion was a skinny little object – Giles's description – sitting by the window, head down, reading a book. He had remembered the book, but not the girl.

Harry met a very different young woman seven years later, when the grammar school joined Red Maids' for a combined school production of *Romeo and Juliet*. It was Elizabeth Barrington, Emma's mother, who noticed that they continued to hold hands after they'd left the stage.

When the curtain came down on the final performance, Harry admitted to his mother that he'd fallen in love with Emma and wanted to marry her. It had come as a shock that Maisie didn't seem delighted by the prospect. Emma's father, Sir Hugo Barrington, made no attempt to hide his feelings, although his wife couldn't explain why he was so vehemently opposed to any suggestion of them marrying. Surely he couldn't be that much of a snob? But despite both their parents' misgivings, Harry and Emma became engaged just before they went up to Oxford. Both virgins, they didn't sleep together until a few weeks before the wedding.

But the wedding ended in tears because when the college chaplain said, '*If any man can show any just cause why they may not lawfully be joined together, let him now speak, or else hereafter, forever hold his peace,*' Old Jack, Harry's mentor and friend, hadn't held his peace, and told the congregation why he feared he had just cause.

When Harry learned the truth about who his father might be, he was so distraught he immediately left Oxford and joined the Merchant Navy, unaware that Emma was pregnant, or that, while he was crossing the Atlantic, England had declared war on Germany.

It wasn't until he'd been released from prison, joined the US Army and been blown up by a German landmine, that he finally returned to England to be reunited with Emma, only to discover that he had a three-year-old son called Sebastian. Even then, it was still another two years before the highest court in the land decided that Sir Hugo Barrington was not Harry's father, but, despite the ruling, both he and Emma were aware that there would always be a lingering doubt about the legitimacy of their marriage in an even higher court.

Harry and Emma had desperately wanted to have a second child, but they agreed not to tell Sebastian why they had decided against it. Harry never, even for a moment, placed any blame on his beloved mother. It hadn't taken a lot of digging to discover that Maisie had not been the first factory worker to be seduced by Hugo Barrington on the annual works outing to Weston-super-Mare.

When Sir Hugo died in tragic circumstances, Giles inherited his title along with the estates, and the natural order of things was finally restored. However, while Harry had remained happily married to Emma, Giles had been through two divorces, and his political career now seemed to be in tatters.

◄o►

Emma had spent the past three months preparing for the 'big event', and nothing had been left to chance. Harry was even made to deliver a dress rehearsal of his speech in their bedroom the night before.

Three hundred guests beat a path to the Manor House for a black-tie dinner to celebrate Maisie's seven decades, and when she made her entrance on Harry's arm, it wasn't difficult for anyone to believe that she must have been one of the great beauties of her day. Harry sat down beside her and beamed with pride, although he became more and more nervous as the moment approached when he would have to propose his mother's health. Performing in front of a packed audience no longer troubled him, but in front of his mother . . .

He began by reminding the guests of his mother's formidable achievements, against all the odds. She had progressed from being a waitress in Tilly's tea room, to manager of the city's Grand Hotel – the first woman to hold that position. After she had reluctantly retired at the age of sixty, Maisie had enrolled as a mature student at Bristol University, where she read English, and three years later graduated with honours; something Harry, Emma and Sebastian hadn't achieved – all for different reasons.

When Maisie rose to reply, the whole room rose with her. She opened her speech like a seasoned pro, not a note, not a tremor. 'Mothers always believe their sons are special,' she began, 'and I'm no exception. Of course I'm proud of Harry's many achievements, not only as a writer but, more importantly, as President of English PEN and as a campaigner on behalf of his less fortunate colleagues in other countries. In my opinion, his campaign to have Anatoly Babakov released from a Siberian gulag is a far greater achievement than topping the *New York Times* bestseller list.

'But the cleverest thing Harry has ever done was to marry Emma. Behind every great man . . .' Laughter and applause suggested that the audience agreed with Maisie. 'Emma is a remarkable woman in her own right. The first female chairman of a public company, yet she still somehow manages to be an exemplary wife and mother. And then of course there's my grandson, Sebastian, who I'm told will be the next governor of the Bank of England. That must be right, because it was Sebastian himself who told me.'

'I'd rather be chairman of Farthings Bank,' Seb whispered to his aunt Grace, who was seated beside him.

'All in good time, dear boy.'

Maisie ended with the words, 'This has been the happiest day of my life, and I count myself lucky to have so many friends.'

Harry waited for the applause to subside before he rose again to propose Maisie's long life and happiness. The assembled guests raised their glasses and continued to cheer as if it was the last night of the Proms.

'I'm sorry to see you on your own again, Seb,' said Grace once the applause had died down and everyone had resumed their seats. Seb didn't respond. Grace took her nephew's hand. 'Hasn't the time finally come for you to accept that Samantha is married and has another life?'

'I wish it was that easy,' said Seb.

'I regret not marrying and having children,' Grace confided, 'and that's something I've not even told my sister. But I do know that Emma wants so much to be a grandmother.'

'She already is,' whispered Seb. 'And like you, that's something I've never told her.'

Grace's mouth opened, but no words came out. 'Sam has a little girl called Jessica,' Seb said. 'I only needed to see her once to know she was my daughter.'

'Now I begin to understand,' said Grace. 'Is there really no chance you and Samantha can be reconciled?'

'Not while her husband is still alive.'

'I'm so sorry,' said Grace, squeezing her nephew's hand.

◄o►

Harry was delighted to see his brother-in-law chatting amiably to Griff Haskins, the Labour Party agent for Bristol Docklands. Perhaps the wily old pro could still persuade Giles to allow his name to go forward, despite Major Fisher's poisonous intervention. After all, Giles had been able to show that the letter was peppered with half-truths and was clearly an attempt to settle old scores.

'So have you finally made a decision about the by-election?' asked Harry, when Giles broke away from Griff to join him.

'I've not been left with a lot of choice,' said Giles. 'Two divorces and a dalliance with an East German woman, who may even be a Stasi spy, doesn't make one the ideal candidate.'

'But the press seem convinced that whoever the Labour candidate is, they're certain to win by a landslide while this Tory government remains so unpopular.'

'It's not the press or even the electorate who will select the candidate but a group of men and women who make up the local selection committee, and I can tell you, Harry, there's nothing more conservative than a Labour Party selection committee.'

'I'm still convinced they'd back you now they know the truth. Why don't you throw your hat in the ring and let them decide?'

'Because if they asked me how I feel about Karin, they might not like the answer.'

◄o►

'It was kind of you to include me in such an illustrious occasion, Mrs Clifton.'

'Don't be silly, Hakim, your name was one of the first on the guest list. No one could have done more for Sebastian, and after that rather unpleasant experience with Adrian Sloane I shall be forever in your debt, which I know your countrymen don't take lightly.'

'You have to know who your friends are, when you spend so much time looking over your shoulder, Mrs Clifton.'

'Emma,' she insisted. 'And tell me, Hakim, what exactly do you see when you look over your shoulder?'

'An unholy trinity that I suspect has plans to rise from the dead and once again try to take control of Farthings – and possibly even Barrington's.'

'But Mellor and Knowles are no longer on the board of Barrington's, and Sloane has forfeited whatever reputation he had in the City.'

'True, but that hasn't stopped them forming a new company.'

'Mellor Travel?'

'Which I don't imagine will be recommending that their customers book a holiday on the Barrington line.'

'We'll survive,' said Emma.

'And I presume you know that Lady Virginia Fenwick is considering selling her shares in Barrington's? My spies tell me she's a bit strapped for cash at the moment.'

'Is she indeed? Well, I wouldn't want those shares to fall into the wrong hands.'

'You needn't worry about that, Emma. I've already instructed Sebastian to pick them up the moment they come on the market. Be assured that if anyone even thinks about attacking you again, Hakim Bishara and his caravan of camels will be at your disposal.'

—◁○▷—

'It's Deakins, isn't it?' said Maisie, as a thin, middle-aged man with prematurely grey hair came up to her to pay his respects. He was dressed in the suit he must have graduated in.

'I'm flattered that you remember me, Mrs Clifton.'

'How could I ever forget? After all, Harry never stopped reminding me, "Deakins is in my class but, frankly, he's in a different class."'

'And I was proved right, Mother,' said Harry as he joined them. 'Because Deakins is now Regius Professor of Greek at Oxford. And like myself, he mysteriously disappeared during the war. But while I ended up in jail, he was at a place called Bletchley Park. Not that he ever reveals what went on behind those moss-covered walls.'

'And I doubt he ever will,' said Maisie, looking more closely at Deakins.

'"Did you ever see the picture of 'We Three'?"' said Giles, appearing by Deakins' side.

'Which play?' demanded Harry.

'*Twelfth Night*,' said Giles.

'Not bad, but which character says the words and to whom?'

'The Fool, to Sir Andrew Aguecheek.'

'And who else?'

'Sir Toby Belch.'

'Impressive,' said Deakins, smiling at his old friend, 'but for an alpha, which act and which scene?'

Giles fell silent.

'Act two, scene three,' said Harry. 'But did you spot the one-word mistake?'

'Did you *never* see,' said Maisie.

This silenced the three of them, until Emma came across and said, 'Stop showing off and circulate. This isn't an old boys' reunion.'

'She always was a bossy little thing,' said Giles as the old school chums split up and began to mingle with the other guests.

'When a woman shows some leadership,' said Maisie, 'she's immediately branded as bossy, but when a man does exactly the same thing, he's described as decisive, and a born leader.'

''Twas ever thus,' said Emma. 'Perhaps we should do something about it.'

'You already have, my dear.'

—◦—

After the last guest had departed, Harry and Emma accompanied Maisie back to her cottage.

'Thank you for the second happiest day of my life,' said Maisie.

'In your speech, mother,' Harry reminded her, 'you said it was the happiest day of your life.'

'No, not even close,' replied Maisie. 'That will always be reserved for the day I discovered you were still alive.'

5

HARRY ALWAYS ENJOYED visiting his New York publisher, but he wondered if anything would have changed now that Aaron Guinzburg had taken over from his father as chairman.

He took the lift to the seventh floor, and when the doors slid open, he found Kirsty, Harold's long-suffering former secretary, waiting for him. At least that hadn't changed. Kirsty led him briskly down the corridor to the chairman's office. A gentle tap on the door before she opened it, to allow Harry to enter another world.

Aaron, like his father before him, considered it must have been a clerical error by the Almighty that he had not been born on the other side of the Atlantic. He wore a double-breasted, pin-striped suit, probably tailored in Savile Row, a white shirt with a starched collar and a Yale tie. Harry could have been forgiven for thinking Aaron's father had been cloned. The publisher jumped up from behind his desk to greet his favourite author.

Over the years the two of them had become close friends and, once Harry had sat down in the ancient leather armchair on the other side of the publisher's large desk, he spent a few moments taking in the familiar surroundings. The oak-panelled walls were still covered in sepia photographs – Hemingway, Faulkner, Buchan, Fitzgerald, Greene, and more recently Saul Bellow. Harry couldn't help wondering if he would ever join them. He'd already outsold most of the authors on the wall, but the Guinzburgs didn't measure success by sales alone.

'Congratulations, Harry.' The same warm, sincere voice.

'Number one again. William Warwick becomes more popular with every book, and having read Babakov's revelations that Khrushchev had a hand in killing Stalin, I can't wait to publish *Uncle Joe*. I'm confident that book is also heading for the top spot, albeit on the non-fiction list.'

'It's a truly amazing work,' replied Harry. 'I only wish I'd written it.'

'I suspect you did write a great deal of it,' said Aaron, 'because I detect your hand on almost every page.' He looked questioningly at Harry.

'Every word is Anatoly's. I am nothing more than his faithful scribe.'

'If that's the way you want to play it, that's fine by me. However, your most ardent fans just might notice your style and phraseology creeping in from time to time.'

'Then we'll both have to stick to the same hymn sheet, won't we?'

'If you say so.'

'I do,' said Harry firmly.

Aaron nodded. 'I've drawn up a contract for *Uncle Joe* which will require Mrs Babakova's signature as her husband's representative. I'm willing to offer her a one-hundred-thousand-dollar advance on signing, against a ten per cent royalty.'

'How many copies do you think you'll sell?'

'A million, possibly more.'

'Then I want the royalty to rise to twelve and a half per cent after the first hundred thousand sales, and fifteen per cent once you've sold a quarter of a million.'

'I've never given such good terms for a first book,' protested Aaron.

'This isn't a first book, it's a last book, a one-off, a one and only book.'

'I accept your terms,' said Aaron, 'but on one condition.' Harry waited. 'When the book is published, you'll do an author tour, because the public will be fascinated to know how you managed to smuggle the manuscript out of the Soviet Union.'

Harry nodded, and the two men stood up and shook hands.

Something else Aaron had in common with his father: a hand-shake was quite enough to show that the deal had been closed. In a Guinzburg contract, there were no get-out clauses.

'And while you're over here, I need to finalize a new three-book contract for the William Warwick series.'

'On the same terms as Babakov,' said Harry.

'Why, will he be writing those as well?'

Both men laughed, before shaking hands a second time.

'Who's publishing *Uncle Joe* in England?' asked Aaron, as he sat back down.

'Billy Collins. We closed the deal last week.'

'Same terms?'

'Wouldn't you like to know? Mind you, when I get home he's certain to ask me the same question.'

'And he'll get the same reply, no doubt. Now, Harry, your timing couldn't be better, because I need to speak to you on another subject in the strictest confidence.'

Harry leaned back in his chair.

'I've always wanted Viking to merge with an appropriate paperback house, so I don't have to make separate deals the whole time. Several other companies have already gone down that road, as I'm sure you know.'

'But if I remember correctly, your father was always against the idea. He feared it would stifle his independence.'

'And he still feels that way. But he's no longer chairman, and I've decided it's time to move up a gear. I've recently been offered an attractive deal by Rex Mulberry of Mulberry House.'

'"The old order changeth, yielding place to new".'

'Remind me.'

'Tennyson, "Morte d'Arthur".'

'So, are you prepared to yield to new?'

'Although I don't know Rex Mulberry, I'll happily back your judgement,' said Harry.

'Good. Then I'll have both contracts drawn up immediately. If you can get Mrs Babakova to sign hers, I'll have yours ready by the time you get back from Pittsburgh.'

'She'll probably resist taking an advance payment, or even

royalties, so I'll just have to remind her that the last thing Anatoly said before they dragged him off was "Make sure Yelena doesn't have to spend the rest of her life in a different kind of prison."'

'That should do the trick.'

'Possibly. But I know she still considers it nothing less than her duty to suffer the same deprivation her husband is experiencing.'

'Then you must explain to her that we can't publish the book if she doesn't sign the contract.'

'She will sign the contract, but only because she wants the whole world to know the truth about Joseph Stalin. I'm not convinced she'll ever cash the cheque.'

'Try deploying that irresistible Clifton charm.' Aaron rose from behind his desk. 'Lunch?'

'The Yale Club?'

'Certainly not. Pa still eats there every day, and I don't want him to find out what I'm up to.'

◄○►

Harry rarely read the business section of any newspaper, but today he made an exception. The *New York Times* had devoted half a page to the merger between the Viking Press and Mulberry House, alongside a photograph of Aaron shaking hands with Rex Mulberry.

Viking would have 34 per cent of the new company, while Mulberry, a far bigger house, would control 66 per cent. When the *Times* asked Aaron how his father felt about the deal, he simply replied, 'Curtis Mulberry and my father have been close friends for many years. I am delighted to have formed a partnership with his son, and look forward to an equally long and fruitful relationship.'

'Hear, hear, to that,' said Harry, as a dining car waiter poured him a second cup of coffee. He glanced out of the window to see the skyscrapers of Manhattan becoming smaller and smaller as the train continued on its journey to Pittsburgh.

Harry sat back, closed his eyes, and thought about his meeting with Yelena Babakova. He just hoped she would fall in with her husband's wishes. He tried to recall Anatoly's exact words.

—◦—

Aaron Guinzburg had risen early, excited by the prospect of his first day as deputy chairman of the new company.

'Viking Mulberry,' he murmured into the shaving mirror. He liked the billing.

His first meeting that day was scheduled for twelve o'clock, when Harry would report back on his visit with Mrs Babakova. He planned to publish *Uncle Joe* in April, and was delighted that Harry had agreed to go on tour. After a light breakfast – toast and Oxford marmalade, a three-and-a-half-minute boiled egg and a cup of Earl Grey tea – Aaron read the article in the *New York Times* for a second time. He felt it was a fair reflection of his agreement with Rex Mulberry and was pleased to see his new partner repeating something he'd said to Aaron many times: *I am proud to be joining a house with such a fine literary tradition.*

As it was a clear, crisp morning, Aaron decided to walk to work and savour the thought of starting life anew. He wondered how long it would be before his father admitted he'd made the right decision if the company were to play in the major leagues. He crossed the road on to Seventh Avenue, his smile broadening with each step he took. As he walked towards the familiar build-ing he noticed two smartly dressed doormen standing at the entrance. Not an expense his father would have approved of. One of the men stepped forward and saluted.

'Good morning, Mr Guinzburg.' Aaron was impressed that they knew his name. 'We have been instructed, sir, not to allow you to enter the building.'

Aaron was struck dumb. 'There must be some mistake,' he eventually managed. 'I'm deputy chairman of the company.'

'I'm sorry, sir, but those are our instructions,' said the second guard, stepping forward to block his path.

'There must be some mistake,' repeated Aaron.

'There is no mistake, sir. Our instructions were clear. If you attempt to enter the building, we are to prevent you from doing so.'

Aaron hesitated for a moment before taking a pace back. He stared up at the newly minted sign declaring *Viking Mulberry*, then attempted to enter the building once again, but neither guard budged an inch. Reluctantly, he turned away and hailed a cab, giving the driver his home address. There must be a simple explanation, he kept telling himself as the taxi headed towards 67th Street.

Once he was back in his apartment, Aaron picked up the phone and dialled a number he didn't need to look up.

'Good morning, Viking Mulberry, how can I help you?'

'Rex Mulberry.'

'Who's calling please?'

'Aaron Guinzburg.' He heard a click, and a moment later another voice said, 'Chairman's office.'

'This is Aaron Guinzburg. Put me through to Rex.'

'Mr Mulberry is in a meeting.'

'Then get him out of the meeting,' said Aaron, finally losing his temper.

Another click. He'd been cut off. He dialled the number again, but this time he didn't get any further than the switchboard. Collapsing into the nearest chair, he tried to gather his thoughts. It was some time before he picked up the phone again.

'Friedman, Friedman and Yablon,' announced a voice.

'This is Aaron Guinzburg. I need to speak to Leonard Friedman.' He was immediately put through to the senior partner. Aaron took his time explaining what had happened when he'd turned up at his office that morning, and the result of his two subsequent phone calls.

'So your father was right all along.'

'What do you mean?'

'A handshake was always good enough for Curtis Mulberry, but when you deal with his son Rex, just make sure you read the small print.'

'Are you suggesting Mulberry's got right on his side?'

'Certainly not,' said Friedman, 'just the law. As long as he controls sixty-six per cent of the company's stock, he can call the shots. We did warn you at the time of the consequences of being a minority shareholder, but you were convinced it wouldn't be a problem. Although I have to admit, even I'm shocked by the speed with which Mulberry has taken advantage of his position.'

Once Friedman had taken his client though the relevant details of the contract, Aaron wished he'd read Law at Harvard and not History at Yale. 'Still,' said the lawyer, 'we did manage to insert clause 19A, which Mulberry will surely now live to regret.'

'Why is clause 19A so important?'

After Friedman had explained the significance of the get-out clause in great detail, Aaron put the phone down and walked across to the drinks cabinet. He poured himself a whisky – before twelve o'clock for the first time in his life. Twelve o'clock, the time of his appointment with Harry. He glanced at his watch: 11.38. He put down his drink, and ran out of the apartment.

He cursed the slow lift as it trundled down to the ground floor, where he hurled back the grille and ran out on to the street. He hailed a yellow cab, never a problem on Fifth Avenue, but once he hit Third, Aaron was faced with the inevitable gridlock. Light after light seemed to turn red just as the cab reached the front of the line. When they ground to a halt at the next set of lights, Aaron handed the driver a five-dollar bill and leapt out. He ran the last two blocks, dodging in and out of the traffic, horns blaring, as he tried to stay on the move.

The two guards were still stationed outside the building, almost as if they were expecting him to return. Aaron checked his watch on the run: four minutes to twelve. He prayed that Harry would be late. Harry was never late. Then he saw him about a hundred yards away, striding in his direction, but he arrived at the front of the building just moments before Aaron. The guards stood aside and allowed him to pass. Someone else they were expecting.

'Harry! Harry!' shouted Aaron, now only a few strides from the front door, but Harry had already entered the building. 'Harry!' Aaron screamed again as he reached the entrance, but the two guards marched forward and blocked his path just as Harry stepped into a lift.

—◦—

When the lift door opened, Harry was surprised not to find Kirsty waiting for him. Funny how you get used to something, he thought, even take it for granted. He made his way across to the reception desk and told an unfamiliar young woman his name. 'I have an appointment with Aaron Guinzburg.'

She checked her day sheet. 'Yes, you're down to see the chairman at twelve, Mr Clifton. You'll find him in Mr Guinzburg's old office.'

'His old office?' said Harry, unable to mask his surprise.

'Yes, the room at the far end of the corridor.'

'I know where it is,' Harry replied, before heading off towards Aaron's office. He knocked on the door and waited.

'Come in,' said a voice he didn't recognize.

Harry opened the door and immediately assumed he'd walked into the wrong room. The walls had been stripped of their magnificent oak panelling and the distinguished authors' photographs replaced by a set of gaudy prints of SoHo. A man he'd never met before, but whom he recognized from his photograph in that morning's *New York Times*, rose from behind a trestle table and thrust out a hand.

'Rex Mulberry. Delighted to meet you at last, Harry.'

'Good morning, Mr Mulberry,' said Harry. 'I have an appointment with my publisher, Aaron Guinzburg.'

'I'm afraid Aaron doesn't work here any longer,' said Mulberry. 'I'm the chairman of the new company, and the board decided that the time had come for Viking to make some radical changes. But, let me assure you, I'm a great admirer of your work.'

'So you're a fan of Wilfred Warwick, are you?' said Harry.

'Yes, I'm a huge fan of Wilfred's. Have a seat.' Harry reluctantly sat down opposite the new chairman. 'I've just been over your latest contract, which I'm sure you'll agree is generous by normal publishing standards.'

'I have only ever been published by Viking, so I've nothing to compare it with.'

'And of course we will honour Aaron's most recent contract in the Wilfred Warwick series, as well as the one for *Uncle Joe*.'

Harry tried to think what Sebastian would have done in these circumstances. He was aware that the contract for *Uncle Joe* was in his inside pocket and, after some considerable persuasion, had been signed by Yelena Babakova.

'Aaron had agreed to prepare a new three-book contract, which I had intended to go over with him today,' he said, playing for time.

'Yes, I have it here,' said Mulberry. 'There are a few minor adjustments, none of them of any real significance,' he added as he pushed the contract across the table.

Harry turned to the last page, to find Rex Mulberry's signature already on the dotted line. He took out his fountain pen – a gift from Aaron – removed the top and stared down at the words, *On behalf of the author*. He hesitated, before saying the first thing that came into his head.

'I need to go to the lavatory. I came straight from Grand Central as I didn't want to be late.' Mulberry forced a smile, as Harry placed the elegant Parker on the table beside the contract. 'I won't be long,' Harry added as he rose from his seat and casually left the room.

Harry closed the door behind him, walked quickly down the corridor, past the reception desk and didn't stop until he reached the lobby, where he stepped inside the first available lift. When the doors opened again on the ground floor, he joined the bustle of office workers who were making their way out of the building for their lunch break. He glanced at the two guards, but they didn't give him a second look as he passed them. They seemed to be focused on someone standing sentinel-like on the opposite side of the street. Harry turned his back on Aaron and hailed a cab.

'Where to?'

'I'm not sure yet,' said Harry, 'but could you drive across to the far corner and pick up the gentleman who's standing there.'

The cabbie came to a halt on the other side of the street. Harry wound down the window. 'Jump in,' he shouted.

Aaron looked suspiciously inside, but when he saw Harry, he quickly joined him in the back.

'Did you sign the contract?' were his first words.

'No, I did not.'

'What about the Babakov contract?'

'I still have it,' said Harry, touching the inside pocket of his jacket.

'Then we just may be in the clear.'

'Not yet. I persuaded Mrs Babakova that she should cash Viking's cheque for $100,000.'

'Help,' said Aaron.

'Where to?' demanded the cabbie again.

'Grand Central Station,' said Harry.

'Can't you just phone her?' said Aaron.

'She doesn't have a phone.'

6

'IT'S THE FIRST TIME I've ever known you do something dishonest,' said Emma, as she poured herself a second cup of coffee.

'But surely it's morally defensible,' said Harry. 'After all, the end justified the means.'

'Even that's questionable. Don't forget that Mrs Babakova had already signed the contract and accepted the cheque in payment.'

'But she hadn't cashed it and, in any case, she was under the impression Anatoly's book would be published by Viking.'

'And it still would have been.'

'But not by Aaron Guinzburg, with whom she made the original deal.'

'A High Court judge might consider that an interesting legal dilemma. And who's going to publish William Warwick, now you're no longer with Viking?'

'The Guinzburg Press. Anatoly and I will be the company's first authors, and Aaron will also be presenting me with a new fountain pen.'

'A new pen?'

'It's a long story, which I'll save for when you get back from your board meeting,' said Harry, breaking into the top of his egg.

'I'm still a little surprised that Mulberry hadn't considered the possibility of Aaron setting up his own company and didn't include a clause in the merger document preventing him from poaching any of Viking's authors.'

'I'm sure he did consider it, but if he'd inserted such a clause, Aaron's lawyers would have realized immediately what he was up to.'

'Perhaps he doubted that Aaron would have the resources to set up a new publishing company.'

'Well, he got that wrong,' said Harry. 'Aaron's already had several offers for his shares in Viking Mulberry, including one from Rex Mulberry himself, who clearly doesn't want any of his rivals to get their hands on Aaron's thirty-four per cent stake.'

'What goes around . . .' said Emma. Harry smiled as he sprinkled a little salt on his egg. 'But however much you like Aaron,' continued Emma, 'after his obvious lack of judgement when it came to Mulberry, are you sure he's the right man to be your American publisher? If you were to sign a three-book contract, and then—'

'I admit I had my doubts,' said Harry, 'but I've been reassured by the fact that Aaron's father has agreed to return as president of the new company.'

'Is that a hands-on job?'

'Harold Guinzburg doesn't do hands-off.'

—◦—

'Item number one,' declared Emma in her crisp, clear chairman's voice. 'The latest update on the building of our second luxury liner, the MV *Balmoral*.' She glanced towards the group's new chief executive, Eric Hurst, who was looking down at an already open file.

'The board will be pleased to learn,' he said, 'that despite a few unavoidable hold-ups, which is not unusual in such a major undertaking, we are still well on course to launch the new ship in September. Equally important, we remain within our forecast budget, having anticipated most of the issues that so bedevilled the construction of the *Buckingham*.'

'With one or two notable exceptions,' said Admiral Summers.

'You're right, admiral,' said Hurst. 'I confess that I didn't foresee the need for a second cocktail bar on the upper deck.'

'Passengers are allowed to drink on deck?' said the admiral.

'I'm afraid so,' said Emma, suppressing a grin. 'But it does mean extra money in our coffers.' The admiral didn't attempt to suppress a snort.

'Although I still need to keep a watchful eye on the timing of the launch,' continued Hurst, 'it shouldn't be too long before we can announce the first booking period for the *Balmoral*.'

'I wonder if we've bitten off more than we can chew?' chipped in Peter Maynard.

'I think that's the finance director's department, not mine,' said Hurst.

'It most certainly is,' said Michael Carrick, coming in on cue. 'The company's overall position,' he said, looking down at his pocket calculator, which the admiral had already dismissed as a new-fangled machine, 'is that our turnover is three per cent up on this time last year, and that's despite a substantial loan from Barclays to make sure that we don't miss any payments during the building phase.'

'How substantial?' demanded Maynard.

'Two million,' said Carrick, not needing to check the figure.

'Can we afford to service such a large overdraft?'

'Yes, Mr Maynard, but only because our cash flow is also up on last year, along with increased bookings on the *Buckingham*. It seems the current generation of seventy-year-olds are refusing to die, and have rather taken to the idea of an annual cruise. So much so that we have recently introduced a loyalty programme for customers who've taken a holiday with us on more than three occasions.'

'And what does membership entitle them to?' asked Maurice Brasher, Barclays' representative on the board.

'Twenty per cent off the price of any voyage as long as it's booked more than a year in advance. It encourages our regulars to look upon the *Buckingham* as their second home.'

'What if they die before the year is up?' asked Maynard.

'They get every penny back,' said Emma. 'Barrington's is in the luxury liner business, Mr Maynard, we're not undertakers.'

'But can we still make a profit,' pressed Brasher, 'if we give so many of our customers a twenty per cent discount?'

'Yes,' said Carrick, 'there's still a further ten per cent leeway, and don't forget, once they're on board, they spend money in our shops and bars, as well as the twenty-four-hour casino.'

'Something else I don't approve of,' muttered the admiral.

'What's our current occupancy rate?' asked Maynard.

'Eighty-one per cent over the past twelve months, often a hundred per cent on the upper decks, which is why we're building more staterooms on the *Balmoral*.'

'And what's break-even?'

'Sixty-eight per cent,' said Carrick.

'Very satisfactory,' said Brasher.

'While I agree with you, Mr Brasher, we can't afford to relax,' said Emma. 'Union-Castle are planning to convert the *Reina del Mar* into a luxury liner, and Cunard and P&O have both recently begun construction on ships that will carry over two thousand passengers.'

There followed a long silence, while members of the board tried to take this information in.

'Is New York still our most lucrative run?' asked Maynard, who hadn't appeared particularly interested in the other directors' questions.

'Yes,' said Hurst, 'but the Baltic cruise is also proving popular – Southampton to Leningrad, taking in Copenhagen, Oslo, Stockholm and Helsinki.'

'But now we're launching a second ship and, considering how many other liners are already on the high seas,' continued Maynard, 'do you anticipate any staffing problems?'

Emma was puzzled by the number of questions Maynard was asking. She was beginning to suspect him of having his own agenda.

'That shouldn't be a problem,' said Captain Turnbull, who hadn't spoken until then. 'Barrington's is a popular line to work for, especially with the Filipinos. They remain on board for eleven months, never leaving the ship and rarely spending a thing.'

'What about the twelfth month?' asked Sebastian.

'That's when they go home and hand over their hard-earned

cash to their wives and families. Then they report back for duty twenty-eight days later.'

'Poor blighters,' said Brasher.

'In truth, Mr Brasher,' said Turnbull, 'the Filipinos are the happiest members of my crew. They tell me they'd far rather be with the Barrington line than spending twelve months out of work in Manila.'

'What about the officers? Any problems there, captain?'

'At least six qualified men apply for every available job, admiral.'

'Any women?' asked Emma.

'Yes, we now have our first woman on the bridge,' said Turnbull. 'Clare Thompson. She's the first mate, and proving damned effective.'

'What has the world come to?' said the admiral. 'Let's hope I don't live to see a woman prime minister.'

'Let's hope you do,' said the chairman, gently chiding her favourite director, 'because the world has moved on, and perhaps we should too.' Emma looked at her watch. 'Any other business?'

The company secretary coughed, a sign that he had something he needed to tell the board.

'Mr Webster,' said Emma, sitting back, aware that he was not a man to be hurried.

'I feel I should inform the board that Lady Virginia Fenwick has disposed of her seven and a half per cent shareholding in the company.'

'But I thought—' began Emma.

'And the shares have been registered at Companies House in the name of the new owner.'

'But I thought—' repeated Emma, looking directly at her son.

'It must have been a private transaction,' said Sebastian. 'I can assure you her shares never came up for sale on the open market. If they had, my broker would have picked them up immediately on behalf of Farthings, and Hakim Bishara would have joined the board as the bank's representative.'

Everybody in the room began to speak at once. They were all

asking the same question. 'If Bishara didn't buy the shares, who did?'

The company secretary waited for the board to settle before he answered their collective cry. 'Mr Desmond Mellor.'

There was immediate uproar, which was silenced only by Sebastian's curt interjection. 'I have a feeling Mellor won't be returning as a member of the board. It would be far too obvious, and wouldn't suit his purpose.' Emma looked relieved. 'No, I think he'll select someone else to represent him. Someone who's never sat on the board before.'

Every eye was now fixed on Sebastian. But it was the admiral who asked, 'And who do you think that might be?'

'Adrian Sloane.'

7

A BLACK STRETCH limousine was parked outside the Sherry-Netherland. A smartly dressed chauffeur opened the back door as Harry walked out of the hotel. He climbed in and sank on to the back seat, ignoring the morning papers stacked neatly on the cocktail bar opposite him. Who drank at that time in the morning, Harry wondered. He closed his eyes and tried to concentrate.

Harry had told Aaron Guinzburg several times that he didn't need a stretch limo to take him on the short journey from the hotel to the studio, a yellow cab would have been just fine.

'It's all part of the service the *Today* programme gives its headline guests.'

Harry gave in, although he knew Emma would not have approved. 'An extravagant waste of the company's money,' as NBC would have discovered, if Emma had been its chairman.

Harry recalled the first time he'd appeared on an American breakfast radio show, more than twenty years before, when he had been promoting his debut William Warwick novel. It had been a fiasco. His already brief spot was cut short when the previous two guests, Mel Blanc and Clark Gable, both overran their allotted time, and when it was finally his turn in front of the microphone, Harry had forgotten to mention the title of his book, and it quickly became clear that his host, Matt Jacobs, hadn't read it. Two decades later, and he accepted that was par for the course.

Harry was determined not to suffer the same fate with *Uncle Joe*, which the *New York Times* had already described as the most anticipated book of the season. All three morning shows had offered him their highest rated spot, at 7.24 a.m. Six minutes didn't sound a long time, but in television terms, only ex-presidents and Oscar winners could take it for granted. As Aaron pointed out, 'Just think how much we'd have to pay for a six-minute peak-time advertisement.'

The limo came to a halt outside the glass-fronted studio on Columbus Avenue. A smartly dressed young woman was standing on the sidewalk waiting for him.

'Good morning, Harry,' she said. 'My name is Anne and I'm your special assistant. I'll take you straight through to make-up.'

'Thank you,' said Harry, who still hadn't got used to people he'd never met calling him by his Christian name.

'As you know, you're on at 7.24 for six minutes, and your interviewer will be Matt Jacobs.'

Harry groaned. Would he have read the book this time? 'Great,' he said.

Harry hated make-up. He'd showered and shaved only an hour before, but it was a ritual he knew he couldn't refuse, despite insisting, 'As little as possible, please.' After a liberal amount of cream was applied to his cheeks, and powder dabbed on his forehead and chin, the make-up girl asked, 'Shall I remove those stray grey hairs?'

'Certainly not!' said Harry. She looked disappointed, and satisfied herself with trimming his eyebrows.

Once he'd escaped, Anne escorted him through to the green room, where he sat quietly in a corner while a B-movie star, whose name he didn't catch, was telling an attentive audience what it was like to share a scene with Paul Newman. At 7.20, the door swung open and Anne reappeared to carry out her most important function of the day. 'Time to take you through to the studio, Harry.'

Harry jumped up and followed her down a long corridor. He was far too nervous to speak, which she was clearly accustomed to. She stopped outside a closed door on which a notice declared: DO NOT ENTER WHEN RED LIGHT IS ON. When the light turned green, she heaved open the heavy door and led him into a studio the size of an aircraft hangar, crammed with arc lights and cameras, with technicians and floor staff running in every direction during the ad break. Harry smiled at the studio audience, who from the blank expressions on their faces clearly didn't have a clue who he was. He turned his attention to the host, Matt Jacobs, who was seated on a sofa looking like a spider waiting for a passing fly. A studio assistant handed him a copy of *Uncle Joe* while a second powdered his nose. Jacobs glanced at the cover before turning to the back flap to check the author's biography. He finally turned to the front flap and read the synopsis of the book. This time Harry was prepared. While he waited to be taken to his place, he studied his inquisitor carefully. Jacobs didn't seem to have aged in the past twenty years, although Harry suspected the make-up girl had been allowed to use her considerable skills to defy the passage of time. Or had he succumbed to a facelift?

The studio manager invited Harry to join Jacobs on the sofa. He was graced with a 'Good morning, Mr Clifton,' but then his host became distracted by a note yet another assistant placed in front of him.

'Sixty seconds to transmission,' said a voice from somewhere beyond the arc lights.

'Where will it be?' asked Jacobs.

'The page will come up on camera two,' said the floor manager.

'Thirty seconds.'

This was the moment when Harry always wanted to get up and leave the studio. *Uncle Joe, Uncle Joe, Uncle Joe*, he repeated under his breath. Don't forget to keep mentioning the title of the book, Aaron had reminded him, because it's not your name on the cover.

'Ten seconds.'

Harry took a sip of water as a hand appeared in front of his face, displaying five splayed fingers.

'Five, four . . .'

Jacobs dropped his notes on the floor.

'Three, two . . .'

And looked straight into the camera.

'One.' The hand disappeared.

'Welcome back,' said Jacobs, reading directly from the tele-prompter. 'My next guest is the crime novelist Harry Clifton, but today we're not discussing one of his works, but a book he smuggled out of the Soviet Union.' Jacobs held up his copy of *Uncle Joe*, which filled the whole screen.

Good start, thought Harry.

'But let me make it clear,' continued Jacobs, 'that it was not the book itself that Mr Clifton smuggled out, just the words. He says that while he was locked up in a Russian prison cell with Anatoly Babakov, *Uncle Joe*'s author, he learnt the entire manuscript by heart in four days, and after he had been released he wrote it out word for word. Some people might find this hard to believe,' said Jacobs, before turning to face Harry for the first time, and from the incredulous look on his face, he was clearly one of them.

'Let me try and understand what you're suggesting, Mr Clifton. You shared a cell with the distinguished author Anatoly Babakov, a man you'd never met before.'

Harry nodded, as the camera swung on to him.

'During the next four days he recited the entire contents of his banned book, *Uncle Joe*, an account of the eleven years he worked in the Kremlin as Joseph Stalin's interpreter.'

'That is correct,' said Harry.

'So when you were released from prison, four days later, like a professional actor, you knew your part off by heart.'

Harry remained silent, as it was now clear that Jacobs had his own agenda.

'I'm sure you'll agree, Mr Clifton, that no actor, however seasoned, could be expected to remember forty-eight thousand words after only four days of rehearsal.'

'I am not an actor,' said Harry.

'Forgive me,' said Jacobs, not looking as if he wanted to be forgiven, 'but I suspect that you are a very accomplished actor who has invented this whole story for no other purpose than to promote your latest book. If that's not the case, perhaps you'll allow me to put your claim to the test.'

Without waiting for Harry to respond, Jacobs turned to another camera and, holding up the book, said, 'If your story is to be believed, Mr Clifton, you shouldn't have any difficulty in reciting whichever page I select from Mr Babakov's book.' Harry frowned as Jacobs added, 'I'm going to turn to a page at random, which will appear on the screen so that all our viewers can see it. You will be the one person who won't be able to.'

Harry's heart reached a thumping pace, because he hadn't read *Uncle Joe* since he'd handed in the manuscript to Aaron Guinzberg some time ago.

'But first,' said Jacobs turning back to face his guest, 'let me ask you to confirm that we have never met before.'

'Just once,' Harry replied. 'You interviewed me on your radio programme twenty years ago, but you've clearly forgotten.'

Jacobs looked flustered, but quickly recovered. 'Then let's hope your memory is better than mine,' he said, not making any attempt to hide his sarcasm. He picked up the book, and flicked through several pages before stopping at random. 'I'm going to read out the first line of page 127,' he continued, 'and then we'll see if you can complete the rest of the page.' Harry began to concentrate. '*One of the many subjects no one ever dared to raise with Stalin—*'

Harry tried to gather his thoughts, and as the seconds passed, the audience began murmuring among themselves, while Jacobs' smile became broader. He was just about to speak again, when Harry said, '*One of the many subjects no one ever dared to raise with Stalin was the role he played during the siege of Moscow, when the outcome of the Second World War still hung in the balance. Did he, like most of the government ministers and their officials, beat a hasty retreat to Kuibyshev on the Volga, or did he, as he claimed, refuse to leave the capital and remain in the Kremlin, personally organizing the defence of the city? His version became legend, part of the official Soviet history, although several people saw him on the platform moments before the train departed for Kuibyshev, and there are no reliable reports of anyone seeing him in Moscow again until the Russian army had driven the enemy from the gates of the city. Few of those who expressed any doubts about Stalin's version lived to tell the tale.'* Harry looked into the camera and continued to deliver the next twenty-two lines without hesitation.

He knew he'd come to the end of the page when the studio audience burst into applause. Jacobs took a little longer to recover his composure, but eventually managed, 'I might even read this book myself,' with an ingratiating smile.

'That would make a change,' said Harry, immediately regretting his words, although some of the studio audience laughed and applauded even louder, while others just gasped.

Jacobs turned to face the camera. 'We'll take a short break, and return after these messages.'

When the green light came on, Jacobs yanked off his lapel mic, jumped up from the sofa and marched across to the floor manager. 'Get him off the set now!'

'But he's got another three minutes,' said the floor manager, checking his clipboard.

'I don't give a fuck. Wheel on the next guest.'

'Do you really want to interview Troy Donahue for six minutes?'

'Anyone but that guy,' he said, gesturing in Harry's direction before beckoning Anne. 'Get him off the set now,' he repeated.

Anne hurried across to the sofa. 'Will you please come with me, Mr Clifton,' she said, not sounding as if it was a request. She led Harry out of the studio and didn't stop until they were back on the sidewalk, where she abandoned her headline guest, although there was no sign of a chauffeur waiting by an open limo door.

Harry hailed a cab and on the way back to the Sherry-Netherland he checked page 127 of his copy of *Uncle Joe*. Had he left out the word 'hasty'? He couldn't be sure. He went straight up to his room, removed his make-up and took his second shower of the morning. He didn't know if it was the huge arc lights or Jacobs' hectoring manner that had caused him to sweat so profusely.

Once he'd put on a clean shirt and his other suit, Harry took the lift to the mezzanine floor. When he walked into the dining room, he was surprised how many people gave him a second look. He ordered breakfast, but didn't open the *New York Times*, as he thought about how angry the Guinzburgs would be after he'd humiliated one of breakfast TV's leading presenters. He was due to meet them in Aaron's office at nine to discuss the details of his national tour, but Harry assumed he'd now be heading back to Heathrow on the next available flight.

Harry signed the check, and decided to walk to Aaron's new office on Lexington Avenue. He left the Sherry-Netherland just after 8.40, and by the time he reached Lexington, he was just about ready to face the headmaster's wrath. He took the elevator to the third floor, and when the doors opened, Kirsty was standing there. She said only 'Good morning, Mr Clifton' before leading him through to the chairman's office.

She knocked and opened the door to reveal a carbon copy of the office Harry had such fond memories of. Hemingway, Fitzgerald, Greene and Buchan all stared down at him from the oak-panelled walls. Harry stepped inside to see father and son seated opposite each other at the partners' desk. The moment they saw him they stood and applauded.

'Hail the conquering hero,' said Aaron.

'But I thought you'd be—'

'Ecstatic,' said Harold Guinzburg, slapping him on the back. 'The phone's been ringing off the hook for the past hour, and you're set to be on every major talk show across the country. But be warned, everyone's going to pick a different page after your triumph this morning.'

'But what about Jacobs?'

'He's turned you into an overnight star. You may never be invited back on to his show, but all the other networks are chasing you.'

◄○►

Harry spent the next seven days flying from airport to airport: Boston, Washington, Dallas, Chicago, San Francisco and Los Angeles. He was rushed from studio to studio in an attempt to fulfil every commitment on his revised schedule.

Whenever he was in the air, in the back of a limousine or in a green room, even in bed, he read and re-read *Uncle Joe*, astounding audiences right across the country with his prodigious memory.

By the time he touched down in Los Angeles to be Johnny Carson's headline guest on *The Tonight Show*, journalists and television crews were turning up at the airports, hoping to grab an interview with him, even on the move. Exhausted, Harry finally returned on the red-eye to New York, only to be whisked off in yet another limo to his publisher's office on Lexington Avenue.

When Kirsty opened the door of the chairman's office, Harold and Aaron Guinzburg were holding up a copy of the *New York Times* bestseller list. Harry leapt in the air when he saw that *Uncle Joe* had hit the top spot.

'How I wish Anatoly could share this moment.'

'You're looking at the wrong list,' said Aaron.

Harry looked across to the other side of the page to see that *William Warwick and the Smoking Gun* headed the fiction list.

'This is a first even for me,' said Harold as he opened a bottle of champagne. 'Number one in fiction and non-fiction on the same day.'

Harry turned, to see Aaron placing a framed photograph of Harry Clifton on the wall, between John Buchan and Graham Greene.

GILES BARRINGTON

1971

8

'I'M AFRAID THAT won't be possible,' said Giles.

'Why not?' demanded Griff. 'Most people won't even remember what happened in Berlin, and, let's face it, you wouldn't be the only Member of Parliament who's been divorced.'

'Twice, and both times for adultery!' said Giles. This silenced his parliamentary agent for a moment. 'And I'm afraid there's another problem I haven't told you about.'

'Go on, surprise me,' said Griff with an exaggerated sigh.

'I've been trying to get in touch with Karin Pengelly.'

'You've been what?'

'In fact, I'm on my way to Cornwall to find out if her father can help.'

'Are you out of your tiny mind?'

'Quite possibly,' admitted Giles.

The Labour agent for Bristol Docklands covered his face with his hands. 'It was a one-night stand, Giles. Or have you forgotten?'

'That's the problem. I haven't forgotten, and there's only one way to find out if it was more than that for her.'

'Is this the same man who won an MC escaping from the Germans, then built a formidable reputation as a cabinet minister, and when he's thrown a lifeline which would allow him to return to the House of Commons, rejects it?'

'I know it doesn't make any sense,' said Giles. 'But if it was just a one-night stand, I have to tell you I've never spent a night like it.'

'For which she was undoubtedly well rewarded.'

'So what will you do, now I've made my decision?' Giles said, ignoring the comment.

'If you're really not going to fight the seat, I'll have to appoint a sub-committee to select a new candidate.'

'You'll have a flood of applications, and while inflation is at ten per cent and the Tories' only solution is a three-day-week, a poodle wearing a red rosette would be elected.'

'Which is precisely why you shouldn't just throw in the towel.'

'Haven't you been listening to a word I've said?'

'Every word. But if you really have made up your mind, I hope you'll be available to advise whoever we select as candidate.'

'But what can I possibly tell them that you can't, Griff? Let's face it, you were organizing elections when I was still in short trousers.'

'But not as the candidate, that's a unique experience. So will you accompany him—'

'Or her—' said Giles, smiling.

'—or even her,' said Griff, 'when they're out walking the streets and canvassing the estates?'

'If you think it will help, I'll make myself available whenever you want me.'

'It could make the difference between just winning, and securing a large enough majority to make it tough for the Tories to overturn at the next election.'

'My God, the Labour Party's lucky to have you,' said Giles. 'I'll do everything I can to help.'

'Thank you,' said Griff. 'I apologize for my earlier outburst. Truth is, I've always been a cynic. Goes with the territory, I suppose. So let's hope I'm wrong this time. Mind you, I've never gone much on fairy tales. So if you do change your mind about standing, I can hold off appointing a selection committee for at least a couple of weeks.'

'Won't you ever give up?'

'Not while there's the slightest chance of you being the candidate.'

◄o►

As Giles sat alone in the first-class carriage on the way to Truro, he thought carefully about what Griff had said. Was he sacrificing his whole political career for a woman who might not even have given him a second thought since Berlin? Had he allowed his imagination to override his common sense? And if he did meet Karin again, would the bubble burst?

There was also the possibility – the strong possibility, which he tried to push to the back of his mind – that Karin had been no more than a Stasi plant, simply doing her job, proving that his veteran agent was not a cynic, but simply a realist. By the time the *Penzance Flyer* pulled into Truro station just after six, Giles was none the wiser.

He took a taxi to the Mason's Arms, where he had agreed to meet John Pengelly later that evening. Once he had signed the register, he climbed the stairs to his room and unpacked his over-night bag. He had a bath, changed his clothes and went down to the bar a few minutes before seven, as he didn't want to keep Karin's father waiting.

As Giles walked into the bar, he spotted a man seated at a corner table, at whom he wouldn't have taken a second look had he not immediately stood and waved.

Giles strode across to join him and shook his outstretched hand. No introduction was necessary.

'Let me get you a drink, Sir Giles,' said John Pengelly, with an unmistakable West Country burr. 'The local bitter's not half bad, or you might prefer a whisky.'

'A half of bitter will be just fine,' said Giles, taking a seat at the small, beer-stained table.

While Karin's father was ordering the drinks, Giles took a closer look at him. He must have been around fifty, perhaps fifty-five, although his hair had already turned grey. His Harris Tweed jacket was well worn, but still fitted perfectly, suggesting he hadn't put on more than a few pounds since his army days, and probably exercised regularly. Although he appeared reserved, even diffident, he clearly wasn't a stranger to these parts, because one of the locals seated at the bar hailed him as if he were a long-lost brother. How cruel that he had to live alone, thought Giles, with his wife and daughter unable to join him, for no other reason than that they were on the wrong side of a wall.

Pengelly returned a few moments later carrying two half-pints, one of which he placed on the table in front of Giles. 'It was kind of you to make such a long journey, sir. I only hope you'll feel it's been worthwhile.'

'Please call me Giles, as I hope we'll not only be friends, but that we'll be able to help each other's causes.'

'When you're an old soldier—'

'Not so old,' said Giles, taking a sip of his beer. 'Don't forget we both served in the last war,' he added, trying to put him at ease. 'But tell me, how did you first meet your wife?'

'It was after the war, when I was stationed with the British forces in Berlin. I was a corporal in the supply depot where Greta was a stacker. The only work she could get. It must have been love at first sight, because she couldn't speak a word of English, and I couldn't speak any German.' Giles smiled. 'Bright though. She picked up my language much quicker than I got the hang of hers. Of course, I knew from the start that it wasn't going to be plain sailing. Not least because my mates thought any Kraut skirt was only good for one thing, but Greta wasn't like that. By the time my tour of duty came to an end, I knew I wanted to marry her, whatever the consequences. That's when my problems began. A leg over behind the Naafi canteen is one thing, but wanting to marry one of them was considered nothing less than fraternization, when neither side would trust you.

'When I told the orderly officer that I intended to marry Greta, even if it meant I had to stay in Berlin, they put every possible obstacle in my path. Within days I was handed my demob papers and told I would be shipped out within a week. I became desperate, even considered deserting, which would have meant years in the glasshouse if they'd caught me. And then a barrack room lawyer informed me they couldn't stop me marrying Greta if she was pregnant. So that's what I told them.'

'Then what happened?' asked Giles.

'All hell broke loose. My discharge papers arrived a few days later. Greta lost her job, and I couldn't find any work. It didn't help that a few weeks later she really was pregnant, with Karin.'

'I want to hear all about Karin, but not before I've ordered another round.' Giles picked up the two empty glasses and made his way over to the bar. 'Same again please, but make them pints this time.'

Pengelly took a long draught before he continued with his story. 'Karin made all the sacrifices bearable, even the suspicion and ridicule we'd both had to endure. If I adored Greta, I worshipped Karin. It must have been about a year later that my old duty officer at the depot asked me to fill in for someone who was on sick leave – time is a great healer – and I was invited to act as a civilian liaison officer between the British and German workers, because by then, thanks to Greta, my German was pretty fluent. The British have many fine qualities, but they're lazy when it comes to learning someone else's language, so I quickly made myself indispensable. The pay wasn't great, but I spent every spare penny on Karin, and every spare moment with her. And like all women, she knew I was a sucker for a cuddle. It may be a cliché, but she had me wound round her little finger.'

Me too, thought Giles, taking another sip of his beer.

'To my delight,' said Pengelly, 'the English school in Berlin allowed Karin to sit the entrance exam, and a few weeks later she was offered a place. Everyone assumed she was English. Even had my Cornish accent, as you may have noticed. So from then on, I never had to worry about her education. In fact, when she reached sixth form, there was even talk of her going to Oxford, but that was before the wall went up. Once that monstrosity had been erected, Karin had to settle for a place at the East German School of Languages, which frankly is nothing more than a Stasi recruitment centre. The only surprise came when she chose to study Russian as her first language, but by then her English and German were already degree standard.

'When Karin graduated, the only serious offer she got as an interpreter came from the Stasi. It was them or be out of work, so she didn't have much choice. Whenever she wrote she would say how much she enjoyed her work, especially the international conferences. It gave her the opportunity to meet so many inter-esting people from all four sectors of the city. In fact, two Americans and one West German proposed to her, but she told Greta that it wasn't until she met you that she'd fallen in love. It amused her that you had picked up her accent straight away, although she's never been outside Berlin.'

Giles smiled as he recalled the exchange.

'Despite several attempts to return to my family, the East German authorities won't let me back, even though Greta has recently become seriously ill. I think they distrust me even more than the British.'

'I'll do everything I can to help,' said Giles.

'Karin writes regularly, but only a few of her letters get through. One that did said she'd met someone special but that it was a disaster because, not only was he married, he was English, and had only been in Berlin for a few days. And worst of all, she wasn't even sure if he felt the same way as she did.'

'How wrong she was,' said Giles softly.

'She didn't mention your name, of course, or why you were visiting the Russian sector, because she was only too aware that the authorities would be reading her letters. It wasn't until you contacted me that I realized it must be you she'd been writing about.'

'But how did Alex Fisher become involved?'

'A few days after you'd resigned as a minister, he turned up in Truro unannounced. Once he'd tracked me down, he told me that you had publicly disowned Karin, implying that she was either a prostitute or a Stasi spy, and you'd made it clear to the Whips' Office that you had no interest in ever seeing her again.'

'But I tried desperately to contact her, I even travelled to Berlin, but I was turned back at the border.'

'I know that now, but at the time . . .'

'Yes,' sighed Giles, 'Fisher could be very persuasive.'

'Especially when he's a major, and you're just a two-stripe corporal,' said Pengelly. 'Of course, I followed every day of Mrs Clifton's libel trial in the papers, and like everyone else, I read the letter Fisher wrote before committing suicide. If it would help, I'd be happy to tell anyone there was no truth in it.'

'That's good of you, John, although I'm afraid it's too late for that.'

'But I heard on the radio only yesterday, Sir Giles, that you were still thinking about standing in the Bristol by-election.'

'Not any more. I've withdrawn my name. I can't think of doing anything until I've seen Karin again.'

'Of course, as her father I think she's worth it, but it's still one hell of a sacrifice.'

'You're worse than my agent,' said Giles, laughing for the first time. He took a sip of beer and they sat in silence for some time, before he asked, 'Is Karin really pregnant?'

'No, she's not. Which made me realize that everything else Fisher had said about you was a pack of lies, and his only interest was revenge.'

'I wish she were pregnant,' said Giles quietly.

'Why?'

'Because it would be far easier to get her out.'

'Last orders, gentlemen.'

9

'WHAT A FUNNY OLD game politics is,' said Giles. 'I'm marooned in the wilderness, while you're the West German Foreign Minister.'

'But our positions could be reversed overnight,' said Walter Scheel, 'as you know only too well.'

'That would take some change of fortune for me, as I'm not even standing in the by-election and my party isn't in power.'

'But why aren't you standing?' said Walter. 'Even with my rudimentary knowledge of your parliamentary system, it looks as if Labour is certain to win back your old seat.'

'That might well be so, but the local party has already selected a capable young candidate called Robert Fielding to take my place. He's bright-eyed and bushy-tailed, with all the enthusiasm of a recently appointed school prefect.'

'Just like you used to be.'

'And still am, if the truth be known.'

'Then why did you decide not to stand?'

'It's a long story, Walter. In fact, it's the reason I wanted to see you.'

'Let's order first,' said Walter, opening the menu. 'Then you can take your time telling me why you could possibly need the assistance of a West German Foreign Minister.' He began to peruse the fare. 'Ah, the dish of the day is roast beef and York-shire pudding. My favourite,' he whispered. 'But don't tell any of your countrymen, or mine for that matter, or my guilty secret will be out. So what's your guilty secret?'

By the time Giles had fully briefed his old friend about Karin and his failure to be allowed back into East Germany, they were both enjoying a coffee.

'And you say she was the young woman who was in your hotel room when we had that private meeting?'

'You remember her?'

'I certainly do,' said Walter. 'She's interpreted for me in the past but never gave me a second look, although it wasn't through lack of trying on my part. So tell me, Giles, are you willing to fight a duel over this young woman?'

'Name your weapon, and your second.'

Walter laughed. 'More seriously, Giles, do you have any reason to believe she wants to defect?'

'Yes, her mother has recently died, and the East German authorities won't allow her father, who's English and lives in Cornwall, back into the country.'

Walter took a sip of coffee while he considered the problem. 'Would you be able to fly to Berlin at a moment's notice?'

'On the next plane.'

'Impetuous as ever,' said Walter as a waiter placed a brandy in front of him. He swirled it around in the balloon before saying, 'Do you have any idea if she speaks Russian?'

'Fluently. It was her degree subject at language school.'

'Good, because I'm hosting a bilateral trade meeting with the Russians next month, and they just might agree—'

'Can I do anything to help?'

'Just make sure she's got a British passport.'

—◦—

'My name is Robert Fielding, and I'm the Labour candidate for the Bristol Docklands by-election on May twentieth.' The young man tried to shake hands with a woman who was laden down with shopping bags.

'What are you doing about Concorde?' she asked.

'Everything in my power to make sure the plane will be built at Filton and not Toulouse,' said Fielding.

The woman looked satisfied. 'Then I'll be voting for you. But

I'd rather have voted for him,' she said, pointing at Giles. As she walked away, the young man looked despondent.

'Don't worry about her. On May twenty-first you'll be the member and I'll be history.'

'And Concorde?'

'You gave the only credible response. The French will put up a hell of a fight, but then they have every right to, and in the end I suspect the work will be divided fairly equally between the two countries. Just be sure you never spell it with an "e",' said Giles. 'You might have asked if her husband worked at Filton because I suspect that's why she asked the question.'

'Of course. I should have thought of that. Anything else?'

'Perhaps Bob Fielding rather than Robert. Don't want to continually remind your supporters that you went to a public school and Oxford.'

Fielding nodded and turned to the next passer-by. 'Hello, my name's Bob Fielding, and I'm the Labour candidate for the by-election on May twentieth. I hope you'll be supporting me.'

'Sorry you're not standing, Sir Giles.'

'That's kind of you, sir, but we've chosen an excellent candidate. I hope you'll be voting for Bob Fielding on Thursday May twentieth.'

'If you say so, Sir Giles,' said the man as he hurried away.

'Thursday, Thursday, Thursday. Always say Thursday,' said Fielding. 'God knows you've told me often enough.'

'Don't worry about it,' said Giles. 'It will soon become a habit, and frankly you're a much better candidate than I was at my first election.'

The young man smiled for the first time. 'Hello, my name is Bob Fielding, and I'm the Labour candidate for the by-election on Thursday May twentieth,' he said as Emma walked up to join her brother.

'Are you beginning to regret not standing?' she whispered, continuing to hand out leaflets. 'Because it's pretty clear that the voters have either forgiven or forgotten Berlin.'

'But I haven't,' said Giles, shaking hands with another passer-by.

'Has Walter Scheel been back in touch?'

'No, but that man won't call until he's got something to say.'

'Let's hope you're right,' said Emma, 'otherwise you really are going to regret it.'

'Yes, but what you going to do about it?' another constituent was demanding.

'Well, bringing the country to a standstill with a three-day week isn't the answer,' said Fielding, 'and the Labour party's first priority has always been unemployment.'

'Never unemployment,' whispered Giles. '*Employment*. You must always try to sound positive.'

'Good morning, my name is Bob . . .'

'Is that who I think it is?' said Emma, looking across the road.

'It most certainly is,' said Giles.

'Will you introduce me?'

'You must be joking. Nothing would please the lady more than to have her photo on every front page tomorrow morning shaking hands with the former member.'

'Well, if you won't, I'll have to do it myself.'

'You can't—'

But Emma was already halfway across the road. Once she was on the other side, she walked straight up to the Secretary of State for Education and Science and thrust out her hand.

'Good morning, Mrs Thatcher. I'm the sister of Sir Giles—'

'And more important, Mrs Clifton, you were the first woman to chair a public company.'

Emma smiled.

'Women should never have been given the vote!' shouted a man, shaking his fist from a passing car.

Mrs Thatcher waved and gave him a magnanimous smile.

'I don't know how you cope with it,' said Emma.

'In my case, I've never wanted to do anything else,' said Thatcher. 'Although I confess that a dictatorship might make one's job a little easier.' Emma laughed, but Mrs Thatcher didn't. 'By the way,' she said, glancing across the road, 'your brother was a first-class MP as well as a highly respected minister both at home and abroad. He's sadly missed in the House – but don't tell him I said so.'

'Why not?' said Emma.

'Because it doesn't fit in with his image of me and I'm not sure he'd believe it.'

'I wish I could tell him. He's rather low at the moment.'

'Don't worry, he'll be back in one house or the other soon enough. It's in his blood. But what about you? Have you ever considered going into politics, Mrs Clifton? You have all the right credentials.'

'Never, never, never,' said Emma vehemently. 'I couldn't handle the pressure.'

'You handled it well enough during your recent trial, and I suspect pressure doesn't worry you when it comes to facing up to your fellow directors.'

'That's a different kind of pressure,' said Emma. 'And in any case—'

'I'm sorry to interrupt you, Secretary of State,' said an agitated minder, 'but the candidate seems to be in a spot of trouble.'

Mrs Thatcher looked up to see an old woman jabbing a finger at the Tory candidate. 'That's not a spot of trouble. That lady probably remembers this street being bombed by the Germans – now that's what I call a spot of trouble.' She turned back to Emma. 'I'll have to leave you, Mrs Clifton, but I do hope we'll meet again, perhaps in more relaxed circumstances.'

'Secretary of State?'

'Yes, yes, I'm coming,' said Mrs Thatcher. 'If he can't handle one old lady without me having to hold his hand, how's he ever going to cope with the baying opposition in the Commons?' she added before hurrying away.

Emma smiled and walked back across the road to re-join her brother, who was telling a military-looking gentleman the sanitized version of why he wasn't standing in the by-election.

'So what did you think of her?' asked Giles once he'd broken away.

'Remarkable,' said Emma. 'Quite remarkable.'

'I agree,' said Giles. 'But don't ever tell her I said so.'

◄○►

The call came when he least expected it. Giles turned on the light by the side of his bed to find it was a few minutes after five, and wondered who could possibly be phoning him at that time in the morning.

'Sorry to ring you so early, Giles, but this is not a call I can make from my office.'

'I understand,' said Giles, suddenly wide awake.

'If you can be in Berlin on May twenty-second,' said Walter, 'I may be able to deliver your package.'

'That's wonderful news.'

'But not without some considerable risk, because it will require a bit of luck, and a lot of courage from two young women in particular.'

Giles swung his legs on to the floor, sat on the edge of the bed and listened carefully to what the West German Foreign Minister expected him to do. By the time Walter had finished, it was no longer dark outside.

◄○►

Giles dialled the number again, hoping he'd be in. This time the phone was picked up immediately.

'Good morning, John.'

'Good morning, Sir Giles,' said Pengelly, immediately recognizing the voice.

Giles wondered how long it would be before he dropped the 'sir'. 'John, before I get in touch with the relevant department at the Home Office, I need to know if Karin has ever applied for a British passport.'

'Yes – or at least I did on her behalf, when she was still thinking of going to Oxford,' said Pengelly.

'Don't tell me it's locked away somewhere in East Berlin?'

'No, I picked it up from Petty France myself, and intended to take it back when I returned to East Germany but of course never did. That was some years ago so heaven knows where it is now. Even if I could lay my hands on it, it's probably out of date.'

'If you can find it, John, it's just possible you may be seeing your daughter far sooner than you'd expected.'

—◦—

Although Griff Haskins invited Giles to attend the count in the Council House, he couldn't face it. Having tramped the streets with the candidate for the past four weeks, attended countless public meetings and even delivered eve-of-poll leaflets on the Woodbine Estate, when ten o'clock struck on Thursday 20 May, Giles shook hands with Bob Fielding, wished him luck and drove straight back to Barrington Hall.

On arriving home, he poured himself a large glass of whisky and ran a warm bath. He fell asleep within minutes of climbing into bed. He woke just after six, the most sleep he'd had in a month. He got up, strolled into the bathroom and covered his face with a cold, wet flannel, then put on a dressing gown and slippers and padded downstairs.

A black Labrador strolled into the drawing room, his tail wagging, assuming it must be time for his morning walk. What other reason could the master have for being up so early? Giles said, 'Sit!', and Old Jack sat down beside him, tail thumping the carpet.

Giles switched on the radio and settled back in a comfortable armchair to listen to the morning news. The Prime Minister was in Paris holding talks with the French president on the possibility of Britain joining the EEC. Normally, Giles would have been the first to acknowledge the historic significance of such a meeting, but not at this particular moment. All he wanted to know was the result of the Bristol Docklands by-election. 'Mr Heath dined with President Pompidou at the Elysée Palace last night, and although no official communiqué has been released, it's clear that now General De Gaulle is no longer a political force to be reckoned with, Britain's application is finally being taken seriously.'

'Get on with it,' said Giles and, as if he'd heard him, the newsreader stayed with Ted Heath, but returned to England.

'Another setback for the Tories,' he declared, 'who lost the by-election in Bristol Docklands last night to the Labour Party. The seat had become vacant following the death of Major Alex Fisher, the sitting Conservative member. We now join our West Country correspondent in Bristol, for the latest news.'

'In the early hours of this morning, Bob Fielding, the Labour candidate, was declared the winner of the by-election here in Bristol Docklands by a majority of 3,127, representing a swing of eleven per cent from Conservative to Labour.'

Giles leapt in the air, and the dog stopped wagging its tail.

'Although the turnout was low, this was a resounding victory for Mr Fielding, who, at the age of thirty-two, will be one of the youngest members in the House. This is what he had to say following the announcement of the result: "I'd first like to thank the returning officer and his staff for the exemplary way they have—"'

The telephone on the table beside him began to ring. Giles cursed, turned off the radio and picked up the phone, assuming it had to be Griff Haskins, who he knew wouldn't have gone to bed.

'Good morning, Giles, it's Walter Scheel . . .'

10

GILES COULDN'T SLEEP the night before he was due to fly to Berlin. He was up long before the sun rose, didn't bother with breakfast and took a taxi from his home in Smith Square to Heathrow hours before his flight was due to depart. First flights in the morning were almost the only aircraft guaranteed to take off on time. He picked up a copy of the *Guardian* in the first-class lounge, but didn't get beyond the front page as he drank a cup of black coffee and went over Walter's plan again and again. It had one fundamental weakness, what he'd described as a necessary risk.

Giles was among the first to board the aircraft and, even though the plane took off on time, kept checking his watch every few minutes throughout the flight. The plane touched down in Berlin at 9.45 a.m. and, as Giles had no luggage, he was sitting in the back of another taxi twenty minutes later.

'Checkpoint Charlie,' he said to the driver, who gave him a second look before joining the early morning traffic heading into the city.

Soon after they'd passed the dilapidated Brandenburg Gate, Giles spotted the white Mercedes coach Walter had told him to look out for. As he didn't want to be the first person to board, he asked the taxi driver to stop a couple of hundred yards from the crossing point. Giles paid the fare and began to stroll around as if he were a tourist, not that there were any sites to look out for, other than a graffiti-covered wall. He didn't start to make his way towards the coach until he'd seen several other delegates climb aboard.

Giles joined the line of foreign dignitaries and political journalists who had travelled from all over Europe to attend a ceremonial lunch and hear a speech by Erich Honecker, the new General Secretary of the Socialist Unity Party. He still wondered if he might once again be prevented from crossing the border and be left with no choice but to return on the next flight back to Heathrow. But Walter had assured him that since he was representing the British Labour Party as a former Foreign Minister, he would be made most welcome by his hosts. The East German regime, Walter explained, had been unable to open any meaningful dialogue with the present Conservative government and was desperate to forge some worthwhile alliances with the Labour Party, especially as it looked likely that they would soon be returning to power. When Giles reached the front of the queue he handed his passport to an official, who gave it a cursory glance before ushering him on board. The first hurdle crossed.

As Giles walked down the aisle, he spotted a young woman sitting alone near the back, looking out of the window. He didn't need to check her seat number.

'Hello,' he said.

She looked up and smiled. He didn't know her name, and perhaps it was better that he didn't. All he knew was that she spoke fluent English, was an interpreter by profession, roughly the same age as Karin, and would be wearing an identical outfit to hers. But there was one thing Walter hadn't explained. Why was she willing to take such a risk?

Giles looked around at his fellow delegates. He didn't recognize any of them, and was pleased to see that no one showed the slightest interest in him. He sat down by his blind date, slipped a hand into an inside pocket and pulled out Karin's passport. There was one thing missing, and that would remain in his wallet until the return journey. Giles leant forward to shield the young woman as she bent down and took a tiny square photo and a tube of glue out of her handbag. She completed the process in a couple of minutes. It was clear she had practised the exercise several times.

Once she'd placed the passport in her handbag, Giles took a closer look at the woman sitting next to him. He could immediately see why Walter had chosen her. She was a similar age and build to Karin, possibly a couple of years older and a few pounds heavier, but roughly the same height, with the same dark eyes and auburn hair, which she'd arranged in Karin's style. Clearly as little as possible had been left to chance.

Giles checked his watch again. It was almost time for them to leave. The driver conducted a head count. He was two short.

'I'll give them another five minutes,' he said, as Giles glanced out of the window to see a couple of figures running towards the bus. He recognized one of them as a former Italian minister, although he couldn't recall his name. But then, there were a lot of former Italian ministers.

'*Mi dispiace*,' the man said as he climbed aboard. Once the two late-comers were seated, the doors closed with a soft hiss of air and the coach set off at a pedestrian pace towards the border crossing.

The driver came to a halt in front of a red-and-white striped barrier. The coach door swung open to allow two smartly dressed American military policemen to climb aboard. They carefully checked each passport, to make sure the temporary visas were in order. Once they'd completed their task, one of them said, 'Have a good day,' without any suggestion that he meant it.

The coach never got out of first gear as it progressed another three hundred yards towards the East German border, where it once again came to a halt. This time three officers in bottle-green uniforms, knee-length leather boots and peaked caps climbed on board. Not a smile mustered between them.

They took even longer checking each passport, making sure every visa was correctly dated and stamped, before one of them placed a tick against a name on his clipboard and moved on to the next passenger. Giles displayed no emotion when one of the officers asked to see his passport and visa. He checked the document carefully, then placed a tick by the name of Barrington. He took considerably longer looking at Karin's passport, and then asked her a couple of questions. As Giles couldn't understand a word the guard was saying, he became more anxious by the second, until a tick was placed next to the name Karin Pengelly. Giles didn't speak until all three officers had disembarked, the door had been closed and the coach had crossed a wide yellow line which indicated that they had crossed the border.

'You're welcome to East Berlin,' said the driver, clearly unaware of the irony of his words.

Giles looked up at the tall brick towers manned by armed guards who stared down on the crude concrete wall crowned with razor wire. He felt sorry for its jailed inhabitants.

'What did he ask you about?' asked Giles.

'He wanted to know where I lived in England.'

'What did you tell him?'

'Parson's Green.'

'Why Parson's Green?'

'That's where I had digs when I was studying English at London University. And he must have thought I was your mistress, because your wife's name is still on your passport as next of kin. Fortunately, being someone's mistress isn't a crime in East Germany. Well, not yet.'

'Who would take a mistress to East Berlin?'

'Only someone who was trying to get one out.'

Giles hesitated before he asked his next question. 'Shall we go over the details of what will happen once we reach the hotel?'

'That won't be necessary,' she replied. 'I met up with Karin a few days ago when the minister was holding bilateral talks with his opposite number, so all you have to do is stay in your seat during lunch, make sure everyone thinks you're enjoying the meal and keep applauding during the general secretary's speech. Leave the rest to us.'

'But—' began Giles.

'No buts,' she said firmly. 'It's better that you don't know anything about me.'

Giles would have liked to ask her what else she knew about

Karin, but decided that was probably also *verboten*. Although he still remained curious why . . .

'I can't tell you how much I appreciate what you're doing,' whispered Giles, 'both for me and Karin.'

'I'm not doing it for either of you,' she said matter-of-factly. 'I'm doing it for my father, who was shot down trying to climb over that wall, just three days after it had been built.'

'I'm so sorry,' said Giles. 'Let's hope it will come down one day,' he added as he looked back at the grey concrete monstrosity, 'and sanity will return.'

'Not in my lifetime,' she said, in the same impassive voice, as the coach trundled on towards the centre of the city.

Eventually they pulled up outside the Adlon Hotel, but it was some time before they were allowed to disembark. When the doors finally opened, they were shepherded off the coach by a posse of tall uniformed policemen accompanied by snarling Alsatians on short leads. The delegates remained corralled until they had reached the dining room, where they were released into a large pen. The East Germans' idea of making you feel at home.

Giles checked the seating plan displayed on a board to one side of the double doors. Sir Giles Barrington and interpreter were on table number 43 near the back of the room, where they wouldn't attract attention, Walter had explained. He and his companion found their places and sat down. Giles tried subtly, and then crudely, to find out her name and what she did, but came up against another brick wall. It was clear that her identity had to remain secret, so he satisfied himself with talking about London and the theatre, to which she happily responded, until several people around them stood up and began to applaud – some more loudly than others.

Giles stood to see the diminutive figure of Comrade Honecker enter the room surrounded by a dozen bodyguards who towered over him, so that he only occasionally bobbed into view. Giles joined in the applause, as he didn't want to draw attention to himself. The general secretary walked towards the top table and, as he climbed the few steps up on to the platform, Giles spotted Walter applauding about as enthusiastically as he was.

The West German Foreign Minister was seated just two places away from the general secretary, and it wasn't difficult for Giles to work out that the man between them had to be Walter's Russian counterpart, because he was clapping more enthusiastically than anyone else at the top table.

When everyone in the room finally sat down, Giles saw Karin for the first time. She was seated behind the two Foreign Ministers. He was immediately reminded why he'd been so captivated by her. During the meal he couldn't stop staring in her direction, but she never once returned the compliment.

The three-course meal was both interminable and inedible: nettle soup followed by boiled beef and soggy cabbage, and finally a slab of brick-hard cake covered in custard that any self-respecting schoolboy would have left untouched. His companion began asking him questions, clearly trying to distract him from constantly staring at Karin. She asked which musicals were on in London. He didn't know. Had he seen *Oh! Calcutta!*? No, he hadn't. What was showing at the Tate Gallery? He had no idea. She even asked if he'd met Prince Charles.

'Yes, once, but only briefly.'

'Who's the lucky girl who will marry him?'

'No idea, but it will have to be someone the Queen approves of.'

They continued chatting, but she never once mentioned Karin or asked how they had met.

At last the waiters began to clear away the pudding; there was enough left over to feed the five thousand. The chairman, the mayor of East Berlin, rose slowly from his place and tapped his microphone several times. He didn't begin to speak until he had complete silence. He then announced in three languages that there would be a ten-minute break before the General Secretary of the Socialist Unity Party would address them.

'Good luck,' she whispered, and was gone before he had time to thank her. He watched as she disappeared into the crowd, not sure what was going to happen next. He had to grip the sides of his chair to stop himself trembling.

The ten minutes seemed an eternity. And then he spotted her walking between the tables towards him. She was wearing the same dark suit as his erstwhile companion, an identical red scarf, and black high-heeled shoes, but that was where the similarity ended. Karin sat down beside him, but said nothing. Interpreters don't hold real conversations, she had once told him.

Giles wanted to take her in his arms, feel the warmth of her body, her gentle touch, smell her perfume, but she remained detached, professional, giving nothing away, nothing that would draw attention to how he felt about her.

Once everyone had resumed their places and coffee had been served, the chairman rose for a second time and only had to tap the microphone once before the audience fell silent.

'It is my privilege as your host to introduce our speaker today, one of the world's great statesmen, a man who has single-handedly . . .' When the chairman sat down twenty minutes later, Giles could only wonder how long the general secretary's speech was going to be.

Honecker began by thanking all the foreign delegates and distinguished journalists who had travelled from many parts of the world to hear his speech.

'That's not the reason I came,' murmured Giles.

Karin ignored the comment and faithfully continued to translate the general secretary's words. 'I am delighted to welcome you all to East Germany,' said Karin, 'a beacon of civilization which is a benchmark for all those nations who aspire to emulate us.'

'I want to touch you,' whispered Giles.

'I am proud to announce that in East Germany we enjoy full employment,' said Karin. A smattering of applause from some well-placed apparatchiks allowed the general secretary to pause and turn another page of his thick script.

'There's so much I want to talk to you about, but I realize it will have to wait.'

'In particular, our farming programme is an example of how to use the land to benefit those most in need.'

'Stop staring at me, Sir Giles,' whispered Karin, 'and concentrate on the leader's words.'

Reluctantly Giles turned his attention back to Honecker, and tried to look engrossed.

'Our hospitals are the envy of the West,' said Karin, 'and our doctors and nurses the most highly qualified in the world.'

Giles turned back, just for a moment, only to be greeted with, 'Let me now turn to the construction industry, and the inspiring work our first-class engineers are doing building new homes, factories, bridges, roads . . .'

'Not to mention walls,' said Giles.

'Be careful, Sir Giles. You must assume every other person in this room is a spy.'

He knew Karin was right. The masks must remain in place until they had crossed the border and reached the freedom of the West.

'The Communist vision is being taken up by millions of comrades across the globe – in Cuba, Argentina, France and even Great Britain, where membership of the Communist Party doubled last year.'

Giles joined in the orchestrated applause, although he knew it had halved.

When he could bear it no longer, he turned and gave Karin a bored glance, and was rewarded with a stern look, which kept him going for another fifteen minutes.

'Our military might, supported by Mother Russia, has no equal, making it possible for us to face any challenge . . .'

Giles thought he would burst, and not with applause. How much longer could this rubbish go on, and how many people present were taken in by it? It was an hour and a half before Honecker finally sat down, having delivered a speech that seemed to Giles to rival Wagner's *Ring Cycle* in length, with none of the opera's virtues.

What Giles hadn't been prepared for was the fifteen-minute standing ovation that followed Honecker's speech, kept alight by several planted apparatchiks and henchmen who had probably enjoyed the cake and custard. Finally the general secretary left the stage, but he was held up again and again as he shook hands with enthusiastic delegates, while the applause continued even after he'd left the hall.

'What a remarkable speech,' said the former Italian minister, whose name Giles still couldn't remember.

'That's one way of describing it,' said Giles, grinning at Karin, who scowled back at him. Giles realized that the Italian was looking at him closely. 'A remarkable feat of oratory,' he added, 'but I'll need to read it carefully to make sure I didn't miss any key points.' A copy of Honecker's speech was immediately thrust into Giles's hands, which only reminded him how vigilant he needed to be. His remarks seemed to satisfy the Italian, who was distracted when another delegate marched up to him, gave him a bear hug and said, 'How are you, Gian Lucio?'

'So what happens now?' whispered Giles.

'We wait to be escorted back to the bus. But it's important that you continue to look as if you were impressed by the speech, so please make sure to keep complimenting your hosts.'

Giles turned away from Karin and began shaking hands with several European politicians who Griff Haskins would have refused to share a pint with.

Giles couldn't believe it. Someone actually blew a whistle to attract the attention of the foreign delegates. They were then rounded up and, like unruly schoolchildren, led back to the bus.

When all thirty-two passengers were safely on board and had once again been counted, the bus, accompanied by four police motorcycle outriders, their sirens blaring, began its slow journey back to the border.

He was about to take Karin's hand, when a voice behind him said, 'It's Sir Giles Barrington, isn't it?' Giles looked round to see a face he recognized, although he couldn't recall the name.

'Keith Brookes.'

'Ah yes,' said Giles, 'the *Telegraph*. Good to see you again, Keith.'

'As you're representing the Labour Party, Sir Giles, can I assume you still hope to return to front-line politics?'

'I try to keep in touch,' said Giles, not wanting to hold a lengthy conversation with a journalist.

'I'm sorry you didn't stand at the by-election,' said Brookes. 'Fielding seems a nice enough chap, but I miss your contributions from the front bench.'

'There wasn't much sign of that when I was in the House.'

'Not the paper's policy, as you well know, but you have your admirers on the news desk, including Bill Deedes, because I can tell you we all feel the present bunch of shadow ministers are pretty colourless.'

'It's fashionable to say that about every new generation of politicians.'

'Still, if you do decide to make a comeback, give me a call.' He handed Giles a card. 'You just might be surprised by our attitude to your second coming,' he added before resuming his place.

'He seemed nice enough,' said Karin.

'You can never trust the *Torygraph*,' said Giles, placing the card in his wallet.

'Are you thinking of making a comeback?'

'It wouldn't be that easy.'

'Because of me?' said Karin, taking his hand as the coach came to a halt at a barrier just a few hundred yards from freedom. He would have replied, but the door swung open, letting in a gust of cold air.

Three uniformed officers climbed on board again. Giles was relieved to see that the morning shift had clearly changed. As they began slowly and meticulously checking every passport and visa, Giles suddenly remembered. He whipped out his wallet, retrieved the small photo of Karin and quickly handed it to her. She cursed under her breath, took her passport out of her bag and, with the help of a nail file, began to carefully peel off the morning's photograph.

'How could I have forgotten?' Karin whispered, as she used the same small tube of glue to fix her own photograph back in place.

'My fault, not yours,' said Giles, peering down the aisle to keep a watchful eye on the guards' slow progress. 'Let's just be thankful that we aren't sitting at the front of the bus.'

The guards were still a couple of rows away by the time Karin had completed the transfer. Giles turned to see that she was shaking, and gripped her firmly by the hand. Fortunately, the guards were taking far longer to check each name than they had when he'd entered the country, because despite Honecker's boastful claims, the wall proved that more people wanted to get out of East Germany than get in.

When a young officer appeared by their side, Giles nonchalantly handed over his passport. After the guard had turned a few pages and checked the Englishman's visa, he handed it back and put a tick by Giles's name. Not as bad as he'd feared.

As the guard opened Karin's passport, Giles noticed that her photograph was slightly askew. The young lieutenant took his time studying the details, date of birth, next of kin – at least this time they were accurate. Giles prayed that he wouldn't ask her where she lived in England. However, when he did begin to question her, it quickly became clear from his tone of voice that he wasn't convinced by her answers. Giles didn't know what to do. Any attempt to intervene would only draw even more attention to them. The guard barked an order, and Karin rose slowly from her place. Giles was about to protest, when Brookes leapt up from behind them and began taking photographs of the young officer. The other two guards immediately charged forward to join their colleague. One grabbed the camera and ripped out the film, while the other two dragged Brookes unceremoniously off the coach.

'He did that on purpose,' said Karin, who was still shaking. 'But why?'

'Because he'd worked out who you are.'

'What will happen to him?' asked Karin, sounding anxious.

'He'll spend the night in jail and then be deported back to England. He'll never be allowed to return to East Germany. Not much of a punishment, and well worth it for an exclusive.'

Giles became aware that everyone on the bus was now looking in their direction, while trying to work out, in several tongues, what had just happened. Gian Lucio beckoned to Giles that he and Karin should join him at the front of the coach. Another risk, but one Giles felt was worth taking.

'Follow me,' said Giles.

They took the two empty seats across the aisle from Gian Lucio, and Giles was explaining to the former minister what had happened when two of the guards reappeared, but not the one who'd questioned Karin. He was probably having to explain to a higher authority why he'd dragged a Western journalist off the bus. The two guards moved to the back of the coach and quickly checked the few remaining passports and visas. Someone must have explained to them that they didn't need a diplomatic incident on the day the supreme leader had made a ground-breaking speech.

Giles continued chatting to Gian Lucio as if they were old friends while one of the officers did another head count. Thirty-one. He stood to attention and saluted, then he and his colleagues climbed off the bus. As the door closed behind them the passengers broke into a spontaneous round of applause for the first time that day.

The coach drove a couple of hundred yards across no-man's land, an acre of bare wasteland that neither country laid claim to, before coming to a halt in the American sector. Karin was still shaking when a US marine sergeant stepped on to the bus.

'Welcome back,' he said in a voice that sounded as if he meant it.

11

'Is this what politicians in the East mean, when they describe the West as decadent?'

'Decadent?' said Giles, pouring Karin another glass of champagne.

'Staying in your hotel room until eleven o'clock in the morning and then ordering breakfast in bed.'

'Certainly not,' said Giles. 'If it's eleven o'clock, it's no longer breakfast, but brunch, and therefore quite acceptable.'

Karin laughed as she sipped her champagne. 'I just can't believe I've escaped and will finally be reunited with my father. Will you come and visit us in Cornwall?'

'No, I intend to give you a job in London as my housekeeper.'

'Ah, Professor Higgins.'

'But your English is already perfect and, don't forget, they didn't have sex.'

'They would have done if Shaw was writing today.'

'And the play would have ended with them getting married,' said Giles, taking her in his arms.

'What time's our flight?'

'Three twenty.'

'Good, then we have more than enough time,' said Karin, as her hotel dressing gown fell to the floor, 'to re-write the last act of *Pygmalion*.'

◂◦▸

The last time Giles had been greeted by a bank of television cameras, photographers and journalists on returning to England was when it had looked as if he might be the next leader of the Labour Party.

As he and Karin walked down the aircraft steps, Giles placed an arm around her shoulder and guided her gently through the assembled pack of journalists.

'Karin! Karin! What's it feel like to have escaped from East Germany?' shouted a voice as the cameras flashed, and the television crews tried to stay a yard ahead of them while walking backwards.

'Say nothing,' said Giles firmly.

'Has Sir Giles proposed to you, Miss Pengelly?'

'Will you be standing for Parliament again, Sir Giles?'

'Are you pregnant, Karin?'

Karin, looking flustered, glared at the journalist and said, 'No, I am not!'

'Can you be sure after last night?' whispered Giles.

Karin smiled, and was about to kiss him on the cheek when he turned towards her and their lips brushed for a brief moment, but that was the photograph that appeared on most front pages, as they discovered over breakfast the following morning.

◄○►

'Keith Brookes has been as good as his word,' said Karin, looking up from the *Telegraph*.

'I agree, surprisingly generous. And the leader even more so.'

'The leader?'

'An editorial opinion on one of the leading stories of the day.'

'Ah. We never used to get those on our side of the wall. All the papers delivered the same message, written by a party spokesman, and printed by the editor, if he hoped to keep his job.'

'That would make life easier,' said Giles, as Markham appeared carrying a rack of warm toast, which he placed on the table.

'Is Markham decadent?' asked Karin once the butler had closed the door behind him.

'He certainly is,' said Giles. 'I know for a fact he votes Conservative.'

Giles was reading *The Times*' leader when the phone rang.

Markham reappeared. 'It's Mr Harold Wilson on the line, sir,' he said, handing him the phone.

'Is he going to send me back?' said Karin.

Giles wasn't sure if she was joking. 'Good morning, Harold.'

'Good morning, Giles,' said an unmistakable Yorkshire voice. 'I wondered if you could find the time to drop into the Commons today as there's something I need to discuss with you.'

'When would be convenient?' asked Giles.

'I've got a gap in my diary at eleven, if that would suit you.'

'I'm sure that's fine, Harold, but can I check?'

'Of course.'

Giles placed a hand over the mouthpiece and said, 'Karin, when's your father expected?'

'Around ten, but I'll have to buy some clothes before then.'

'We can go shopping this afternoon,' said Giles. He removed his hand and said, 'I'll see you in the Commons at eleven, Harold.'

'And what am I expected to wear until then?' Karin asked once he'd put the phone down.

The butler coughed.

'Yes, Markham?'

'Mrs Clifton always leaves a change of clothes in the guest bedroom, sir, in case of an emergency.'

'This is unquestionably an emergency,' said Giles, taking Karin by the hand and leading her out of the room.

'Won't she object?' asked Karin as they climbed the stairs to the first floor.

'It's difficult to object to something you don't know about.'

'Perhaps you should call her?'

'I have a feeling Emma might be doing something a little more important than worrying about which clothes she left in London,' said Giles as he opened the door to the guest bedroom.

Karin pulled open a large wardrobe to find not one, but several suits and dresses, not to mention a rack of shoes she would never have seen in a worker's cooperative.

'Come and join me downstairs once you're ready,' said Giles.

He spent the next forty minutes trying to finish the morning papers, while being regularly interrupted by phone calls offering congratulations or trying to arrange interviews. He even found the odd moment to speculate about why Harold Wilson wanted to see him.

'Mr Clifton is on the line, sir,' said Markham, passing him the phone once again.

'Harry, how are you?'

'I'm fine, but having read the morning papers, I'm just calling to find out how you are after escaping from the Germans a second time.'

Giles laughed. 'Never better.'

'I presume being reunited with Miss Pengelly is the cause of you sounding so pleased with yourself.'

'Got it in one. As well as being beautiful, Karin's the most delightful, kind, thoughtful and considerate creature I've ever met.'

'Isn't it a little early to be making such an unequivocal judgement?' suggested Harry.

'No. This time, I've really struck gold.'

'Let's hope you're right. And how do you feel about the press describing you as a cross between Richard Hannay and Douglas Bader?'

'I see myself more as Heathcliff,' said Giles, laughing.

'So when are we going to be allowed to meet this paragon?'

'We'll be driving down to Bristol on Friday evening, so if you and Emma are free for lunch on Saturday—'

'Sebastian's coming down on Saturday, and Emma's hoping to talk to him about taking over as chairman. But you're welcome to join us.'

'No, I think I'll skip that, but why don't you all come over to the Hall for lunch on Sunday?'

'Isn't that putting a little too much pressure on Karin?' said Harry.

'When you've been living under a Communist regime for most of your life, I don't think you'd consider having lunch with the Cliftons as pressure.'

'If you're sure, then we'll see you both on Sunday.'

'I'm sure,' said Giles, as the front door bell rang. 'Got to dash, Harry.' He put the phone down and checked his watch. Could it possibly be ten o'clock already? He almost ran into the hall to find Markham opening the front door.

'Good morning, Mr Pengelly, Sir Giles is expecting you.'

'Good morning,' said Pengelly, giving the butler a slight bow.

'Come on in,' said Giles, as they shook hands. 'Markham, can you rustle up some fresh coffee while I take Mr Pengelly through to the drawing room.'

'Of course, sir.'

'Karin should be down in a moment. It's a long story, but she's trying to decide which of my sister's clothes to wear.'

Pengelly laughed. 'Women have enough trouble deciding which of their own clothes to wear.'

'Did you have any difficulty finding us?'

'No, I left it all to the taxi driver. A rare experience for me, but this is a special occasion.'

'It certainly is,' said Giles. 'The chance to be reunited with your daughter when you thought you might never see her again.'

'I'll be eternally grateful to you, Sir Giles. And if the *Telegraph* is to be believed, it was a close-run thing.'

'Brookes exaggerated the whole incident,' said Giles, as the two of them sat down, 'but one can hardly blame the man after what they put him through.'

Markham returned carrying a tray of coffee and shortbread biscuits, which he placed between them on the drawing room table.

'Comrade Honecker won't be best pleased that you upstaged him,' said Pengelly, looking down at the *Telegraph* headline. 'Not that there was anything in the speech that we haven't all heard before.'

'Several times,' said Giles, as the door opened and Karin burst in. She ran towards her father, who leapt up and took her in his arms. Funny, thought Giles, I never noticed that simple white dress when my sister wore it.

Father and daughter clung on to each other, but it was Mr Pengelly who burst into tears.

'Sorry to make such a fool of myself,' he said, 'but I've been looking forward to this moment for so long.'

'Me too,' said Karin.

Giles looked at his watch. 'I apologize, but I'll have to leave you both, as I have a meeting in the Commons at eleven. But I know you have a great deal to catch up on.'

'When will you be back?' asked Karin.

'Around twelve, possibly earlier, then I'll take you both out to lunch.'

'And after lunch?'

'We're going shopping. I haven't forgotten.' Giles kissed her gently on the lips, while Pengelly looked away. 'See you both around twelve,' he said as he walked out into the hall where the butler was holding his overcoat. 'I'm expecting to be back in about an hour, Markham. Don't disturb them, as I suspect they'll appreciate having some time to themselves.'

—◦►—

Karin and her father remained silent as they waited for the front door to close, and even then they didn't speak until they heard Markham close the kitchen door.

'Did everything go to plan?'

'Almost everything,' said Karin. 'Until we reached the border, when an over-zealous young officer started asking far too many questions.'

'But I personally briefed the border guards,' said Pengelly. 'I even told Lieutenant Engel that he was to give you a hard time before ticking off your name, so Barrington would be even more convinced you'd been lucky to escape.'

'Well, it didn't work out quite as you planned, comrade, because a Fleet Street journalist decided to poke his nose in, and even started taking photographs.'

'Keith Brookes. Yes, I gave orders for him to be released soon after you crossed the border. I wanted to be sure he didn't miss his deadline,' Pengelly added as he looked down at the *Telegraph* headline:

SIR GILES BARRINGTON RESCUES GIRLFRIEND FROM BEHIND THE IRON CURTAIN

'But we can't afford to relax,' said Karin. 'Despite the lovelorn look, Giles Barrington is nobody's fool.'

'From what I've just witnessed, you seem to have him eating out of your hand.'

'For now, yes, but we can't assume that will last, and we'd be unwise to ignore his record when it comes to women. He isn't exactly reliable.'

'He managed ten years with his last wife,' said Pengelly, 'which should be more than enough time for what our masters have in mind.'

'So what's the immediate plan?'

'There's no immediate plan. Marshal Koshevoi looks upon this as a long-term operation, so just be sure you give him everything his two previous wives obviously failed to do.'

'That shouldn't be too difficult, because I think the poor man is actually in love with me. Can you believe that last night was the first time he'd ever had oral sex?'

'And I'm sure there are one or two other experiences he can look forward to. You must do everything in your power to keep it that way, because we'll never have a better chance of getting a foot in the British establishment's door.'

'I won't be satisfied with getting my foot in the door,' said Karin. 'I intend to break it down.'

'Good. But for now, let's concentrate on your other responsibilities. We must develop a simple system for passing on messages to our agents in the field.'

'I thought I was only going to deal directly with you.'

'That might not always be possible as I'll have to remain in Cornwall for a lot of the time if Barrington's not to become suspicious.'

'So what should I do if I need to contact you urgently?'

'I've installed a second phone line for your exclusive use, but it's only for emergencies. Whenever you want to get in touch with your "father", use the listed number, and only ever speak in English. If you need to call the private line – and I stress, only in emergencies – I'll speak in Russian and you should respond in German. So there are only two numbers you'll need to remember.'

The front door slammed, and a moment later they heard Giles's voice in the hallway. 'Are they still in the drawing room?'

'Yes, sir.'

'And I'll never forgive myself,' Pengelly was saying, 'for not being by your mother's side when—'

Giles burst into the room. 'I wanted you to be the first to know, my darling. Harold Wilson has offered me a place in the House of Lords.'

Both of them looked pleased.

LADY VIRGINIA FENWICK

1971

12

THE EARL OF FENWICK wrote to his daughter and summoned her to Scotland. Almost a royal command.

Virginia dreaded the thought of having to face her father. As long as she kept herself out of the gossip columns and within her budget, the old man didn't seem to care too much about what she got up to in London. However, her high court libel action against her ex-sister-in-law Emma Clifton had been extensively reported in the *Scotsman*, the only paper the noble earl ever read.

Virginia didn't arrive at Fenwick Hall until after dinner, and immediately retired to bed in the hope that her father would be in a better mood following a night's sleep. He wasn't. In fact, he barely uttered a word throughout breakfast, other than to say, 'I'll see you in my study at ten,' as if she were an errant schoolgirl.

She was standing outside Papa's study at five minutes to ten, but didn't knock on the door until she heard the clock in the hall strike the hour. She was painfully aware that her father expected one to be neither early nor late. When she did knock, she was rewarded with the command, 'Come!' She opened the door and walked into a room she only ever entered when she was in trouble. Virginia remained standing on the other side of the desk, waiting to be invited to sit. She wasn't. She still didn't speak. Children should be seen and not heard, was one of her father's favourite maxims, which may have been the reason they were almost strangers.

While Virginia waited for him to open the conversation, she took a closer look at the old man who was seated behind his desk, attempting to light a briar pipe. He'd aged considerably since she'd last seen him. The lines on his face were more deeply etched. But despite being well into his seventies, his grey hair was still thick, and his finely clipped moustache served to remind everyone he was of a past generation. The earl's smoking jacket was the lovat green of his highland clan, and he considered it a virtue that he rarely ventured beyond the borders. He'd been educated at Loretto School in Edinburgh before graduating to St Andrews. The golf club, not the university. At general elections, he supported the Conservative Party, not out of conviction, but because he considered the Tories the lesser of several evils. However, as his Member of Parliament had been Sir Alec Douglas-Home, he wasn't without influence. He visited the House of Lords on rare occasions, and then only when a vote was required on a piece of legislation that affected his livelihood.

Once he'd lit his pipe and taken a few exaggerated puffs, he reluctantly turned his attention to his only daughter, whom he considered to be one of his few failures in life. The earl blamed his late wife for indulging the child during her formative years. The countess had favoured the carrot rather than the stick, so that by the age of eighteen, the only carats Virginia knew were to be found at Cartier and not the local greengrocers.

'Let me begin by asking you, Virginia,' said the earl between puffs, 'if you have finally settled all the legal bills that arose from your reckless libel action?'

'Yes, I have, Papa. But I had to sell all my shares in Barrington's in order to do so.'

'No more than poetic justice,' commented the earl, before taking another puff on his ancient pipe. 'You should never have allowed the case to get to court after Sir Edward advised you that your chances were no better than fifty-fifty.'

'But it was in the bag until Fisher wrote that unfortunate letter.'

'Another example of your lack of judgement,' spat out the earl. 'Fisher was always going to be a liability, and you should never have become involved with him.'

'But he was a major in the army.'

'A rank you reach only after the war office has decided it's time for you to retire.'

'And a Member of Parliament.'

'Who rate above only second-hand car salesmen and cattle thieves for reliability.' Virginia opted for silence in a battle she knew she couldn't win. 'Please assure me, Virginia, that you haven't thrown your hand in with any more ne'er-do-wells.'

She thought about Desmond Mellor, Adrian Sloane and Jim Knowles, to whom she knew her father wouldn't have given house room. 'No, Papa, I've learnt my lesson, and won't be causing you any more trouble.'

'I'm glad to hear it.'

'But I must admit that it's quite difficult to live in London on only two thousand pounds a month.'

'Then come back and live in Kinross, where one can exist quite comfortably on two thousand a year.'

Virginia knew only too well that was the last thing her father would want, so she decided to take a risk. 'I was rather hoping, Papa, you might see your way to raising my allowance to three thousand a month.'

'You needn't give that a second thought,' came back the immediate reply. 'In fact, after your most recent shenanigans, I was thinking of cutting your allowance in half.'

'But if you did that, Papa, how could I hope to survive?' She wondered if this was the moment to burst into tears.

'You could behave like the rest of us and learn to live within your means.'

'But my friends rather expect—'

'Then you've got the wrong friends. Perhaps the time has come for you to join the real world.'

'What are you suggesting, Papa?'

'You could start by dismissing your butler and housekeeper, who are in my opinion an unnecessary expense, and then move into a smaller flat.' Virginia looked shocked. 'And you could even go out and look for a job.' Virginia burst into tears. 'Although that, come to think of it, would be pointless, as you're not qualified to do anything apart from spending other people's money.'

'But, Papa,' Virginia said, dabbing away a tear, 'another thousand a month would solve all my problems.'

'But not mine,' said the earl. 'So you can begin your new regime by taking a bus to the station and travelling back to London – second class.'

◄○►

Virginia had never entered a second-class carriage and, despite her father's admonition, had no intention of doing so. However, during the long journey back to King's Cross, she did give considerable thought to her current predicament, and what choices had been left open to her if she was not to further exhaust the old man's patience.

She had already borrowed small amounts from several friends and acquaintances, and one or two of them were beginning to press her for repayment, while others seemed resigned to the fact that she hadn't considered the money a loan, more of a gift.

Perhaps she could learn to live without a butler and a cook, visit Peter Jones more often than Harrods, and even board the occasional bus, rather than hail a taxi. However, one thing she could never agree to do was to travel on the tube. She didn't care to go underground, unless it was to visit Annabel's. Her weekly visit to the hair salon was also non-negotiable, and white wine in place of champagne was unthinkable. She also refused to consider giving up her box at the Albert Hall, or her debenture seats at Wimbledon. She'd been told by Bofie Bridgwater that some of his friends rented them out when they weren't using them. So vulgar, although she had to admit it would be marginally better than losing them altogether.

However, Virginia had noticed recently that she'd been receiving more brown envelopes through the letterbox. She left them unopened in the vain hope that they would go away, whereas in truth they were often followed by a solicitor's letter warning of an impending writ if their client's bills were not paid within fourteen days. As if that wasn't enough, she had that morning opened a letter from her bank manager asking to see her ladyship at her earliest convenience.

Virginia had never met a bank manager, and it certainly wasn't convenient. But when she returned to Cadogan Gardens and opened her front door, she discovered that the brown envelopes on the hall table now outnumbered the white. She took the letters through to the drawing room, where she divided them into two piles.

After dropping into the waste-paper basket a second request from her bank manager for an urgent meeting, she turned her attention to the white envelopes. Several invitations from chums inviting her to spend a weekend in the country, but she'd recently sold her little MGB and no longer had any means of transport. Balls, at which she couldn't possibly be seen in the same dress twice. Ascot, Wimbledon, and of course the garden party at Buckingham Palace. But it was Bofie Bridgwater's embossed invitation that intrigued her most.

Bofie was, in her father's opinion, a waste of space. However, he did have the virtue of being the youngest son of a viscount, which allowed him to mix with a class of people who were only too happy to foot the bill. Virginia read Bofie's attached letter. Would she care to join him for lunch at Harry's Bar (which certainly meant he wouldn't be paying) to meet an old American chum (they'd probably met quite recently), Cyrus T. Grant III, who was visiting London for the first time and didn't know his way around town?'

'Cyrus T. Grant III,' she repeated. Where had she come across that name before? Ah, yes, William Hickey. She picked up the previous day's *Daily Express* and turned to the gossip column, as a gambler turns to the racing pages. *Cyrus T. Grant III will be visiting London this summer to take in the season,* Hickey informed her. *In particular, to watch his filly, Noble Conquest, race in the King George VI and Queen Elizabeth Stakes at Ascot. He will be flying to London on his Lear jet, and staying in the Nelson suite at the Ritz. Forbes Magazine has listed Grant as the 28th richest man in America.* A multi-millionaire – Virginia liked the word 'multi' – who had made his fortune in the canning industry – she didn't care for the word 'industry'. Hickey went on to say that *Vogue* had described him as one of the most eligible bachelors on the planet. But how old are you?, mumbled Virginia, as she studied the photo of the tycoon below the story. She guessed forty-five, and hoped fifty, and although he wasn't what you might have called handsome, or even presentable, the number 28 stuck in her mind.

Virginia dropped Bofie a hand-written billet accepting his kind invitation, and added how much she was looking forward to meeting Cyrus T. Grant III. Perhaps she could sit next to him?

◄o►

'You called, my lady?' said the butler.

'Yes, Morton. I'm sorry to say that I have been left with no choice but to terminate your employment at the end of the month.' Morton didn't look surprised, as he hadn't been paid for the past three months. 'Of course, I shall supply you with an excellent reference, so you should have no difficulty in finding another position.'

'Thank you, my lady, because I confess these have not been the easiest of times.'

'I'm not sure I understand you, Morton.'

'Mrs Morton is expecting again.'

'But you told me only last year that you felt three children was more than enough.'

'And I still do, my lady, but just let's say this one wasn't planned.'

'One must organize one's life more carefully, Morton, and learn to live within one's means.'

'Quite so, my lady.'

◄o►

Virginia could no longer put off visiting her bank manager after an embarrassed Mayfair hairdresser presented her with a bounced cheque.

'A clerical error,' Virginia assured her, and immediately wrote out another cheque. But once she'd left the salon, she hailed a taxi and asked the cabbie to take her to Coutts in the Strand.

Mr Fairbrother rose from behind his desk as Lady Virginia

marched into his office unannounced. 'No doubt you have a simple explanation for this?' she said, placing the REFER TO DRAWER cheque on the manager's desk.

'I fear, my lady, that you are well above your agreed overdraft limit,' said Fairbrother, not commenting on the fact that she hadn't made an appointment. 'I have written to you several times requesting a meeting to discuss the present situation, but you have clearly been very busy.'

'I rather assumed that as my family has banked with Coutts for over two hundred years, I might be given a little more latitude.'

'We have been as obliging as we felt able in the circumstances,' said Fairbrother, 'but as there are several other transactions pending, I'm afraid you left us with little choice.'

'If that is the case, you have left me with no choice but to make arrangements to move my account to a more civilized establishment.'

'As you wish, my lady. And perhaps in the fullness of time you would be kind enough to let me know to which bank we should transfer your overdraft. Meanwhile, we will, I fear, be unable to honour any of your current outstanding cheques until we have received his lordship's monthly payment.'

'That's fortunate really,' said Virginia, 'as I've recently visited my father in Scotland, and he agreed to raise my allowance to three thousand pounds a month.'

'That is indeed good news, my lady, and will unquestionably help to alleviate your current short-term problem. However, I should point out that following that meeting with your father, his lordship wrote to inform the bank that he was no longer willing to guarantee your overdraft. And he made no mention of any increase in your monthly allowance.'

13

Virginia spent the morning at a new hairdresser, had her nails manicured and picked up her favourite Chanel outfit from the dry-cleaners before returning to Cadogan Gardens.

As she stared at herself in a full-length mirror, she felt she didn't look too bad for forty-two, well, forty-three . . . well . . . She took a taxi to Harry's Bar just before 1 p.m., and when she mentioned the name Cyrus T. Grant III to the concierge, she was immediately accompanied to the private dining room on the second floor.

'Welcome, my darling,' said Bofie as she entered the room. He quickly took her to one side and whispered, 'I know Cyrus is just dying to meet you. I've already told him you're a member of the royal family.'

'I'm a distant niece of the Queen Mother, whom I've only met at official functions, though it's true my father occasionally plays bridge with her when she stays at Glamis Castle.'

'And I told him you had tea with the Queen only last week.'

'Buck House or Windsor?' asked Virginia, joining in the game.

'Balmoral. So much more exclusive,' said Bofie as he grabbed another glass of champagne from a passing waiter.

Virginia pretended not to notice the guest of honour, who was surrounded by admirers, and wondered if they would have been hanging on his every word had he not been the twenty-eighth richest man in America.

Cyrus couldn't have been an inch over five foot five, and sadly didn't have Gary Cooper's looks to compensate. He was wearing a red-and-white check jacket, blue jeans, a pale blue silk shirt and a leather bootlace tie. His Cuban heels made him almost the same height as Virginia. She wanted to giggle, but somehow managed to keep a straight face.

'Cyrus, may I introduce my dear friend, the Lady Virginia Fenwick?'

'Nice to meet you, my lady,' said Cyrus.

'Please call me Virginia, all my friends do.'

'Thank you, Ginny. You can call me Cyrus, everyone does.'

Virginia didn't comment. Bofie clapped his hands, and once he had everyone's attention, said, 'I'm sure you're all ready for a spot of lunch.'

'I sure am,' said Cyrus, who left the ladies standing. Virginia was both appalled and delighted to find herself sitting on the right-hand side of the honoured guest.

'How long do you plan to be in England?' she ventured.

'Just a few weeks. I'm here for what you people call the season, so I'll be going to Wimbledon, Henley and, most important, Royal Ascot. You see, I have a filly running in the King George VI and Queen Elizabeth Stakes.'

'Noble Conquest.'

'Well, I'll be damned,' said Cyrus. 'That's impressive, Ginny.'

'Not really. I never miss Ascot, and your horse is already being talked about.'

'I'd invite you to be my guest,' said Cyrus, 'but I guess you'll be in the royal box.'

'Not every day,' said Virginia.

'I asked if you could sit next to me today,' confided Cyrus, as a plate of smoked salmon was placed in front of him, 'because I've got a problem, and I have a feeling you're the right person to solve it for me.'

'I will certainly do anything I can to help.'

'I don't know how to get dressed, Ginny.' Virginia looked surprised, until he added, 'And I'm told you have to wear a special outfit before you can enter the royal enclosure.'

'Top hat and tails,' said Virginia. 'And if you're lucky enough to have a winner, Her Majesty will present you with the cup.'

'That would be the greatest honour of my life. May I call her Liz?'

'Certainly not,' said Virginia firmly. 'Even her family address her as "Your Majesty."'

'Will I be expected to bow?'

'First things first,' said Virginia, warming to her task. 'You'll need to visit Gieves and Hawkes in Savile Row, who will be able to kit you out.'

'Kit me out?'

'Make sure that you're appropriately attired.'

A waiter appeared by Cyrus's side and refilled his glass with whisky, while another offered Virginia a glass of champagne.

'It's just a shame they don't have my favourite brand,' said Cyrus after he'd emptied his glass.

'Your favourite brand?'

'Maker's Mark. I haven't been able to find a hotel or restaurant in this city that stocks it,' he said, as a waiter leaned forward and lit his cigar. Cyrus took a few puffs and blew out a cloud of smoke, before saying, 'I hope you don't mind, Ginny.'

'Not at all,' said Virginia, as another waiter whisked away the empty plates. 'Is your wife travelling with you?' she added, casting a fly.

'I'm not married, Ginny.'

Virginia smiled.

'But I plan to get myself hitched just as soon as I'm back in Louisiana.'

Virginia frowned.

'I've known Ellie May since we were in high school together but, goddamn it, I was too slow off the mark first time round, so Wayne Halliday upped and married her. They got divorced last year, so I'm not going to let her get away a second time.' Cyrus took out his wallet and produced a photo of Ellie May, who didn't look likely to win any beauty pageants, but then perhaps she had other, more tangible, assets.

'Quite beautiful,' said Virginia.

'I think so.'

Virginia needed to reconsider her strategy.

'And that's another thing I've got to do while I'm in London, Ginny, get myself an engagement ring. You see, I couldn't risk buying a ring in Baton Rouge, because if I did, half the county would know an hour later, which wouldn't make it much of a surprise for Ellie May. And I've no idea where to start,' he added as a T-bone steak almost the size of the plate was put in front of him.

Virginia sipped her champagne while she considered this new piece of information.

Cyrus picked up his knife and fork and glared at the steak before attacking it. 'It has to be a bit special, Ginny, because Ellie May's family came over on the *Mayflower*. She can trace her ancestors back nine generations. Bit like you, I guess.'

'The first recorded Fenwick was farming in Perthshire in 1243,' said Virginia, 'but I confess we're unable to trace anyone with certainty before that.'

Cyrus laughed. 'You got me there. I know who my granddaddy was, 'cause he founded the company, but before that it gets a bit hazy.'

'Every great dynasty has to begin somewhere,' said Virginia, touching his hand.

'That's kind of you to say so,' said Cyrus. 'And to think I was nervous about sitting next to a member of the royal family.' He put down his knife and fork, but only to pick up his cigar and take another gulp of whisky.

When Bofie asked Cyrus a question, Virginia turned to the person on her right, in the hope of finding out more about Cyrus T. Grant III. Mr Lennox turned out to be Cyrus's trainer. It took Virginia a few moments to realize that Mr Lennox trained Cyrus's horses, not Cyrus himself, which may have explained why his boss looked unlikely to be up for a morning gallop. She pumped Lennox for information, and quickly learned that thoroughbreds were the real love of Cyrus's life. After his grandfather had died, his father Cyrus T. Grant II had continued to build up the family company, and when he died, Cyrus T. Grant III was made an offer that allowed him to give up the canning business and concentrate on his stud farm. He'd already won the Kentucky Derby, and he now had his eyes set on the King George VI and Queen Elizabeth Stakes.

Once Virginia had gleaned all the information she needed, she turned her attention back to Cyrus, who may not have cared that much for Scotch whisky, but still seemed quite happy to consume several drams of the golden nectar between each mouthful of steak. An idea was beginning to form in Virginia's mind.

'If you're not doing anything particular this afternoon, Cyrus, why don't I take you to Bond Street and see if we can find something a little special for Ellie May?'

'What a swell idea. Are you sure you can spare the time?'

'I'll just have to rearrange my diary, won't I, Cyrus.'

'Gee, Ginny, and to think the folks back home kept telling me the English are so uptight and stand-offish. Won't I have something to tell them when I get back to Baton Rouge.'

'I do hope so.'

When Cyrus eventually turned to his left to speak to Bofie again, Virginia slipped out of her seat and went across to have a word with the maître d'.

'Would you be kind enough to send one of your waiters to Fortnum's and pick up two bottles of Maker's Mark. Put them in a bag, and hand them to me as I leave.'

'Of course, my lady.'

'And put them on the bill.'

'As you wish, my lady.' She handed the maître d' a pound note, painfully aware that he was probably better off than she was.

'Thank you, my lady.'

Virginia returned to her place and quickly guided Cyrus back on to his favourite subject – Cyrus. She allowed him to talk about himself for the next twenty minutes, only interrupting with carefully prepared questions.

Over coffee, Virginia leant across to Bofie and said, 'I'm going to take Cyrus shopping this afternoon.'

'Where will you start?' he asked.

'Asprey, Cartier, and possibly Cellini.'

'Cellini?' said Bofie. 'Aren't they a little nouveau?'

'I'm sure you're right, Bofie, but I'm told they now have the finest selection of stones.'

'Then let's start there,' said Cyrus as he got up from the table, seemingly unaware that several of the guests hadn't yet been served coffee. While he was being helped on with his raincoat, the maître d' deftly handed her ladyship a Fortnum's bag. Once Virginia had kissed Bofie on both cheeks, she linked her arm into Cyrus's and led him up the path to Bond Street.

They glanced in the windows of Cartier and Asprey, but didn't go in, as Cyrus seemed set on Cellini. When they arrived outside the thick glass door displaying a large golden 'C', Virginia rang the bell and a moment later a man appeared, dressed in tailcoat and striped trousers. When he saw Virginia, he immediately unlocked the door and stood aside to allow them to enter.

'Mr Cyrus T. Grant and I,' she whispered, 'are looking for an engagement ring.'

'Many congratulations, madam,' said the assistant, whom Virginia didn't disillusion. 'Perhaps you'd allow me to show you our latest collection.'

'Thank you,' said Virginia. They were guided towards a pair of comfortable leather chairs next to the counter, before the assistant disappeared into a back room.

Cyrus, clearly not a man who liked to be kept waiting, began to fidget, but he perked up the moment the assistant returned carrying a tray displaying a large selection of magnificent diamond rings.

'Wow,' he said. 'Now that's what I call spoilt for choice. Where do I start?'

'They're all so beautiful,' purred Virginia. 'But I'll leave you to decide, my darling,' she said, choosing her words carefully.

Cyrus stared down at the sparkling stones for some time before he selected one.

'A fine choice, if I may say so,' said the assistant. 'Every other woman will be certain to admire it.'

'They'll be as jealous as hell,' said Cyrus.

Virginia certainly agreed with that.

'Shall we try it on the lady's finger, so you can see how it looks?'

'Good idea,' said Cyrus as the assistant placed the ring on the third finger of Virginia's left hand.

'And its provenance?' asked Virginia, looking more closely at the huge diamond.

'The stone is South African, my lady, from the Transvaal. 6.3 carat, certified rare yellow, unblemished. VVH2.'

'How much?' asked Cyrus.

The young man checked his coded stock list and said, 'Fourteen thousand pounds, sir,' as if it were loose change for a customer who shopped at Cellini.

Cyrus whistled through his teeth.

'I agree,' said Virginia, as she admired the ring on her finger. 'I expected it to be far more, and it certainly would have been, had we gone to Cartier or Asprey. How clever of you, Cyrus, to have chosen Cellini.' Cyrus hesitated. 'If someone wanted to marry me,' she said taking his hand, 'this is exactly the sort of ring I would want.'

'God damn it you're right, Ginny,' he said, taking out his cheque book. 'Wrap it up.'

'Thank you, sir.'

Cyrus wrote out a cheque and placed it on the counter. 'Do you have a men's room?'

'Yes, sir, down the stairs on the right. You can't miss it.'

As Cyrus slowly pushed himself up out of his chair, Virginia thought he might. She stared lovingly down at the ring before removing it from her finger and placing it in its smart leather box, also embossed with a gold 'C'.

'If I were to change my mind . . .' she said casually.

'Just come back whenever it's convenient, my lady. We'll always be happy to accommodate you.'

Virginia was pulling on her leather gloves when Cyrus reappeared. She gave him one look before saying, 'I think we'd better get you back to your hotel, my darling. Lucky it's so close.'

'Good idea, Ginny,' said Cyrus as he took her arm.

The assistant handed her a small bag which contained the even smaller leather box, before accompanying them to the door. As she stepped out on to the street, Virginia checked the opening times printed discreetly on the window.

'Ellie May is going to be so excited,' Virginia said as they walked slowly down Old Bond Street towards the Ritz.

'All thanks to you,' said Cyrus, clinging firmly on to her while she guided him across Piccadilly.

'I always enjoy afternoon tea at the Ritz,' said Virginia. 'But you may not feel up to it.'

'Of course I'm up to it,' said Cyrus, staggering unsteadily up the steps and into the hotel.

'Perhaps the first thing you should do,' she added as they passed the tea room, 'is put Ellie May's ring in the safe in your room.'

'You think of everything, Ginny. Let me get my key.'

When Virginia saw the size of the Nelson Suite, she suggested they take tea in its large drawing room rather than go back downstairs to the crowded Palm Court.

'Suits me,' said Cyrus. 'Why don't you make the order while I go to the john?'

Virginia picked up the phone and ordered tea and buttered scones for two. She then took one of the bottles of Maker's Mark out of the bag and placed it in the centre of the table. When Cyrus walked back into the drawing room it was the first thing he saw. 'Where did you get that?'

'I didn't tell you, it's also my favourite.'

'Then let's have a small one to celebrate,' said Cyrus.

When Virginia saw what Cyrus meant by a small one, she was glad she'd ordered two bottles.

A gentle knock on the door and a trolley was wheeled in. A smartly dressed waitress set up tea for two on the table by the sofa. Virginia poured two cups, as Cyrus sat down next to her. She sipped her tea while Cyrus poured himself another whisky. He clearly had no interest in Earl Grey. She moved a little closer, letting her skirt ride up well above her knees. He stared down at her legs, but didn't move. She edged even closer and placed a hand on his thigh. He quickly downed his glass and refilled it, which gave her enough time to undo a couple of buttons of her silk blouse, while moving her other hand further up his leg. He didn't resist when she began to unbuckle his cowboy belt and unbutton his shirt.

'What about Ellie May?' he murmured.

'I'm not going to tell her, if you don't,' whispered Virginia, as she pulled down the zip on his jeans and placed a hand inside his pants. He took another swig of whisky straight from the bottle, before lunging at her.

Virginia continued to focus on the job at hand and, after she had pulled off his boots and socks, she deftly removed the rest of his clothing, until he was naked. She looked down at him and smiled. She'd never seen anything so small. He took another swig and slipped off the sofa and on to the floor, his head narrowly missing the table. Virginia sank down on to the carpet beside him. She was about to pull him on top of her, when he passed out. She rolled him over gently, so he was sprawled on the carpet.

She jumped up, ran to the door, opened it a few inches and hung the DO NOT DISTURB sign on the outside doorknob. She returned to Cyrus's side, fell to her knees and, gathering all her strength, placed her arms under his shoulders and dragged him across the carpet and into the bedroom. She left him on the floor as she pulled back the sheets and blanket on the vast king-sized bed. She then knelt down beside him and, with one final Herculean effort, pulled him up off the floor and on to the mattress, grateful that he was only five foot five. He was snoring contentedly as she covered him gently with the sheet and blanket. She filled another glass with Maker's Mark and placed it on the small table by his side of the bed. Virginia then closed the bedroom door, drew the heavy curtains and turned out all the lights one by one until the room was in total darkness.

When she finally climbed into bed beside him, she was only wearing one thing.

14

VIRGINIA SPENT MOST of the night wide awake, listening to Cyrus's thunderous snores. He tossed and turned, and when he did wake, it was only for a few moments before the snores erupted again. She couldn't believe Ellie May had ever slept with this man.

Virginia lay there, for hour upon hour, realizing it could be a long night. Not only was Cyrus drunk, but probably suffering from jet lag. She spent her time preparing a plan that would be set into motion the moment he awoke. She even rehearsed the lines she would deliver until they were word perfect.

He woke just after six the next morning, but it was some time before he properly entered this world, which gave Virginia time to carry out an undress rehearsal. A few minutes before seven, Cyrus stretched out an arm and, after some fumbling, managed to switch on his bedside light, the cue for Virginia to close her eyes, turn over and let out a soft sigh. When Cyrus looked around and saw her lying next to him, she heard a voice say, 'What the hell?'

Virginia yawned and stretched her arms, pretending to wake slowly. When she opened her eyes, she was greeted with a vision of Bottom: an unshaven face, mouth wide open, sweating profusely and stinking of whisky. All Cyrus needed was a pair of ass's ears to complete the image.

'Good morning, my darling,' said Virginia. She leant across and kissed him, catching a full waft of his morning breath, but she didn't recoil, just smiled, and wrapped her arms around his damp, podgy body. She began to move a hand up his leg.

'You were magnificent last night, my little dumpling,' she said. 'A lion, a veritable lion.'

'What happened last night?' Cyrus managed, snatching at the sheet to cover his naked body.

'You were unstoppable. I don't know how many times we made love, and it was so romantic when you told me you'd never met anyone like me and we must spend the rest of our lives together.'

'I said what?'

'"But what about Ellie May?" I insisted. "How could I even think about Ellie May now I've met a goddess," you replied. "I shall make you the Queen of Louisiana." Then you got out of bed, fell on one knee and asked me to be your wife.'

'I did what?'

'You proposed, and I confess I was overwhelmed by the thought of spending the rest of my life with you in Baton Rouge. You then placed the ring on my finger.' She held up her left hand.

'I did?'

'You did, and now we must let the world share our happiness.' Cyrus's mouth remained open. 'I'll tell you what I'm going to do, my darling,' continued Virginia, getting out of bed and pulling open the curtains to let the sun flood in. Cyrus's mouth remained open as he stared at her naked body. 'As soon as I'm dressed, I'm going home to change. After all, even though I'm now your fiancée, we wouldn't want anyone to see me in the same clothes I was wearing last night, would we, my little dumpling.' She giggled as she leant over and kissed him on the mouth.

Virginia picked up the phone by his side of the bed. 'Breakfast for one,' she said. 'Tea, toast and Oxford Marmalade, and perhaps a Virgin Mary. My fiancé has a dreadful hangover. Thank you, yes, as soon as possible.' She put the phone down. 'I'll be back around ten, dumpling,' she promised, 'and then we can go shopping. I think we should start at Moss Bros. You'll need a top hat and tails for Ascot, and perhaps a grey silk cravat if you're going to be seen regularly in the royal box. And then you can join me while I spend a little time looking at Hartnell's spring collection. I'll need to find something worthy of the winner of the King George VI and Queen Elizabeth Stakes,' she added as she pulled on her skirt and did up her blouse.

There was a knock at the door. Virginia left the bedroom and opened the door to allow a waiter pushing a trolley to enter.

'My fiancé is still in bed. Do go through. Your breakfast has arrived, my darling,' Virginia said as she followed the waiter into the bedroom. 'And be sure to drink your Virgin Mary,' she added as the tray was placed on his lap, 'because we've got a busy day ahead of us.' Once again she leant over and kissed Cyrus, who was now sitting bolt upright and staring blankly at her. 'I must also give some thought to the wording of our engagement announcement in the Court Circular. Something simple but dignified,' she said, 'letting the world know the significance of our two families coming together. Of course everyone will expect a society wedding at St Margaret's, Westminster, although I'd prefer a quiet affair, perhaps in Baton Rouge.' The waiter proffered the bill. 'I'll sign it,' said Virginia, who, before ushering him out, added 20 per cent, to make sure the young man couldn't possibly forget what he had just witnessed. She then gave Cyrus one final kiss and said, 'See you in a couple of hours, dumpling.'

She had slipped out of the room before he could reply.

Virginia walked quickly down the long corridor, purpose in her stride, and took the lift to the ground floor. As she passed the reception desk, none of the porters gave her a second look. They were well accustomed to ladies slipping out of the hotel early in the morning, some paid, others not – and certainly Virginia intended to be paid in full. A liveried porter opened the front door for her and asked if she needed a taxi.

'Yes, please.'

He raised an arm, let out a piercing whistle and a taxi miraculously appeared a moment later.

Virginia did as she'd told Cyrus she would. She returned home, where she spent some considerable time soaking in a warm bath, before washing her hair and changing her clothes. She then selected an appropriate outfit for returning to the Ritz.

Over breakfast, she took her time reading the morning papers. After all, the shop she intended to visit didn't open until ten. She left her flat in Cadogan Gardens just after nine forty, and took another taxi, this time to Bond Street, which looked like a desert at that time in the morning. She was dropped outside the House of Cellini a few minutes after ten.

Virginia pressed the bell, took out her handkerchief, and was pleased to see the same assistant step forward to open the door. She bowed her head and dabbed away an imaginary tear.

'Is everything all right, madam?' he asked solicitously.

'No, I'm afraid it isn't,' she said, her voice quivering. 'My beloved has changed his mind and asked me to return this,' she said, removing the engagement ring from her finger.

'I'm so sorry, my lady.'

'Not as sorry as I am,' she said placing the ring on the counter. 'He asked me if you could return his cheque.'

'That won't be possible, madam, we banked it immediately, and as you had taken the ring with you, we requested same-day clearance.'

'Then I'll need a cheque for the full amount in compensation. After all, you witnessed him giving me the ring, and I've agreed with his lawyers not to pursue the matter any further. Always so unpleasant when the press become involved, don't you think?' The assistant looked anxious. 'None of us need that sort of publicity, do we? And of course, it's possible my beloved might change his mind again, in which case I'll be back. So perhaps you could put the ring on one side for a few days.'

The assistant hesitated before saying, 'Who shall I make the cheque out to, my lady?'

'The Lady Virginia Fenwick,' she said, giving him a warm smile.

The assistant disappeared into the back office and didn't reappear for what seemed to Virginia like an eternity. He finally returned and handed her a cheque for £14,000. As Virginia placed the cheque in her handbag, he came round from behind the counter, opened the front door and said, 'Good day, my lady. I hope we'll be seeing you again soon.'

'Let's hope so,' said Virginia as she walked out on to the pavement. She hailed a taxi and instructed the cabbie to take her to Coutts in the Strand. Once again she prepared her words carefully for whatever his name was.

On arrival at the bank, she told the driver to wait as she would only be a few minutes. She got out, walked into Coutts and headed straight for the manager's office. She marched in to find him dictating a letter to his secretary.

'You can leave us, Mrs Powell,' said Mr Fairbrother. He was about to tell her ladyship that he wasn't willing to see her again unless she made an appointment, when Virginia placed the cheque on the desk in front of him. He stared at the figure of £14,000 in disbelief.

'Be sure to clear every one of my outstanding cheques without delay,' she said. 'And please don't bother me again in the future.' Before he could respond, Virginia had left the office and closed the door behind her.

'The Ritz,' she told the waiting cabbie. The taxi swung round on to the other side of the road and headed for Piccadilly. They came to a halt outside the hotel ten minutes later. Virginia handed over her last pound, walked up the steps and made her way to the reception desk.

'Good morning, madam, how may I help you?'

'Would you please call Mr Cyrus T. Grant in the Nelson Suite, and tell him that Lady Virginia Fenwick is waiting for him in reception.'

The concierge looked puzzled. 'But Mr Grant checked out over an hour ago, my lady. I ordered a limousine to take him to Heathrow.'

SEBASTIAN CLIFTON

1971

15

'YOUR MOTHER TOLD me I'd never get you to take the day off,' said Giles as his nephew joined him in the front seat.

'Especially to watch a game of cricket,' said Sebastian scornfully, pulling the door closed.

'This isn't just any old game of cricket,' said Giles. 'It's the opening day of a Lord's Test match against India, one of our oldest rivals.'

'It was still difficult to explain to my chairman, who's Scottish, and to the bank's owner, who's Turkish and refuses to believe any sporting encounter could go on for five days and then end up without a result.'

'A draw is a result.'

'You try explaining that to Hakim Bishara. However, when I told him I'd be your guest, he was keen for me to accept the invitation.'

'Why?' asked Giles.

'Hakim and Ross Buchanan are both great admirers of yours, and Ross asked me to find out if there was any chance you would consider becoming a director of Farthings.'

'Why would he suggest that, when I know as much about banking as he does about cricket?'

'I don't think your cricketing prowess is the reason they want you to join the board. But you do have certain skills that could be of benefit to the bank.'

'Like what?' asked Giles, as they turned off Hyde Park Corner and headed up Park Lane.

'You were a senior minister at the Foreign Office in the last government, and you currently sit in the Shadow Cabinet. Just think of the political contacts you've made over the years. And if we're going to join the EEC, imagine the doors you could open that would be closed to our rivals.'

'I'm flattered,' said Giles, 'but frankly I'm a politician at heart, and if we win the next election – and I'm convinced we will – I would hope to be appointed a minister again, and would there-fore have to give up any directorships.'

'But that might not be for another three or four years,' said Seb, 'during which time we could make good use of your know-ledge, contacts and expertise to expand our interests in Europe.'

'What would my responsibilities be?'

'You'd have to attend a board meeting every quarter, and be on the end of a phone if Hakim or Ross need to seek your advice. Not too onerous, so I hope you'll at least give it some thought.'

'A Labour politician on the board of a bank.'

'That might even be an advantage,' said Seb. 'Show you don't all hate business.'

'The first thing I'd need to do is find out how my colleagues in the Shadow Cabinet would react.'

As they drove around Marble Arch, Seb asked, 'And how are you enjoying the Lords?'

'It's not the Commons.'

'What does that mean?'

'The real power will always be in the Lower House. They instigate the bills, while we just revise them, which must be right while we're an unelected chamber. Frankly I made a mistake not standing in the by-election. But I'm not complaining. It means I get to spend more time with Karin, so in a way I've ended up with the best of both worlds. And you, Seb?'

'The worst of both worlds. The woman I love lives on the wrong side of the Atlantic and, as long as her husband's alive, there's not a lot I can do about it.'

'Have you told your parents about Jessica?'

'No, not in so many words, but I have a feeling Dad already knows. He came to my office a few weeks ago to take me to lunch and spotted a painting on the wall entitled "My Mom", signed "Jessica".'

'And he put two and two together?'

'It wouldn't have been difficult. "My Mom" couldn't be anyone but Samantha.'

'But that's wonderful on one level.'

'And dreadful on another, because Sam would never consider leaving her husband Michael while he's lying in a coma in hospital.'

'Perhaps it's time for you to move on.'

'That's what Aunt Grace keeps telling me, but it's not quite that easy.'

'After two failed marriages, I can hardly claim to be a role model,' said Giles. 'But I did get lucky the third time, so there must still be some hope for you.'

'And the whole family's delighted by how it's worked out. Mum particularly likes Karin.'

'And your father?' asked Giles, as he drove into St John's Wood Road.

'He's cautious by nature, so he may take a little longer. But that's only because he's got your best interests at heart.'

'Can't blame him. After all, he and your mother have been married for over twenty-five years, and they still adore each other.'

'Tell me more about today's game,' said Seb, clearly wanting to change the subject.

'For the Indians, cricket is not a game, it's a religion.'

'And we're guests of the president of the MCC?'

'Yes, Freddie Brown and I both played for the MCC, and he went on to captain England,' Giles said as he parked his car on a yellow line outside the ground. 'However, you're about to find that cricket is a great leveller. There's sure to be an interesting mix of guests in the president's box, who only have one thing in common – a passion for the game.'

'Then I'll be the odd one out,' said Seb.

–◦–

'The Cabinet Office.'

'It's Harry Clifton. Could I have a word with the Cabinet Secretary?'

'Hold on please, sir, I'll find out if he's free.'

'Mr Clifton,' said a voice a few moments later. 'What a pleasant surprise. I was only asking your brother-in-law the other day if there had been any progress in getting Anatoly Babakov released.'

'Sadly not, Sir Alan, but that wasn't the reason I was calling. I need to see you fairly urgently, on a private matter. I wouldn't bother you unless I considered it important.'

'If you say it's important, Mr Clifton, I'll see you whenever it's convenient, and I don't always say that, even to cabinet ministers.'

'I'm in London today to visit my publishers, so if by any chance you could fit me in for fifteen minutes this afternoon . . .'

'Let me check my diary. Ah, I see the Prime Minister is at Lord's to watch the Test match, where he'll have an unofficial meeting with Indira Gandhi, so I don't expect him back at No.10 much before six. Would four fifteen suit you?'

◄o►

'Good morning, Freddie. It was kind of you to invite us.'

'My pleasure, Giles. Nice to be on the same side for a change.'

Giles laughed. 'And this is my nephew, Sebastian Clifton, who works in the City.'

'Good morning, Mr Brown,' said Sebastian, as he shook hands with the president of the MCC. He looked out on to the magnificent ground, which was quickly filling up in anticipation of the opening salvoes.

'England won the toss and have elected to bat,' said the president.

'Good toss to win,' said Giles.

'And is this your first visit to the home of cricket, Sebastian?'

'No, sir, as a schoolboy I saw my uncle score a century for Oxford on this ground.'

'Not many people have achieved that,' said the president, as two of his other guests entered the box and came across to join them.

Sebastian smiled, although he was no longer looking at the former captain of England.

'And this,' said the president, 'is an old friend of mine, Sukhi Ghuman, not a bad spin bowler in his time, and his daughter Priya.'

'Good morning, Mr Ghuman,' said Giles.

'Do you enjoy cricket, Priya?' Seb asked the young woman, whom he tried not to stare at.

'That's a rather silly question to ask an Indian woman, Mr Clifton,' said Priya, 'because there wouldn't be anything to talk to our men about if we didn't follow cricket. How about you?'

'Uncle Giles played for the MCC, but when bowlers see me, they don't expect it to be a lasting experience.'

She smiled. 'And I heard your uncle say you work in the City.'

'Yes, I'm at Farthings Bank. And you, are you over here on holiday?'

'No,' said Priya. 'Like you, I work in the City.'

Sebastian felt embarrassed. 'What do you do?' he asked.

'I'm a senior analyst at Hambros.'

Let's wind back, Seb wanted to say. 'How interesting,' he managed, as a bell rang and rescued him.

They both looked out on to the ground to see two men in long white coats striding down the pavilion steps, a signal to the packed crowd that battle was about to commence.

—◄o►—

'Mr Clifton, what a pleasure to see you again,' said the Cabinet Secretary as the two men shook hands.

'What's the teatime score?' asked Harry.

'England are seventy-one for five. Someone called Bedi is taking us apart.'

'I rather hope they beat us this time,' admitted Harry.

'That's nothing less than high treason,' said Sir Alan, 'but I'll pretend I didn't hear it. And by the way, congratulations on the worldwide success of Anatoly Babakov's book.'

'You played your own role in making that possible, Sir Alan.'

'A minor role. After all, cabinet secretaries are not meant to appear on the stage, but be satisfied with prompting others from the wings. Can I get you a tea or coffee?'

'No, thank you,' said Harry, 'and as I don't want to take up any more of your time than necessary, I'll get straight to the point.' Sir Alan leant back in his chair. 'Some years ago, you asked me to travel to Moscow on behalf of Her Majesty's government, to carry out a private mission.'

'Which you did in an exemplary manner.'

'You may recall that I was required to memorize the names of a group of Russian agents operating in this country, and to pass those names on to you.'

'And most useful that has proved to be.'

'One of the names on that list was an agent called Pengelly.' The Cabinet Secretary reverted to being an expressionless mandarin. 'I was rather hoping that is no more than a coincidence.' The wall of silence prevailed. 'How stupid of me,' said Harry. 'Of course you'd already worked out the significance of that particular name.'

'Thanks to you,' said Sir Alan.

'Has my brother-in-law been informed?' Another question that remained unanswered. 'Is that entirely fair, Sir Alan?'

'Possibly not, but espionage is a dirty business, Mr Clifton. One doesn't exchange calling cards with the enemy.'

'But Giles is deeply in love with Pengelly's daughter, and I know he wants to marry her.'

'She is not Pengelly's daughter,' said Sir Alan. It was Harry's turn to be struck dumb. 'She's a highly trained Stasi agent. The whole operation was a set-up from the beginning, which we're monitoring closely.'

'But Giles is bound to find out in time, and then all hell will be let loose.'

'You may be right, but until then my colleagues have to consider the bigger picture.'

'As you did with my son Sebastian, some years ago.'

'I will regret that decision for the rest of my life, Mr Clifton.'

'And I suspect you will regret this one too, Sir Alan.'

'I don't think so. If I were to tell Lord Barrington the truth about Karin Brandt, many of our agents' lives would be put in danger.'

'Then what's to stop me telling him?'

'The Official Secrets Act.'

'Are you absolutely confident that I wouldn't go behind your back?'

'I am, Mr Clifton, because if I know one thing about you, it's that you would never betray your country.'

'You're a bastard,' said Harry.

'That's part of my job description,' said Sir Alan.

—◦—

Harry would often visit his mother at her cottage on the estate during his four to six p.m. writing break, when they would enjoy what Maisie described as high tea: cheese and tomato sandwiches, hot scones with honey, éclairs and Earl Grey tea.

They would discuss everything from the family – her greatest interest – to the politics of the day. She didn't care much for Jim Callaghan or Ted Heath, and only once, straight after the war, had voted anything other than Liberal.

'A wasted vote, Giles never stopped reminding you.'

'A wasted vote is when you don't vote, as I've told him many times.'

Harry couldn't help but notice that since her late husband had died, his mother had slowed down. She no longer walked the dog every evening, and recently she'd even cancelled the morning papers, unwilling to admit her eyesight was failing.

'Must get back to my six to eight session,' said Harry. As he rose from his seat by the fire, his mother handed him a letter.

'Not to be opened until they've laid me to rest,' she said calmly.

'That won't be for some years, Mother,' he said as he bent down and kissed her on the forehead, although he didn't believe it.

—◦—

'So, are you glad you took the day off?' Giles asked Sebastian as they walked back through the Grace Gates after stumps.

'Yes, I am,' said Seb. 'Thank you.'

'What a glorious partnership between Knott and Illingworth. They may have saved the day for England.'

'I agree.'

'Did you have a chance to chat to Mick Jagger?'

'No, I didn't speak to him.'

'What about Don Bradman?'

'I shook his hand.'

'Peter O'Toole?'

'I couldn't understand a word he said.'

'Paul Getty?'

'We exchanged cards.'

'What about the Prime Minister?'

'I didn't realize he was there.'

'From this scintillating exchange, Sebastian, should I conclude that you were distracted by a certain young lady?'

'Yes.'

'And are you hoping to see her again?'

'Possibly.'

'Are you listening to a word I'm saying?'

'No.'

—◦—

The three of them met once a week, ostensibly to discuss matters concerning Mellor Travel, on whose board they all sat. But as they didn't always want their fellow directors to know what they were up to, the meeting was neither minuted nor official.

The Unholy Trinity, as Sebastian referred to them, consisted of Desmond Mellor, Adrian Sloane and Jim Knowles. They only had one thing in common: a mutual hatred of anyone named Clifton or Barrington.

After Mellor had been forced to resign from the board of Barrington's and Sloane was dismissed as chairman of Farthings Bank, while Knowles departed from the shipping company without any 'regrets' being minuted, they had become bound together by a common thread – to gain control of Farthings Bank, and then take over Barrington's shipping company, by fair means or foul.

'I am able to confirm,' said Mellor as they sat quietly in the corner of one of the few London clubs that would have them as members, 'that Lady Virginia has reluctantly sold me her seven and a half per cent holding in Barrington's Shipping, which will allow one of us to take a seat on the board.'

'Good news,' said Knowles. 'I'm only too happy to volunteer for the job.'

'No need to be in such a rush,' said Mellor. 'I think I'll leave our fellow directors to consider the possible consequences of whoever I might select, so that every time the boardroom door opens, Mrs Clifton will wonder which one of us is about to appear.'

'That's a job I would also relish,' chipped in Sloane.

'Don't hold your breath,' said Mellor, 'because what neither of you know is that I already have a representative on the board. One of Barrington's longest-serving directors,' he continued, 'is experiencing a little financial difficulty, and has recently approached me for a fairly hefty loan that I feel sure he has no chance of repaying. So from now on, not only will I be getting the minutes of every board meeting, but also any inside information Mrs Clifton doesn't want recorded. So now you know what I've been up to during the past month. What have you two got to offer?'

'Quite a bit,' said Knowles. 'I recently heard that Saul Kaufman only retired as chairman of Kaufman's after everyone at the bank, including the doorman, realized he had Alzheimer's. His son Victor, who couldn't organize a piss-up in a brewery, has temporarily taken his place while they look for a new chairman.'

'Then this must be our best chance to make a move?' said Mellor.

'I wish it were that easy,' said Knowles, 'but unfortunately young Kaufman has begun negotiating a merger with Farthings. He and Sebastian Clifton were at school together, even shared a study, so Clifton's got the inside track.'

'Then let's make sure he trips up as he comes round the final bend,' said Sloane.

'I also picked up another useful piece of information,' continued Knowles. 'It seems that Ross Buchanan intends to step down as chairman of Farthings some time in the New Year, and Hakim Bishara will take his place, with Clifton as CEO of the newly formed Farthings Kaufman Bank.'

'Will the Bank of England go along with such a cosy little arrangement?'

'They'll turn a blind eye, especially now Bishara has ingratiated himself with the City. He's somehow managed to get himself accepted as part of the establishment.'

'But,' interjected Mellor, 'doesn't the new government legislation demand that any proposed bank merger has to be vetted by the City regulators? So there's nothing to stop us putting in a counter-bid and stirring things up.'

'What's the point, when we couldn't begin to challenge Bishara's deep pockets? All we could do is hold the process up, and even that wouldn't come cheap, as we found to our cost last time.'

'Is there anything else we can do to prevent the merger?' asked Mellor.

'We could so damage Bishara's reputation with the Bank of England,' said Sloane, 'that they wouldn't consider him a fit and proper person to run one of the City's larger financial institutions.'

'We tried that once before,' Mellor reminded him, 'and failed.'

'Only because our plan wasn't foolproof. This time I've come up with something that will make it impossible for the City regulators to allow the merger to go ahead, and Bishara would have to resign as chairman of Farthings.'

'How can that be possible?' asked Mellor.

'Because convicted criminals are not allowed to serve on the board of a bank.'

16

'AM I UGLY?'

'Need you ask?' said Clive Bingham as he sat at the bar sipping a pint of beer.

'And stupid?'

'Never in any doubt,' said Victor Kaufman.

'Then that explains it.'

'Explains what?' asked Clive.

'My uncle took me to Lord's last Thursday.'

'To watch England thrash the Indians.'

'True, but I met this girl . . .'

'Ah, the fog is lifting,' said Victor.

'And you fancied her,' said Clive.

'Yes, and what's more, I thought she quite liked me.'

'Then she must be dumb.'

'But when I called her the next day and asked her to dinner, she turned me down.'

'I like the sound of this woman.'

'So as we both work in the City, I suggested lunch.'

'And she still spurned you?'

'Out of hand,' said Seb. 'So I asked her if she—'

'Would consider dispensing with the meals and—'

'No, if she'd like to see Laurence Olivier in *The Merchant of Venice.*'

'And she still turned you down?'

'She did.'

'But you can't get tickets for that show even from touts,' said Victor.

'So I'll ask you again. Am I ugly?'

'We've already established that,' said Clive, 'so all that's left to discuss is which one of us will be your date for *Merchant*.'

'Neither of you. I haven't given up yet.'

⊸◦⊱

'I thought you told me you liked Sebastian?'

'I did. He was wonderful company for a day I'd been dreading,' said Priya.

'So why did you turn him down?' asked her flatmate.

'It was just unfortunate that on all three days he asked me out, I already had something else on.'

'And you couldn't rearrange any of them?' asked Jenny.

'No, my father had invited me to the ballet on Wednesday evening. Margot Fonteyn in *Swan Lake*.'

'OK, I'll accept that one. Next?'

'On Thursday, my boss asked me to attend a lunch he was giving for an important client who was flying in from New Delhi.'

'Fair enough.'

'And on Friday I always do my hair.'

'Pathetic.'

'I know! But by the time I'd thought about it, he was no longer on the line.'

'Pathetic,' Jenny repeated.

'And worse, Dad rang the next day to say something had come up and he had to fly to Bombay, and would I like the tickets. Fonteyn in *Swan Lake*. Can I tempt you, Jenny?'

'You bet. But I'm not going with you, because you are going to call Sebastian, tell him your father can't make it and ask him if he'd like to join you.'

'I can't do that,' said Priya. 'I couldn't possibly phone a man and ask him out.'

'Priya, it's 1971. It's no longer frowned upon for a woman to ask a man out.'

'It is in India.'

'But we're not in India, just in case you hadn't noticed. And what's more, you phone men all the time.'

'No, I do not.'

'Yes you do. It's part of your job, and you're rather good at it.'

'That's different.'

'So it would be all right to call Sebastian and discuss the drop in interest rates, but not to invite him to the ballet.'

'Perhaps he'll call me again.'

'And perhaps he won't.'

'Are you sure you don't want to see Fonteyn?'

'Of course I do. And if you give me the tickets I'll phone Sebastian and ask him if he'd like to be my date.'

◄○►

'There's a Jenny Barton on line one, Mr Clifton.'

'Jenny Barton, Jenny Barton . . . Doesn't ring a bell. Did she say which company she's from?'

'No, she said it was a personal matter.'

'I can't place her, but I suppose you'd better put her through.'

'Good morning, Mr Clifton. You don't know me, but I share a flat with Priya Ghuman.' Seb nearly dropped the phone. 'You rang Priya yesterday and invited her to dinner.'

'And lunch, and the theatre, all of which she turned down.'

'Which she now regrets, so if you were to call her again, I think you'll find she might be free on Wednesday night after all.'

'Thank you, Miss Barton,' said Seb. 'But why didn't she call herself?'

'You may well ask. Because after what she told me about you, I certainly wouldn't have turned you down.' The line went dead.

◄○►

'I had no idea you were interested in the ballet, Sebastian. I always think of you as more of a theatre buff.'

'You're quite right, Mother. In fact it will be my first visit to the Royal Opera House.'

'Then be warned, don't bother to have lunch.'

'What are you talking about?'

'It's all very civilized at Covent Garden. You have dinner throughout the evening. They serve the first course before the curtain goes up, the main course during the long interval, and coffee, cheese and biscuits after the curtain comes down. Who are you taking?'

'I'm not. I'm a guest.'

'Anyone I know?'

'Stop fishing, Mother.'

◄○►

Sebastian arrived at the Royal Opera House a few minutes before seven, surprised by how nervous he felt. But then, as Clive had so helpfully reminded him, it was his first date for some time. He scanned the crowd streaming through the front doors, and then he saw her. Not that he could have missed her. Priya's long dark hair and deep brown eyes were complemented by a striking red silk dress that made him feel she should be gracing the cover of *Vogue* rather than hidden away analysing profits and losses in the deep recesses of a bank. Her face lit up the moment she spotted him.

'Wow,' he said. 'You look stunning.'

'Thank you,' Priya replied, as Seb kissed her on the cheek as if she were his aunt Grace.

'I'm sure you've been to the House many times before,' she said, 'so you'll be familiar with the routine.'

'No, it's my first visit,' admitted Seb. 'In fact, I've never been to the ballet before.'

'Lucky you!'

'What do you mean?' asked Seb as they entered the restaurant on the ground floor.

'You'll either be hooked for life, or you won't ever want to come again.'

'Yes, I know what you mean,' said Seb.

Priya stopped at the entrance. 'We have a booking in the name of Ghuman.'

'Please follow me, madam,' said the maître d', who led them

to their table and, once they were seated, handed each of them a menu.

'They serve the first course before the curtain goes up, and we have to order the main course at the same time so they can have it ready for us at the interval.'

'Are you always this organized?'

'I'm so sorry,' said Priya. 'I was only trying to help.'

'And I was only teasing,' said Seb. 'But then, when you've got a mother like mine, it goes with the territory.'

'Your mother is a remarkable lady, Seb. I wonder if she knows just how many women look upon her as a role model?'

A waiter appeared at their side, his order pad open.

'I'll have the asparagus, and Dover sole,' said Priya.

'And I'll have the duck pâté, and a lamb chop,' said Seb, 'and I'd like to order a bottle of wine.'

'I don't drink,' said Priya.

'I'm sorry. What would you like?'

'Water will be fine, thank you. But don't let me stop you.'

Seb checked the wine list. 'I'll have a glass of Merlot,' he said.

'As a banker,' said Priya, 'you'd approve of how well this place is run. Most of the courses are simple and easy to prepare, so when you return to your table at the end of each act, they can serve you quickly.'

'I can see why you're an analyst.'

'And you head up the property division of Farthings, which must be quite a responsibility for someone—'

'—of my age? As you well know, banking is a young man's game. Most of my colleagues are burnt out by forty.'

'Some at thirty.'

'And it still can't be easy for a woman to make headway in the City.'

'One or two of the banks are slowly coming round to accepting that it's just possible a woman might be as bright as a man. However, most of the older establishments are still living in the dark ages. Which school you went to, or who your father is, often outranks ability or qualifications. Hambros is less Neanderthal than most, but they still don't have a woman on the board, which is also true of every other major bank in the City, including Far-things.'

Three bells rang.

'Does that mean the players are about to come out on to the pitch?'

'As you're a regular theatre-goer, you'll know that's the three-minute bell.'

Seb followed her out of the restaurant and into the auditor-ium as she seemed to know exactly where she was going. He wasn't surprised when they were shown to the best seats in the house.

From the moment the curtain rose and the little swans flut-tered out on to the stage, Seb was transported into another world. He was captivated by the dancers' skills and artistry, and just when he thought it couldn't get any better, the prima ballerina made her entrance, and he knew he would be returning again and again. When the curtain fell at the end of the second act and the applause had died down, Priya led him back to the restaurant.

'Well, what do you think?' she asked as they sat down.

'I was spellbound,' he said, looking directly at her. 'And I enjoyed Margot Fonteyn's performance as well.'

Priya laughed. 'My father first took me to the ballet when I was seven years old. Like all little girls, I left the theatre wanting to be one of the four cygnets, and it's been an unbroken love affair ever since.'

'I had the same feeling when my father first took me to Strat-ford to see Paul Robeson in *Othello*,' Seb said as a lamb chop was placed in front of him.

'How fortunate you are.' Seb looked puzzled. 'You'll now be able to see all the great ballets for the first time. Mind you, start-ing with Fonteyn won't make it easy for those who follow her.'

'My father once told me,' said Seb, 'that he wished he'd never read a word of Shakespeare until he was thirty. Then he could have seen all thirty-seven plays without knowing the endings. I now realize exactly what he meant.'

'I just don't get to the theatre enough.'

'I did invite you to *The Merchant of Venice*, but—'

'I had something on that night. But I can now get out of it, so I'd love to go with you. Assuming you haven't offered the ticket to someone else.'

'I'm sorry, but two of my friends were desperate to see Olivier, so . . .'

'I understand,' said Priya.

'But I turned them down.'

'Why?'

'They both have hairy legs.'

Priya burst out laughing.

'I know you—'

'Where do you—'

'No, you first,' said Priya.

'I just have so many questions I want to ask you.'

'Me too.'

'I know you went to St Paul's and then Girton, but why banking?'

'I've always been fascinated by figures and the patterns they create, especially when you have to explain their significance to men, who so often are only interested in a short-term gain.'

'Like me, perhaps?'

'I hope not, Seb.'

It could have been Samantha speaking. He wouldn't make the same mistake a second time. 'How long have you been with Hambros?'

'Just over three years.'

'So you must be thinking about your next move?'

'So like a man,' said Priya. 'No, I'm very happy where I am, although I do get depressed when inadequate men are promoted to positions above their actual ability. I wish banking was like the ballet. If it was, Margot Fonteyn would be governor of the Bank of England.'

'I don't think Sir Leslie O'Brien would make a very good black swan,' said Seb as the three-minute bell rang. He quickly drained his glass of wine.

Priya was right, because Seb couldn't take his eyes off the

black swan, who mesmerized the entire audience with her bril-
liance, and when the curtain fell at the end of act three, he was
desperate to find out what would happen in the final act.

'Don't tell me, don't tell me,' he said as they returned to their
table.

'I won't,' said Priya. 'But savour the moment, because sadly
you can only have this unique experience once.'

'Perhaps you'll have the same experience when I take you to
The Merchant of Venice.'

> *'How sweet the moonlight sleeps upon this bank!*
> *Here will we sit and let the sounds of music*
> *Creep in our ears. Soft stillness and the night*
> *Become the touches of sweet harmony.*
> *Sit, Jessica, look how—'*

Sebastian bowed his head.

'I'm so sorry,' said Priya. 'What did I say?'

'Nothing, nothing. You just reminded me of something.'

'Or someone?'

Seb was rescued by the tannoy. 'Ladies and gentlemen, would
you please take your seats, the final act is about to begin.'

The final act was so moving, and Fonteyn so captivating, that
when Seb turned to see if it was having the same effect on Priya,
he thought he saw a tear trickling down her cheek. He took her
hand.

'Sorry,' she whispered. 'I'm making a fool of myself.'

'That wouldn't be possible.'

When the curtain finally fell, Seb joined in the ten-minute
standing ovation, and Margot Fonteyn received so many curtain
calls and bouquets she could have opened a flower shop. As they
left the auditorium, he took Priya's hand as they strolled back to
the restaurant, but she seemed nervous and didn't speak. Once
coffee had been served, Priya said, 'Thank you for a wonderful
evening. Being with you was like seeing *Swan Lake* for the first
time. I haven't enjoyed a performance so much in a long time.'
She hesitated.

'But something is worrying you.'

'I'm a Hindu.'

Seb burst out laughing. 'And I'm a Somerset yokel, but it's never worried me.'

She didn't laugh. 'I don't think I can come to the theatre with you, Seb.'

'But why not?'

'I'm frightened of what might happen if we see each other again.'

'I don't understand.'

'I told you my father had to return to India.'

'Yes, I assumed on business.'

'Of a kind. My mother has spent the past few months selecting the man I will be expected to marry, and I think she's made her final choice.'

'No,' said Seb, 'that can't be possible.'

'All that's needed now is my father's approval.'

'You have no choice, no say in the matter?'

'None. You have to understand, Seb, it's part of our tradition, our heritage and our religious beliefs.'

'But what if you were to fall in love with someone else?'

'I would still have to honour my parents' wishes.' Seb leant across the table to take her hand, but she quickly withdrew it. 'I will never forget the night I saw *Swan Lake* with you, Seb. I will cherish the memory for the rest of my life.'

'And so will I, but surely . . .' But when he looked up, like the black swan, she had disappeared.

17

'So how did last night go?' asked Jenny, as she placed two eggs in a saucepan of warm water.

'It couldn't have been much worse,' Priya replied. 'Didn't work out at all as I'd planned.'

Jenny turned round to see her friend on the verge of tears. She rushed across, sat down beside her and put an arm around her shoulder. 'That bad?'

'Worse. I liked him even more the second time. And I blame you.'

'Why me?'

'Because if you'd agreed to come to the ballet with me, none of this would have happened.'

'But that's good.'

'No, it's awful. At the end of the evening I walked out on him, after telling him I never wanted to see him again.'

'What did he do to make you so angry?'

'He made me fall in love with him, which wasn't what I intended.'

'But that's fantastic, if he feels the same way.'

'But it can only end in disaster when our parents—'

'I'm pretty sure Seb's parents will welcome you as a member of their family. Everything I've ever read about them suggests they're extremely civilized.'

'It's not his parents I'm worried about, it's mine. They just wouldn't consider Sebastian a suitable—'

'We're living in the modern world, Priya. Mixed-race marriage is becoming quite the thing. You should take your parents to see *Guess Who's Coming to Dinner.*'

'Jenny, a black man wanting to marry a white woman in 1960s America is nothing compared to a Hindu falling in love with a Christian, believe me. Did you notice in that film, they never once discussed religion, only the colour of his skin? I realize it's not unknown for an Indian to marry someone of a different race, especially if they're both Christians. But it's not something a Hindu would ever consider. If only I hadn't gone to that cricket match.'

'But you did,' said Jenny, 'so you'll have to deal with reality. Would you rather try and build a worthwhile relationship with Sebastian, or please your parents by marrying a man you've never met?'

'I just wish it was that simple. I tried to explain to Seb last night what it's like to be brought up in a traditional Hindu house-hold, where heritage, duty—'

'What about love?'

'That can come after marriage. I know it did for my mother and father.'

'But your father's met Sebastian, so surely he'd understand.'

'The possibility of his daughter marrying a Christian will never even have crossed his mind.'

'He's an international businessman who sent you to St Paul's, and was so proud when you won a place at Cambridge.'

'Yes, and he made it possible for me to achieve those things, and has never asked for anything in return. But when it comes to who I should marry, he'll be immovable, and I'll be expected to obey him. I've always accepted that. My brother was married to someone he'd never met, and my younger sister is already being prepared to go through the same process. I could face defying my parents if I felt that in time they might come round, but I know they never will.'

'But surely they must accept that there's a new world order and things have changed?'

'Not for the better, as my mother never tires of telling me.'

Jenny ran across to the stove as the water bubbled over the

rim of the saucepan and rescued two very hard-boiled eggs. They both laughed. 'So what are you going to do about it?' asked Jenny.

'There's nothing I can do. I told him we couldn't see each other again, and I meant it.'

There was a firm rap on the front door.

'I'll bet that's him,' said Jenny.

'Then you have to answer it!'

'Sorry. Got another egg to boil, and can't afford to make the same mistake twice.'

A second rap on the door, even firmer.

'Get on with it,' said Jenny, remaining by the stove.

Priya prepared a little speech as she walked slowly into the hall.

'I'm sorry, but—' she began as she opened the front door to find a young man standing on the doorstep holding a red rose.

'Are you Miss Priya Ghuman?' he said.

'Yes.'

'I was asked to give you this.'

Priya thanked him, closed the door and returned to the kitchen.

'Was it him?' asked Jenny.

'No, but he sent this,' she said, holding up the rose.

'I really must start going to more cricket matches,' said Jenny.

—◦—

'On the hour, every hour?' asked Clive.

'That's right,' said Seb.

'And for just how long do you intend to keep sending her a rose on the hour, every hour?' asked Victor.

'For as long as it takes.'

'There's got to be one very happy florist out there somewhere.'

'Tell me, Vic, do Jewish parents feel as strongly about their children marrying outside their faith?'

'I have to admit,' said Vic, 'when my parents invited Ruth to dinner three Fridays in a row, I knew the only thing I was going to be allowed to choose was the vegetables.'

'How can we even begin to understand the pressure Priya must be facing?' said Clive. 'I feel for her.'

'On a lighter note, Seb,' said Victor, 'does this mean you won't be taking her to *The Merchant of Venice* at the National tonight?'

'It seems unlikely, so you may as well have my tickets.' He took out his wallet and handed them to Clive. 'Hope you both enjoy it.'

'We could toss a coin,' said Victor, 'to decide which one of us goes with you.'

'No, I have other plans for tonight.'

◄○►

'It's Miss Jenny Barton on line three, Mr Clifton.'

'Put her through.'

'Hi, Seb. I was just calling to say hang in there. She's weakening.'

'But she hasn't replied to any of my letters, doesn't answer my calls, won't acknowledge—'

'Perhaps you should try to see her.'

'I see her every day,' said Seb. 'I'm standing outside Hambros when she turns up for work in the morning, and again when she catches her bus in the evening. I'm even there when she gets back to her flat at night. If I try any harder, I could be arrested for stalking.'

'I'm visiting my parents in Norfolk this weekend,' said Jenny, 'and I won't be back until Monday morning. I can't do much more to help, so get on with it.'

◄○►

It was raining when Priya left the bank on Friday evening. She put up her umbrella and kept her head down, looking out for puddles as she made her way to the bus stop. Of course he was waiting for her, as he had been every night that week.

'Good evening, Miss Ghuman,' he said, and handed her a rose.

'Thank you,' she replied before joining the queue.

Priya climbed on board the bus and took a seat on the top

deck. She glanced out of the window and for a moment thought she spotted Seb hiding in the shadows of a shop doorway. When she got off the bus in Fulham Road, another young man, another rose, another thank you. She ran to the flat as the rain became heavier by the minute. By the time she put her key in the front door she was frozen. She'd decided on a quick supper, a warm bath and early bed, and tonight she would even try and get some sleep.

She was taking a yogurt out of the fridge when the door bell rang. She smiled, and checked her watch: the last rose of the day, which would join all the others in the vase on the hall table. Wondering just how long Seb would keep this up, she walked quickly to the door, not wanting the young man to get drenched. She opened it to find him standing there, an umbrella in one hand, a rose in the other.

Priya slammed the door in his face, sank to the floor and burst into tears. How could she continue to treat him so badly, when she was the one to blame? She sat in the hallway, hunched up against the wall. It was some time before she slowly picked herself up and made her way back to the kitchen. The light was fading, so she walked across to the window and drew the curtains. It was still raining – what the English describe as cats and dogs. And then she saw him, head down, sitting on the kerb on the far side of the road, rain cascading off his umbrella into the gutter. She stared at him through the tiny gap in the curtain, but he couldn't see her. She must tell him to go home before he caught pneumonia. She ran to the door, opened it and shouted, 'Sebastian.' He looked up. 'Please go home.'

He stood up, and she knew she should have closed the door immediately. He began walking slowly across the road towards her, half expecting the door to be slammed in his face again. But she didn't close it, so he stepped forward and took her in his arms.

'I don't want to go on living if I can't be with you,' he said.

'I feel the same way. But you must realize it's hopeless.'

'I'll go and see your father as soon as he comes back from India. I can't believe he won't understand.'

'It won't make any difference.'

'Then we'll have to do something about it before he returns.'

'The first thing we're going to have to do is get you out of that suit. You're soaking.' As she took off his jacket, he leaned forward and began to undo the tiny buttons on her blouse.

'I'm not soaking,' she said.

'I know,' he whispered, as they continued to undress each other. He took her in his arms and kissed her for the first time. They fumbled around like teenagers, discovering each other's bodies, slowly, gently, so when they finally made love, for Sebastian it was as if it was for the first time. For Priya it was the first time.

◄○►

For the rest of the weekend they never left each other, even for a moment. They ran together in the park each morning, she cooked while he laid the table, they went to the cinema, not watching much of the film, laughed and cried, and lost count of how many times they made love. The happiest weekend of her life, she told him on Monday morning.

'Let me tell you about my master plan,' he said as they sat down for breakfast.

'Does it begin with making love in the corridor?'

'No, but let's do that every Friday night. I'll stand out in the rain.'

'And I'll tell you to go home.'

'Home. That reminds me, my master plan. Next weekend I want to take you down to the West Country so you can meet my parents.'

'I'm so worried they won't—'

'Think I'm good enough for you? They'd be right. I suspect the real problem will be convincing your father that I'll ever be good enough for you, but I'll go and see him the moment he's back in England.'

'What will you say to him?'

'I've fallen in love with your daughter, and I want to spend the rest of my life with her.'

'But you haven't even proposed.'

'I would have done at Lord's, but I knew you'd only laugh at me.'

'He won't laugh. He'll only ask you one thing,' she said softly.

'And what will that be, my darling?'

Her words were barely audible. 'Have you slept with my daughter?'

'If he does, I'll tell him the truth.'

'Then he'll either kill you, or me, or both of us.'

Seb took her back in his arms. 'He'll come round once he sees how much we care for each other.'

'Not if my mother's already chosen a suitable man for me to marry, and the two families have come to an understanding. Because just before my father flew to India, I gave him my word I was still a virgin.'

–◄o►–

During the week, Seb spoke to his mother and father, and they were not only delighted by his news, but couldn't wait to meet their future daughter-in-law. Priya was heartened by their response, but couldn't hide how anxious she was about how her father would react. He phoned her on Thursday to say he was on his way back to England and had some exciting news to share with her.

'And we have some exciting news to share with him,' said Seb, trying to reassure her.

–◄o►–

On Friday evening, Seb left the bank early, only stopping off on the way to buy another bunch of roses. He then continued across town to the Fulham Road to pick up Priya before they travelled down to the West Country together. He couldn't wait to introduce her to his parents. But first he must thank Jenny for all she'd done to make it possible, and this time he would give the roses to her. He parked outside the flat, jumped out of the car and rang the doorbell. It was some time before the door opened, and when it did he felt his legs give way. Jenny stood there shaking uncontrollably, a red swelling on her cheek.

'What's happened?' he demanded.

'They've taken her away.'

'What do you mean?'

'Her father and brother turned up about an hour ago. She put up a fight, and I tried to help, but the two of them dragged her out of the flat, threw her in the back of a car and drove off.'

18

'It was good of you to see us at such short notice, Varun,' said Giles. 'Especially on a Saturday morning.'

'My pleasure,' said the High Commissioner. 'My country will always be in your debt for the role you played as foreign minister when Mrs Gandhi visited the United Kingdom. But how can I help, Lord Barrington? You said on the phone the matter was urgent.'

'My nephew, Sebastian Clifton, has a personal problem he'd like your advice on.'

'Of course. If I can assist in any way, I will be happy to do so,' he said, turning to face the young man.

'I've come up against what seems to be an intractable problem, sir, and I don't know what to do about it.' Mr Sharma nodded. 'I've fallen in love with an Indian girl, and I want to marry her.'

'Congratulations.'

'But she's a Hindu.'

'As are eighty per cent of my countrymen, Mr Clifton, myself included. Therefore should I assume the problem is not the girl, but her parents?'

'Yes, sir. Although Priya wants to marry me, her parents have chosen someone else to be her husband, someone she hasn't even met.'

'That's not uncommon in my country, Mr Clifton. I didn't meet my wife until my mother had selected her. But if you think it might help, I will be happy to have a word with Priya's parents and try to plead your case.'

'That's very kind of you, sir. I'd be most grateful.'

'However, I must warn you that if the family has settled the contract with the other parties concerned, my words may well fall on deaf ears. But please,' continued the High Commissioner as he picked up a notepad from the table by his side, 'tell me everything you can about Priya, before I decide how to approach the problem.'

'Yesterday evening, Priya and I had planned to drive down to the West Country so she could meet my parents. When I arrived at her flat to pick her up, I found that she had, quite literally, been kidnapped by her father and brother.'

'May I know their names?'

'Sukhi and Simran Ghuman.'

The High Commissioner shifted uneasily in his chair. 'Mr Ghuman is one of India's leading industrialists. He has very strong business and political connections, and I should add that he also has a reputation for ruthless efficiency. I choose my words carefully, Mr Clifton.'

'But if Priya is still in England, surely we can prevent him from taking her back to India against her will? She is, after all, twenty-six years old.'

'I doubt if she's still in this country, Mr Clifton, because I know Mr Ghuman has a private jet. But even if she were, proving a father is holding his child against her wishes would involve a long legal process. I have experienced seven such cases since I took up this post, and although I'm convinced all seven young women wished to remain in this country, four of them were back in India long before they could be questioned, and the other three, when interviewed, said they no longer wanted to claim asylum. But if you wish to pursue the matter, I can call the chief inspector at Scotland Yard who is responsible for such cases, though I should warn you that Mr Ghuman will be well aware of his legal rights and it won't be the first time he's taken the law into his own hands.'

'Are you saying there's nothing I can do?'

'Not a great deal,' admitted the High Commissioner. 'And I only wish I could be more helpful.'

'It was good of you to spare us so much of your time, Varun,' said Giles as he stood up.

'My pleasure, Giles,' said the High Commissioner. The two men shook hands. 'Don't hesitate to be in touch if you feel I can be of any assistance.'

As Giles and Seb left Varun Sharma's office and walked out on to the Strand, Giles said, 'I'm so sorry, Seb. I know exactly what you're going through, but I'm not sure what you can do next.'

'Go home and try to get on with my life. But thank you, Uncle Giles, you couldn't have done more.'

Giles watched as his nephew strode off in the direction of the City, and wondered what he really planned to do next, because his home was in the opposite direction. Once Seb was out of sight, Giles headed back up the steps and into the High Commissioner's office.

◄O►

'Rachel, I need five hundred pounds in rupees, an open-ended return ticket to Bombay and an Indian visa. If you call Mr Sharma's secretary at the High Commission, I'm sure she'll speed the whole process up. Oh, and I'll need fifteen minutes with the chairman before I leave.'

'But you have several important appointments next week, including—'

'Clear my diary for the next few days. I'll phone in every morning, so you can keep me fully briefed.'

'This must be one hell of a deal you're trying to close.'

'The biggest of my life.'

◄O►

The High Commissioner listened carefully to what his secretary had to say.

'Your nephew has just called and applied for a visa,' he said after putting the phone down. 'Do I speed it up, or slow it down?'

'Speed it up,' said Giles, 'although I admit I'm quite anxious about the boy. Like me, he's a hopeless romantic, and at the moment he's thinking with his heart and not his head.'

'Don't worry, Giles,' said Varun. 'I'll see that someone keeps an eye on him while he's in India and tries to make sure he doesn't get into too much trouble, especially as Sukhi Ghuman is involved. No one needs that man as an enemy.'

'But when I met him at Lord's, he seemed quite charming.'

'That's half the reason he's so successful.'

◄o►

It wasn't until later that evening, when Seb had fastened his seatbelt and the plane had taken off, that he realized he didn't have a plan. All he knew for certain was that he couldn't spend the rest of his life wondering if this journey just might have made a difference. The only piece of useful information he picked up from the chief steward during the flight was the name of the best hotel in Bombay.

Seb was dozing when the captain announced that they were about to begin their descent into Bombay. He looked out of the cabin window to see a vast, sprawling mass of tiny houses, shacks and tenement blocks, filling every inch of space. He could only wonder if Bombay had any planning laws.

As he left the aircraft and walked down the steps, he was immediately overwhelmed by the oppressive humidity, and once he'd entered the airport, he quickly discovered the local pace of everything – slow or stop. Having his passport checked, the longest queue he'd ever seen; waiting for his luggage to be unloaded from the hold, he nearly fell asleep; being held up by customs, although he only had one suitcase; and then trying to find a taxi when there wasn't an official rank – they just seemed to come and go.

When Seb finally set off for the city, he discovered why no one was ever booked for speeding in Bombay, because the car rarely got out of first gear. And when he asked about air conditioning, the driver wound down his window. He stared out of the open window at the little shops – no roofs, no doors, trading everything from spare tyres to mangos – while the citizens of Bombay went about their business. Some were dressed in smart suits that hung loosely on their bodies and ties that wouldn't have been out of place in the Square Mile, while others wore spotless loincloths, bringing to mind the image of Gandhi, one of his father's heroes.

Once they'd reached the outskirts of the city, they came to a halt. Seb had experienced traffic jams in London, New York and Tokyo, but they were Formula One racetracks compared to Bombay. Broken-down lorries parked in the fast lane, over-crowded rickshaws on the inside lane, and sacred cows munched happily away in the centre lane, while old women crossed the road seemingly unaware what it had originally been built for.

A little boy was standing in the middle of the road carrying a stack of paperback books. He walked up to the car, tapped on the window and smiled in at Sebastian.

'Harold Robbins, Robert Ludlum and Harry Clifton,' he said, giving him a beaming grin. 'All half price!'

Sebastian handed him a ten-rupee note and said, 'Harry Clifton.'

The boy produced his father's latest book. 'We all love William Warwick,' he said, before moving on to the next car. Would his father believe him?

It took another hour before they drew up outside the Taj Mahal Hotel, by which time Seb was exhausted and soaked with perspiration.

When he stepped inside the hotel, he entered another world and was quickly transported back to the present day.

'How long will you be staying with us, sir?' asked a tall, elegant man in a long blue coat, as Seb signed the registration form.

'I'm not sure,' said Seb, 'but at least two or three days.'

'Then I'll leave the booking open-ended. Is there anything else I can help you with, sir?'

'Can you recommend a reliable car hire firm?'

'If it's a car you require, sir, the hotel will happily supply you with a chauffeur-driven Ambassador.'

'Will it be possible to keep the same driver for the whole visit?'

'Of course, sir.'

'He'll need to speak English.'

'In this hotel, sir, even the cleaners speak English.'

'Of course, I apologize. I have one more request – could he possibly be a Hindu?'

'Not a problem, sir. I believe I have the ideal person to meet all your requirements, and I can recommend him highly, because he's my brother.' Seb laughed. 'And when would you want him to start?'

'Eight o'clock tomorrow morning?'

'Excellent. My brother's name is Vijay and he'll be waiting for you outside the main entrance at eight.' The receptionist raised a hand and a bellboy appeared. 'Take Mr Clifton to room 808.'

19

WHEN SEBASTIAN left his hotel at eight o'clock the following morning, he spotted a young man standing beside a white Ambassador. The moment he saw Seb heading towards him, he opened the back door.

'I'll sit in the front with you,' said Seb.

'Of course, sir,' said Vijay. Once he was behind the wheel he asked, 'Where would you like to go, sir?'

Seb handed him an address. 'How long will it take?'

'That depends, sir, on how many traffic lights are working this morning and how many cows are having their breakfast.'

The answer turned out to be just over an hour, although the milometer indicated that they had covered barely three miles.

'It's the house on the right, sir,' said Vijay. 'Do you want me to drive up to the front door?'

'No,' said Seb as they passed the gates of a house that was so large it might have been mistaken for a country club. He admired Priya for never having mentioned her father's wealth.

Vijay parked in an isolated spot, down a side road from where they could see anyone coming in or out of the gates, while they would be unlikely to be noticed.

'Are you very important?' asked Vijay an hour later.

'No,' said Seb. 'Why do you ask?'

'Because there's a police car parked just down the road, and it hasn't moved since we arrived.'

Seb was puzzled but tried to dismiss it as a coincidence, even though Cedric Hardcastle had taught him many years ago to always be wary of coincidences.

They remained seated in the car for most of the day, during which time several cars and a van passed in and out of the gates. There was no sign of Priya, although at one point a large Mercedes left the grounds with Mr Ghuman seated in the back talking to a younger man Seb assumed must be his son.

In between the comings and goings, Vijay gave Seb a further insight into the Hindu religion, and he began to realize just how difficult it must have been for Priya even to consider defying her parents.

He was about to call it a day when two men, one carrying a camera, the other a briefcase, came strolling down the drive from the house and stopped outside the main gate. They were dressed smartly but casually, and had a professional air about them. They hailed a taxi and climbed into the back.

'Follow that cab, and don't lose them.'

'It's quite difficult to lose anyone in a city where bicycles overtake you,' said Vijay as they progressed slowly back towards the city centre. The taxi finally came to a halt outside a large Victorian building that proclaimed above its front door: *The Times of India*.

'Wait here,' said Sebastian. He got out of the car and waited until the two men had entered the building before following them inside. One of them waved to a girl on the reception desk as they headed towards a bank of lifts. Sebastian made his way over to the desk, smiled at the girl and said, 'How embarrassing. I can't remember the name of the journalist who's just getting into the lift.'

She glanced around as the lift door closed. 'Samraj Khan. He writes a society column for the Sunday paper. But I'm not sure who that was with him.' She turned to her colleague.

'He's freelance. Works for Premier Photos, I think. But I don't know his name.'

'Thanks,' said Sebastian, before making his way back to the car.

'Where now?' asked Vijay.

'Back to the hotel.'

'That police car is still following us,' said Vijay, as he eased into a long line of traffic. 'So you're either very important, or very dangerous,' he suggested, displaying a broad grin.

'Neither,' said Seb. Like Vijay, he was puzzled. Did Uncle Giles's influence stretch this far, or were the police working for the Ghumans?

Once Seb was back in his room, he asked the switchboard to get Premier Photos on the line. He had his story well prepared by the time the operator called back. He asked to be put through to the photographer who was covering the Sukhi Ghuman story.

'Do you mean the wedding?'

'Yes, the wedding,' said Sebastian, hating the word.

'That's Rohit Singh. I'll put you through.'

'Rohit Singh.'

'Hi, my name is Clifton. I'm a freelance journalist from London, and I've been assigned to cover Priya Ghuman's wedding.'

'But it's not for another six weeks.'

'I know, but my magazine wants background material for a colour spread we're doing, and I wondered if you'd be able to supply some photographs to go with my piece.'

'We'd need to meet and discuss terms. Where are you staying?'

'The Taj.'

'Would eight o'clock tomorrow morning suit you?'

'Look forward to seeing you then.'

No sooner had he put the phone down than it rang again.

'While you were on the line, sir, your secretary called. She asked if you would ring a Mr Bishara at the bank urgently. She gave me the number. Shall I try and get him on the line?'

'Yes please,' said Seb, then put the phone down and waited. He checked his watch, and hoped Hakim hadn't already gone to lunch. The phone rang.

'Thanks for calling back, Seb. I realize you've got a lot on your mind at the moment, but I have some sad news. Saul Kaufman has died. I thought you ought to know immediately, not just because of the takeover deal we're in the middle of, but, more important, I know Victor is one of your oldest friends.'

'Thank you, Hakim. How very sad. I greatly admired the old man. Victor will be my next call.'

'Kaufman's shares have fallen sharply, which is hard to explain, seeing Saul hasn't been in to the office for over a year.'

'You and I know that,' said Seb, 'but the public doesn't. Don't forget, Saul founded the bank. His name is still at the top of the notepaper, so investors who don't know any better will wonder if it's a one-man band. But taking into account the bank's strong balance sheet, and its considerable assets, in my opinion Kaufman's shares were already well below market value even before Saul's death.'

'Do you think they might fall even further?'

'No one gets in at the bottom and out at the top,' said Seb. 'If they fall below three pounds – and they were £3.26 when I left – I'd be a buyer. But remember Farthings already has six per cent of Kaufman's stock, and if we go over ten per cent, the bank of England will require us to make a full takeover bid, and we're not quite ready for that.'

'I think there may be someone else in the market.'

'That will be Desmond Mellor, but he's only a spoiler. He doesn't have the sort of capital to make a real impact. Believe me, he'll run out of steam.'

'Unless he has someone else backing him.'

'No one in the City would consider backing Mellor, as Adrian Sloane and Jim Knowles have already discovered.'

'Thanks for the advice, Seb. I'll buy a few more Kaufman's shares if they fall below three pounds, and then we can look at the bigger picture once you get back. By the way, how's it all going out there?'

'I wouldn't buy shares in Clifton Enterprises.'

—◦—

Seb was gradually coming to terms with the oppressive heat and even the traffic jams, but he couldn't handle the fact that being on time simply wasn't part of the Indian psyche. He had been pacing up and down the lobby of the Taj since 7.55, but Rohit Singh didn't come strolling through the revolving doors until a few minutes before nine, offering only a shrug of the shoulders and a smile. He uttered the single word, 'Traffic,' as if he had never driven in Bombay before. Sebastian didn't comment, as he needed Singh on his team.

'So who do you work for?' Singh asked once they'd sat down in a pair of comfortable seats in the lounge.

'*Tatler*,' said Sebastian, who had decided on the magazine overnight. 'We want to do a centre-page spread on the wedding. We've got quite a bit on Priya Ghuman, because she's been living in London for the past three years, but we don't even know the name of the man she's going to marry.'

'We only found out ourselves yesterday, but no one was surprised to hear it was Suresh Chopra.'

'Why?'

'His father is chairman of Bombay Building, so the marriage is more about the joining of two companies than of two people. I've got a picture of him if you'd like to see it.' Singh opened his briefcase and took out a photograph. Sebastian stared at a man who looked around fifty, but might have been younger, because he was certainly fifty pounds overweight.

'Are he and Priya old friends?' he asked.

'Their parents are, but I'm not sure they themselves have ever met. I'm told the official introductions will be made next week. That's a ceremony in itself, to which we won't be invited. Can I ask about payment?' said Singh, changing the subject.

'Sure. We'll pay you the full agency rate,' replied Seb, without any idea what that meant, 'and an advance payment to make sure you don't share your pictures with anyone else in England.' He passed over five 100-rupee notes. 'Is that fair?'

Singh nodded and pocketed the cash in a way that would have impressed the Artful Dodger.

'So when do you want me to start?'

'Will you be photographing any members of the family in the near future?'

'Day after tomorrow. Priya's got a fitting at Brides of Bombay on Altamont Street at eleven o'clock. Her mother wanted me to take a few shots for a family album she's preparing.'

'I'll be there,' said Seb. 'But I'll keep my distance. I gather Sukhi Ghuman doesn't care much for London hacks.'

'He doesn't care for us either,' said Singh, 'unless it suits his purpose. Be warned, Mrs Ghuman will almost certainly accompany her daughter. That will mean at least two armed guards, which the family have never bothered with in the past. Perhaps Mr Ghuman just wants to remind everyone how important he is.'

Not everyone, thought Seb.

20

SEBASTIAN WALKED over to the reception desk.

'Good morning, Mr Clifton. I trust you're enjoying your stay with us.'

'Yes, thank you.'

'And my brother is proving satisfactory?'

'Couldn't be better.'

'Excellent. And how can I help you today?'

'First, I'd like you to replace the Ambassador with a motorbike.'

'Of course, sir,' said the receptionist, not sounding surprised. 'Anything else?'

'I need a florist.'

'You'll find one downstairs in the arcade. Fresh flowers were delivered about an hour ago.'

'Thank you,' said Seb. He jogged down the steps to the arcade, where he spotted a young woman arranging a bunch of vivid orange marigolds in a large vase. She looked up as he approached.

'I'd like to buy a single rose.'

'Of course, sir,' she said, gesturing towards a selection of different-coloured roses. 'Would you like to choose one?'

Seb took his time picking a red one that was just starting to bloom. 'Can I have it delivered?'

'Yes, sir. Would you like to add a message?' she asked, handing him a pen.

Seb took a card from the counter, turned it over and wrote:

To Priya Ghuman,

Congratulations on your forthcoming marriage.

From all your admirers at the Taj Hotel.

He gave the florist Priya's address and said, 'Please charge it to room 808. When will it be delivered?'

She looked at the address. 'Some time between ten and eleven, depending on the traffic.'

'Will you be here for the rest of the morning?'

'Yes, sir,' she replied, looking puzzled.

'If anyone calls and asks who sent the rose, tell them it was the guest who's staying in room 808.'

'Certainly, sir,' said the florist, as he handed her a fifty-rupee note.

Seb ran back upstairs, aware that he had only a couple of hours to spare, three at the most. When he walked out of the hotel he was pleased to see that the receptionist had carried out his instructions and replaced the Ambassador with a motorbike.

'Good morning, sir. Where would you like to go today?' asked Vijay, displaying the same irrepressible smile.

'Santacruz airport. The domestic terminal. And I'm not in a hurry,' he emphasized as he climbed on to the back of the bike.

He carefully observed the route that Vijay took, noting the occasional blue and white airport signs dotted along the way. Forty-two minutes later Vijay screeched to a halt outside the domestic terminal. Seb jumped off, saying, 'Hang around, I'll only be a few minutes.' He walked inside and checked the departures board. The flight he required was leaving from Gate 14B, and the word 'Boarding' was flashing next to the words 'New Delhi'. He followed the signs, but when he arrived at the gate, he didn't join the queue of passengers waiting to board the plane. He checked his watch. It had taken forty-nine minutes from the moment he'd left the hotel to reaching the gate. He retraced his steps to find Vijay waiting patiently for him.

'I'll take us back,' said Seb, grabbing the handlebars.

'But you don't have a licence, sir.'

'I don't think anyone will notice.' Seb flicked on the ignition, revved up and waited for Vijay to climb on behind him before he joined the traffic heading into Bombay.

They were back outside the hotel forty-one minutes later. Seb checked his watch. The rose should be delivered any time now.

'I'll be back, Vijay, but I can't be sure when,' he said before walking quickly up the steps and into the hotel. He took the lift to the eighth floor, went straight to his room, poured himself a cold Cobra and sat down next to the phone. So many jumbled thoughts flooded through his mind. Had the rose been delivered? If it had, would Priya even see it? If she did see it, would she realize who'd sent it? At least he felt confident about that. She would recognize his handwriting, and with one call to the florist she would discover which room he was in. It was clear that her family weren't letting her out of the house unaccompanied, possibly not even out of their sight. Checking his watch every few minutes he paced up and down the room, occasionally stopping to take a sip of his beer. He glanced at the front page of the *Times of India*, but didn't get beyond the headlines. He thought about ringing his uncle Giles, and bringing him up to date, but decided he couldn't risk the line being busy when she called.

When the phone made a loud metallic sound, Seb grabbed it. 'Hello?'

'Is that you, Seb?' Priya whispered.

'Yes it is, black swan. Can you talk?'

'Only for a minute. What are you doing in Bombay?'

'I've come to take you back to England.' He paused. 'But only if that's what you want.'

'Of course it's what I want. Just tell me how.'

Seb quickly explained exactly what he had planned, and although she remained silent, he felt confident she was listening intently. Suddenly she spoke, her voice formal. 'Thank you, yes. You can expect my mother and me around eleven—' A pause. 'I'm also looking forward to seeing you.'

'Don't forget to bring your passport,' said Seb, just before she put the phone down.

'Who was that?' Priya's mother asked.

'Brides of Bombay,' said Priya, casually, not wanting her mother to become suspicious. 'Just confirming our appointment for tomorrow,' she added, trying to conceal her excitement. 'They suggested I wear something casual, as I'll be trying on several outfits.'

Seb made no attempt to disguise how euphoric he felt. He punched the air and shouted 'Hallelujah!' as if he'd just scored the winning goal in the cup final. Once he'd recovered, he sat down and thought about what needed to be done next. After a few moments, he left his room and went downstairs to the front desk.

'Did you find what you were looking for at the florist, Mr Clifton?'

'She couldn't have been more helpful, thank you. Now I'd like to book two first-class tickets on Air India's flight to New Delhi at two twenty tomorrow afternoon.'

'Certainly, sir. I'll ask our travel desk to send the tickets up to your room as soon as they're confirmed.'

Seb sat alone in the hotel restaurant, picking at a curry as he went over his plan again and again, trying to eradicate any possible flaws. After lunch he left the hotel to find Vijay sitting on the bike. He could have given a lapdog lessons in loyalty.

'Where to now, sir?'

'Back to the airport,' said Seb, as he grabbed the handlebars and climbed on.

'Do you require me, sir?'

'Oh yes. I need someone sitting behind me.'

Seb knocked three minutes off their previous time to the airport, and once again walked across to Gate 14B, where he double-checked the departure board. On the return trip to the hotel, he knocked another minute off his time, without ever breaking the speed limit.

'See you at ten tomorrow morning, Vijay,' said Seb, knowing he was talking to someone who didn't need to be reminded to be on time.

Vijay gave a mock salute as Sebastian entered the hotel and

returned to his room. He ordered a light supper and tried to relax by watching *Above Us the Waves* on television. He finally climbed into bed just after eleven, but didn't sleep.

21

Despite a sleepless night, Sebastian wasn't tired when he pulled open the curtains the following morning, letting the first rays of the sun flood into his room. He now knew what an athlete must feel like the morning before an Olympic final.

He took a long cold shower, put on a pair of jeans, a T-shirt and a pair of trainers. He ordered breakfast in his room, but only to kill time. He would have called his uncle Giles to bring him up to date if it hadn't been the middle of the night in London. He went down to the front desk just after ten and asked for his bill.

'I hope you enjoyed your stay with us, Mr Clifton,' said the concierge, 'and will be returning soon.'

'I hope so too,' said Seb as he handed over his credit card, although he couldn't imagine what circumstances would make it possible for him ever to return. When the receptionist handed him back his credit card, he asked, 'Shall I send someone up to collect your luggage, Mr Clifton?'

Seb was momentarily thrown. 'No, I'll pick it up later,' he stammered.

'As you wish, sir.'

When Seb stepped out of the hotel, he was pleased, though not surprised, to see Vijay leaning on the motorbike.

'Where to this time, sir?'

'114 Altamont Street.'

'Posh shopping area. You buy present for your girlfriend?'

'Something like that,' said Seb.

They arrived outside Brides of Bombay at twenty minutes

past ten. This was never going to be an appointment Seb would be late for. Vijay didn't comment when Seb asked him to park out of sight, but he was surprised by his next instruction.

'I want you to take a bus to the airport and wait for me outside the entrance to the domestic terminal.' He took 500 rupees from his wallet and handed over the well-worn notes to Vijay.

'Thank you, sir,' said Vijay, before walking away looking even more bemused.

Seb kept the engine turning over as he remained hidden behind a dilapidated old lorry. He couldn't decide whether it had been dumped or parked.

A large black Mercedes drew up outside Brides of Bombay a few minutes after eleven. The chauffeur opened the back door to allow Mrs Ghuman and her daughter to step out. Priya was wearing jeans, a T-shirt and flat shoes, as Seb had recommended. It didn't matter what Priya wore, she always looked stunning.

One guard accompanied them as they entered the bridal shop, while the other remained in the front seat of the car. Seb had assumed that once the chauffeur had delivered his passengers, he would drive off and come back later. But the car remained parked in a restricted zone, and clearly wasn't going to move until his charges returned; Seb's first mistake. He had also thought both guards would accompany Mrs Ghuman into the shop. His second mistake. He switched off the bike's engine, not wanting to draw attention to himself. His third mistake. He wondered how long it might be before Priya reappeared, and whether she would be alone or accompanied by the guard.

A few minutes later he spotted Rohit Singh in his wing mirror. The photographer was strolling nonchalantly along the pavement, camera slung over one shoulder, clearly content to be fashionably late. Seb watched as he disappeared into the shop. The next twenty minutes felt like an hour, with Seb continually glancing at his watch. He was sweating profusely. Thirty minutes. Had Priya lost her nerve? Forty minutes. Could she have changed her mind? Fifty minutes. Much longer and they'd miss their flight. And then suddenly, without warning, there she was, running out on to the pavement on her own. She paused briefly, before anxiously looking up and down the road.

Seb switched on the ignition and revved the engine, but he was only at the side of the lorry by the time the second guard stepped out of the Mercedes and began walking towards the boss's daughter. The chauffeur was opening the rear door as Seb pulled up by the car. He waved frantically at Priya, who ran out into the street, jumped on to the back of the bike and clung on to him. The guard reacted immediately and charged towards them. Seb was trying to accelerate away when he lunged at him, causing Seb to swerve and almost unseat his passenger. The guard narrowly avoided being hit by a passing taxi and landed spread-eagled in the street.

Seb quickly recovered and manoeuvred the bike into the centre lane with Priya clinging on. The guard leapt up and gave chase, but it was an unequal contest. Once he had seen which way the bike turned at the end of the street, Seb's fourth mistake, the guard immediately changed direction and ran into the shop.

When Mrs Ghuman was told the news, she screamed at a petrified shop assistant, 'Where's the nearest phone?' Before she could reply, the manager, hearing the outburst, reappeared and led Mrs Ghuman into her office. She closed the door and left her alone, while her customer dialled a number she rarely phoned. After several rings a voice said, 'Ghuman Enterprises.'

'It's Mrs Ghuman. Put me through to my husband immediately.'

'He's chairing a board meeting, Mrs Ghuman—'

'Then interrupt it. This is an emergency.' The secretary hesitated. 'Immediately, do you hear me?'

'Who is this?' demanded the next voice.

'It's Simran, we have a problem. Priya has run off with Clifton.'

'How can that be possible?'

'He was waiting for her on a motorbike outside the shop. All I can tell you is that they turned left at the end of Altamont Street.'

'They must be heading for the airport. Tell the chauffeur to take both guards to the international terminal and await my instructions.' He slammed down the phone and quickly left the room, leaving twelve bewildered directors sitting around the boardroom table. As he swept through to his office he shouted at his secretary, 'Find out the time of the next flight to London. And quickly!'

Ghuman's secretary picked up the phone on her desk and called special services at the airport. A few moments later she pressed the intercom button that connected her to the chairman's desk.

'There are two flights out of Bombay today, both of them Air India.' She glanced down at her pad. 'One in forty minutes' time, at 12.50, so you couldn't possibly make it to the airport in time, and one—'

'—but a man on a motorbike could,' said Ghuman without explanation. 'Get me the duty controller at the airport.'

Ghuman paced around the room as he waited to be put through. He snatched at the phone the moment it rang.

'It's Patel, in accounts, sir. You asked me to—'

'Not now,' said Ghuman. He slammed the phone down and was just about to ask his secretary what was taking so long when it rang again.

'Who is this?' he demanded as he picked the phone up.

'My name is Tariq Shah, Mr Ghuman. I am Air India's senior controller at Santacruz airport. How may—'

'I have reason to believe that a Mr Sebastian Clifton and my daughter, Priya, are booked on your 12.50 flight to London. Check your manifest immediately and let me know if they've already boarded the plane.'

'Can I call you back?'

'No, I'll hold on.'

'I'll need a couple of minutes, sir.'

Two minutes turned into three, and as Ghuman could no longer pace around his office while he held on to the phone, he grabbed the letter-opener on his desk and began stabbing his blotting pad in frustration. Finally a voice said, 'Neither Mr Clifton nor your daughter are on that flight, Mr Ghuman, and the boarding desk has already closed. Do you want me to check the 18.50 flight?'

SEBASTIAN CLIFTON

'No, they won't be on that one,' Ghuman said before adding, 'What a clever young man you are, Mr Clifton.'

'I beg your pardon?' said Shah.

'Listen carefully, Shah. I want you to check every other flight that's leaving India for London tonight, whatever the airport, and then ring me straight back.'

—◄○►—

Seb and Priya pulled up outside the domestic terminal just before one o'clock, to find Vijay standing on the pavement looking out for them.

'Take the bike back to the garage, Vijay, then go home and stay put for the rest of the day. Don't report back to work until tomorrow morning. Is that clear?'

'Crystal,' said Vijay.

Seb handed him the keys to the bike and another 500 rupees.

'But you have already given me more than enough money, sir.'

'Nowhere near enough,' said Seb. He took Priya by the hand and led her quickly into the terminal and straight to Gate 14B, where some passengers were already boarding. He was glad he'd carried out two dress rehearsals, but it didn't stop him continually looking over his shoulder to check if anyone was following them. With a bit of luck, Ghuman's thugs would be heading for the international terminal.

They joined the queue of passengers boarding the flight to New Delhi, but Seb didn't feel safe even when the stewardess asked everyone to fasten their seatbelts. Not until the wheels had left the ground did he breathe a sigh of relief.

'But we won't be safe even when we're back in London,' said Priya, who was still shaking. 'My father won't give up while he thinks there's the slightest chance of getting me to change my mind.'

'That will be pretty difficult, if we're already married.'

'But we both know that won't be possible for some time.'

'Have you ever heard of Gretna Green?' said Seb, not letting go of her hand. 'It's like Vegas without the gambling, so by this time tomorrow, you will be Mrs Clifton. Which is why we're taking a plane to Glasgow this evening, and not London.'

'But even if we do that, my father will only take some other kind of revenge.'

'I don't think so. Because when he returns to London he's going to have a visit from Mr Varun Sharma, the Indian High Commissioner, as well as a chief inspector from Scotland Yard.'

'How did you manage that?'

'I didn't. But when you see my uncle Giles again, you can thank him.'

—◦—

The airport controller was back on the line forty minutes after Ghuman had put the phone down.

'There are five other flights scheduled for London this evening, Mr Ghuman. Three out of New Delhi, one from Calcutta and the other from Bangalore. Neither Mr Clifton nor your daughter are booked on any of them. However, there's a BOAC flight to Manchester and another to Glasgow that are leaving New Delhi later this evening, and the booking desks for both are still open.'

'Clever, Mr Clifton, very clever indeed. But there's one thing you've overlooked. Mr Shah,' said Ghuman, 'I need to know which of those flights they're booked on. Once you've found out, make sure they don't board the plane.'

'I'm afraid that won't be possible, Mr Ghuman, because they are both British carriers, and I have no way of checking their manifests, unless I can show a crime has been committed.'

'You can tell them Clifton is attempting to kidnap my daughter, and that you'll hold the flight up if they allow them to board the plane.'

'I don't have the authority to do that, Mr Ghuman.'

'Listen carefully, Mr Shah. If you don't do it, by this time tomorrow you won't have any authority at all.'

—◦—

The flight from Bombay to New Delhi landed a couple of hours later, leaving Seb and Priya with almost two hours to kill before they could board their connecting flight. They didn't waste any time making their way over to the international terminal, where they joined the queue at BOAC's booking desk.

'Good afternoon, sir, how can I help you?' asked the clerk.

'I'd like two seats on your flight to Glasgow.'

'Certainly, sir. First or economy?'

'First,' said Seb.

'Economy,' said Priya. They tossed a coin. Priya won.

'Is this the way it's going to be for the rest of our married life?' said Seb.

'Are you on your honeymoon?' asked the booking clerk.

'No,' said Seb. 'We're getting married tomorrow.'

'Then I shall be delighted to upgrade you to first class.'

'Thank you,' said Priya.

'But first I need to see your passports.' Sebastian handed them over. 'Do you have any bags to check in?'

'None,' said Seb.

'Fine. And could I have a credit card please?'

'Do we also toss for that?' asked Seb, looking at Priya.

'No, I'm afraid you're about to marry a girl who comes without a dowry.'

'You're in seats 4A and 4B. The flight is scheduled to leave on time, and the gate opens in forty minutes. You might like to take advantage of our first-class lounge, which is on the other side of the hall.'

Seb and Priya held hands as they nervously nibbled nuts and drank endless cups of coffee in the first-class lounge, until they finally heard the announcement they had been waiting for.

'This is the first call for BOAC flight 009 to Glasgow. Will all passengers please make their way to Gate number eleven.'

'I want us to be the first on the plane,' said Seb, as they walked out of the lounge. He had always known that this would be the only unscripted moment, but he was confident that once they'd boarded the plane, even Mr Ghuman wouldn't be able to have them taken off a British carrier. In the distance he spotted two armed policemen standing by the departure gate. Were they always there, or were they on the lookout for him? And then he remembered the police car that had been stationed outside Mr Ghuman's house and had then continuously followed him and Vijay. Ghuman was a man with political influence and power, especially in his own country, the High Commissioner had warned.

Seb slowed down, looking first to his right and then his left as he searched for an escape route. The two policemen were now staring at them and, when they were just a couple of yards from the barrier, one of the officers stepped forward as if he'd been waiting for them.

Seb heard a commotion behind him and swung round to see what was going on. He immediately knew that he'd made the wrong decision and should have kept on walking. His fifth mistake. He stood, mesmerized, as Ghuman's two bodyguards charged towards them. How could they have got there so quickly? Of course, Ghuman had a private jet – something else the High Commissioner had warned him about. Seb was surprised how calm he felt, even when one of them pulled out a gun and pointed it directly at him.

'Drop that gun and get on your knees!' shouted one of the policemen. The crowd scattered in every direction, leaving the six of them stranded in their own no-man's land. Seb realized that the police had always been on his side. Barrington *v*. Ghuman – no contest. One of Ghuman's guards immediately fell to his knees and slid his gun across the floor towards the two policemen. The other thug, the one who'd failed to dislodge Priya from the motorbike, ignored the order, never taking his eyes off his quarry.

'Move away, black swan,' said Seb firmly, pushing Priya to one side. 'It's not you he's after.'

'Put down your weapon and get on your knees or I will fire,' said one of the policemen standing behind them.

But the man didn't lower his gun and didn't fall on his knees. He squeezed the trigger.

Seb felt the bullet hit him. As he stumbled back, Priya shouted, 'No!' and threw herself between Seb and the gunman. The second bullet killed her instantly.

LADY VIRGINIA FENWICK

1972

22

WHEN THE MONEY began to dry up, Virginia wondered if she could return to the same watering hole a second time.

Without informing her father, she had employed a new butler and housekeeper and returned to her old way of life. £14,000 might have seemed like a lot of money at the time, but that was before she checked her recent dress account, spent a month at the Excelsior Hotel in Tenerife with a totally unsuitable young man, made a foolish loan to Bofie that she knew he'd never repay and backed a string of fillies at Ascot that never had any intention of entering the winners' enclosure. She had refused to place a bet on Noble Conquest for the King George VI and Queen Elizabeth Stakes, and then watched her romp home at 3/1. Her owner, Cyrus T. Grant III, was inexplicably absent, so Her Majesty presented the cup to his trainer.

Virginia opened yet another letter from Mr Fairbrother, a man she had sworn never to speak to again, and reluctantly accepted that she was facing the same temporary embarrassment as she'd experienced six months previously. Her father's monthly allowance had put her bank balance temporarily back in the black, so she decided to invest a hundred pounds seeking the advice of Sir Edward Makepeace QC. After all, it wasn't his fault she'd lost her libel case against Emma Clifton. Alex Fisher was to blame for that.

◄o►

'Let me try to understand what you're telling me,' said Sir Edward after Virginia had come to the end of her story. 'You met a Mr Cyrus T. Grant III, a Louisiana businessman, at a lunch party at Harry's Bar in Mayfair hosted by the son of Lord Bridgwater. You then accompanied Mr Grant back to his hotel –' Sir Edward checked his notes – 'the Ritz, where you had tea in his private suite, and later both of you drank a little too much . . . presumably not tea?'

'Whisky,' said Virginia. 'Maker's Mark, his favourite brand.'

'And you ended up spending the night together.'

'Cyrus can be very persuasive.'

'And you say that he proposed to you that evening, and when you returned to the Ritz the following morning he had, to quote you, "done a runner". By which you mean he had settled his account with the Ritz and taken the first flight back to America.'

'That is exactly what he did.'

'And you are seeking my legal opinion as to whether you have a claim for breach of promise against Mr Grant that would stand up in a court of law?' Virginia looked hopeful. 'If so, I have to ask, do you have any proof that Mr Grant actually proposed to you?'

'Such as?'

'A witness, someone he told or, even better, an engagement ring?'

'We had planned to go shopping for a ring that morning.'

'I apologize for this indelicacy, Lady Virginia, but are you pregnant?'

'Certainly not,' said Virginia firmly. She paused for a moment, before adding, 'Why? Would it make any difference?'

'A considerable difference. Not only would we have proof of your liaison but, more importantly, you could seek a maintenance order, claiming that Mr Grant had an obligation to bring up the child in a style and manner commensurate with his considerable wealth.' He looked at his notes again, 'As the twenty-eighth richest man in America.'

'As reported in *Forbes Magazine*,' confirmed Virginia.

'That would have been good enough for most courts of law in both countries. However, as you are not pregnant, and have no proof that he proposed to you other than your word against his, I cannot see any course of action open to you. I would therefore advise you not to consider suing Mr Grant. The legal expense alone could prove crippling and, after your recent experience, I suspect that isn't a road you'd want to travel down a second time.'

Her hour was up, but Virginia considered it £100 well spent.

◄◦►

'And when is the baby due, Morton?' asked Virginia.

'In about two months, my lady.'

'Do you still plan to have it adopted?'

'Yes, my lady. Although I've found a new position in a good household, while Mrs Morton is unable to work we simply can't afford the expense of another child.'

'I sympathize with you,' said Virginia, 'and am keen to help if I can.'

'That's very kind of you, my lady.'

Morton remained standing while Virginia outlined, in some detail, a proposition that she hoped might solve her problem as well as his. 'Would that be of any interest to you?' she asked finally.

'It certainly would, my lady, and if I may say so, it is most generous.'

'How do you think Mrs Morton will react to such a proposal?'

'I'm sure she'll fall in with my wishes.'

'Good. However, I must stress that should you and Mrs Morton accept my offer, neither of you would be able to have any contact with the child again.'

'I understand.'

'Then I will have the necessary documents drawn up by my lawyer and engrossed ready for you both to sign. And be sure to keep me regularly informed about Mrs Morton's health, in particular when she plans to go into hospital.'

'Of course, my lady. I can't tell you how grateful I am.'

Virginia stood up and shook hands with Morton, something she'd never done before.

◄◦►

Virginia had the *Baton Rouge State-Times* airmailed to her from Baton Rouge once a week. This allowed her to keep up with the 'wedding of the year'. The latest edition devoted a whole page to the forthcoming marriage of Ellie May Campbell to Cyrus T. Grant III.

Invitations had already been sent out. The guests included the state governor, The Hon Hayden Rankin, both US senators, several congressmen and the mayor of Baton Rouge, as well as most of the leading society figures in the state. The ceremony would be conducted by Bishop Langdon, in St Luke's Episcopal Church, and would be followed by a five-course banquet at the bride's family ranch for the four hundred guests who were expected to attend.

'Four hundred and one,' said Virginia, although she wasn't quite sure how she was going to lay her hands on an invitation. She turned next to page four of the *State-Times*, and read about the outcome of a divorce case she had been following with great interest.

Despite meticulous preparation, there were still one or two obstacles that Virginia needed to overcome before she could consider setting off for the New World. Bofie, who seemed to have contacts in both the Upper House and the lower classes, had already supplied her with the name of a struck-off doctor and a lawyer who had appeared more than once in front of the Bar Council's Ethics Committee. Mellor Travel had organized her flights to and from Baton Rouge, and booked her into the Commonwealth Hotel for three nights. The hotel was sadly unable to offer her ladyship a suite as they had all been taken by guests attending the wedding. Virginia didn't complain, as she had no wish to be the centre of attention – well, only for a few minutes.

For the next month she prepared, double-checked and rehearsed everything that needed to be covered during her three days in Baton Rouge. Her final plan would have impressed General Eisenhower, although she only needed to defeat Cyrus T. Grant III. The week before she was due to fly to Louisiana, Virginia visited a branch of Mothercare in Oxford Street, where she purchased three outfits that she only ever intended to wear once. She paid in cash.

◄o►

Lady Virginia Fenwick was picked up from her flat in Cadogan Gardens and driven to Heathrow in a private hire car arranged by Mellor Travel. When she checked in at the BOAC counter, she was told her flight to New York was running a few minutes late, but there would still be more than enough time to catch the connecting flight to Baton Rouge. She hoped so, because there was something she needed to do while she was at JFK.

A slim, smartly dressed, middle-aged woman stepped on to a plane bound for New York, while a heavily pregnant woman boarded the connecting flight to Baton Rouge.

On arrival in the capital of Louisiana, the pregnant woman took a taxi to the Commonwealth Hotel. As she stepped out of the back of the yellow cab, two porters rushed across to assist her. When she booked in, it wasn't hard to tell, from the conversations all around her, that the hotel was packed with guests looking forward to the special occasion. She was shown up to a single room on the third floor and, as there was nothing more she could do that night, Virginia collapsed on to the bed exhausted and fell into a deep sleep.

When she woke at 4 a.m., 10 a.m. in Cadogan Gardens, she thought about the meeting she had arranged later that morning with a Mr Trend, the man who would decide if her plan was realistic. She had phoned him a week earlier, and his assistant had called back to confirm her appointment with the senior partner. She hoped to have a little more success with her new lawyer than she had managed with Sir Edward.

Virginia took an early breakfast in her room and devoured that morning's *State-Times*. The wedding of the year had advanced to the front page. However, she learnt nothing that hadn't already been reported several times during the past month, except that security at both the church and the bride's family's ranch would be vigilant. The local police chief assured the paper's reporter that anyone who attempted to gatecrash the ceremony or the lunch would be ejected and end up spending the night in the city jail. Photographs of the bridesmaids and a copy of the lunch menu made a centre-page spread – but would Virginia be there to witness the ceremony? After she'd read the article twice and poured herself a third cup of coffee, she became restless, although it was still only 7.20 a.m.

After breakfast she selected a maternity outfit that made her, with a little assistance, look about seven months pregnant. She left the hotel at 9.40 a.m. and took a taxi to Lafayette Street, where she entered a monument to glass and steel and, after checking the directory on the wall, took a lift to the twenty-first floor. She told the receptionist her name was Fenwick and she had an appointment with Mr Trend. The young woman's southern drawl made English sound like a foreign language to Virginia, but she was rescued by a voice from behind her.

'Welcome to Baton Rouge, ma'am. I do believe it's me you're looking for.'

Virginia turned round to see another man who evidently considered that a check jacket, jeans and a string tie inspired confidence. She would have explained to Mr Trend that in England, only members of the royal family and police superintendents were addressed as ma'am, but she let it pass. They shook hands. 'Come through to my office.'

Virginia followed him past a row of offices that seemed to be getting larger and larger with each stride he took. Finally, Trend opened a door at the end of the corridor and ushered her in.

'Have a seat,' he said as he took his place behind a large mahogany desk. The walls were covered with photographs of Mr Trend and triumphant clients who couldn't have looked more guilty. 'Now you can imagine,' said Trend as he leant forward, 'how intrigued I was to receive a call from an English lady wanting to seek my advice, and also to find out how she'd ever come across my name in the first place.'

'It's a long story, Mr Trend,' which she proceeded to tell. Virginia explained to her prospective counsel how she'd met Cyrus T. Grant III on his brief visit to London. She did not mention the ring, but assured Mr Trend that her present condition was the result of that liaison.

The lawyer began licking his lips. 'Some questions, if I may, Lady Virginia,' he said, leaning back in his chair. 'First, and most important, when is the baby due to pop out?'

Once again Virginia was reminded of Cyrus. 'In about two months.'

'So I assume this liaison took place at the Ritz in London some seven months ago.'

'Almost to the day.'

'And may I ask you a delicate question?' he said, not waiting for her to reply. 'Could anyone else be the father?'

'As I hadn't slept with anyone for over a year before I met Cyrus, it seems unlikely.'

'I'm sorry if I've offended you, ma'am, but it's the first question Mr Grant's attorney will ask.'

'And you have your answer.'

'That being the case, it appears we do indeed have a paternity claim against Mr Grant. But I need to ask you another delicate question. Do you want this matter made public? Because if you do, you'd sure hit the front pages at the moment, considering who's involved. Or would you prefer me to try to reach a private settlement?'

'I would much prefer a private settlement. The less my friends in London know about this whole affair the better.'

'That's fine by me. In fact, we might even be able to get the best of both worlds.'

'I'm not sure I understand, Mr Trend.'

'Well, if you were to attend the wedding—'

'But surely it won't come as a surprise to you that I haven't been invited. And I read only this morning that security will be extremely tight.'

'Not if you have an invitation.'

'Does that mean you're going?'

'No, I was the lawyer who acted on behalf of Ellie May's first husband, so you won't see me there.'

'Which is the reason I chose you to represent me, Mr Trend.'

'I'm flattered. But before I agree to take on your case, there's another crucial matter we need to discuss. My fees, and how you intend to pay them. I charge one hundred dollars an hour, plus expenses, and I expect a down payment of ten thousand dollars on appointment.' Virginia realized their short meeting was about to be terminated. 'There is an alternative,' continued Trend, 'although I know it's frowned upon on your side of the pond. It's called the contingent fee option.'

'And how does that work?'

'I agree to take on your case and, if you win, I get twenty-five per cent of the final settlement.'

'And if I lose?'

'I get nothing. But you don't end up with a bill.'

'I like the sound of that.'

'Good, then that's settled. Now, my immediate problem is to make sure you get an invitation to the nuptials, and I think I know exactly who to call. Where can I contact you later today?'

'The Commonwealth Hotel, Mr Trend.'

'Call me Buck.'

23

'Mrs Kathy Frampton.'

'Who's she?' asked Virginia.

'A distant cousin of Ellie May Campbell,' replied Trend.

'Then someone at the wedding is certain to know her.'

'Unlikely. Her invitation was returned from Seattle unopened, with "Not known at this address" stamped across the envelope.'

'But surely someone who works for the wedding planners will know Mrs Frampton didn't reply to her invitation.'

'Yes, and that person just happens to be in charge of the guest list, and also the place settings for lunch at the ranch. And I can promise you, she won't be telling anyone.'

'How can you be so sure?' asked Virginia, sounding unconvinced.

'Let's just say she was delighted with the divorce settlement I negotiated for her.'

Virginia smiled. 'So how do I get hold of Mrs Frampton's invitation?'

'I slipped it under the door of your room an hour ago. Didn't want to disturb you.'

Virginia dropped the phone, jumped out of bed, ran to the door and picked up a large cream envelope. She ripped it open, to find an invitation from Mr and Mrs Larry Campbell to the wedding of their only daughter, Ellie May Campbell, to Cyrus T. Grant III.

Virginia picked the phone back up. 'I've got it.'

'Be sure to make it a memorable occasion for Cyrus,' said Trend. 'I look forward to hearing all about it when we meet up again tomorrow morning.'

◄○►

'Ellie May, will you take this man to be your . . .'

Virginia was seated in the eighth row of the congregation, among the cadet branch of the Campbell family. She had an excellent view of the nuptials, and had to give Ellie May some credit because Cyrus looked almost acceptable in morning dress, and may even have shed a few pounds. And from the look on his face, he clearly adored the about-to-be-pronounced Mrs Grant. Although, in truth, even a devoted mother would have been hard pressed to describe the bride as anything other than plain, which gave Virginia some satisfaction.

Virginia had taken a seat as close to the aisle as possible, in the hope that Cyrus would spot her as he and his bride left the church. But at the last moment, a family of three rushed in and edged her towards the centre of the pew. Despite her staring fixedly at the groom as the new Mr and Mrs Cyrus T. Grant proceeded down the aisle together, Cyrus appeared oblivious to anyone other than his bride and marched happily straight past her.

After Virginia had left the church, she checked the instructions neatly printed on the back of her invitation card. She was on coach B, which, along with seven other buses, countless limousines and even the odd car, stretched as far as the eye could see. She climbed on board and selected a seat near the back.

'Hello,' said an elegant white-haired old lady, offering a gloved hand as Virginia sat down next to her. 'I'm Winifred Grant. Cyrus is my nephew.'

'Kathy Frampton,' said Virginia. 'I'm a cousin of Ellie May.'

'I don't think I've seen you before,' said Winifred as the bus moved off.

'No, I hail from Scotland, and I don't get over to the States that often.'

'I see you're expecting.'

'Yes, in a couple of months.'

'Are you hoping for a girl or a boy?'

Virginia hadn't given a moment's thought to any questions she might be asked about being pregnant. 'Whatever the good Lord decides,' she said.

'How very sensible, my dear.'

'I thought the ceremony went rather well,' said Virginia, wanting to change the subject.

'I agree, but I do wish Cyrus had married Ellie May twenty years ago. It was what both families had always planned.'

'Then why didn't he?'

'Cyrus was always shy. He didn't even ask Ellie May to be his date for the school prom, so he lost out to Wayne Halliday. Wayne was the school's star quarterback and, frankly, he could have had any girl he wanted, and probably did. But she let him sweep her off her feet and, let's face it, it can't have been her looks that first attracted him to Ellie May.'

'Where's Wayne now?'

'I have no idea, but with the settlement he ended up with, he's probably lounging on a South Sea island drinking piña coladas, surrounded by skimpily clad maidens.'

Virginia didn't need to ask who Wayne Halliday's lawyer was. She had followed the case in the *State-Times* with great interest and been impressed with the size of the settlement Mr Trend had pulled off on behalf of his client.

The bus swung off the road and drove through a vast set of wrought-iron gates before proceeding down a long drive lined with tall pine trees that led to a massive colonial mansion surrounded by hundreds of acres of manicured lawns.

'What's Cyrus's ranch like?' asked Virginia.

'About the same size, I would guess,' said Winifred. 'So he didn't have to bother with a pre-nup. A marriage made not in heaven, but on the New York Stock Exchange,' she added with a smile.

The bus came to a halt outside a vast Palladian mansion. Virginia climbed off and joined the long line of guests who were having their invitations carefully checked. When she reached the front of the queue, she was handed a small white envelope by a woman who seemed to know exactly who she was.

'You're on table six,' she whispered. 'No one there for you to worry about.'

Virginia nodded and followed the other guests into the house. A row of white-jacketed waiters holding trays of champagne created a path all the way to the ballroom where a lunch for four hundred was waiting to be served. Virginia studied the layout of the room like a Grand National jockey considering which fences might bring him down.

A long table, clearly reserved for the family and their most important guests, ran down one side of the room. In front of it was a dance floor and, beyond that, forty circular tables filled the rest of the room. Virginia was still taking all this in when a gong sounded and a toastmaster dressed in a red tailcoat announced, 'Please take your places so we can all welcome the family and their distinguished guests.'

Virginia went in search of table six, which she found on the edge of the dance floor, right in front of the top table. She introduced herself to the two middle-aged men seated on either side of her. It turned out that like her, they were cousins, but of the Grants, not the Campbells. Buck Trend clearly wasn't taking any chances.

No sooner was everyone seated than they were on their feet again to applaud the bride and groom, who were accompanied by their parents, brothers and sisters, the best man, the bridesmaids and several distinguished guests.

'That's our governor,' said the man on Virginia's right, 'Hayden Rankin. Mighty fine fellow, much admired by the folks of Louisiana.' But Virginia was more interested in the seating at the top table. Although she had a clear view of Cyrus, she doubted he would spot her on the other side of the dance floor. How was she going to attract his attention without it being too obvious?

'I'm a cousin of Ellie May,' she eventually replied as they sat back down. 'And you?'

'My name's Nathan Grant. I'm a cousin of Cyrus, so I guess

we're now kith and kin.' Virginia couldn't think of a suitable response. 'Is your husband with you?' Nathan asked politely.

Another question Virginia hadn't anticipated. 'No, I'm afraid he's attending a business conference he couldn't get out of, so I came with Great-aunt Winifred instead.' She waved, and Winifred returned the compliment.

'So what line of business is he in?' Virginia looked puzzled. 'Your husband?'

'He's an insurance broker.'

'And what's his specialty?'

'Horses,' Virginia said, looking out of the window.

'How interesting. I'd like to meet him. Perhaps he could give me a better deal than the guy who's currently robbing me.'

Virginia didn't respond, but turned to the man sitting on her left. By switching her attention from one to the other at regular intervals, she avoided having to answer too many awkward questions. She received an occasional wave from Great-aunt Winifred, but Cyrus never once glanced in her direction. How was she going to make him aware she was there? And then the question was answered for her.

She was chatting to Nathan about her other child, her first-born, giving him a name – Rufus, aged eight – and even the school he was attending – Summerfields – when an attractive young woman from another table strolled past. Virginia noticed that several pairs of male eyes followed her progress. By the time she'd reached the other side of the dance floor, Virginia had worked out how to be sure that Cyrus couldn't miss her. However, her timing needed to be perfect, because she didn't want any rivals on the catwalk at the same time. Especially one who was younger and had longer legs.

After the third course had been cleared away, the toastmaster banged his gavel and silence prevailed once again. 'Ladies and gentlemen, Mr Larry Campbell, the father of the bride.'

Mr Campbell rose from his place at the centre of the top table. He began by welcoming his guests on behalf of his wife and . . .

Virginia anticipated Mr Campbell's speech would last for

about ten minutes. She needed to select the exact moment to make her move, because she knew she would only get one chance. While the father of the bride was welcoming Governor Rankin and the two US senators was clearly not that moment. She waited until Campbell began a long anecdote about some minor incident Ellie May had been involved in when she was at school. The punchline was greeted with far more laughter and applause than it deserved, and Virginia took advantage of the pause in his speech. Rising from her place and clutching her stomach, she walked slowly around the edge of the dance floor. She gave Mr Campbell an apologetic glance before staring, but only for a moment, directly at Cyrus. He turned chalk white, before she turned her back on him and made her way towards an exit sign on the far side of the room. The look on Cyrus's face suggested that Banquo's ghost could not have made a more effective appearance.

Virginia knew her re-entry needed to be just as powerful. She waited patiently in the wings for the best man's speech to finish before the toastmaster finally called on the bridegroom, Cyrus T. Grant III, to reply on behalf of the guests. As Cyrus rose, every-one burst into applause, which was the moment Virginia chose to re-enter the arena. She moved swiftly across the dance floor and back to her seat, trying to give the impression that she didn't want to hold up the bridegroom's speech. Cyrus was not a natu-rally gifted speaker at the best of times, and these weren't the best of times. He stumbled through his text, repeating several lines and, when he finally sat down, he received only muted applause, along with a gracious smile from an uninvited guest.

Cyrus turned round and began talking animatedly to a secu-rity guard who was stationed behind the top table. The square-shouldered giant of a man nodded and beckoned to two of his colleagues. Virginia suddenly realized she didn't have an exit strategy. When the band struck up, Nathan Grant rose gallantly from his place and was about to ask Kathy for the first dance, only to find she was already weaving her way nimbly between the tables towards the entrance.

When Virginia reached the far side of the room, she glanced

round to see one of the security guards pointing at her. Once she'd left the ballroom, her walk turned into a run. She shot along the corridor, out of the front door and on to the terrace at a speed no pregnant woman could possibly have managed.

'Can I help you, ma'am?' asked an anxious-looking young man stationed at the front door.

'I think the baby's coming,' said Virginia, clutching her stomach.

'Follow me, ma'am.' He ran down the steps ahead of her and quickly opened the back door of a guest limousine. Virginia climbed inside and collapsed on to the seat, just as two security guards came charging through the front door.

'Our Lady medical centre, and step on it!' said the young man to the chauffeur.

As the car accelerated down the drive Virginia turned round and, looking out of the back window, saw the two guards chasing after her. She waved at them as if she were royalty, confident that Cyrus T. Grant III knew she was in town.

─◄o►─

'You must have made quite an impression,' said Trend, even before Virginia had sat down. 'Because when I called Cyrus Grant's attorney this morning, he didn't seem surprised to hear from me. We've agreed to meet at his office at ten tomorrow.'

'But I'm flying back to London this afternoon.'

'Which is just dandy, because a case this important won't be settled in a hurry. Don't forget, Cyrus is on his honeymoon, and we wouldn't want to spoil that, would we? Although I have a feeling he'll be calling his lawyers from time to time.'

'So what am I expected to do?'

'Go home, prepare for the birth of your child and wait until you hear from me. And just a word of warning, Ginny. They're certain to have a detective in London keeping an eye on you.'

'What makes you say that?'

'Because it's exactly what I'd do.'

─◄o►─

Virginia boarded the 4.40 p.m. flight from Baton Rouge to New York. The plane landed at Kennedy just after 10 p.m.

She made her way to Gate 42 and thought she'd stop on the way to pick up a copy of *Vogue*. But when she saw the Barnes & Noble window was dominated by two bestselling books, she marched straight past. She didn't have long to wait before passengers were asked to board the plane for London.

Virginia was met at Heathrow by a chauffeur once again supplied by Mellor Travel, who drove her down to Hedley Hall in Hampshire, the country home of Bofie Bridgwater. Bofie was there to greet her as she stepped out of the car.

'Did you pull it off, my darling?'

'I don't know yet. But one thing's for certain – when I return to London, I'm going to have to give birth.'

24

BUCK TREND PHONED Virginia the following day to tell her that two Pinkerton detectives were on their way to England to watch her every move and report back to Grant's lawyers. One mistake, he warned her, and there would be no settlement. Was there even a possibility that Trend suspected she wasn't pregnant?

If Virginia was going to convince the two detectives that she was about to give birth, she would need the help of someone who was shrewd, resourceful and unscrupulous; in short, a man who considered fooling detectives and bending the law as simply part of his everyday life. She'd only ever met one person who fitted that description and, although she despised the man, Virginia didn't have a lot of choice if the next eight weeks were to go as planned.

She knew only too well that he would expect something in return, and it wasn't money, because he already had enough for both of them. But there was one thing Desmond Mellor didn't have, and wanted desperately – recognition. Having identified his Achilles heel, all Virginia had to do was convince him that as the daughter of the Earl of Fenwick, and a distant niece of the Queen Mother, she had the key to unlock that particular door and fulfil his ambition to be tapped on the shoulder by Her Majesty and hear the words, 'Arise, Sir Desmond'.

◄○►

'Operation Childbirth' was run like a military campaign, and the fact that Desmond Mellor had never risen above the rank of sergeant in the pay corps, and had never set eyes on the enemy, made it even more remarkable. Virginia spoke to him twice a day, although they never met in person, once he'd confirmed that the two detectives had arrived in London and were watching her apartment night and day.

'You must be sure they see exactly what they would expect to see,' he told her. 'Behave like any normal mother-to-be, with only a few weeks to go before she gives birth.'

Virginia continued to see Bofie and his chums regularly, for lunch, even dinner, at which she munched sticks of cucumber and drank glasses of carrot juice, eschewing champagne for the first time in her life. And when pressed, she never even hinted who the father might be. The gossip columns settled on Anton Delouth, the unsuitable young French man who had accompanied her to Tenerife, never to be seen again. The *Express* kept reprinting the one blurred photograph they had of them lying on a beach together.

Virginia relentlessly carried out her daily routine, with touches of sheer genius supplied by Desmond Mellor. A chauffeur-driven car picked her up once a week from Cadogan Gardens and drove her slowly to 41A Harley Street, never running a red light, never seeking a faster lane. After all, she was heavily pregnant and, more important, she didn't want the two Pinkerton detectives to lose sight of her. On arrival at 41A, a large, five-storey Georgian town house with seven brass name plates by its door, Virginia reported to reception for her weekly appointment with Dr Keith Norris.

Dr Norris and his assistant then examined her for over an hour before she returned to the car and was driven home. Desmond had assured her that the doctor was completely reliable and would personally deliver the child in his private clinic.

'How much did you have to pay him to keep his mouth shut?'

'Not a penny,' replied Desmond. 'In fact, he only hopes that I'll keep my mouth shut.' He let her wait for a moment before he added, 'When Dr Norris's attractive young nurse became pregnant, he certainly didn't want Mrs Norris to find out why he'd chosen Mellor Travel to organize her trip to a clinic in Sweden.'

Virginia was reminded once again that she didn't need this man as an enemy.

'There are two more people who must be informed of the impending birth,' said Mellor, 'if you want the world to believe you're pregnant.'

'Who?' asked Virginia suspiciously.

'Your father and Priscilla Bingham.'

'Never,' said Virginia defiantly.

–◄o►–

'Never' turned out to be a week later, in the case of Priscilla Bingham. When Virginia rang her old friend in Lincolnshire, Priscilla was reserved and somewhat distant – they had parted on sour terms after Virginia had caused the break-up of her marriage – until Virginia burst into tears and said, 'I'm pregnant.'

Priscilla's ex-husband Bob Bingham, like everyone else, was curious to know who the father might be, but that was the one thing Priscilla couldn't prise out of Virginia, even during a long lunch at the Mirabelle.

Virginia took a little longer to obey Desmond's second command, and even as the *Flying Scotsman* pulled into Edinburgh Waverley she was still considering returning to King's Cross without leaving the train. However, she concluded she couldn't win either way. If she told her father she was pregnant, he would probably cut off her allowance. On the other hand, if Buck Trend failed to secure a settlement and Papa were to discover she'd never been pregnant in the first place, he would undoubtedly disown her.

When Virginia walked into her father's study at ten o'clock that morning, looking eight months pregnant, she was shocked by his reaction. The earl assumed the *Daily Express* had got it right and Anton Delouth was the father, and the cad had run off and deserted her. He immediately doubled her allowance to £4,000 a month and only asked one thing in return: that once Virginia had given birth, she might consider visiting Fenwick Hall more often.

'A grandson at last,' were the words he kept repeating.

For the first time, Virginia didn't curse the fact that she had three brothers who'd only sired daughters.

◄o►

On Priscilla's advice, Virginia placed an advertisement for a nanny in *The Lady*, and was surprised by how many replies she received. She was looking for someone who would take complete responsibility for the child: mother, governess, mentor and companion, as she had no intention of fulfilling any of these obligations. Priscilla helped her prune the applicants down to a shortlist of six, and Desmond Mellor suggested she interview them on separate days, so the two detectives would have something new to report back to Grant's lawyers in Baton Rouge.

After Virginia and Priscilla had interviewed the final five – one of them didn't turn up – they both agreed that only one of the candidates ticked all the required boxes. Mrs Crawford was a widow and the daughter of a clergyman. Her husband, a captain in the Scots Guards, had been killed in Korea, fighting for Queen and country. Mrs Crawford turned out to be the eldest of six children and had spent her formative years raising the other five. Equally important, she had no children of her own. Even the earl approved of his daughter's choice.

◄o►

It occurred to Virginia that if she was to play out this charade to its ultimate conclusion, she needed to look for a larger establishment that would accommodate not only a butler and housekeeper but also the redoubtable Mrs Crawford, along with her new-born child.

After viewing several desirable residences in Kensington and Chelsea, closely observed by the two detectives, she settled on a town house in Onslow Gardens that had a top floor Mrs Crawford assured her would make a satisfactory nursery. When Virginia looked out of the drawing-room window, she noticed one of the detectives taking a photograph of the house. She smiled and told the estate agent to take the property off the market.

The only slight problem Virginia now faced was that despite

her father's generously increased allowance, she certainly didn't have enough money in her bank account to pay for a nanny, a butler and a housekeeper, let alone the deposit on the house in Onslow Gardens. Her former butler, Morton, had phoned earlier in the week – he was no longer allowed to visit the flat – to say that Dr Norris had provisionally booked Mrs Morton into the clinic in a fortnight's time. As Virginia climbed into bed that night, she decided she would have to call her lawyer in the morning. Moments after she'd fallen into a deep sleep, the phone rang. Only one person would consider calling her at that time of night, because he would still be sitting at his desk.

Virginia picked up the phone and was delighted to hear the deep southern drawl on the other end of the line.

'I guess you'll be pleased to know we've finally agreed terms with Grant's lawyers,' said Buck Trend. 'But there are conditions.'

'Conditions?'

'There always are with a settlement this large.' Virginia liked the word 'large'. 'But we may still have a problem or two.' She didn't care so much for 'problem or two'. 'We've agreed on a settlement of one million dollars, along with a maintenance order of ten thousand a month for the child's upbringing and education.'

Virginia gasped. Not in her wildest dreams . . . 'How can that possibly be a problem?' she asked.

'You must agree not to reveal the identity of the father to anyone, and that means anyone.'

'I'm happy to agree to that.'

'You and the child will never be allowed to set foot in Louisiana, and if either of you ever decide to travel to the United States, Grant's lawyers must be informed at least a month in advance.'

'I've only been to the States once in my life,' said Virginia, 'and I have no plans to return.'

'The child's surname must be Fenwick,' continued Trend, 'and Mr Grant has to approve the Christian names you select.'

'What's he worried about?'

'He wants to make sure that if it's a boy, you don't call him Cyrus T. Grant IV.'

Virginia laughed. 'I've already selected the name if it's a boy.'

'And if any of these conditions are broken at any time, all payments will immediately cease.'

'That's quite an incentive to keep to the agreement,' said Virginia.

'All payments will automatically cease in 1995, by which date it is assumed the child will have completed his or her full-time education.'

'I'll be nearly seventy by then.'

'And finally, Mr Grant's attorneys will be sending a doctor and a nurse to England to witness the birth.'

Virginia was glad Trend couldn't see her face. Once she'd put the phone down, she immediately rang Desmond Mellor to ask him how they could possibly get round that seemingly intractable problem. When the phone rang again at 7.45 the following morning, Desmond had come up with a solution.

'But won't Dr Norris object?' asked Virginia.

'Not while there's a chance he might have to explain to his wife and children why he's been struck off the medical register.'

-◄o►-

Virginia waited until she heard the siren before she called her lawyer in Baton Rouge.

'The baby's going to be born prematurely,' she screamed down the phone. 'I'm on my way to the hospital now!'

'I'll inform Grant's attorneys immediately.'

A few minutes later there was a loud knock on the door. When the butler answered it, one of the paramedics picked up Virginia's overnight case, while the other took her gently by the arm and guided her to a waiting ambulance. She glanced across the road to see two men clambering into a car. When the ambulance arrived at 41A Harley Street, the two paramedics opened the back door and led their patient slowly into the private clinic, to find Dr Norris and a staff nurse waiting for them. Norris left instructions that he should be told immediately the American doctor and his assistant arrived. He only needed fifteen minutes.

Nobody took any notice of the couple who slipped out of the back door of the clinic and took a taxi for the first time in their lives. But then, it wasn't every day the Mortons were handed a thousand pounds in cash.

Virginia undressed quickly and put on a nightgown. After she had climbed into the bed the nurse dabbed some rouge on her cheeks and sprayed a little moisture on her forehead. She lay back, trying to look exhausted. Twenty-two minutes later the nurse rushed back in.

'Dr Langley and his assistant have just arrived and are asking if they can witness the birth.'

'Too late,' said Dr Norris, who left the patient to welcome his American colleagues.

'We heard it was an emergency,' Dr Langley said. 'Is the baby all right?'

'I can't be sure yet,' said Norris, looking concerned. 'I had to perform an emergency caesarean. The baby's in an incubator, and I've given Lady Virginia a sedative to help her sleep.'

Dr Norris led them through to a room where they could observe the new-born infant in the incubator, seemingly fighting for its life. A narrow plastic tube inserted into one nostril was connected to a ventilator, and only the steady beeps of the heart monitor showed the child was actually alive.

'I'm feeding the little fellow through a gastric tube. We just have to pray his fragile body will accept it.'

Dr Langley examined the child closely for some time before asking if he could see the mother.

'Yes, of course,' said Norris. He led the two Americans through to the private room where Virginia was lying in bed, wide awake. Immediately the door opened, she closed her eyes, lay still and tried to breathe evenly.

'I'm afraid it's been rather an ordeal for the poor lady, but I'm confident she'll recover quickly. I wish I could say the same for her child.'

Virginia was relieved they only stayed for a few minutes, and she didn't open her eyes until she heard the door close behind them.

'If you'd like to remain overnight, we have a guest room, but if you return first thing in the morning, I'll be able to give you my written report.'

The Americans took one more look at the baby before leaving.

Later that evening, Dr Langley reported back to Grant's lawyers that he doubted the child would make it through the night. But then, he had no way of knowing that the baby had never needed to be in intensive care in the first place.

◄○►

Dr Langley and his assistant returned to 41A Harley Street the following morning, when Norris was able to report a slight improvement in the child's condition. His mother was sitting up in bed enjoying her breakfast. She looked suitably anguished and pale when they visited her.

Other visitors dropped in during the week, including Virginia's father and her three brothers, as well as Bofie Bridgwater, Desmond Mellor and Priscilla Bingham, who were all delighted by the child's progress. Virginia was surprised how many people said, 'He's got your eyes.'

'And your ears,' Bofie added.

'And the ancestral Fenwick nose,' pronounced the earl.

On the seventh day, mother and child were allowed to go home, where the responsibility for the infant was taken over by Nanny Crawford. However, Virginia had to wait another three weeks before she could begin to relax, and that was only after she had been told, courtesy of Mellor Travel, that Dr Langley and his assistant had boarded a plane for New York, accompanied by one of the detectives.

'Why hasn't the other one gone back with them?' she asked Mellor.

'I don't know yet, but I'll find out.'

◄○►

A wire transfer for $750,000 arrived at Coutts three days later, and was credited to the account of Lady Virginia Fenwick. Mr Fairbrother rang and asked if her ladyship wanted the dollars converted into pounds.

'What's the spot rate as we speak?' Virginia asked.

'Two sixty-three to the pound, my lady,' said a surprised Fairbrother.

'So what amount in sterling would be credited to my account?'

'£285,171, my lady.'

'Then go ahead, Mr Fairbrother. And send me confirmation the moment you've completed the transaction,' she added, before putting the phone down.

Desmond Mellor smiled. 'Word perfect.'

◄o►

Virginia and a healthy little boy moved into No.9 Onslow Gardens sixteen days later, along with Nanny Crawford, the butler and a housekeeper. Virginia inspected the nursery briefly and then handed the child over to its willing new devotee, before disappearing downstairs.

The christening was held at St Peter's, Eaton Square, and was attended by the Earl of Fenwick, who made one of his rare visits to London, Priscilla Bingham, who had reluctantly agreed to be a godmother, and Bofie Bridgwater, who was delighted to be a godfather. Desmond Mellor kept a wary eye on a solitary figure seated at the back of the church. The vicar held the baby over the font and dipped a finger in the holy water, before making a sign of the cross on the child's forehead.

'Christ claims you for his own. Frederick Archibald Iain Bruce Fenwick, receive the sign of his cross.'

The earl beamed, and Mellor looked around to see the lone detective had disappeared. He had honoured his part of the bargain, and now he expected Virginia to keep hers.

MAISIE CLIFTON

1972

25

WILLIAM WARWICK was just about to arrest the wrong person when there was a gentle tap on the door.

The rule was sacrosanct in the Clifton household. It had to be a serious matter – a very serious matter – before any member of the family would consider interrupting Harry while he was writing. In fact, he could recall the three occasions it had occurred during the past twenty-five years.

The first had been when his beloved daughter Jessica had won a scholarship to the Slade School of Fine Art in Bloomsbury. She had burst into the room without knocking, waving the letter of acceptance, and Harry had dropped his pen and opened a bottle of champagne to celebrate. The second was when Emma had won the casting vote over Major Alex Fisher to become chairman of Barrington's Shipping, and the first woman to chair a public company; another bottle of champagne. And the third he still considered to be marginal. Giles had barged in to announce that he'd been offered a peerage by Harold Wilson and would be taking the title Lord Barrington of Bristol Docklands.

Harry put his pen down on his desk and swivelled his chair round to face the intruder. Emma walked in, her head bowed, tears streaming unchecked down her cheeks. Harry didn't need to be told that his mother was dead.

◄○►

Harry spent more hours working on the eulogy for his mother's funeral than he had on any lecture, address or speech he'd ever delivered in the past. His final draft, the fourteenth, in which he felt he'd captured her indomitable spirit, ran for twelve minutes.

He visited St Luke's the morning before the service so he could see where he would be sitting and how far it was from the pulpit. He then tested the acoustics to find out how well his voice carried. The Dean of St Luke's pointed out that if there was a large congregation, his words might be a little muffled. A useful warning, thought Harry, because the church turned out to be so packed that if the family hadn't had reserved seats, they would have had to stand at the back. The order of service had been chosen in advance by Maisie, so no one was surprised that it was traditionally English, and very Maisie: 'Rock Of Ages', 'Abide With Me', 'To Be A Pilgrim' and of course 'Jerusalem', ensured that the congregation sang with heart and voice.

Sebastian had been selected to read the first lesson. During the last verse of 'Abide With Me', he walked slowly up to the lectern, no longer trying to disguise a slight limp that had taken longer to recover from than the Indian surgeon had predicted. No one could predict how long it would take to recover from the last funeral he'd attended.

He began to read 1 Corinthians, *Though I speak with the tongues of men and of angels, but have not charity,* and Giles delivered the second reading, a poem by Kipling, *If you can keep your head when all about you . . .* while the choir sang 'O Rejoice That The Lord Has Risen'. By the time Harry rose from his place in the front row and made his way to the pulpit during the last verse of 'Abide With Me', there was a sense of anticipation as he climbed the pulpit steps. He placed his text on the small brass lectern and checked the opening sentence, though in truth he knew the whole script by heart. He looked up and, once the congregation had settled, he began.

'How proud my mother would have been to see so many of you here today, some who have travelled from far and wide to celebrate her amazing life. "You just can't fill the churches nowadays," she used to say. Can't understand it myself, because when I was a child the sermons went on for over an hour. Dear Mother,' Harry said, looking up at the ceiling, 'I promise mine won't be over an hour, and by the way, the church is packed.' A ripple of laughter broke out, allowing Harry to relax a little.

'Maisie was born in 1901, in the reign of Queen Victoria, and died at the age of 71, during the reign of Queen Elizabeth the Second. My bookends, is how she used to describe the two Queens. She began life at 27 Still House Lane, in the back streets of the Bristol docks, and my father, Arthur Clifton, a docker, who was born in 1898, lived at number 37. They didn't even have to cross the road to bump into each other. My father died when I was only one, so I never knew him, and the responsibility for bringing me up fell squarely on the shoulders of my mother. Maisie was never ambitious for herself, but that didn't stop her spending those early years scrimping and saving farthings, yes, farthings, to ensure that I was never hungry, and never went without. Of course I had no idea of the sacrifices she had to endure to make it possible for me to attend St Bede's as a choral scholar, and later to go on to Bristol Grammar School before being offered a place at Oxford, a city she visited only once.

'If Maisie had been born today, it would have been a city that would have welcomed her with open arms. How can I be so sure of that? Because at the age of sixty-two, when most people are preparing for retirement, Maisie enrolled at Bristol University, and three years later graduated with a first-class honours degree. She remains to this day the only member of the Clifton family to have managed that distinction. Imagine what she might have achieved if she had been born a generation later.

'My mother was a regular churchgoer until the day she died, and I once asked her if she thought she'd go to heaven. "I certainly hope so," she told me, "as I need to have a word with St Peter, St Paul and our Lord." You will not be surprised to hear that I asked her what she intended to say to them. "I shall point out to St Peter that none of the women who were close to our Lord ever denied him, let alone three times. Typical man."' This time the laughter was sustained. Harry, now feeling in control of his audience, didn't continue until he had complete silence. '"And when it comes to St Paul," Maisie said, "I shall ask him why it took him so long to get the message." And our Lord? I asked her. "If you are the son of God, could you please point out to the Almighty that the world would be a far better place if there had only been one religion, because then we could have all sung from the same hymn sheet."' Harry had never experienced applause in a church before, and he knew it would have delighted his mother.

'When someone close to you dies, you remember all the things you wished you'd said and it's suddenly too late to say. I wish I'd understood, appreciated and been fully aware of the sacrifices my mother made, which have allowed me to live such a privileged life, a life I fear I sometimes take for granted. When I first went to St Bede's, dressed in my smart navy blazer and long grey trousers, we took the tram from Chapel Street, and I never understood why we got off a few hundred yards from the school. It was because my mother didn't want the other boys to see her. She thought I would be ashamed of her.

'I am ashamed,' said Harry, his voice cracking. 'I should have paraded this great lady, not hidden her. And when I went to Bristol Grammar School, she continued to work full-time as a waitress at the Royal Hotel during the day, and as a hostess at Eddie's Club every evening. I didn't realize it was because that was the only way she could afford the school fees. But, like St Peter, whenever any of my school chums asked if it was true that my mother worked in a nightclub, I denied her.' Harry's head dropped, and Emma looked on anxiously as the tears ran down his cheeks.

'What hardships did she have to endure without ever once, ever once . . . burdening me with her problems. And now it's too late to let her know.' Harry's head dropped again. 'To tell her . . .' he said, desperately searching for his place. He gripped the side of the pulpit. 'And when I went to Bristol Grammar School . . . I didn't realize.' He furiously turned back a page. 'I never realized . . .' He turned another page. 'Whenever any of my school chums asked me . . .'

Giles rose slowly from his place in the front row, walked across to the pulpit and climbed the steps. He placed an arm around his friend's shoulder, and guided him back to his place in the front pew.

Harry took Emma's hand and whispered, 'I let her down when she most needed me.'

Giles didn't whisper when he replied, 'No son has ever paid his mother a greater compliment, and right now she's telling St Peter, "That's my boy Harry down there."'

After the service, Harry and Emma stood by the door of the church, shaking hands with a long line of well-wishers. Harry had still not fully recovered, but it quickly became clear that the congregation universally agreed with Giles's sentiments.

Family and friends returned to the Manor House and raised glasses as they swapped stories about a remarkable woman, who touched the lives of everyone with whom she came into contact. Finally, when the last guest had departed, Harry, Emma and Sebastian were left alone.

'Let's drink to my mother's memory,' said Harry. 'I think it's time to open the '57 Merlot that Harold Guinzburg said should be saved for a special occasion. But before we do,' he added as he uncorked the bottle, 'I have to tell you that my mother gave me a letter a few weeks ago that she said was not to be opened until after her funeral.' He removed an envelope from his inside pocket with a flourish, tore it open and pulled out several hand-written pages in Maisie's bold, unmistakable script.

Emma sat down, feeling a little apprehensive, while Seb perched on the edge of his seat as if he were back at school before Harry began to read.

Dearest Harry,

These are no more than a few rambling thoughts from an old woman who should know better, so you are most welcome to dismiss them as such.

Let me begin with my dear grandson, young Sebastian. I still think of him as young, despite all that he's achieved in such a short period of time. Achievements that have been earned by ability combined with prodigious hard work, and I am sure he will realize his aim of becoming a millionaire

*by the age of forty. Commendable, no doubt, but Sebastian,
by the time you reach my age you will have learned that
acquiring great wealth is unimportant if you have no one
to share it with. Samantha was among the kindest, most
generous people I have ever known, and you were foolish to
part with such a gem. If that was not enough, it has been a
great sadness to me that I never met my great-granddaughter,
Jessica, because if she was anything like your sister, I know
I would have adored her.*

'How could she possibly have known about Jessica?' said Seb.
'I told her,' admitted Harry.

*I would also like to have known Priya, who by all accounts
was a very special young woman, who loved you so dearly
she was willing to sacrifice her life for you. And what a
compliment to your parents that the colour of her skin never
crossed your mind, because you were in love with her, so
her race and religion were irrelevant, which would not have
been possible for someone of my generation. You lost Priya
because of her parents' prejudice. Make sure you don't lose
Sam and Jessica because you are too proud to make the
first move.*

Sebastian bowed his head. He knew she was right.

*And now to you, dear Emma. Frankly, people should never
listen to their mothers-in-law. Behind every successful man,
they say, is a surprised mother-in-law. Harry owes so much
of his success to your loving support, as both a wife and
mother. But, and you knew there would be a 'but', you have,
in my opinion, by no means achieved your potential. Proust
said, we all end up doing the thing we're second best at.
There is no doubt that you have been an outstanding
chairman of Barrington's Shipping, as your directors,
shareholders and the City of London readily acknowledge.
But that should not be enough for someone with your*

*remarkable talents. No, I believe the time has come for you
to use some of your vision and energy for the public good.
There are so many causes that could flourish under your
leadership. Simply giving money to charity is the easy way
out. Giving time is much more precious. So make it your aim
that, when you die, people will not remember you only as
the chairman of Barrington's.*

'Why didn't she tell me that when she was alive?' said Emma.
'Perhaps she thought you were too busy to listen, my darling.'
'I can't wait to hear what she has to say to you, Dad.'

*And finally, my beloved son, Harry. For a mother to say
that she is proud of her son is only human. However, I could
never have dreamed of the happiness your success, both as
a novelist and as a campaigner for those who don't know
freedom, would bring me.*

*Although I believe, as I know you do, that your
courageous fight for Anatoly Babakov is your finest
achievement, I know you will not be satisfied until he
is a free man and can join his wife in America.*

*Have you ever told Emma you turned down a
knighthood, an honour you would not consider accepting
while Babakov was still in prison? I am proud of you for
that, even though I would have enjoyed hearing my son
addressed as Sir Harry.*

'You never told me,' said Emma.
'I never told anyone,' said Harry. 'Giles must have somehow
found out.' He returned to the letter.

*And now to William Warwick, who has entertained so many
people, for so many years. Harry, perhaps it's time for him
to retire, so that you can finally stretch yourself to reach
even greater heights. You told me once, many years ago, the
rough outline of a novel you had always wanted to write, but
had never got round to. You never got round to it because*

Harold Guinzburg, that wicked old publisher, kept tempting you with bigger and bigger advances. Perhaps the time has now come for you to write a book that will bring happiness for generations to come, whose reputation will outlive any bestseller list and make it possible for you to join that handful of authors whose names will never die.

Rant over. All that is left for me to say is thank you for making my final years so peaceful, comfortable and enjoyable. And when the time comes for any of you to write a similar letter, please don't be like me and feel you could have done so much more with your life.

Your loving mother,
Maisie

Harry poured three glasses of the '57 Merlot and handed one each to Emma and Seb. He raised his own glass and said, 'To Maisie. Shrewd old thing.'

'To Maisie,' repeated Emma and Seb, raising their glasses.

'Ah, and I nearly forgot,' said Harry, picking the letter back up. 'There's a postscript.'

P.S. Please remember me to your dear friend Giles, who can consider himself lucky that I didn't write about him, because had I done so, it would have been a far longer letter.

EMMA CLIFTON

1972–1975

26

'GOOD MORNING, Mrs Clifton. My name is Eddie Lister. We met briefly at your mother-in-law's funeral, but there's no reason you should remember me.'

'How did you know Maisie, Mr Lister?' Emma asked, because he was right, she couldn't place him.

'I'm chairman of the governors of the Bristol Royal Infirmary. She was one of our volunteers and will be sadly missed by patients and staff alike.'

'I had no idea,' said Emma. 'What did she do?'

'She was in charge of the lending library and organized the daily rota for the book trolley to be taken around the wards. More people read books at BRI than in almost any other hospital in the country.'

'Why am I not surprised,' said Emma. 'Are you looking for someone to replace her, because if you are, I'd certainly be happy to do so.'

'No, thank you, Mrs Clifton, that isn't the reason I'm calling.'

'But I'm confident I could organize the library and, what's more, my family has had a close association with the hospital for many years. My grandfather, Sir Walter Barrington, was chairman of the governors, my husband was nursed back to health at BRI after being seriously wounded by a German landmine in 1945, and my mother spent the last months of her life there under the care of Dr Raeburn. What's more, I was born at the Royal Infirmary.'

'I'm impressed, Mrs Clifton, but I still don't think you're the right person to organize the book trolley.'

'May I ask why you won't even consider me?'

'Because I was rather hoping you'd agree to become a governor of the hospital.'

Emma was momentarily silenced. 'I'm not altogether sure I know what a hospital governor does.'

'Every major NHS hospital – and ours is one of the largest in the country – has a board of governors drawn from the local community.'

'And what would my responsibilities be?'

'We hold a meeting every quarter, and I also invite each trustee to take an interest in one particular department of the hospital. I thought nursing might appeal to you. Our senior matron, Mima Puddicombe, represents the two thousand nurses who work full- or part-time at BRI. I should mention that if you agree to become a governor, there is no remuneration or expenses. I realize you are a busy woman, Mrs Clifton, with many responsibilities, but I do hope you'll give some thought to my proposal before you make—'

'I've thought about it.'

Mr Lister sighed. 'Yes, I feared you'd be too busy with all your other commitments, and of course I thoroughly understand—'

'I'd be delighted to become a governor of the hospital, Mr Chairman. When do I start?'

–◀○▶–

'Marshal Koshevoi is becoming somewhat restless, Comrade Brandt. He thinks it's time you came up with something a little more tangible. After all, you've been living with Barrington for the past year and all you've produced so far is the minutes of the Labour Party's weekly meetings in the House of Lords. Hardly illuminating.'

'I have to be careful, comrade director,' said Karin as they walked arm in arm down a quiet country lane. 'If Barrington were to become suspicious and my cover was blown, all our painstaking preparations would have been for nothing. And while he's in opposition, and not a member of the government, he isn't privy to what's going on in Whitehall. But if the Labour Party wins the next election, and Barrington is confident they will, that could all change overnight. And if I recall your exact words when I took on this assignment, "We are not in a hurry, we're in this for the long game."'

'That is still the case, comrade. However, I'm becoming concerned that you might be enjoying your bourgeois existence as Barrington's mistress a little too much, and have forgotten where your true allegiance lies.'

'I joined the party when I was still at school, comrade director, and have always been dedicated to our cause. You have no reason to question my loyalty.'

Tap, tap, tap. They fell silent when they saw an elderly gentleman approaching.

'Good afternoon, colonel,' said Pengelly.

'Afternoon, John. How nice to see your daughter again,' said the old man, raising his hat.

'Thank you, colonel,' said Pengelly. 'She's just down for the day, and we thought a breath of country air wouldn't do us any harm.'

'Capital,' said the colonel. 'I rarely miss my constitutional. Gets me out of the house. Well, must be getting along, or the memsahib will be wondering where I am.'

'Of course, sir.' Pengelly didn't speak again until they could no longer hear the tap, tap, tap of the colonel's walking stick. 'Has Barrington asked you to marry him?' he asked, taking Karin by surprise.

'No, comrade director, he has not. After two failed marriages, I don't think he'll be rushing into a third.'

'Perhaps if you were to become pregnant?' he said as they turned off the road and followed a path that led to a disused tin mine.

'What use would I be to the party then, if I had to spend all my time bringing up a child? I'm a trained operative, not a babysitter.'

'Then let's see some proof of it, Comrade Brandt, because I can't go on telling my masters in Moscow tomorrow, tomorrow, tomorrow, like a parrot.'

'Barrington is attending an important meeting in Brussels next Monday, when he'll witness the signing of the treaty that will make Britain a member of the EEC. He's asked me to accompany him. I may be able to pick up some useful information as there will be a lot of foreign delegates around.'

'Good. With so many ambitious politicians all trying to prove how important they are, be sure to keep your ears open, especially at dinners and casual get-togethers. They have no idea how many languages you speak. And don't switch off in the evening, when they'll be relaxed after a drink or two and more likely to say something they might later regret, especially to a beautiful woman.'

Karin looked at her watch. 'We'd better turn back. I'm supposed to be in Bristol in time for dinner with Giles and his family.'

'Wouldn't want you to miss that,' said Pengelly, as they began to retrace their steps. 'And do remember to wish Giles . . . a happy Christmas.'

—◄◦►—

On the journey back from Truro to Bristol, Karin couldn't stop thinking about the dilemma she now faced. During the past year she had fallen deeply in love with Giles and had never been happier in her life, but she'd become trapped, playing a role she no longer believed in, and she couldn't see a way out of the maze. If she suddenly stopped supplying information for the Stasi, her masters would call her back to Berlin, or worse. If she lost Giles, she would have nothing to live for. By the time she drove through the gates of the Manor House, the dilemma hadn't been resolved, and wouldn't be, unless . . .

—◄◦►—

'Is Karin joining us for dinner?' asked Emma as she poured her brother a whisky.

'Yes, she's driving up from Cornwall. She's been to visit her father, so she may be a little late.'

'She's so bright and full of life,' said Emma. 'I can't imagine what she sees in you.'

'I agree. And it's not as if she doesn't know how I feel about her, because I've asked her to marry me enough times.'

'Why do you think she keeps turning you down?' asked Harry.

'With my track record, who can blame her? But I think she may be weakening.'

'That's good news, and I'm so pleased you'll both be joining us for Christmas.'

'And how are you enjoying the Lords these days?' asked Harry, changing the subject.

'It's been fascinating shadowing Geoffrey Rippon, who's been in charge of our application to join the EEC. In fact I'm off to Brussels next week to witness the signing of the treaty.'

'I read your speech in Hansard,' said Harry, 'and I agreed with your sentiments. Let me see if I can remember your exact words, "Some talk of the economy, others of trade relations, but I will vote for this bill if for no other reason than it will ensure that our country's youth will only have to read about two world wars, and will never have to experience a third".'

'I'm flattered.'

'And what does the new year hold for you, Giles?' asked Emma, filling up his glass.

'I've been drafted on to the general election team and put in charge of the marginal seats campaign. Even better news, Griff Haskins has agreed to come out of retirement and act as my chief of staff.'

'So the two of you will be roaming around the country doing what, exactly?' asked Emma.

'Visiting the sixty-two marginal seats that will determine the outcome of the next election. If we win them all – which is most unlikely – we'll end up with a majority of around thirty.'

'And if you lose them all?'

'The Conservatives will remain in power. I'll be history, and I suspect your friend Margaret Thatcher will be the next Chancellor of the Exchequer.'

'I can't wait,' said Emma.

'Did you take up her offer to meet again?'

'She's invited me to have a drink with her in the Commons in a couple of weeks' time.'

'Not lunch?' said Harry.

'She doesn't do lunch,' said Giles.

Emma laughed. 'So don't regard anything you tell me as private, because I've got both feet firmly in the enemy's camp.'

'My own sister, plotting against me.'

'You'd better believe it.'

'No need to get too worried,' said Harry. 'Emma's just been appointed a governor of the Bristol Royal Infirmary so she isn't going to have a lot of time left over for politics.'

'Congratulations, sis. Eddie Lister is a first-class chairman and you'll enjoy serving under him. But what made you agree to take on such a demanding commitment?'

'Maisie. It turns out she was a hospital volunteer, in charge of the library. I didn't even know.'

'Then you can be sure every book had to be properly stamped and back on time if you didn't want to be fined.'

'She'll be a hard act to follow, as everyone continually reminds me. I've already discovered that a hospital is a fascinating twenty-four-hour operation. It rather puts Barrington Shipping in the shade.'

'Which department has Eddie asked you to shadow?'

'Nursing. The senior matron and I are already meeting once a week. An NHS hospital is very different from a public company because no one thinks about profits, only patients.'

'You'll end up a socialist yet,' said Giles.

'Not a hope. The bottom line still dictates the success or failure of any organization, so I've asked Sebastian to trawl through the hospital's annual accounts to see if he can spot any ways of cutting costs or making savings.'

'How's Sebastian doing,' asked Giles, 'remembering all he's been through?'

'He's more or less fully recovered physically, but I suspect that mentally it will take considerably longer.'

'That's understandable,' said Giles. 'First Sam, and then Priya. How can we even begin to understand how he's coping?'

'He's simply immersed himself in work,' said Emma. 'Since he's become the bank's chief executive he's been working hours that make no sense. In fact he doesn't seem to have any personal life at all.'

'Have either of you raised the delicate subject of Samantha?' asked Giles.

'Once or twice,' said Harry, 'but it's always the same response. He won't consider getting in touch with her while Michael is still alive.'

'Does that also apply to Jessica?'

'I'm afraid so, although I never mention our granddaughter unless he does.'

'But your mother was right,' said Emma. 'The years are slipping by and, at this rate, Jessica will be a young woman before any of us get to meet her.'

'Sadly that may well be the case,' said Harry. 'But we have to remember it's Seb's life that's been thrown into turmoil, not ours.'

'Speaking of people whose lives have been thrown into turmoil,' said Emma, turning to her brother, 'I often wonder how your ex-wife is coping with motherhood.'

'Not very well, I suspect,' said Giles. 'And has anybody ever found out who the father is?'

'No, that remains a mystery. But whoever it is, little Freddie doesn't seem to have interfered with Virginia's lifestyle. I'm told she's back on the circuit, and the drinks are on her.'

'Then the father has to be an extremely wealthy man,' said Harry.

'He does,' agreed Giles. 'Wealthy enough to have bought her a house in Onslow Gardens, and for her to employ a nanny, who I gather can be seen wheeling the Hon. Frederick Archibald Iain Bruce Fenwick in his pram down Rotten Row every morning.'

'How do you know that?' asked Emma.

'We socialists don't confine ourselves to *The Times* and

Telegraph, sis, and what's more—' Giles was interrupted by a knock on the front door. 'That must be Karin back from Corn-wall,' he said as he rose from his chair and left the room.

'Why don't you like Karin?' asked Emma once Giles was out of earshot.

'What makes you say that?' asked Harry.

'You imagine I don't know what you're thinking, after more than forty years? Giles adores her, and it upsets him that you won't accept her.'

'Is it that obvious?'

'I'm afraid so.'

Giles and Karin strolled into the room chatting and holding hands. Harry stood up to greet her. If she wasn't in love with Giles, he thought, she's a damn good actress.

27

EMMA HADN'T ENTERED the Palace of Westminster since their lordships had decided she was free to marry the man she loved. Giles had invited her to join him for lunch many times, but she just couldn't face it. She hoped a visit to the Commons would finally exorcise the ghosts of the past and, in any case, she was looking forward to meeting Mrs Thatcher again.

With the help of a policeman and a messenger, she found her way to the tea room, where Margaret Thatcher was standing by the door waiting for her.

'Come and join me,' she said, before leading her guest to an empty table. 'I've already ordered tea as I had a feeling you were the kind of person who wouldn't be late.'

Margaret, as she insisted on Emma calling her, bombarded her with questions about her thoughts on education, the NHS and even Jacques Delors. When Emma asked Margaret, if Ted Heath were to lose the next election and was forced to resign, whether she would consider standing as party leader, she didn't hesitate in giving her opinion.

'A woman can never hope to be prime minister of this country,' she said without hesitation. 'At least not in my lifetime.'

'Perhaps the Americans will show us the way.'

'It will take the Americans even longer to elect a woman president,' said Thatcher. 'They are still at heart a frontier society. There are only fifteen women in Congress, and not even one in the Senate.'

'What about the Labour Party?' said Emma. 'Some people are suggesting that Shirley Williams—'

'Not a hope. The unions wouldn't stand for it. They'd never allow a woman to be their general secretary. No, we elected the first Jewish prime minister, and the first bachelor, so we'll elect the first woman, but not in my lifetime,' Thatcher repeated.

'But other countries have already chosen women to be their PM.'

'Three of them,' said Thatcher.

'So if you can't be the fourth, and we do win the next election, what job are you hoping to get?'

'It's not a question of what I'm hoping to get, it's what Ted will reluctantly offer me. And remember, Emma, in politics it's never wise to let anyone know what you want. That's the quickest way to make enemies and detractors. Just look surprised any time anyone offers you anything.' Emma smiled. 'So tell me, what's your brother Giles up to?'

'He's been put in charge of the marginal seats campaign, so he spends most of his life trudging up and down the country trying to make sure Harold Wilson is returned to No.10.'

'A brilliant choice. He fought and won Bristol Docklands against the odds again and again, and there are many on our side who would have preferred to see him back in the House rather than that second-rater, Alex Fisher. And if Labour were to win, Giles might well become Leader of the Lords, which would see him back in the Cabinet. Anyway, that's enough politics. Tell me what's happening in the real world. I see Barrington's Shipping had another record year.'

'Yes, but I'm beginning to feel I'm repeating myself. It may not be too long before I'm ready to hand over to my son.'

'Then what will you do? You don't strike me as the type who'll take up golf or start attending basket-weaving classes.'

Emma laughed. 'No, but I've recently been appointed a governor of the Bristol Royal Infirmary.'

'A great hospital, but I'm sure you will already have discovered, unlike my socialist colleagues, that there just isn't enough money to give every hospital not only what it would like, but even what it needs, with the development of so many new drugs. The biggest problem the health service faces is that we are no longer conveniently dying at the age of seventy, but many more people are living to eighty, ninety, even a hundred. Whoever wins the next election will have to face that problem head on, if they're not going to saddle future generations with a mountain of debt they will never be able to repay. Perhaps you could help, Emma.'

'How?'

Thatcher lowered her voice. 'You may have heard the rumours that if we win, I'll be offered Health. It would be helpful to have a friend who works at the coalface and not just go on attending endless meetings with experts who have three degrees and no hands-on experience.'

'I'd be delighted to help in any way I can,' said Emma, flattered by the suggestion.

'Thank you,' said Margaret. 'And I know it's asking rather a lot, but it might prove useful in the long term to have an ally on the West Country area Conservative committee.'

A loud, continuous bell began clanging, almost deafening Emma. The door of the tea room swung open and a man in a black jacket marched in and shouted, 'Division!'

'Back to work, I'm afraid,' said Thatcher. 'It's a three-line whip, so I can't ignore it.'

'What are you voting on?'

'No idea, but one of the whips will guide me into the right corridor. We were told there wouldn't be any more votes today. This is what's called an ambush: a vote on an amendment that we thought wasn't controversial and would go through on the nod. I can't complain, because if we were in opposition, we'd be doing exactly the same thing. It's called democracy, but you already know my views on that subject. Let's keep in touch, Emma. We Somerville girls must stick together.'

Margaret Thatcher stood up and shook hands with Emma before joining the stampede of members who were deserting the tea room to make sure they reached the division lobbies within eight minutes, otherwise the door would be slammed in their faces.

Emma sank back into her chair, feeling simultaneously exhilarated and exhausted, and wondered if Margaret Thatcher had the same effect on everyone.

◄○►

'Good of you to pop over, John. I wouldn't have asked for a meeting at such short notice if there hadn't been a development.'

'Not a problem, Alan, and thank you for the tip-off, because it allowed me to dig out the relevant file.'

'Perhaps you could start by bringing me up to date on Miss Brandt.'

Sir John Rennie, Director General of MI6, opened the file on the table in front of him. 'Miss Brandt was born in Dresden in 1944. She joined the communist youth party at the age of sixteen, and, when she left school, went to the East German School of Languages to study Russian. After graduating, the Stasi recruited her as an interpreter at international conferences, which we assumed was no more than a front. But there's no proof that she did much more than pass on fairly mundane information to her superiors. In fact, we were of the opinion that she'd fallen out of favour until the Giles Barrington affair.'

'Which I assume was a set-up.'

'Yes. But who was being set up? Because she certainly wasn't on our list of operatives who specialize in that sort of thing and, to be fair to Barrington, he's steered well clear of any honey traps while on government trips behind the Iron Curtain, despite several opportunities.'

'Is it just possible that she really did fall for him?' asked the Cabinet Secretary.

'There's nothing in your file to suggest you're a romantic, Alan, so I'll take your question at face value. It would certainly explain several incidents that have taken place since she arrived in the UK.'

'Such as?'

'We now know that Giles Barrington's rescue of a damsel in distress from the other side of the Iron Curtain was actually nothing of the sort. In fact, it was a well-organized operation overseen and approved by Marshal Koshevoi.'

'Can you be sure of that?'

'Yes. When Brandt was attempting to cross the border with Barrington by bus, she was questioned by a young officer who nearly blew the whole operation. He was posted to Siberia a week later. That was what caused us to suspect they'd always wanted her to cross the border, although it's just possible she only fell in with their plans because she really did want to escape.'

'What a devious mind you have, John.'

'I'm head of MI6, Alan, not the boy scouts.'

'Do you have any proof?'

'Nothing concrete. However, at a recent meeting Brandt had with her handler in Truro, our observer reported that Pengelly's body language suggested he wasn't at all pleased with her. Which isn't surprising, because one of our double agents recently passed some information to her that Pengelly would certainly have reported to his masters back in Moscow, and I can tell you he didn't, which means she didn't.'

'That's a risky game she's playing. It won't take them long to work out she isn't keeping her side of the bargain.'

'Agreed. And once they do, she'll be on the next flight back to East Berlin, never to be heard of again.'

'Perhaps she'd make a good candidate for turning,' suggested Sir Alan.

'Possibly, but I still need to be convinced she's not taking us for fools. I plan to use the same agent to feed her with a piece of information Pengelly will be desperate to hear about, so I'll know within a few days if she's passed the message on to him.'

'Has the time come to let Barrington know he's sleeping with the enemy? If Labour win the next election he'll certainly be back in the Cabinet, and then someone is going to have to brief the Prime Minister.'

'Let's clear that hurdle when . . .'

◄○►

'What are you up to today, darling?'

'A little shopping this morning. Your socks either have holes in them, or they don't match.'

'How exciting,' said Giles. 'And to think I'm only opposing the new education bill.'

'I'm also hoping to find something for your sister's birthday,' she added, ignoring the comment. 'Any ideas?'

'A soap box? We're barely on speaking terms at the moment.'

'It's not her fault. You spend your life attacking Mrs Thatcher.'

'Not Mrs Thatcher, but the government's philistine education policy. It's never personal. You save that for your own side.'

'And I've been invited to have tea in the Lords' this afternoon with Baroness Forbes-Watson, but I'm not altogether sure why.'

'She's a sweet old bat, used to be something in the Foreign Office a hundred years ago but since her husband died she's rather lost the plot. I know she likes to invite members' wives to tea from time to time.'

'But I'm not your wife.'

'That's hardly my fault,' said Giles, giving her a kiss. 'I'll try and drop into the tea room after the vote. You may need rescuing,' he added as he picked up *The Times*. He smiled when he saw the headline. 'I must call Emma.'

◄○►

'She's the statutory woman,' said Harry, pouring himself another cup of coffee.

'What did you just say?'

'I didn't say it. Ted Heath did. *The Times*,' he continued, picking his morning paper back up, 'reports him as saying, "If it's necessary to have a woman in the Cabinet, it may as well be Margaret".'

Emma was speechless, but only for a moment. 'That's certain to endear him to fifty per cent of the electorate,' she finally managed.

'Fifty-two per cent, according to *The Times*.'

'Sometimes I despair for the Tory party,' said Emma, as the phone rang.

Harry put down his paper, walked across to the sideboard and picked up the phone. 'Hello, Giles, yes, I did read the piece about Margaret Thatcher in *The Times*. Yes, of course. It's your brother on the line, wants to have a word with you,' said Harry, unable to hide a smirk.

Emma folded her napkin, put it back in its ring, stood up and made her way slowly out of the room. 'Tell him I'm out canvassing.'

◄o►

After Karin had bought six pairs of grey woollen socks, size nine, and a black leather handbag that she knew Emma coveted, she boarded a bus in Sloane Square and headed for the Palace of Westminster. A badge messenger directed her to the Lords' tea room. 'Never step off the red carpet, madam, and you won't go far wrong.'

As she entered the tea room, Karin immediately spotted a grey-haired old lady hunched up in the corner looking as if she might have been Margaret Rutherford's older sister. She managed a wave, and Karin walked across to join her.

'Cynthia Forbes-Watson,' the old lady said, trying to rise from her place.

'No, no,' said Karin quickly, sitting down opposite her hostess.

'How lovely to meet you,' said the old lady, offering a thin, bony hand, although her voice was strong. 'I read about your amazing escape from behind the Iron Curtain. That must have been quite an ordeal.'

'It would never have been possible without Giles.'

'Yes, he's a fine man, if occasionally impetuous,' she said as a waiter appeared by their side. 'Tea for two, Stanley, and a couple of those awful crumpets, slightly burnt. And don't be mean with the butter.'

'Certainly, my lady.'

'I see you've been shopping.'

'Yes, Giles needed some socks. It's also his sister's birthday and he forgot to get her a present. She and her husband are joining us for dinner this evening.'

'It's never easy to find the right present for another woman,' said the baroness, as a tray of tea and two slightly burnt crumpets was placed on the table between them. 'I'll be mother. Milk?'

'Yes, please,' said Karin.

'Sugar?'

'No, thank you.'

'How sensible,' said the baroness as she put two heaped spoonfuls in her own cup. 'But then it's a bit late for me to be worrying about my figure.' Karin laughed dutifully. 'Now, you must be wondering why I wanted to see you.'

'Giles told me you regularly hold little tea parties.'

'Not like this one I don't.'

'I'm not sure I understand.'

The baroness put down her cup and looked directly at Karin. 'I want you to listen very carefully to what I'm about to say, young lady.' Although she spoke softly, her words were clear. 'This will be the only time we ever meet, unless you follow my instructions to the letter.'

Karin wondered if she was joking, but it was obvious from her manner she was serious.

'We British like to give the impression of being bumbling amateurs, but some of us aren't that easily fooled, and although it made an exciting story for the press, your escape from East Berlin was just a little too convenient.'

Karin felt herself shaking.

'If the Labour Party were to win the next election, you would be well placed to cause considerable embarrassment, not only for the government, but for this country.'

Karin gripped the arms of her chair.

'We've known for some time that John Pengelly isn't your father, and that he reports directly to Marshal Koshevoi. But what puzzles us is that although you've been living in this country for more than two years, you don't appear to have passed any information of real significance to the other side.'

Karin wished Giles would come and rescue her, but she knew there was no chance of that.

'I'm relieved you're not foolish enough to deny it, because

there is a way out of this mess, as long as you're willing to co-operate.'

Karin said nothing.

'I'm going to give you the chance to work for this country. I will personally make sure that you are regularly supplied with information that will keep the Stasi convinced you're still working for them. But in return we will expect to know everything Pengelly is up to, and I mean everything.'

Karin picked up her cup but her hand was trembling so much she put it straight back down.

'I will be your handler,' the baroness continued, 'and what better cover could you have than the occasional tea with a silly old bat from the House of Lords? That's the story you'll tell Giles, unless you want him to find out the truth.'

'No, that's the last thing I want,' stammered Karin.

'Then let's keep it that way. My husband, dear man, went to his grave thinking I was an under-secretary at the FCO, which indeed I was, to all intents and purposes. He would have burst out laughing if you'd suggested I was a spy. I should warn you, Miss Brandt, that if you feel unable to go along with our plan, you will be on the next flight back to East Berlin, and I will be the one who has to tell Lord Barrington the truth.' She paused. 'I see you have some feeling for Giles.'

'I adore him,' said Karin without guile.

'So, Sir John got that right. You really did want to escape from East Germany to be with him. Well, you'll just have to go on fooling most of the people most of the time. Ah, I see Giles heading towards us. If I receive a thank-you note from you tomorrow, I'll know which side you're on. If I don't, you and Pengelly had better be on a flight to East Germany before dusk.'

'Cynthia, you don't look a day over forty,' said Giles.

'And you're still an incorrigible flirt and flatterer, Giles Barrington.'

'Guilty. It was kind of you to invite Karin to tea.'

'We've had a most interesting conversation.'

'And now I must drag her away as we're taking my sister out to dinner tonight.'

'To celebrate her birthday, Karin tells me. I won't detain you any longer.'

Karin got up unsteadily, picked up her shopping bag and said, 'Thank you for tea.'

'I do hope you'll come again, Karin.'

'I'd like that.'

'A remarkable old biddy,' said Giles as they walked down the corridor, 'although no one seems to be quite sure what she did at the Foreign Office. More important, did you remember to buy me some socks?'

'Yes, I did, darling. Cynthia told me that she was an under-secretary at the FCO.'

'I'm sure she was . . . And did you manage to find a present for Emma?'

28

EMMA WAS RUNNING late for her meeting. Attempting to juggle three balls at once was a skill she'd had to learn very quickly, and for the first time in her life there had been moments when she wondered if she had taken on more than she could handle.

Chairing the family company remained her first priority, and what she described to Harry as the day job. However, her responsibilities as a governor of the hospital were taking up far more of her time than she had originally anticipated. Officially, she was expected to attend four board meetings a year and to devote two days a month to hospital business. But it hadn't been long before she found herself doing two days a week. There was no one but herself to blame, because she enjoyed every minute of her responsibilities as the governor overseeing the nursing staff.

The hospital employed over two thousand nurses and hundreds of doctors, and the senior matron, Mima Puddicombe, was not old school, but ancient school. Florence Nightingale would happily have taken her to the Crimea. Emma enjoyed learning about the day-to-day problems Mima faced; at one end of the scale were grandiose consultants who imagined they were omnipotent, while at the other were patients who knew their rights. Somewhere in between were the nurses, who were expected to take care of both, while making sure a smile never left their faces. It was no wonder Mima had never married. She had two thousand anxious daughters, and a thousand unruly sons.

Emma had soon become engrossed in the daily routines of

the hospital and was touched that Mima not only sought her advice, but treated her as an equal, sharing her anxieties and ambitions for the hospital to which she had devoted her life. But the meeting Emma was running late for had nothing to do with her duties at the hospital.

Earlier that morning, the Prime Minister had visited the Queen at Buckingham Palace and sought her permission to dissolve Parliament, so that a general election could be called. Emma had kept her promise to Margaret Thatcher and joined the election committee that oversaw the seventy-one constituencies in the West Country. She represented Bristol, with its seven seats, two of which were marginal, one of them her brother's old stomping ground. For the next three weeks she and Giles would be standing on opposite sides of the road, imploring the electorate to support their cause.

Emma was thankful the campaign would be over in a month because she had to accept that Barrington's and the hospital were not going to see a lot of her until after polling day. Harry never got used to her creeping into bed after midnight and then disappearing before he woke the following morning. Most men would have suspected their wife had a lover. Emma had three.

‹o›

It was a bitterly cold afternoon and the two of them put on heavy coats, scarves and gloves before they went out for their usual walk. They only spoke of inconsequential matters until they reached the abandoned tin mine, where there would be no colonels, tourists or noisy children to disturb them.

'Do you have anything worthwhile to report, Comrade Brandt, or is this another wasted journey?'

'The Home Fleet will be carrying out exercises off Gibraltar on February twenty-seventh and twenty-eighth, when the Royal Navy's new nuclear submarine will be in service for the first time.'

'How did you get hold of that piece of information?' said Pengelly.

'Barrington and I were invited to dine with the First Sea Lord at Admiralty House. I've found that if you remain silent long enough you blend into the background, like wallpaper.'

'Well done, comrade. I knew you'd come good in the end.'

'Can I seek your advice on another matter, comrade director?' After double-checking that there was no one who could overhear them, Pengelly nodded. 'Barrington has asked me to be his wife. How would the party want me to respond?'

'You should accept, of course. Once you're married, they'd never be able to expose you because it could bring down the government.'

'If that's what you want, comrade director.'

◄○►

Emma returned home at ten o'clock on the evening of the election, and she and Harry sat up through the night following the results from all over the country. It quickly became clear after the first count was declared in Billericay that the outcome was going to be too close to call, and when the last seat was announced in County Down in Northern Ireland just after 4.30 the following afternoon, the Labour Party had captured the most seats, 301 to 297, although the Tories had won the popular vote, by over 200,000.

Ted Heath refused to resign as prime minister, and spent the next few days trying to cobble together a coalition with the Liberals, which would have given the Tories an overall majority. But it fell apart when Jeremy Thorpe, the Liberal leader, demanded as part of their acquiescence that proportional representation had to be enacted in law before the next election. Heath knew his backbenchers wouldn't deliver, so he returned to Buckingham Palace and informed the Queen that he was unable to form a government.

The following morning, Her Majesty called for the Labour leader and invited him to form a minority government. Harold Wilson took up residence at No.10 Downing Street and spent the rest of the day appointing his Cabinet.

Emma was delighted when the television cameras followed Giles walking up Downing Street to keep an appointment with the Prime Minister. He came out of No.10 twenty minutes later, as Leader of the House of Lords. She called her brother to congratulate him on the appointment.

'Double congratulations are in order,' said Giles. 'Karin has finally agreed to marry me.'

Emma could not have been more pleased, but when she told Harry the news that evening, he didn't seem to share her enthusiasm. She would have probed as to why he was always so negative about Karin if the phone hadn't rung and interrupted her. The local paper was on the line asking if she wanted to make a statement, not about the minority government or her brother's appointment, but the tragic death of Eddie Lister.

—◦—

Emma attended an emergency meeting of the hospital's governors the following evening. The meeting opened with a minute's silence in memory of the late chairman, who had suffered a heart attack while climbing in the Alps with his two sons. Emma's thoughts were with Eddie's wife Wendy, who had flown out to Switzerland to be with her children and bring her husband's body home.

The second item on the agenda was to elect a new chairman. Nick Caldercroft, Eddie's long-serving deputy, was proposed, seconded and elected *nem. con.* to take Eddie's place. He spoke warmly of the man he had had the honour of serving under and pledged to carry on with his legacy.

'But,' he emphasized, 'that task will be made a lot easier if we select the right person to be my deputy. None of you will be surprised to learn that my first choice is Emma Clifton.'

Emma wasn't surprised, she was shocked, as the idea had never crossed her mind. However, as she looked around the boardroom table, it appeared that everyone agreed with the new chairman. Emma began mentally composing a few words about how she was flattered by their confidence in her but sadly it wasn't possible at the present time because . . . But then she looked up and saw the photograph of her grandfather staring down at her. Sir Walter Barrington was giving her that gimlet-eyed look she remembered so well from her schooldays, when she'd been caught doing something naughty.

'Thank you, Mr Chairman. It's a great honour and I shall try to prove worthy of your confidence.'

Returning home later that evening she had to explain to Harry why she was clutching a thick bundle of files. He didn't look surprised. 'After all,' he said, 'you were the obvious choice.'

When the phone rang, Emma said firmly, 'If it's the Queen, say thank you but I just haven't the time to be prime minister.'

'It isn't the Queen,' said Harry, 'but she might just be the next prime minister,' he added as he handed Emma the phone.

'I wanted to call and thank you, Emma,' said Margaret Thatcher, 'for all the hard work you did for the party in the West Country during the campaign, and to warn you that I'm pretty sure there will be another election within a few months, when we will need to call on your help again.'

◄○►

Mrs Thatcher's prediction turned out to be correct, because the Labour Party were unable to win every vote in the division lobby, night after night, often having to rely on the support of some of the smaller parties, and on one occasion even bringing a member in on a stretcher. It came as no surprise when in September Harold Wilson asked the Queen to dissolve Parliament for the second time within a year. Three weeks later, fighting under the banner *Now you know Labour government works,* Wilson was returned to No.10 Downing Street with a Commons majority of three.

Emma's first call was not to Giles to congratulate him on retaining his seat in the Cabinet, but to Margaret Thatcher at her home in Flood Street, Chelsea.

'You have to stand for the leadership of the party, Margaret.'

'There isn't a vacancy,' Mrs Thatcher reminded her, 'and there's no suggestion that Ted is considering giving up the post.'

'Then kick him into touch,' said Emma firmly. 'Perhaps it's time to remind him he's lost us three elections out of four.'

'True,' said Thatcher, 'but the Tories are not known for ditching their leaders, as you'll discover when you talk to the party faithful at your next area committee meeting. By the way, Ted has spent the last week calling every constituency chairman one by one.'

'It's not the constituency chairmen who will choose the next leader of the party,' said Emma, 'but your colleagues in the House. They're the only ones who have a vote. So perhaps you should be calling them one by one.'

◄○►

Emma watched from a distance as speculation over the party leadership became more and more rife. She'd never read so many newspapers, listened to so many radio discussions or watched so many television debates, often late into the night.

Apparently oblivious to what was going on around him, Ted Heath, like Nero, went on playing his fiddle. But then, in an attempt to stamp his authority on the party, he called a leadership election for 4 February 1975.

Over the next few days Emma tried repeatedly to call Margaret Thatcher, but her line was constantly engaged.

When she finally got through, Emma didn't bother with pleasantries. 'You'll never have a better chance of leading the party than now,' she said. 'Not least because Heath's old cabinet chums aren't willing to stand against him.'

'You may be right,' said Margaret, 'which is why some of my colleagues in the Commons are trying to gauge my chances, should I decide to throw my hat into the ring.'

'You have to make your move now, while the men still think they're part of an old boys' club that would never allow a woman to become a member.'

'I know you're right, Emma, but I only have a few cards to play and must be careful about which ones I select and when to show them. One mistake, and I could be on the back benches for the rest of my political career. But please keep in touch. You know how much I value your opinion as someone who's not holed up in the Westminster village, only thinking about what's in it for them.'

Emma turned out to be right about the 'old boys' club',

because all the big beasts in the party remained loyal to Heath, along with the *Telegraph* and *Mail*. Only the *Spectator* kept pressing Mrs Thatcher to stand. And when, to Emma's delight, she finally did allow her name to go forward, the announcement was met by Heath's inner circle with ridicule and contempt, while the press refused to take her challenge seriously. In fact, Heath told anyone who would listen that she was no more than a stalking horse.

'He's about to discover that she's a thoroughbred,' was all Emma had to say on the subject.

–◦–

On the day of the vote, Giles invited his sister to join him for lunch in the House of Lords so she would be among the first to learn the result. Emma found the atmosphere in the corridors of power electric, and understood for the first time why so many otherwise rational human beings couldn't resist the roar of the political jungle.

She accompanied Giles up to the first floor so she could watch the Tory members as they entered committee room 7 to cast their votes. There was no sign of any of the five candidates, just their acolytes swarming around, trying to persuade last-minute waverers that their candidate was certain to win.

At six o'clock, the door to committee room 7 slammed shut so the chairman of the 1922 Committee could preside over the count. Fifteen minutes later, even before Edward du Cann had a chance to announce the result, a loud cheer went up from inside the committee room. Everyone standing in the corridor fell silent as they waited for the news.

'She's won!' went up the cry, and like falling dominoes, the words were repeated again and again until they reached the crowds on the street outside.

Emma was invited to join the victor for a celebratory drink in her room.

'I haven't won yet,' said Thatcher after Airey Neave had raised a glass to the new Leader of the Opposition. 'Let's not forget that was only the first round, and someone else is bound to stand against me. Not until then will we discover if a woman can not only lead the Tory party, but become prime minister. Let's get back to work,' she added, not allowing her glass to be refilled.

It wasn't until later, much later, that Emma called Harry to explain why she'd missed the last train to Bristol.

◄o►

On the journey back to the West Country the following morning, Emma began to think about her priorities and the allocation of her time. She had already decided to resign as area chairman of the Conservative Association if Ted Heath had been re-elected as leader, but she accepted that, having trumpeted Margaret Thatcher's cause, she would now have to remain in her post until after the next general election. But how would she juggle being chairman of Barrington's and deputy chairman of the hospital's trustees, along with her responsibilities to the party, when there were only twenty-four hours in each day? She was still wrestling with the problem when she got off the train at Temple Meads and joined the taxi queue. She was no nearer solving it by the time the cabbie dropped her outside the Manor House.

As she opened the front door, she was surprised to see Harry come rushing out of his study during a writing session.

'What is it, darling?' she asked, worried that it could only be bad news.

'Nick Croft has called three times and asked if you'd ring him the moment you got back.'

Emma picked up the phone in the hall and dialled the number Harry had written down on the pad next to the phone. Her call was answered after only one ring.

'It's Emma.' She listened carefully to what the chairman had to say. 'I'm so very sorry, Nick,' she said eventually. 'And of course I understand why you feel you have to resign.'

SEBASTIAN CLIFTON

1975

29

'THERE'S A DR WOLFE on line one for you,' said Rachel.

Although Sebastian hadn't spoken to the lady for some time, it wasn't a name he was likely to forget.

'Mr Clifton, I'm calling because I thought you'd like to know that Jessica has several paintings in the school's end-of-term exhibition that prove she's been well worthy of your scholarship. There is one piece that I consider quite exceptional, called *My Father.*'

'When does the exhibition take place?'

'This weekend. It opens on Friday evening and runs through Sunday. I appreciate that it would be a long way to travel just to see half a dozen pictures so I've put a catalogue in the post.'

'Thank you. Are any of Jessica's pictures for sale?'

'All the works are for sale, and this year the children have chosen to give the proceeds to the American Red Cross.'

'Then I'll buy all of them,' said Sebastian.

'I'm afraid that won't be possible, Mr Clifton. Other parents would rightly complain if any of the pictures were sold before the show opens, and that is a rule I'm not willing to break.'

'What time does the show open?'

'Five o'clock on Friday.'

Seb flicked open his diary and looked down at what he had planned for the weekend. Victor had invited him to White Hart Lane to see Spurs play Liverpool, and Uncle Giles was holding a drinks party at the Lords. Not a difficult decision. 'I'll fly over on

Friday morning. But I don't want Jessica or her mother to know I'm in town while her husband is still alive.'

There was a long pause before Dr Wolfe said, 'But Mr Brewer died over a year ago, Mr Clifton. I'm so sorry, I assumed you knew.'

Sebastian collapsed back into his chair as if he'd been floored by a heavyweight boxer. He tried to catch his breath while he took in her words.

'I apologize, but—'

'You have nothing to apologize for, Dr Wolfe. But I'd still prefer them not to know I'm coming over.'

'As you wish, Mr Clifton.'

Sebastian looked up to see his secretary standing in the doorway waving frantically at him.

'I have to leave you, Dr Wolfe, something's come up. Thank you for calling, and I look forward to seeing you at the weekend,' he said before putting the phone down. 'Rachel, I'm flying to Washington on Friday morning, probably returning Sunday. I'll need a first-class return, fifteen hundred dollars in cash, and please book me into the Mayflower.' Seb paused. 'You have that exasperated look on your face, Rachel.'

'Mr Hardcastle arrived fifteen minutes ago and they're all waiting for you in the chairman's office so the documents can be signed.'

'Of course, the signing ceremony. How could I have forgotten?' Seb ran out of the room and down the corridor. He burst into the chairman's office to find Hakim Bishara, Victor Kaufman and Arnold Hardcastle poring over the merger documents.

'I apologize, chairman. An unexpected call from the States.'

'No problem, Seb,' said Hakim. 'By the way, have you ever been to jail?'

'Is that a trick question?' asked Seb, grinning.

'No, it certainly is not,' said Arnold Hardcastle. 'Although it's only a formality in your case, it's one of the questions the Bank of England asks whenever an application for a new banking licence is submitted.'

'No, I have never been to jail,' said Seb, hoping he sounded suitably chastised.

'Good,' said Arnold. 'Now all that's required is for Mr Bishara and Mr Kaufman to sign all three documents, with Mr Clifton acting as a witness.'

It amused Seb that Arnold Hardcastle would never have considered addressing him by his Christian name while they were in the chairman's office, although they were old family friends and Arnold had been the firm's legal advisor for as long as Seb could remember. How like his late father he was, thought Seb, whom he had never once called Cedric.

'Before I part with my mess of pottage,' said Victor, 'perhaps Mr Hardcastle would be kind enough to explain once again the implications of my signing this document. Something my father always insisted on.'

'And quite rightly so,' said Arnold. 'When your father died, he owned fifty-one per cent of the shares in Kaufman's Bank, which he bequeathed to you, thus giving you a majority shareholding. That was the position when Mr Clifton, on behalf of Farthings Bank, approached you to suggest that the two banks should merge. Following a long period of negotiation, it was agreed that you would become a twenty-five per cent shareholder of the new bank, Farthings Kaufman, and a full board director, while retaining your position as head of the foreign exchange department – a post you've held at Kaufman's for the past eight years. It was also agreed that Mr Bishara would remain as chairman, with Mr Clifton continuing as chief executive.'

'Is there anything I should be worrying about?' asked Victor.

'Not that I'm aware of,' said Hardcastle. 'Once all three of you have signed the merger document, all that's left is for you to await the Bank of England's approval, which I'm assured by the bank's compliance officer is a mere formality. He expects the paperwork to be completed within a month.'

'My father would have been delighted to see our two banks merge,' said Victor. 'Where do I sign?'

Hakim Bishara, on behalf of Farthings, and Victor Kaufman on behalf of Kaufman's, signed all three documents, with Sebastian adding his name as a witness. Once Arnold had gathered up all the documents, Hakim walked across to the drinks cabinet, opened a small fridge and took out a bottle of champagne. He popped the cork and poured three glasses.

'To Farthings Kaufman,' he said. 'Possibly not the biggest bank on the block, but unquestionably the latest.' The three laughed and raised their glasses. 'To Farthings Kaufman.'

'Right, let's get back to work,' said the chairman. 'What's next on my schedule?'

'Clive Bingham has an appointment to see you in half an hour, chairman,' said Hardcastle, 'to discuss a press statement he's working on. I know everyone in the Square Mile considers it's a done deal, but I'd still like to see the merger well covered by the financial press. Clive tells me that both the *FT* and *Economist* have requested to do profiles on you.'

'And to think it's less than a decade ago that the Bank of England refused to grant me a secondary banking licence.'

'We've all come a long way since then,' said Seb.

'We have indeed,' said Hakim. 'And the merging of our two banks is just the next stage of what I have planned.'

'Amen to that,' said Victor, raising his glass a second time.

'Seb,' said the chairman when he failed to raise his glass, 'you seem a little preoccupied.'

'It's nothing, chairman. But I should let you know that I'll be flying to Washington on Friday morning. I expect to be back in the office by Monday.'

'A deal I ought to know about?' asked Hakim, raising an eyebrow.

'No. I'm thinking of buying some pictures.'

'Sounds interesting,' said Hakim, but Seb didn't rise to the bait. 'I'm off to Lagos tomorrow,' Hakim added, 'for a meeting with the oil minister. The government wants to build a larger port to handle the demand for so many foreign oil tankers following the discovery of several new oil fields off the Nigerian coast. They've invited Farthings – sorry, Farthings Kaufman – to act as their financial advisors. Like you, Seb, I hope to be back at my desk by Monday at the latest, as I have another heavy week ahead of me. So, Victor, we'll leave the shop in your hands while we're away. Just be sure there are no surprises when we return.'

◄○►

'Quite a coup,' said Desmond Mellor once he'd read the press statement. 'I'm not sure there's much we can do about it.'

'How large is our holding in Farthings Kaufman?' asked Jim Knowles.

'We own six per cent of Farthings,' said Adrian Sloane. 'But that will be reduced to three per cent of the new bank when the merger goes through, which wouldn't entitle us to a place on the board.'

'And although Mellor Travel has had another good year,' said Desmond, 'I just don't have the financial clout to take on Bishara.'

'One of my contacts at the Bank of England,' said Knowles, 'tells me he expects the merger to be ratified within the next couple of weeks.'

'Unless the Bank of England felt unable to ratify it,' said Sloane.

'What reason would they have not to?' asked Mellor.

'If a director didn't fulfil one of the Bank's statutory regulations.'

'Which regulation do you have in mind, Adrian?'

'That he'd been to jail.'

30

SEBASTIAN WALKED out of Dulles airport and joined the short queue for a yellow cab.

'The Mayflower Hotel, please,' he said to the driver. Seb always enjoyed the drive from Dulles into the capital. A long, winding road that stretched between wooded forests before crossing the Potomac and passing the magnificent marble monuments of past presidents that dominated the landscape like Roman temples. Lincoln, Jefferson and finally Washington, before the cab drew up outside the hotel.

Sebastian was impressed when the clerk on the front desk said, 'Welcome back, Mr Clifton,' as he'd only stayed at the Willard once before. 'Is there anything I can do to assist you?'

'How long will it take me to get to Jefferson School?'

'Fifteen minutes, twenty at most. Shall I book you a cab?'

Seb checked his watch. Just after 2 p.m. 'Yes, let's make it for four twenty?'

'Four twenty it is, sir. I'll call your room the moment the car arrives.'

Seb made his way to the ninth floor and, as he looked across at the White House, he realized they'd even given him the same room as before. He unpacked his small suitcase and placed a thousand dollars in the wall safe, which he assumed would be more than enough to buy all of Jessica's pictures. He undressed, took a shower, lay down on the bed and put his head on the pillow.

The phone was ringing. Seb opened his eyes and tried to remember where he was. He picked up the receiver.

'Your cab is waiting at the front entrance, sir.'

Seb checked his watch: 4.15 p.m. He must have fallen asleep. Damn jet lag. 'Thank you, I'll be right down.' He quickly put on some clean clothes before making his way downstairs. 'Can you get me there before five?' he asked the driver.

'Kinda depends where "there" is.'

'Sorry, Jefferson School.'

'No sweat.' The cab moved off to join the early evening traffic.

Seb had already worked on two plans. If, when he arrived at the school, he spotted either Samantha or Jessica, he would wait until they'd left before going into the exhibition. But if they weren't there, he would take a quick look at his daughter's work, select the pictures he wanted and be on his way back to the Willard before they even realized he'd been there.

The cab pulled up outside the school entrance a few minutes before five. Seb remained in the back seat and watched as a couple of parents, accompanied by a child, made their way up the path and into the building. He then paid the fare and tentatively followed them, searching all the time for two people he didn't want to see. When he entered the building, he was greeted by a large red arrow with the words ART EXHIBITION pointing down the corridor.

He kept looking in every direction but there was no sign of them. In the exhibition hall there must have been over a hundred pictures filling the walls with bold splashes of colour, but so far there were only about half a dozen parents, who were clearly interested only in their own offspring's efforts. Seb stuck to plan A and walked quickly around the room. It wasn't difficult to pick out Jessica's work; to quote one of his father's favourite expressions when describing his old school friend Mr Deakins, she was 'in a different class'.

Every few moments he glanced towards the door, but as there was no sign of them, he began to study his daughter's work more carefully. Although only ten, she already had a style of her own;

the brushwork was bold and confident with no suggestion of second attempts. And then he stopped in front of the painting entitled *My Father* and understood why Dr Wolfe had singled it out as quite exceptional. The image of a man and woman holding hands seemed to Seb to have been influenced by René Magritte. The woman could only have been Samantha, the warm smile and the kind eyes and even the tiny birthmark that he would never forget. The man was dressed in a grey suit, white shirt and blue tie, but the face hadn't been filled in, just left blank. Seb felt so many emotions: sadness, stupidity, guilt, regret but, most of all, regret.

He quickly checked the door again before walking over to a desk where a young woman was sitting behind a sign that read SALES. Sebastian turned the pages of his catalogue, then asked for the price of items, 9, 12, 18, 21, 37 and 52. She checked her list.

'With the exception of number thirty-seven, they are all a hundred dollars each. And, of course, all the money goes to charity.'

'Please don't tell me number thirty-seven has already been sold?'

'No, sir. It is for sale, but I'm afraid it's five hundred dollars.'

'I'll take all six,' said Seb, as he removed his wallet.

'That will be one thousand dollars,' said the woman, making no attempt to hide her surprise.

Seb opened his wallet and realized immediately that, in his rush to get the cab, he'd left most of his cash in the hotel safe. 'Can you reserve them for me?' he asked. 'I'll make sure you have the money long before the show closes.' He didn't want to explain to her why he couldn't just sign a cheque. That wasn't part of plan A.

'I'm sorry, sir, but I can't do that,' she said. Just then, he felt a hand on his shoulder.

Seb froze and turned in panic to see Dr Wolfe smiling at him.

'Miss Tomkins,' she said firmly. 'That will be quite all right.'

'Of course, headmistress.' Looking back at Seb, she asked, 'What name shall I put on the sales sheet?'

'Put them all in my name,' said Dr Wolfe before Seb could reply.

'Thank you,' said Seb. 'When can I collect them?'

'Any time on Sunday afternoon,' said Miss Tomkins. 'The show closes at five.'

'Thank you again,' said Seb, before turning back to Dr Wolfe.

'I came to warn you that I've just spotted Samantha and Jessica driving into the car park.' Seb looked across to the door, which seemed to be only one way out. 'If you follow me,' said Dr Wolfe, 'I'll take you to my study.'

'Thank you,' said Seb as she led him to the far end of the hall and through a door marked *Private*.

Once she'd closed her study door, Dr Wolfe asked, 'Why won't you let me tell Samantha that you've flown over specially to see Jessica's work? I'm sure they'd both be delighted to see you and Jessica would be so flattered.'

'I'm afraid that's a risk I'm not willing to take at the moment. But can I ask how Jessica's getting on?'

'As you can see from the paintings you've just bought, your bursary proved a wise investment, and I'm still confident that she'll be the first girl from Jefferson to win a scholarship to the American College of Art.' Seb couldn't hide a parent's pride. 'Now, I'd better get back before they begin to wonder where I am. If you go to the far end of the corridor, Mr Clifton, you'll find a back door leading into the yard, so no one will see you leaving. And if you change your mind before Sunday, you have my number. Just give me a call and I'll do everything I can to help.'

◄○►

Hakim Bishara climbed the aircraft steps, feeling his journey to Nigeria had been a complete waste of time. He was a patient man but on this occasion even his patience had been stretched to the limit. The oil minister had kept him waiting for five hours and, when he was finally ushered into his presence, he didn't seem to be fully briefed on the new port project and suggested they meet again in a couple of weeks' time, as if Bishara's office was just around the corner. Bishara left fifteen minutes later with a promise that the minister would look into the matter and get back to him. He wasn't holding his breath.

He returned to his hotel, checked out and took a taxi to the airport.

Whenever Hakim stepped on to a plane, he always hoped for one of two things: to be seated next to either a beautiful woman who would be spending a few days in a city where she was a stranger, or a businessman he normally would not have come across and who he might be able to interest in opening an account with Farthings. He corrected himself, Farthings Kaufman, and wondered how long it would take him to think it without thinking. Over the years, he'd closed three major deals because of someone he'd sat next to on a plane, and met countless women, one of whom had broken his heart after five idyllic days in Rome when she told him she was married and then flew home. He made his way to seat 3A. In the next seat was a woman of such extraordinary beauty it was hard not to just stare at her. Once he'd fastened his seatbelt, he glanced across to see she was engrossed in a novel Harry Clifton had recommended he should read. He couldn't imagine how a book about rabbits could have any appeal.

Hakim always enjoyed trying to work out a person's nationality, background and profession simply by observing them, a skill his father had taught him, whenever he was trying to sell a customer an expensive carpet. First, check the basics: her jewellery, his watch, their clothes and shoes, and anything else unusual.

The book suggested intelligence, the wedding ring, and even more obviously the engagement ring, spelt understated wealth. The watch was a classic Cartier Tank, no longer in production. The suit was Yves Saint Laurent and the shoes Halston. An untutored observer might have described her as a woman of a certain age; a discerning one, like Sky Masterson, as a classy broad. Her slim, elegant figure and long fair hair suggested she was Scandinavian.

He would have liked to begin a conversation with her, but as she seemed so engrossed in her novel and didn't give him so much as a glance, he decided to settle for a few hours' sleep, although he did wonder if he'd later regret it.

—◄o►—

Samantha walked slowly around the exhibition with a nervous Jessica just a pace behind.

'What do you think, Mom? Will anybody buy one?'

'Well, I will for a start.'

'That's a relief. I don't want to be the only girl who couldn't sell a picture.'

Samantha laughed. 'I don't think that will be your problem.'

'Do you have a favourite?'

'Yes, number thirty-seven. I think it's the best thing you've ever done.' Samantha was still admiring *My Father* when Miss Tomkins came up and placed a red dot next to it. 'But I was hoping to buy that one,' said Samantha, unable to hide her disappointment.

'I'm so sorry, Mrs Brewer, but all of Jessica's pictures were sold within a few minutes of the show opening.'

'Are you sure?' asked Jessica. 'I put a price of five hundred dollars on that picture to make certain nobody would buy it because I wanted to give it to my mom.'

'It was also the gentleman's favourite,' said Miss Tomkins. 'And the price didn't seem to bother him.'

'What was this gentleman's name?' asked Samantha, quietly.

'I've no idea. He came just before the show opened and bought every one of Jessica's pictures.' She looked around the room. 'But he seems to have left.'

'I wish I'd seen him,' said Jessica.

'Why?' asked Samantha.

'Because then I could have filled in the face.'

—◄o►—

'How much?' said Ellie May in disbelief.

'About a million and a half dollars,' admitted Cyrus.

'That must be the most expensive one-night stand in history, and I'm damned if I'm going to let the little hussy get away with it.'

'But she's a lady,' said Cyrus.

'She won't be the first lady who recognizes a sucker when she sees one.'

'But there's still a possibility that little Freddie is mine.'

'I have a feeling,' said Ellie May, 'that little Freddie isn't even hers.'

'So what are you going to do about it?'

'Make damn sure Lady Virginia realizes she hasn't got away with it.'

◄○►

Hakim drifted out of a shallow sleep. He blinked, pressed a button in his armrest and his seat straightened up. Moments later a stewardess offered him a warm flannel. He gently rubbed his eyes, forehead and finally the back of his neck, until he felt half awake.

'Would you like some breakfast, Mr Bishara?' the stewardess asked as she removed the flannel with a pair of tongs.

'Just orange juice and a black coffee, please.'

He glanced at the woman on his right but he could see that she only had a few more pages of her book to read, so he reluctantly decided not to interrupt her.

When the pilot announced they would be landing in thirty minutes, the woman immediately disappeared into the lavatory and didn't re-emerge for some time. Hakim concluded that there had to be a lucky man waiting for her at Heathrow.

Hakim always liked to be among the first passengers to disembark, especially when he was only carrying hand luggage and wouldn't be held up in the baggage hall. His chauffeur would be waiting for him outside the terminal building and, although it was a Sunday, he still intended to go into the office and tackle the mountain of unanswered mail that would have piled up on his desk. Once again, he cursed the Nigerian oil minister.

Since he'd become a British citizen he was no longer held up at passport control and didn't have to endure the lengthy nonresidents queues. He walked past the baggage carousels and headed straight for the green channel as he hadn't purchased anything while he was in Lagos. The moment he put his foot in the corridor, a customs officer stepped forward and blocked his path.

'Can I check your bag, sir?'

'Of course,' said Bishara, putting his small overnight bag on the low slatted table.

Another officer appeared and stood a pace behind his colleague, who was systematically going through Hakim's single piece of luggage. All he found was a wash bag, two shirts, two pairs of pants, two pairs of socks and two silk ties; all he'd needed for a two-day visit. The customs officer then unzipped a small side pocket that Hakim rarely used. Hakim watched in disbelief as the man extracted a cellophane bag packed with a white substance. Although he'd never taken a drug in his life, he knew exactly what it must be.

'Does this belong to you, sir?' asked the officer.

'I've never seen it before in my life,' Hakim answered truthfully.

'Perhaps you'd be kind enough to come with us, sir.'

31

Desmond Mellor smiled when he read the headline in the *Daily Mail*.

CITY BANKER ARRESTED IN HEROIN SWOOP

He was only halfway through the article when he looked up at Adrian Sloane and said, 'This couldn't be much better, Adrian, if you'd written it yourself.'

Sloane tossed over his copy of the *Sun*. 'I think you'll find this one tops it.'

BANKER BISHARA BEHIND BARS

Mellor laughed.

'He can't hope to survive headlines like this,' said Jim Knowles. 'Even the *FT* is saying, and I quote, "The Bank of England confirms that it has not received an application to merge Farthings and Kaufman's banks, and will not be issuing any further statements on the subject".'

'Shorthand for "don't bother us again, we've kicked the ball into the long grass",' said Sloane.

'What a coup,' said Mellor. 'Dare I ask how you managed to pull it off, Adrian?'

'It's probably better that you don't know the details, Desmond, but what I can tell you is that the main participants are already safely back in Nigeria.'

'While Bishara is locked up in Wandsworth prison.'

'What's more, I can't see him enjoying any better accommodation for the next few months.'

'I wouldn't be so sure about that,' said Jim Knowles. 'That smooth-talking QC of his will probably get him out on bail.'

'Not if Bishara's charged with unlawful possession of a Class A drug with intent to supply,' said Sloane.

'And if he's found guilty,' asked Knowles, 'how long could he be sent down for?'

'The minimum sentence is five years, according to *The Times*. I'm not too fussed about the maximum, because I'll be chairman of Farthings long before then,' said Mellor.

'What do you think will happen to the two banks' shares?'

'They'll collapse, but we should hold fire for a few days until they bottom out,' said Mellor. 'That's when I intend to pick up another couple of per cent, before I join the Farthings board. While the trial's taking place I'll position myself as a white knight who's reluctantly willing to come to the rescue of the beleaguered shareholders. And after Bishara's been found guilty, I'll allow myself to be persuaded to return as chairman of Farthings in order to save the bank's reputation.'

'Sebastian Clifton's unlikely to just sit around twiddling his thumbs while all this is going on,' said Knowles.

'He'll hang in there until Bishara's convicted,' said Mellor. 'And once I'm chairman, I'll be the first to commiserate with him and say how sorry I am that he feels he also has to resign.'

⊷⊶

Sebastian was sitting on the steps of the Lincoln Memorial and, like the sixteenth president, was deep in thought. He would have returned to England that morning if the school had been willing to release Jessica's paintings, but Miss Tomkins wouldn't allow him to collect them until Sunday afternoon.

He had decided to go back to the school and have another look at Jessica's work, but not before he had convinced himself it was unlikely that she or Samantha would return on a Saturday afternoon. Or did he actually hope they would?

He finally left Lincoln and went in search of Jefferson. He

took a cab back to the school with the excuse he ought to pay off his debt as soon as possible. As he entered the exhibition hall, he was relieved to see how few parents were there; it was clear from the plethora of red dots that most of them must have attended the opening night. One fixture remained dutifully in place behind her desk. Seb walked across to Miss Tomkins and handed over a thousand dollars in cash.

'Thank you,' she said. 'I'm sure you'd like to know that several people were disappointed not to be able to get hold of any of Jessica's paintings. Including her mother, who had wanted to buy *My Father*. She asked me who'd bought it, but of course I couldn't tell her, because I didn't know your name.'

Seb smiled. 'Thank you. And if I may, I'll collect them all tomorrow afternoon.'

He left Miss Tomkins to have another look at Jessica's paintings. He took his time studying the half dozen works he now owned and, with the satisfaction of a seasoned collector, he ended up in front of *My Father*, which he had already decided would hang over the mantelpiece in his flat. He was just about to leave when a voice behind him said, 'Are you looking in a mirror?'

Sebastian swung round to see his daughter, who immediately threw her arms around him and said, 'What took you so long?'

It was rare for Sebastian to be struck speechless, but he just didn't know what to say, so he clung on to her before she took a step back and grinned up at him. 'Well, say something!'

'I'm so sorry,' he eventually managed. 'You're right. I did see you once, years ago, but I didn't have the courage to say hello. I've been such a fool.'

'Well, we can at least agree on that,' said Jessica. 'But then, to be fair, Mom hasn't exactly covered herself in glory either.' Jessica took his hand and led him out of the room, continuing to chat as if they were old friends. 'Actually, she's just as much to blame as you are. I told her to get in touch with you after my stepfather died.'

'You never thought he was your father?'

'I may not be that good at math, but even I can work out that if I was six and they'd met only five years before . . .'

Seb laughed.

'Just after Michael died, Mom confirmed what I already knew, but I still couldn't persuade her to get in touch with you.'

They walked around the park, arm in arm, dropped into a Farrell's ice-cream parlour and shared a hot fudge sundae, while she chatted about her friends, her painting, her plans for the future. As he listened he wondered hopelessly how he could make up for all the lost years in a couple of hours.

'It's getting late,' he said eventually, looking at his watch. 'Won't your mother be wondering where you are?"

'Sebastian,' she said, placing her hands on her hips, 'I'm ten years old.'

'Well, if you're so grown-up, what do you think I should do next?'

'I've taken care of that. You're taking Mom and me to dinner at the Belvedere tonight. I've already made a reservation for three at seven thirty. Then all we'll need to decide is if we're going to live in London or Washington.'

'But what if I hadn't come back to the school this afternoon?'

'I knew you'd come back.'

'But I didn't know myself.'

'That's not the same thing.'

'You seem to have everything worked out,' said Seb.

'Of course I have. I've had a long time to think about it, haven't I?'

'And is your mother happy to fall in with your plans?'

'I haven't actually told her yet. But we can sort all that out tonight, can't we?'

'Dr Wolfe told me yesterday that you could win a scholarship to the American College of Art.'

'Dr Wolfe will be just as proud when I'm the first girl from Jefferson to go to the Royal College of Art, though I thought I'd go to the Slade first, just like the other Jessica.'

'Will your mother or I have any say in all of this?'

'Let's hope not. After all, you two have made such a mess of everything so far.'

Sebastian laughed.

'Can I ask, do I live up to your expectations?' she said, sounding unsure of herself for the first time.

'You're even more talented and beautiful than I'd imagined. How about me?' asked Seb, grinning.

'Actually I'm a little disappointed,' said Jessica. 'I thought you'd be taller and better-looking. More like Sean Connery.'

Seb burst out laughing. 'You are the most precocious child I've ever met.'

'And you'll be pleased to hear that Mom agrees with you, except she substitutes the word brat for child, which I'm sure you'll do once you get to know me better. Now I must be off. I've got lots to tell Mom about, and I'm looking forward to wearing a new dress tonight I bought especially for the occasion. Where are we having dinner?'

'The Belvedere, seven thirty.'

Jessica threw her arms around him and burst into tears.

'What's the matter?' he asked.

'Nothing. Just be sure you're on time for a change.'

'Don't worry, I will be.'

'You'd better be,' said Jessica, and quickly left him.

◄o►

Mr Arnold Hardcastle QC sat opposite Hakim Bishara in a small private room at HMP Wandsworth.

'I'm going to say something, Hakim, that I've never said to a client before. Even though it's a lawyer's duty to present the best defence possible for his client whether he believes them to be guilty or innocent, I want you to know that I am in no doubt, reasonable or otherwise, that you have been set up. However, I must warn you that because of the government's new guidelines on Class A drugs, the judge will have no choice but to refuse an application for bail.'

'And how long will it be before my case comes to trial?'

'Four months, six at most. Be assured, I'll do everything I can to speed it up.'

'During which time I'll be holed up in here, while the bank could go bust.'

'Let's hope it doesn't come to that.'

'Have you read the morning papers?' said Bishara. 'They couldn't be much worse. When the market opens tomorrow, the vultures will swoop down on the carcass and pick the bones clean. Is there any good news?'

'Ross Buchanan rang me at home last night to say he'd be happy to stand in as temporary chairman until you return. He's already issued a press statement saying he has no doubt that you will be cleared of all the charges.'

'Typical of the man,' said Hakim. 'Accept his offer. We'll also need Sebastian to be at his desk when the market opens.'

'He's in Washington at the moment. I've called his hotel several times, but he wasn't in his room. I left a message asking him to call me urgently. Is there anything else I can do?'

'Yes, there is, Arnold. I need the best private detective you've ever come across, someone who's fearless and won't let anything stop him when it comes to tracking down who was responsible for planting that heroin in my bag.'

'Chief Inspector Barry Hammond is the name that immediately comes to mind, but I've lost touch with him since he left the Met Police.'

'Did he retire?'

'No, he resigned after he was accused of planting evidence on a gangland boss who kept getting away with, quite literally, murder.'

'How did you come across him?'

'I was his defending counsel when the trial came to court. I got him off, but he resigned from the force the next day.'

'Then track him down, because I need to see him as soon as possible.'

'I'll get on to it straight away. Anything else?'

'Get hold of Sebastian.'

◄○►

Seb walked slowly back to the hotel and thought about all the wasted years, and how he intended to make up for them, whatever sacrifices he had to make. If only Samantha would give him a second chance. Was Jessica right? Would they really be willing to live in London? Tonight would be like a first date, and he suspected that Samantha would be just as nervous as he was. After all, her husband had recently died, and Seb had no way of knowing how she felt about seeing him again. Perhaps their young chaperone knew more than she was willing to admit. Another woman he dreaded the thought of being parted from.

When Seb entered the hotel, he went to the desk and asked the receptionist, 'How long does it take to get to the Belvedere restaurant?'

'It's just around the corner, sir, shouldn't take more than a few minutes. Do you have a reservation? They're sure to be fully booked on a Saturday night.'

'Yes, I do,' said Seb confidently.

'And I have an urgent message for you, Mr Clifton. Would you please call a Mr Arnold Hardcastle? He's left a number. Shall I get him on the line and put the call through to your room?'

'Yes, please,' said Seb, before heading for the nearest lift. He'd never known Arnold to use the word 'urgent'. What could possibly be that important? Had he failed to sign one of the pages in the merger document? Had Victor changed his mind at the last moment? Once he was in his room he only had to wait a few moments before the phone rang.

'Sebastian Clifton.'

'Seb. Thank God I've finally got hold of you.'

'What's the problem, Arnold?'

'I'm afraid I have some bad news.'

Seb listened in disbelief as Arnold went over everything that had happened to Hakim since he'd stepped off the plane at Heathrow.

'It has to be a set-up, pure and simple,' said Seb angrily.

'My exact words,' said Arnold. 'But I'm afraid it's not pure, and it certainly isn't simple, while the evidence is so stacked against him.'

'Where is he now?'

'In a cell in Wandsworth. He feels it's essential that you're back at your desk when the market opens on Monday morning.'

'Of course I will be. I'll take the next flight back to Heathrow.'
He put the phone down and immediately dialled the front desk.
'I'll be checking out in the next half hour. Please have my bill
ready, and would you book me on to the first available flight to
London? And can you look up the number of a Mrs Michael
Brewer, get her on the line and put her straight through?'

Seb packed quickly, and then checked that he'd left nothing
behind. He was zipping up his bag when the phone rang again.

'I'm sorry, sir, but Mrs Michael Brewer is unlisted.'

'Then get me Dr Wolfe at Jefferson Elementary School. She's
the headmistress.'

Seb paced around the room. If he could speak to Dr Wolfe,
she would surely have Sam's number . . .

The phone rang again.

'Dr Wolfe is not answering her phone, Mr Clifton, and the
only flight I can get you on takes off in just under two hours, so
you'd have to hurry. All the other London flights are fully booked.'

'Take it. And I'll need a taxi to get me to Dulles.'

On the way to the airport, Seb didn't even notice the towering monuments, the fast-flowing Potomac or the densely wooded
forests. His mind was preoccupied with the thought of Hakim
locked up in a prison cell. Seb accepted that there was no longer
any purpose in Arnold delivering the merger papers to the Bank
of England after he recalled Hakim's light-hearted question,
'Have you ever been to jail?' He wondered who could be behind
something so treacherous. Adrian Sloane immediately came to
mind, but he couldn't have done it on his own.

It was when Seb checked his watch and saw that it was almost
7.30 p.m. that he remembered where he was meant to be at that
time. Jessica would assume he'd let them down again. She would
never believe anything could be more important than . . . He
paid the taxi driver, dashed into the terminal, checked in, then
headed straight for the business-class lounge, where he stepped
into the only available phone booth, pressed a coin into the slot
and dialled directory enquiries.

'This is the first call for passengers travelling to London

Heathrow on the seven fifty-five British Airways flight, will you please make your way . . .'

'A restaurant in Washington called the Belvedere.' A few moments later she gave him the number. Seb dialled it immediately, only to find it was engaged. He decided to pick up his ticket and try again in a few minutes. Perhaps the plane would be delayed.

He ran back to the phone booth and dialled again. Still engaged.

'This is the final call for passengers travelling to London Heathrow on the seven fifty-five British Airways flight. Please . . .'

He pressed the coins back in and dialled the number, praying it wouldn't still be busy. This time he was greeted by a ringing tone.

'Come on, pick it up, pick it up!' he shouted.

'Good evening, this is the Belvedere, how may I help you?'

'This is Sebastian Clifton, and I'm meant to be dining at your restaurant this evening with Samantha and Jessica Brewer.'

'Yes, sir, your party has arrived and are in the lounge waiting for you.'

'I need to speak to Jessica Brewer. Please tell her it's urgent.'

'Certainly, sir, I'll ask her to come to the phone.'

Seb waited, but the next voice he heard said, 'Please put another fifty cents into the slot.'

He searched his pockets for change, but all he could find was ten cents. He shoved it into the slot and prayed. 'Hi Pops, it's Jessie.'

'Jessie, hi—' Beep, beep, beep, click . . . purr.

'Would Mr Sebastian Clifton, travelling to London Heathrow on the seven fifty-five British Airways flight, please report to Gate number fourteen as the gate is about to close.'

32

THE FOUR OF THEM held an unscheduled board meeting at eleven on Monday morning. They sat around a square, vinyl-topped table in a cramped room normally reserved for legal consultations.

Ross Buchanan sat at one end of the table with a sheaf of files on the floor beside him. Hakim Bishara sat opposite him with Arnold Hardcastle on his right and Sebastian on his left.

'Perhaps I should begin,' said Ross, 'by letting you know that – so far at least – Farthings shares haven't lost as much ground as we feared they might.'

'Helped by your robust statement, no doubt,' said Hakim, 'which was reported in all the Sunday papers. Indeed, if anything will keep the bank afloat it's your reputation in the City, Ross.'

'It also looks as if there's a third party involved,' said Seb, 'who's picking up any available stock.'

'A friend or a predator, I wonder,' said Hakim.

'I can't be sure, but I'll let you know the moment I find out.'

'How have Kaufman's shares been faring?'

'Surprisingly,' said Seb, 'they've risen slightly, despite Victor making it clear to anyone who asks that, as far as he's concerned, the merger is still on, and that his late father was a great admirer of yours.'

'That's generous of him,' said Hakim, placing his elbows on the table. 'But how many of our major clients have withdrawn their accounts?'

'Several called to express their concern about the charges

you're facing and to point out that their companies can't afford to be associated with a drug-dealer.'

'And what did you tell them?' asked Arnold, before Hakim could jump in.

'I told them,' continued Ross, 'that Mr Bishara doesn't smoke, doesn't drink and who do they imagine he could possibly be selling drugs to?'

'What about our smaller customers?' said Hakim. 'Are they voting with their feet?'

'A handful have already moved their accounts,' said Seb. 'But ironically I've been trying to get rid of one or two of them for years, and no doubt they'll all come crawling back once you've proved your innocence.'

'And they'll find the door slammed in their faces,' said Hakim, banging the table with a clenched fist. 'What about your private detective?' he asked Arnold. 'Have you managed to track him down?'

'I have, chairman. I found him playing snooker in Romford. He'd read about the case in the *News of the World* and said the word on the street was that it was a stitch-up, but no one seems to know who's got the needle and thread, which convinces him it can't be any of the usual suspects.'

'When is he coming to see me?'

'Six o'clock this evening. Be warned, Barry Hammond isn't the easiest of men. But if he does decide to take on the assignment, I wouldn't want to be the person who set you up.'

'What do you mean, "if"? Who the hell does he think he is?'

'He despises drug-dealers, Hakim,' said Arnold calmly. 'Thinks they should all be strung up in Trafalgar Square.'

'If he were even to suggest that I—'

Sebastian placed a hand on Hakim's arm. 'We all understand what you're going through, chairman, but you have to remain calm, and let Ross, Arnold and me handle the pressure.'

'I'm sorry. Of course you're right, Seb. Don't think I'm not grateful to all of you. I look forward to meeting Mr Hammond.'

'He's bound to ask you some fairly direct questions,' said Arnold. 'Just promise me you won't lose your temper.'

'I'll be sweetness and light.'

'How are you passing your time?' asked Ross, trying to lighten the mood. 'It can't be a pleasant experience, being in here.'

'I spent an hour in the gym this morning, which reminded me just how unfit I am. Then I read the *FT* from cover to cover. I had an hour's walk around the yard yesterday afternoon, in the company of two other bankers who are in for manipulating share prices, and in the evening I played a few games of backgammon.'

'For money?' asked Seb.

'A pound a game. There's a guy in for armed robbery who took a couple of quid off me, but I plan to get it back this evening.'

The three visitors burst out laughing.

◄○►

'I've picked up another two per cent of Farthings stock,' said Sloane, 'so you're now entitled to a place on the board.'

'Those additional shares turned out to be more expensive than you predicted,' said Mellor.

'That's true, but my broker tells me there's a big player out there picking up stock whenever it comes on the market.'

'Any idea who it might be?' asked Knowles.

'Not a clue, but it explains why the shares haven't fallen as much as I'd anticipated. If you let me represent you on the board, Desmond, I'll find out exactly what's going on, and then I'll be able to feed the press with regular unhelpful titbits. In the end, it will be the drip, drip, drip effect that finally scuppers them, believe me.'

'Are you still confident that nothing can be traced back to anyone around this table?'

'I'm positive. We're the only three people who know what's going on, and I'm the one person who knows where the bodies are buried.'

◄○►

After Sebastian left the meeting at Wandsworth prison, he hurried back to the bank to find Rachel standing by his office door.

'Thirty-two customers want to speak to you personally, all of them urgently.'

'Who's the top priority?'

'Jimmy Goldsmith.'

'But the bank's never done any business with Mr Goldsmith.'

'He's a close friend of Mr Bishara. They hang out at the Clermont Club.'

'Right, I'll speak to him first.'

Rachel returned to her office and a few moments later Seb's phone buzzed.

'Mr Goldsmith, this is Sebastian Clifton, returning your call.'

'I hear you visited Hakim in prison today. How is he?'

'He's bearing up.'

'Like your shares.'

'So you're the big player?'

'Let's just say that I'm picking up any stock whenever it falls ten per cent below its mid-point.'

'But why would you do that, Mr Goldsmith? It could end up costing you a fortune.'

'For two reasons, Mr Clifton. One, I've known Hakim since his university days and, like me, he despises people who deal in drugs.'

'And the second reason?'

'Let's just say I owe him.'

'But you're still taking one hell of a risk.'

'It's a gamble, I admit. But when Hakim is proved innocent, and I have no doubt he will be, the bank's shares will rebound, and when I sell them I'll make a killing.'

'Mr Goldsmith, I wonder if you could help me make another killing.'

Goldsmith listened carefully to Sebastian's request. 'When are you holding this emergency board meeting?' he asked.

'Tuesday morning, ten o'clock.'

'I'll be there.'

◄o►

Sebastian spent the rest of the day trying to return all his calls. He felt like the little Dutch boy with his finger in the dyke. Would it suddenly burst and drown them all?

He listened to the same questions again and again, and attempted to reassure each customer that Hakim was not only innocent, but the bank was in safe hands. He was pleasantly surprised by how many people were standing firm and were happy to back the chairman. Seb had made two lists, one of them labelled 'Foul-weather friends' and the other 'Fair-weather friends'. By seven o'clock that night, the 'foul' list far outstripped the 'fair'.

Seb was just about to call it a day when the phone rang again. He thought about ignoring it and going home but reluctantly picked it up.

'It's Lord Barrington on the line,' said Rachel. 'Shall I put him through?'

'Of course.'

'Hello, Seb. I'm sorry to disturb you. You must have had a very trying day. But I wondered if you could spare a moment.'

'Of course,' Seb repeated.

'Some time ago you asked me if I'd like to join the board of Farthings. I'm calling to find out if the offer is still open.'

Sebastian was speechless.

'Are you still there, Seb?'

'Yes,' he managed eventually.

'I would consider it a great honour to serve under Hakim Bishara,' said Giles, 'if he still felt I could be of any assistance.'

◄○►

When the phones were no longer ringing off the hook, Sebastian finally decided to go home, although there was one person he still had to call. But he decided it would be easier to speak to her from the privacy of his flat.

On the way home to Pimlico, he suddenly felt hungry, as he hadn't had any lunch. He couldn't face eating out, and certainly didn't feel like cooking, so he stopped off at a takeaway to pick up a large pepperoni pizza. By the time he'd parked outside his block of flats, his mind had turned to the problems he would have to face at tomorrow's emergency meeting, now that Adrian Sloane was back on the board. He let himself in to Pimlico Mansions, and took the lift to his apartment on the ninth floor. As he opened his door, he could hear the phone ringing.

◄○►

Hakim Bishara looked closely at the man seated across the table from him. Once again, he was playing the game his father had taught him. Mr Hammond's dark blue suit was well tailored but off the peg; his white shirt had been put on less than an hour ago. His tie was crested, probably a rugby club, and his shoes could only have been polished by someone who'd served in the armed forces. His head was shaven, his body slim and agile, and although he must have been in his mid-forties, not many thirty-year-olds would have wanted to step into the ring with him. Hakim waited for him to speak. The voice offers so many more clues.

'I only agreed to see you, Mr Bishara, because you're a friend of Mr Hardcastle.'

Essex, tough, streetwise. Hammond turned to his left and gave Arnold a slight nod.

'And I owe him. He got me off when I was guilty. Are you guilty, Mr Bishara?' he asked, his deep brown eyes focused on Hakim as if he were a python eyeing up his lunch.

Hakim could hear Seb's voice in his ear telling him to stay calm. 'No, I am not guilty, Mr Hammond,' he replied, returning his stare.

'Have you ever taken drugs, Mr Bishara?'

'Never,' said Hakim calmly.

'Then you won't mind rolling up your sleeves, will you?' Hakim carried out the order without question. Hammond's eyes scanned his arms. 'And now your trousers.' He rolled up each leg of his trousers. 'Open your mouth, I want to look at your teeth.' Hakim opened his mouth. 'Wider.' He peered inside. 'Well, one thing's for certain, Mr Hardcastle. Your friend has never taken drugs in his life, so he's passed the first test.' Hakim wondered what the second test would be. 'Now let's find out if he's a dealer.'

◄○►

Sebastian pushed the door closed, dropped his pizza on the hall table and grabbed the phone. He was greeted with a voice he hadn't heard for years.

'I was just about to phone you,' said Seb. 'But thought it unwise to call from the office, given the circumstances.'

'The circumstances?' repeated Samantha in a gentle voice Seb could never forget.

'I'm afraid it's rather a long story.'

Seb then attempted to explain what had happened to Bishara since his abortive phone call from Dulles airport, and when he finally stopped talking he still had no idea how Samantha would react.

'Poor man. I can't begin to imagine what he's going through.'

'It's a nightmare,' said Seb. 'I hope you feel I did the right thing.'

'I would have done exactly the same,' she said. 'Although I must confess I was looking forward to seeing you.'

'I could fly back to Washington on Saturday, pick up my pictures and take you to dinner.'

'I would suggest both of us,' said Sam. 'Jessica has made a plasticine model of you and has been sticking pins into it for the past twenty-four hours.'

'No more than I deserve. Should I speak to her, or will she hang up on me?'

'Don't worry. I have a feeling she'll run out of pins.'

—◦—

'Describe the person who was sitting next to you on the plane,' said Hammond.

'Forty, possibly forty-five, elegant, married—'

'How do you know she was married?'

'She was wearing a wedding ring and an engagement ring.'

'What does that prove?'

'That's she's not available. You, for example, are recently divorced.'

'What makes you say that?'

'There's a thin white line on the third finger of your left hand, which you occasionally try to twist around, as if a ring were still there.'

'What was she wearing?'

'A tailored suit, no other jewellery except an expensive pair of diamond earrings and a Cartier Tank watch.'

'Did you talk to her?'

'No, her body language made it clear she didn't want to be disturbed.'

'Did you speak to any of the other passengers on the flight?'

'No, I'd had a pointless and exhausting journey to Lagos and I just wanted to sleep.'

'I'll need the flight number and the date and time of the booking because it's just possible she's a regular on that route.'

Arnold made a note.

'It couldn't have been her,' said Hakim with conviction.

'Do you remember anything else about her?'

'She was reading *Watership Down* and she wore glasses.'

'Her nationality?'

'Scandinavian. Swedish would be my guess.'

'What makes you say that?'

'No other race on earth has such naturally fair hair.'

'Now I want you to think carefully before you answer my next question, Mr Bishara.' Hakim nodded. 'Can you think of anyone who would benefit from your being in jail?'

'Not that I'm aware of. A lot of people are envious of my success, but I don't regard them as enemies.'

'Is there anybody who would be happy to see the proposed Farthings Kaufman merger fail?'

'Several people. But after what I've been through in the last few days, I'm not willing to accuse someone who, like me, might be totally innocent.'

Arnold made another note.

'Mr Clifton or Mr Kaufman, for example? Don't forget they were at school together. One of them may see himself as the next chairman, and sooner than expected if you were safely out of the way.'

'There's no doubt that one of them will eventually take my place as chairman. But I can assure you, Mr Hammond, they are both one hundred per cent trustworthy and have more than proved their loyalty over the past few days. No, Mr Hammond, you'll have to look further afield than that.'

'What about any other board members?'

'They're either too old, too busy, or well aware that they're not up to the job.'

Arnold Hardcastle allowed himself a smile.

'Well, there's someone out there who wants to see you locked up for a very long time, otherwise why take so much trouble to have you arrested for a crime you didn't commit?'

'But if someone like that had been on the plane, surely I would have recognized them.'

'They wouldn't have been on the plane,' said Hammond. 'He or she would have used someone who was above suspicion, who could get on board that flight with thirteen ounces of heroin without anyone suspecting them. A stewardess perhaps, or even the pilot.'

'But why?' said Hakim.

'Greed or fear is usually the answer to that question, Mr Bishara. Money is almost always the catalyst. Some debt they needed to pay, some piece of information they didn't want revealed. Don't worry, Mr Bishara, I'll find out who it was. But it won't come cheap.'

Hakim nodded. The mention of money and he felt on firmer ground. 'What's it going to cost me?'

'I'll need a small team. Two, possibly three. They'll have to be experts in their fields, and they'll expect to be paid in cash, up front.'

'How much?'

'Five grand.'

'You'll have it later today,' said Hakim, who nodded to Arnold. 'And your payment, Mr Hammond?'

'I've given that some thought, and I'd prefer to be paid on results.'

'What did you have in mind?' asked Hakim, remembering

another of his father's golden rules: in any deal, always wait for the other side to make the opening bid.

'Five thousand pounds if I find the person responsible for planting the heroin. Ten thousand if they're arrested and charged. Twenty thousand if I discover the person or persons behind the operation. And another thousand for every year of their sentence.'

Hakim could have bargained for an hour and probably lowered Hammond's demands by 30, 40 even 50 per cent, but as his father had once told him, sometimes the opening bid is the one you should settle for, especially if the stakes are high. In this case, the stakes couldn't have been higher.

He rose slowly from his chair, offered an outstretched hand and said, 'You have a deal, Mr Hammond.'

◄○►

'This emergency board meeting has been called in most unfortunate circumstances,' said Ross Buchanan. 'But first I must tell you that Mr Bishara has asked me to stand in as chairman until he returns.'

'Shouldn't that be put to a vote?' said Adrian Sloane. 'Can a man who's locked up in prison on a serious drugs charge continue to dictate how a public company is run?'

'I agree with Mr Sloane,' said Giles. 'Such an important decision should be put to a vote. I therefore propose that Mr Ross Buchanan, a distinguished former chairman of this bank, takes on the responsibilities of chairing the board once again, until Mr Bishara returns to his rightful position.'

'But I am also a past chairman of the bank,' protested Sloane.

'I did say distinguished,' said Giles, without even bothering to look at Sloane.

A stony silence followed.

'Will anyone second Mr Clifton's proposal that Mr Ross Buchanan stand in as chairman until Mr Bishara returns?' asked the company secretary.

'I will be delighted to do so,' said Jimmy Goldsmith.

'Those in favour?' asked the company secretary.

Everyone around the table except Sloane raised their hand. 'Those against?'

Sloane raised his hand and said, 'I want it minuted that if Bishara is convicted of drug smuggling, I shall expect every one of you to resign.'

'And if he isn't?' asked Victor Kaufman.

'Then naturally I will have to consider my own position.'

'That's something else I'd like minuted,' said Victor. The company secretary duly wrote down his words.

'Perhaps,' said Ross, 'we should now move on. I'd like to begin by welcoming Lord Barrington and Mr James Goldsmith as members of the board, before asking our chief executive, Sebastian Clifton, to report on the effect recent events have had on the company's finances, and the latest position concerning the merger.'

'Our shares are down by twelve per cent, Mr Chairman,' said Sebastian, 'but I'm pleased to report that the market appears to have steadied, not least because of the intervention of Mr Goldsmith, who clearly not only believes in Mr Bishara's innocence but also in the long-term future of the bank. And can I say how delighted I am that he has taken his place on the board and been able to join us today.'

'But like Mr Buchanan,' said Goldsmith, 'I intend to withdraw as a director as soon as Mr Bishara returns.'

'And if he doesn't return?' said Sloane. 'What will you do then, Mr Goldsmith?'

'I will remain on the board and do everything in my power to make sure that a little shit like you doesn't become chairman.'

'Mr Chairman,' protested Sloane. 'This is the board meeting of a leading City bank, not a casino, where clearly Mr Goldsmith would be more at home.'

'My reason for not wanting Mr Sloane to return as chairman of this bank,' said Goldsmith, 'is not just because he's a shit but, far more important, because the last time he held that position he almost succeeded in bringing Farthings to its knees, and I suspect that is his present purpose.'

'That is a disgraceful slur on my reputation,' said Sloane. 'You have left me with no choice but to place the matter in the hands of my solicitors.'

'I can't wait,' said Goldsmith. 'Because when you were chairman of Farthings and Mr Bishara withdrew his bid for the bank, you stated at a full board meeting, which was minuted, that there was another leading financial institution willing to pay considerably more for Farthings shares than Mr Bishara was offering. It's always been a bit of a mystery to me who that leading financial institution was. Perhaps you would care to enlighten us now, Mr Sloane.'

'I don't have to take any more insults from the likes of you, Goldsmith.' Sloane rose from his place and, as he knew his words would be recorded in the minutes, added, 'You will all have to resign when Bishara is convicted. The next meeting of this board I attend will be as chairman. Good day, gentlemen,' he said, and walked out.

Goldsmith didn't wait for the door to close before saying, 'Never be afraid to attack a bully because they always turn out to be cowards, and the moment they come under any pressure they run away.'

A small round of applause followed. When it had died down, Giles Barrington leant across the table. 'I wonder, Jimmy, if you'd consider joining the Labour Party? There are one or two members of the Shadow Cabinet I'd love to see the back of.'

Ross Buchanan waited for the laughter to subside before he said, 'Sloane was right about one thing. If Hakim is convicted, we'll all have to resign.'

HAKIM BISHARA

1975

33

COURT NUMBER FOUR of the Old Bailey was packed long before ten o'clock on Thursday morning. Counsel were in their places, the press benches were heaving and the gallery above resembled the dress circle of a West End theatre on opening night.

Sebastian had attended every day of the trial, even the morning when the jury was being selected. He hated having to witness Hakim coming up from below to take his place in the dock, a policeman standing on either side of him as if he were a common criminal. The American system, where the defendant sits at a table with his legal team, seemed so much more civilized.

Hakim's counsel was Mr Gilbert Gray QC, while the Crown was represented by Mr George Carman QC. They were like two seasoned gladiators in the Roman Colosseum, cut and thrust, but so far neither had managed to inflict anything more serious than the occasional flesh wound. Sebastian couldn't help thinking that if they were to change sides, all the feigned passion, the barbed insults, the angry protests would still have been displayed in equal measure.

In their opening speeches, Mr Gray and Mr Carman had set out their stalls, and Sebastian was sure the jury hadn't been swayed one way or the other by the time they sat back down. The first three witnesses – the captain of flight 207, the purser and Mrs Aisha Obgabo, a Nigerian stewardess who had supplied written evidence – added little to the case, as none of them could remember the woman seated in 3B, and they certainly hadn't

275

witnessed anyone slipping something into Mr Bishara's bag. So a great deal now rested on the next witness, Mr Collier, a senior customs officer at Heathrow, who had arrested the defendant.

'Call Mr Collier!' bellowed a policeman standing by the entrance to the court.

Sebastian watched with interest as Mr Collier entered the room and made his way to the witness box. He was a little over six foot, with thick dark hair and a beard that gave him the look of a sea captain. He had an open and honest face, and Barry Hammond had written in his report that Collier spent his Sunday mornings refereeing mini rugby. But Barry had dug up something that just might give Mr Gray the chance to draw first blood. However, that would have to wait, because he was the Crown's witness, so Mr Carman would be called to examine him first.

When Mr Collier delivered the oath, he didn't need to read the card held up by the clerk of the court. His voice was firm and confident, with no suggestion of nerves. The jury were already looking at him with respect.

Mr Carman rose slowly from his place, opened a red file in front of him and began his examination. 'Would you please state your name for the record?'

'David Collier.'

'And your occupation?'

'I'm a senior customs officer, currently working out of Heath-row.'

'How long have you been a customs officer, Mr Collier?'

'Twenty-seven years.'

'So it would be fair to say that you are a man who has reached the top of his chosen profession?'

'I would like to think so.'

'Let me go further, Mr Collier, and suggest—'

'You needn't go any further,' interjected Mr Justice Urquhart, glaring down from the bench at senior counsel. 'You have established Mr Collier's credentials, so I suggest you move on.'

'I'm most grateful, my lord,' said Carman, 'for your confirmation of Mr Collier's undoubted qualifications as an expert witness.'

The judge frowned, but made no further comment. 'Mr Collier, can I confirm that you were the senior customs officer on duty on the morning the defendant, Mr Bishara, was arrested and taken into custody.'

'Yes I was, sir.'

'When Mr Bishara entered the green channel, indicating that he had nothing to declare, did you stop him and ask to inspect his baggage?'

'Yes I did, sir.'

'How much luggage was he carrying?'

'Just an overnight bag, nothing else.'

'And was this simply a random check?'

'No, sir. We had received a tip-off that a passenger on flight 207 from Lagos would be attempting to smuggle a consignment of heroin into the country.'

'How was this tip-off made?'

'By phone, sir. About thirty minutes before the plane landed.'

'Did the informant give you his name?'

'No, sir, but that's not unusual because informants in cases of this kind are often drug-dealers themselves. They may want a rival removed or punished for not having paid for a previous consignment.'

'Was the conversation with the informant recorded?'

'All such conversations are taped, Mr Carman, in case they are needed as evidence in a trial at a later date.'

'Might I suggest, my lord,' said Carman, looking up at the bench, 'that this would be an appropriate moment for the jury to hear the tape?'

The judge nodded, and the clerk of the court walked over to a table in the centre of the room where a Grundig tape recorder had been set up. He looked towards the judge, who nodded once again, and pressed the play button.

'*Customs office, Heathrow,*' said a female voice.

'*Put me through to the senior customs officer.*'

'*May I ask who's calling?*'

'*No, you may not.*'

'*I'll see if he's available.*' The hum of the whirring tape continued for some time before another voice came on the line. '*SCO Collier. How can I help you?*'

'*If you're interested, I can tell you about some drugs that a passenger will be trying to smuggle in today.*'

Sebastian noticed that Mr Gray was making copious notes on his yellow pad.

'*Yes, I'm interested,*' said Collier. '*But first, would you tell me your name?*'

'*The passenger's name is Hakim Bishara. He's well known in the trade and is travelling on flight 207 from Lagos. He has thirteen ounces of heroin in his overnight bag.*' Click, burr.

'What did you do next, Mr Collier?'

'I contacted a colleague in passport control and asked him to inform me the moment Mr Bishara had been cleared.'

'And he did so?'

'Yes. When Mr Bishara entered the green channel a few minutes later, I stopped him and inspected his overnight bag, the one piece of luggage in his possession.'

'And did you find anything unusual?'

'A cellophane package secreted in a side pocket of the bag containing thirteen ounces of heroin.'

'How did Mr Bishara react when you found this package?'

'He looked surprised and claimed he had never seen it before.'

'Is that unusual, Mr Collier?'

'I've never known a dealer admit to smuggling drugs. They always look surprised and behave impeccably. It's their only defence should the case come to court.'

'What did you do then?'

'I arrested Mr Bishara, cautioned him in the presence of a colleague and conducted him to an interview room, where I handed him over to an officer from the Drugs Squad.'

'Now, before my learned friend Mr Gray leaps up to tell us all that a doctor has examined Mr Bishara and found that there is no indication he has ever taken drugs in his life, can I ask you, with your twenty-seven years of experience as a customs officer,

Mr Collier, would it be unusual for a drug-dealer not to be a drug-user?'

'It's almost unknown for a dealer to take drugs himself. They are businessmen who run large and complex empires, often using apparently legitimate businesses as a front for their criminal activities.'

'Not unlike a banker?'

Mr Gray did leap up.

'Yes, Mr Gray,' said the judge. 'Mr Carman, that was uncalled for.' Turning to the jury, Mr Justice Urquhart added, 'That last comment will be struck from the record, and you should dismiss it from your minds.'

Sebastian had no doubt that it would be struck from the record, but he was equally certain it would not be dismissed from the jurors' minds.

'I apologize, my lord,' said Mr Carman, who couldn't have looked less apologetic. 'Mr Collier, how many drug-smugglers have you arrested in the past twenty-seven years?'

'One hundred and fifty-nine.'

'And how many of those one hundred and fifty-nine were eventually convicted?'

'One hundred and fifty-five.'

'And of the four who were found innocent, how many were later—'

'Mr Carman, where is this leading?'

'I am just trying to establish, my lord, that Mr Collier doesn't make mistakes. It was simply—'

'Stop there, Mr Carman. Mr Collier, you will not answer that question.'

Sebastian realized that the jury would know only too well what Mr Carman was trying to establish.

'No more questions, my lord.'

◄○►

When the court reconvened at two o'clock that afternoon, the judge invited Mr Gray to begin his cross-examination. If he was surprised by the defence counsel's opening remarks, he didn't show it.

'Mr Collier, I don't have to remind a man of your professional standing that you are still under oath.'

The customs officer bristled. 'No, you don't, Mr Gray.' The judge raised an eyebrow.

'I'd like to return to the tape recording, Mr Collier.' The witness nodded brusquely. 'Did you find your conversation with the anonymous informant somewhat unusual?'

'I'm not sure I understand the question,' said Collier, sounding defensive.

'Were you not surprised that he sounded like a well-educated man?'

'What makes you say that, Mr Gray?'

'When replying to the switchboard operator's question, "May I ask who's calling", he said, "No, you may not."' The judge smiled. 'And didn't you also find it interesting that the informant never once swore or used any bad language during the conversation?'

'Not many people swear at customs officers, Mr Gray.'

'And did you get the feeling he was reading from a script?'

'That's not uncommon. The pros know that if they stay on the line for more than three minutes we have a good chance of tracing the call, so they don't waste words.'

'Words like, "No, you may not?" And didn't you find the caller's expression "well known in the trade" rather strange, given the circumstances?'

'I'm not sure I'm following you, Mr Gray.'

'Then allow me to assist you, Mr Collier. You have been a customs officer for the past twenty-seven years, as my learned friend kept reminding us. So I must ask you, under oath, with your extensive knowledge of the drugs world, have you ever come across the name of Hakim Bishara before?'

Collier hesitated for a moment, before he said, 'No, I have not.'

'He wasn't among the one hundred and fifty-nine drug-smugglers you've arrested in the past?'

'No, sir.'

'And didn't you find it a little strange, Mr Collier, that the thirteen ounces of heroin were in a side pocket of his overnight bag and no attempt had been made to conceal them?'

'Mr Bishara is clearly a confident man,' said Collier, sounding a little flustered.

'But not a stupid one. Even more inexplicable, to my mind, is the fact that the man who gave you the tip-off, the well-educated man, said, and I quote' – Gray paused to glance down at his yellow notepad – '"He has thirteen ounces of heroin in his overnight bag." And thirteen ounces he had. Not fourteen. Not twelve. And, as promised, in his overnight bag.'

'Clearly the informant's contact in Nigeria told him the exact amount of heroin he'd sold to Mr Bishara.'

'Or the exact amount he'd arranged to have planted in Mr Bishara's bag?'

Collier gripped the sides of the witness box, but remained silent.

'Let me return to Mr Bishara's reaction when he first saw the package of heroin and remind you once again, Mr Collier, of your exact words: "He looked surprised, and claimed he had never seen it before".'

'That is correct.'

'He didn't raise his voice, lose his temper or protest?'

'No, he did not.'

'Mr Bishara remained calm and dignified throughout this extremely unpleasant ordeal.'

'No more than I would expect from a professional drug-dealer,' said Collier.

'And no more than I would expect from a totally innocent man,' retorted Mr Gray. Collier didn't comment. 'Allow me to end on a point that my learned friend was so keen the jury should know about, and indeed so am I. You told the court that during your twenty-seven years as a customs officer, you have arrested a hundred and fifty-nine people on drugs-related charges.'

'That is correct.'

'And during that time, have you ever made a mistake and

arrested an innocent person?' Collier pursed his lips. 'Yes or no, Mr Collier?'

'Yes, but on only one occasion.'

'And – correct me if I'm wrong –' said Gray as he opened a separate file, 'the man in question was arrested for being in possession of cocaine.'

'Yes.'

'And was he convicted?'

'Yes,' said Collier.

'What was his sentence?'

'Eight years,' said Collier, his voice barely above a whisper.

'Did this evil merchant of death serve out his full sentence?'

'No, he was released after four years.'

'For good behaviour?'

'No,' said Collier. 'In an unrelated trial some years later, a convicted drug-dealer admitted he'd planted the cocaine on him during a flight from Turkey.' It was some time before Collier added, 'The case still haunts me.'

'I hope, Mr Collier, that this case won't also come back to haunt you. No further questions, my lord.'

Sebastian turned to see that one or two members of the jury were whispering among themselves, while others were making notes.

'Mr Carman,' said the judge, 'do you wish to re-examine this witness?'

'I have only one question, my lord. Mr Collier, how old were you when you made that unfortunate mistake?'

'I was thirty-two. It was almost twenty years ago.'

'So you've only made one misjudgement in one hundred and fifty-nine cases? Considerably less than one per cent.'

'Yes, sir.'

'No more questions, my lord,' said Carman, resuming his seat.

'You may leave the witness box, Mr Collier,' said the judge.

Sebastian watched the senior customs officer as he made his way out of court. He turned to glance at Hakim, who managed a thin smile. Seb then looked at the jury, who were talking among themselves, with the exception of one man who didn't take his eyes off Mr Collier.

'Are you ready to call your next witness, Mr Carman?' asked the judge.

'I am indeed, my lord,' said the prosecution's standard-bearer, as he rose slowly from his place. Mr Carman tugged at the lapels on his long black gown and adjusted his wig before turning to face the jury. Once he was confident that every eye in the court-room was on him, he said, 'I call Mrs Kristina Bergström.'

Chattering broke out in the court as an elegant, middle-aged woman entered the room. Mr Gray swung round to see that his client had been taken by surprise, although he clearly recognized her immediately. He turned back to look more closely at the woman everyone had been searching for, for the past five months. He grabbed a new yellow pad, unscrewed the top of his pen and waited to hear her evidence.

Mrs Bergström took the Bible in her right hand and read from the card with such confidence you would not have known English was her second language.

Mr Carman didn't attempt to remove the Cheshire cat grin from his face until he'd asked the witness his first question.

'Mrs Bergström, would you be kind enough to state your name for the record.'

'Kristina Carla Bergström.'

'And your nationality?'

'Danish.'

'And your occupation?'

'I am a landscape architect.'

'Mrs Bergström, so as not to waste everyone's time, yours included, do you recognize the prisoner standing in the dock?'

She looked straight at Hakim and said, 'Yes, I do. We were seated next to each other on a flight from Lagos to London some four or five months ago.'

'And you are certain that the man you sat next to is the man in the dock?'

'He's a handsome man, Mr Carman, and I remember being surprised that he wasn't wearing a wedding ring.'

One or two smiles greeted this statement.

'During the flight, did you strike up a conversation with the defendant?'

'I thought about it, but he looked exhausted. In fact, he fell asleep within moments of the plane taking off, which I envied.'

'Why did you envy him?'

'I've never acquired the knack of being able to sleep on a plane, and have to pass the time watching a film or reading a book.'

'Which was it on this occasion?'

'I'd read half of *Watership Down* on the flight to Lagos, and I intended to finish it on the way back to London.'

'And did you?'

'Yes, I turned the last page a few moments before the captain told us we were about to begin our descent into Heathrow.'

'So you were awake for the entire journey?'

'Yes.'

'Did you at any time see another passenger, or a member of the crew, open the luggage compartment above you and place something in Mr Bishara's bag?'

'No one opened it during the entire flight.'

'How can you be so sure of that, Mrs Bergström?'

'Because I'd closed a major deal when I was in Lagos, to landscape the oil minister's garden.' Hakim wanted to laugh. So that's why he'd been kept waiting for five hours. 'And to celebrate I bought a Ferragamo handbag in duty-free. I'd placed it in the same overhead locker. If anyone had opened it I think I would have noticed.'

Mr Carman smiled at the women on the jury, one of whom was nodding.

'Was there any time during the flight when you were not sitting next to Mr Bishara?'

'After the captain announced that we were about half an hour from Heathrow, I went to the washroom to freshen up.'

'And Mr Bishara was in his seat at the time?'

'Yes, he'd just been served with breakfast.'

'So while you were gone he would have been able to check

and see if anyone had opened the hold above him and interfered with his bag.'

'I would presume so, but only he can answer that.'

'Thank you, Mrs Bergström. Please remain in the witness box, as I'm sure my learned friend will want to question you.'

When he rose, Mr Gray certainly didn't look as if he wanted to question anyone. 'My lord, I wonder if I might request a short break, as I need some time to consult with my client.'

'Of course, Mr Gray,' said Mr Justice Urquhart. He then leant forward, placed his elbows on the bench and turned to the jury. 'I think this would be a convenient time for us to break for the day. Would you please all be back in your places by ten o'clock tomorrow morning when Mr Gray can cross-examine this witness, if he so wishes.'

—◁◦▷—

'Let me first ask you, Hakim,' said Gray once they were settled in the privacy of one of the court's consultation rooms, 'is that the woman you sat next to on the flight from Lagos?'

'It certainly is. She's not someone you'd easily forget.'

'Then how did Carman get to her before we did?'

'He didn't,' said Arnold Hardcastle. 'Carman was only too happy to tell me that she'd read about the case in the press and immediately contacted her company lawyer.'

'Read about the case?' said Gray in disbelief. 'In the *Copenhagen Gazette*, no doubt.'

'No, the *Financial Times*.'

'We'd have been a lot better off if she hadn't,' muttered Gray.

'Why?' asked Hakim.

'Without her evidence I might have been able to sow some doubt in the jury's minds about the role she played in this whole affair, but now . . .'

'So you're not going to cross-examine her?' asked Arnold.

'Certainly not. That would only remind the jury what a convincing witness she is. No, everything now rests on how Hakim comes over.'

'He'll come over as what he is,' said Sebastian. 'A decent, honest man. The jury won't be able to miss that.'

'I wish it were that simple,' said Mr Gray. 'No one can ever be sure how a witness, especially one who's under so much pressure, will perform once they step into the box.'

'Perform?' repeated Ross.

'I'm afraid so,' said Mr Gray. 'Tomorrow will be pure theatre.'

34

As 10 A.M. STRUCK, Mr Justice Urquhart entered the court. Everyone rose, bowed and, after the judge had returned their salutation, waited for him to be seated in his high-backed red leather chair at the centre of the dais.

'Good morning,' he said, smiling down at the jury. He then turned his attention to defence counsel. 'Mr Gray, do you wish to cross-examine Mrs Bergström?'

'No, my lord.'

Carman stared at the jury, a feigned look of surprise on his face.

'As you wish. Mr Carman, will the prosecution be calling any further witnesses?'

'No, my lord.'

'Very well. In that case, Mr Gray, you may call your first witness.'

'I call Mr Hakim Bishara.'

Everyone's eyes followed the defendant as he stepped out of the dock and made his way to the witness box. He was wearing a navy-blue suit, a white shirt and a Yale tie, just as Mr Gray had recommended. He certainly didn't look like a man who had anything to hide. In fact, Sebastian was impressed by how fit he looked. He might have just flown in from a holiday in Lyford Cay, rather than having spent the past five months in prison. But then, as Hakim had explained to Seb on one of his many visits to HMP Wandsworth, he spent an hour in the gym every morning, then walked around the exercise yard for another hour in the afternoon. Besides which, he was no longer eating business lunches, and the prison didn't have a wine cellar.

'Would you please state your name for the record?' said Mr Gray after Hakim had taken the oath.

'Hakim Sajid Bishara.'

'And your profession?'

'Banker.'

'Would you care to elaborate?'

'I was chairman of Farthings Bank in the City of London.'

'Mr Bishara, can you take us through the events that led to you appearing before us in the witness box today?'

'I had flown to Lagos to attend a meeting with the Nigerian oil minister to discuss the funding of a proposed new port to cope with large oil tankers.'

'And what was your particular role in this operation?'

'The Nigerian government had invited Farthings to be the lead bank.'

'For a layman like myself, what does that mean?'

'When sovereign governments need to borrow large capital sums, in this case, twenty million dollars, one bank will take the prime position and supply the largest portion, possibly as much as twenty-five per cent, and then other banks will be invited to make up the shortfall.'

'And what would your bank charge for heading up such an operation?'

'The standard fee is one per cent.'

'So Farthings stood to make two hundred thousand dollars from this deal.'

'Yes, if it had gone through, Mr Gray.'

'But it didn't?'

'No. Soon after I was arrested, the Nigerian government withdrew their offer and invited Barclays to take our place.'

'So your bank lost two hundred thousand dollars?'

'We have lost considerably more than that, Mr Gray.'

'Don't get angry,' Seb whispered, although he knew Hakim couldn't hear him.

'Are you able to estimate just how much your bank has lost because you are no longer its chairman?'

'Farthings shares have fallen by almost nine per cent, knocking more than two million pounds off the value of the company. Several major clients have closed their accounts, along with a lot of smaller customers who followed in their wake. But far more important, Mr Gray, our reputation, both in the City and with our customers, may never recover unless I clear my name.'

'Quite so. And following your meeting with the oil minister in Lagos, you returned to London. On which airline?'

'Nigeria Airways. The Nigerian government had organized my entire trip.'

'How much luggage did you take on board?'

'Just an overnight bag, which I placed in the compartment above my seat.'

'Was anyone seated next to you?'

'Yes, Mrs Bergström. Although I didn't know her name at the time.'

'Did the two of you speak?'

'No. When I took my seat she was reading. I was exhausted and just wanted to sleep.'

'And when you eventually woke, did you speak to her?'

'No, she was still reading, and I could see that she only had a few pages of her book to go, so I didn't interrupt her.'

'Quite understandable. Did you take anything out of your bag during the flight?'

'No, I did not.'

'Were you aware of anyone tampering with it at any time?'

'No. But then I was asleep for several hours.'

'Did you check the contents of your bag before you left the plane?'

'No, I just grabbed it. I wanted to be among the first off the plane. I didn't have any other luggage so there was nothing to hold me up.'

'And once you'd been cleared by passport control, you headed straight for the green channel.'

'I did, because I had nothing to declare.'

'But you were stopped by a customs officer and asked to open your bag.'

'That is correct.'

'Were you surprised to be stopped?'

'No, I assumed it was just a routine check.'

'And the customs officer has told the court that throughout that check, you remained calm and polite.'

'I had nothing to hide, Mr Gray.'

'Quite. But when Mr Collier opened your bag, he found a cellophane package containing thirteen grams of heroin, with a street value of £22,000.'

'Yes, but I had no idea it was there. And of course I was completely unaware of its street value.'

'That was the first time you'd seen it.'

'It was the first time and only time in my life, Mr Gray, that I've ever seen heroin.'

'So you can't explain how the package came to be there?'

'No, I cannot. In fact, for a moment, I even wondered if I had picked up the wrong bag, until I saw my initials on its side.'

'Are you aware, Mr Bishara, of the important difference between being caught with heroin and being caught with, say, marijuana?'

'I wasn't at the time, but I have since been informed that heroin is a Class A drug, whereas marijuana is Class B, and its importation, while still illegal, is regarded as a less serious offence.'

'Something a drug-smuggler would have—'

'You're prompting the witness, Mr Gray.'

'I apologize, my lord. But I am keen for the jury to realize that having been charged with smuggling a Class A drug, Mr Bishara could be sentenced to fifteen years in jail, whereas a much lower tariff would be imposed had he been found in possession of marijuana.'

'Did I hear you correctly, Mr Gray?' interrupted the judge. 'Are you admitting that your client has at some time smuggled drugs into this country?'

'Certainly not, my lord. In fact, the exact opposite. In this case we are dealing with a highly intelligent, sophisticated banker, who regularly closes large deals that need to be calculated to the last decimal point. If Mr Bishara was also a drug-smuggler, as the Crown is trying to suggest, he would have been well aware that the consequences of being caught with thirteen ounces of heroin in his possession would have put him behind bars for the rest of his working life. It beggars belief to imagine that he would have taken such a risk.'

Sebastian turned to look at the jury. One or two of them were nodding, while others were taking notes.

'Have you ever taken even recreational drugs in the past? Perhaps when you were a student?'

'Never. But I do suffer from hay fever, so I sometimes take antihistamine tablets during the summer.'

'Have you ever sold a drug to anyone, at any time in your life?'

'No, sir. I can't imagine anything more evil than living off the proceeds of other people's misery.'

'No more questions, my lord.'

'Thank you, Mr Gray. Mr Carman, you may begin your cross-examination.'

'What do you think, Arnold?' Seb whispered, as the prosecution counsel gathered up his papers and prepared himself for the main event.

'If the jury were asked to return their verdict now,' said Arnold, 'I have no doubt Hakim would be acquitted. But we don't know what the prosecution has up its sleeve, and George Carman doesn't have a reputation for abiding by the Queensberry Rules. By the way, have you noticed that Adrian Sloane is sitting in the public gallery, following every word?'

35

MR CARMAN ROSE slowly from his place, adjusted his well-worn wig and tugged at the lapels of his long black gown before opening the thick file in front of him. He raised his head and peered at the defendant.

'Mr Bishara, do you consider yourself to be a risk-taker?'

'I don't think so,' Hakim replied. 'I am by nature fairly conservative, and I try to judge every deal on its merits.'

'Then allow me to be more specific. Are you a gambler?'

'No. I always calculate the odds before I take any risk, especially when I'm dealing with other people's money.'

'Are you a member of the Clermont Club in Mayfair?'

Mr Gray was quickly on his feet. 'Is this relevant, my lord?'

'I suspect we're about to find out, Mr Gray.'

'Yes, I am a member of the Clermont.'

'So you are a gambler, at least with your own money?'

'No, Mr Carman, I only ever take a risk when I'm confident the odds are in my favour.'

'So you never play roulette, black jack or poker?'

'No, I do not. They are all games of chance, Mr Carman, in which the banker inevitably ends up the winner. On balance, I prefer to be the banker.'

'Then why are you a member of the Clermont Club if you're not a gambler?'

'Because I enjoy the occasional game of backgammon, in which only two people are involved.'

'But wouldn't that mean the odds were fifty-fifty? Yet you just told the court that you only take a risk when you consider the odds are in your favour.'

'Mr Carman, at the World Backgammon Championships in Las Vegas three years ago, I reached the last sixteen. I know the other fifteen players personally, and I have a policy of avoiding them, which ensures that the odds are always in my favour.'

A ripple of laughter ran through the courtroom. Sebastian was pleased to see that even one or two of the jury were smiling.

Carman quickly changed the subject. 'And before your trip to Nigeria, had you ever been stopped by a customs officer?'

'No, never.'

'So you would have calculated that the odds would be in your favour before you—'

'My lord!' said Gray, leaping up from his seat.

'Yes, I agree, Mr Gray,' said the judge. 'You don't need to introduce an element of speculation, Mr Carman. Just stick to the facts of the case.'

'Yes, my lord. So, let's stick to the facts, shall we, Mr Bishara. You may recall that I asked you a moment ago if you had ever been stopped by a customs officer before, and you replied that you had not. Would you like to reconsider that answer?' Bishara hesitated, just long enough for Carman to add, 'Let me rephrase the question, Mr Bishara, so you are in no doubt of what I am asking you, because I'm sure you wouldn't want to add perjury to the list of charges you're already facing.'

The judge looked as if he was about to intervene when Carman added, 'Mr Bishara, is this the first time you've been arrested for smuggling?'

Everyone in the court fell silent as they waited for Hakim's reply. Sebastian remembered from his mother's libel trial that barristers seldom ask leading questions unless they already know the answer.

'There was one other occasion, Mr Carman, but I confess I had forgotten all about it, perhaps because the charge was later withdrawn.'

'You had forgotten all about it,' repeated Carman. 'Well, now you remember, perhaps you'd be willing to share with the court the details of why you were arrested on that occasion?'

'Certainly. I had closed a deal with the Emir of Qatar to finance the building of an airport in his country and, after the signing ceremony, the Emir presented me with a watch, which I was wearing when I arrived back in England. When I was asked to produce a receipt for it, I was unable to do so.'

'So you hadn't declared it.'

'It was a gift from the head of state, Mr Carman,' said Hakim, his voice rising. 'I would hardly have been wearing the watch if I'd been trying to hide it.'

'And what was the value of that watch, Mr Bishara?'

'I have no idea.'

'Then let me enlighten you,' said Carman, turning a page of his file. 'Cartier valued the timepiece at fourteen thousand pounds. Or perhaps you've conveniently forgotten that as well?' Bishara made no attempt to reply. 'What happened to that watch, Mr Bishara?'

'Customs decided that I could keep it if I was willing to pay five thousand pounds import duty.'

'And did you?'

'No,' said Bishara, raising his left hand. 'I prefer the watch my mother gave me on the day of my graduation from Yale.'

'Apart from thirteen ounces of heroin, what else did the customs officer find in your bag on the most recent occasion on which you were detained, Mr Bishara?' said Carman, changing tack.

'The usual toiletries, a couple of shirts, socks . . . but then I was only staying for the weekend.'

'Anything else?' Carman asked as he penned a note.

'A little money.'

'How much money?'

'I don't recall the exact amount.'

'Then let me once again refresh your memory, Mr Bishara. According to Mr Collier, he found ten thousand pounds in cash in your overnight bag.'

A gasp went up around the court. More than the annual

income of most of those sitting on the jury, was Sebastian's first thought.

'Why would a respectable banker, with an impeccable reputation, need to be carrying ten thousand pounds in cash in his overnight bag, when to quote you' – he once again checked his notes – '"but then I was only staying for the weekend".'

'In Africa, Mr Carman, not everyone has a bank account or a credit card, so the local custom is often to settle transactions in cash.'

'And I imagine that would also be the custom if you wanted to buy drugs, Mr Bishara?'

Gray was quickly on his feet again.

'Yes, yes. I withdraw the question,' said Carman, well aware that he'd made his point. 'Presumably, Mr Bishara, you are aware of the maximum amount of cash you are permitted to bring into this country?'

'Ten thousand pounds.'

'That is correct. How much did you have in your wallet when you were detained by Mr Collier?'

'A couple of hundred pounds perhaps.'

'So you must have known you were breaking the law. Or was that just another calculated risk?' Bishara didn't respond. 'I only ask, Mr Bishara,' said Carman turning to face the jury, 'because my learned friend Mr Gray laid great emphasis on the fact that you were' – he looked down at his notes – 'once again, I quote, "a highly intelligent, sophisticated banker, who regularly closes large deals that need to be calculated to the last decimal point". If that is the case, why were you carrying at least ten thousand two hundred pounds, when you must have known you were breaking the law?'

'With respect, Mr Carman, if I had been trying to buy thirteen ounces of heroin when I was in Lagos, by your calculation I would have needed at least twenty thousand pounds in cash.'

'But like a good banker,' said Carman, 'you could have closed the deal for ten thousand pounds.'

'You may well be right, Mr Carman, but if I had done so I wouldn't have been able to bring the ten thousand back, would I?'

'We only have your word that you took just ten thousand out.'

'We only have your word I didn't.'

'Then let me suggest that a man who isn't squeamish about trying to smuggle thirteen ounces of heroin into this country wouldn't give a second thought to taking out the necessary funds to – how shall I put it? – close the deal.'

Mr Gray bowed his head. How many times had he told Hakim not to take on Carman, however much he riled him, and never to forget the wily QC was playing on his home ground.

The Cheshire cat grin reappeared on Carman's face as he looked up at the judge and said, 'No more questions, my lord.'

'Mr Gray, do you wish to re-examine the witness?'

'I have a few additional questions, my lord. Mr Bishara, my learned friend went to great lengths to suggest that even when you play backgammon, you are, by nature, a gambler. Can I ask what stakes you play for?'

'A hundred pounds a game, which, if my opponent loses, he must donate to the charity of my choice.'

'Which is?'

'The Polio Society.'

'And if you lose?'

'I pay one thousand pounds to the charity of my opponent's choice.'

'How often do you lose?'

'About one game in ten. But then, it's a hobby, Mr Gray, not a profession.'

'Mr Bishara, how much money would you have made if you'd been able to dispose of thirteen ounces of heroin?'

'I had no idea until I saw the charge sheet, which estimated a street value of around twenty-two thousand pounds.'

'How much profit did your bank declare last year?'

'Just over twenty million pounds, Mr Gray.'

'And how much do you stand to lose if you are convicted in this case?'

'Everything.'

'No more questions, my lord.' Mr Gray sat wearily down. To

Sebastian, he didn't look like a man who believed the odds were in his favour.

'Members of the jury,' said the judge, 'I am now going to release you for the weekend. Please do not discuss this case with your families or friends, as it is not them, but you, who must decide the fate of the accused. On Monday I shall be inviting leading counsel to make their closing speeches before I sum up. You will then retire and consider all the evidence before you reach your verdict. Please make sure you are back in your places by ten o'clock on Monday morning. I hope you all have a peaceful weekend.'

◄○►

The four of them gathered in Gilbert Gray's chambers.

'What are you up to at the weekend, Mr Clifton?' Gray asked as he hung up his wig and gown.

'I was going to the theatre, to see *Evita*, but I don't think I can face it. So I'll just stay at home and wait for my daughter to call me reverse charges.'

Gray laughed.

'And you, sir?' asked Seb.

'I have to write my closing address and make sure I cover every single point Carman raised. How about you, Arnold?'

'I'll be sitting by the phone, Gilly, just in case you need me. Dare I ask how you feel it's going?'

'It doesn't matter how I feel, as you well know, Arnold, because everything is now in the hands of the jury who, I must warn you, were very impressed by Mrs Bergström's testimony.'

'How can you be so sure of that?' asked Ross.

'Before she stepped into the witness box, several members of the jury were looking in Hakim's direction from time to time, which is usually a good sign. But since she gave evidence, they've hardly even glanced at him.' Gray let out a long sigh. 'I think we must prepare ourselves for the worst.'

'Will you tell Hakim that?' asked Seb.

'No. Let him at least spend the weekend believing innocent men are never convicted.'

36

IT WOULD BE A long weekend for Sebastian, Ross, Arnold, Victor, Clive, Mr Gray and Mr Carman, as well as for Desmond Mellor and Adrian Sloane – and an endless one for Hakim Bishara.

Sebastian woke early on Saturday morning, after catching moments of intermittent sleep. Although it was still dark outside, he got up, put on a tracksuit and jogged to the nearest newsagent. The headlines in the rack outside the shop didn't make good reading.

MYSTERY WOMAN'S UNHELPFUL EVIDENCE
(*The Times*)

£10,000 CASH FOUND IN HEROIN BAG
(*Daily Mail*)

BISHARA CAUGHT SMUGGLING £14,000 WATCH INTO UK
(*Sun*)

The *Sun* even had a picture of the watch on its front page. Seb bought a copy of every paper before he made his way back to his flat. After he'd poured himself a cup of coffee, he sank back into the only comfortable chair in his living room and read the same story again and again, even if the angle taken was slightly different. And by reporting Mr Carman's damning words in inverted commas, the journalists were all able to steer well clear of the libel laws. But you didn't have to read between the lines to work out what they considered the verdict was likely to be.

Only the *Guardian* offered an unbiased report, allowing its readers to make up their own minds.

Seb couldn't expect every member of the jury to read only the *Guardian*, and he also doubted if many of them would comply with the judge's instruction not to read any newspapers while the trial was taking place. 'Do not forget,' Mr Urquhart had reminded them, 'that no one sitting on the press benches can decide the outcome of this trial. That is your privilege, and yours alone.' Would all twelve of them have heeded his words?

Once Seb had read every word of every article that made even a passing reference to Hakim, he dropped the last paper on the floor. He looked up at the clock on the mantelpiece, but it was still only seven thirty. He closed his eyes.

—◦—

Ross Buchanan only read *The Times* that morning and, although he felt the trial's proceedings had been fairly covered by their court reporter, a betting man might have been forgiven for placing a small wager on a guilty verdict. Although he didn't believe in prayer, he did believe in justice.

When he addressed his final board meeting the week before the trial opened, Ross had told his fellow directors that the next time they met, the chairman would either be Hakim Bishara or Adrian Sloane. He went on to advise them that they would have to consider their own positions as directors if Hakim didn't receive a unanimous verdict. He added ominously, 'Should the trial end with a hung jury, or even with a verdict in Hakim's favour by a majority of ten to two, it would be seen as no more than a pyrrhic victory because there would always be a lingering doubt that he'd got away with it; like the damning Scottish judgement *Not Proven.*' Like any responsible chairman, Ross was preparing for the worst.

—◦—

Desmond Mellor and Adrian Sloane were already preparing for the best. They met at their club for lunch just before one. The dining room was almost empty, which suited their purpose.

Mellor checked the press statement Sloane had prepared and

planned to release moments after Mr Justice Urquhart had passed sentence.

Sloane would be demanding that an extraordinary general meeting of Farthings' shareholders be convened to discuss the implications of the jury's decision, and he was confident that Sebastian Clifton wouldn't be able to oppose the request. He would volunteer his services as temporary chairman of the bank until a suitable candidate could be found. That candidate was sitting on the other side of the table.

The two of them discussed in great detail how they would set about the takeover of Farthings, while at the same time revive the merger with Kaufman's. That way, they could bury all of their enemies in one grave.

◄○►

Arnold Hardcastle spent Saturday afternoon considering two press statements with the bank's public relations advisor, Clive Bingham. One was headed 'Hakim Bishara will appeal and is confident that the verdict will be overturned', while the other would show a photograph of Hakim sitting behind his desk at the bank, with the words, 'Business as usual'.

Neither of them dwelled on which statement was more likely to be released to the press.

◄○►

Mr George Carman QC delivered his peroration while soaking in a hot bath. His wife listened intently from the bedroom.

'Members of the jury, having heard the evidence presented in this case, there is surely only one verdict you can consider. I want you to put out of your mind the smartly dressed banker you saw in the witness box and think instead of the poor wretches who every day suffer untold agonies as a result of their addiction to illegal drugs. I have no doubt that Mr Bishara was telling the truth when he said he had never taken a drug in his life, but that doesn't mean he wasn't prepared to ruin the lives of others less fortunate than himself if he could make a quick profit from their misery. Don't let's forget, he failed to close any other deal while he was in Nigeria, so one is bound to ask, why had he taken so much cash to Lagos in the first place? But that is, of course, for you to decide. So when the time comes, members of the jury, to deliver your verdict, you will have to decide if some phantom of Mr Bishara's imagination put thirteen ounces of heroin in his bag, or did he, as I would submit, always know the drugs were there in the first place. Should that be your conclusion, then there's only one verdict you can consider. Guilty.'

A small round of applause emanated from the bedroom.

'Not bad, George. If I was on the jury, I'd certainly be convinced.'

'Though I'm not sure I am,' said Carman quietly, as he pulled the plug.

◄○►

Gilly Gray didn't speak to his wife over breakfast. He was not a moody man, but Susan had become used to longer and longer silences whenever a trial was drawing to a close, so she didn't comment when he left the table and retreated to his study to prepare his closing remarks to the jury. When the phone rang in the hall, Susan rushed to answer it so he wouldn't be disturbed.

'Members of the jury, is it credible that a man of Mr Bishara's standing could be involved in such a squalid crime? Would someone who had so much to lose entertain for a moment—'

There was a tap at the door. Gilly swung round, knowing that his wife would not have considered interrupting him unless . . .

'There's a Mr Barry Hammond on the line. He says it's urgent.'

◄○►

For Hakim Bishara, it was not a long weekend, but sixty-seven sleepless hours while he waited to be driven back to the court to learn his fate. He could only hope that when the foreman of the jury rose, he would deliver two words, not one.

While he was pacing around the prison yard on Sunday afternoon, accompanied by two bankers who would find it difficult ever to open an account again, several inmates came over to wish him luck.

'Pity one or two of them didn't appear as witnesses in the trial,' said one of his companions.

'How would that have helped?' asked Hakim.

'Rumour on the block is that the drug barons are telling everyone you were never a dealer or a junkie, because they know their customers and suppliers better than any retailer. After all, they can't advertise, and they don't have a shop front.'

'But who would believe them?' asked Hakim.

37

SEBASTIAN ARRIVED at the Old Bailey just after nine thirty on Monday morning. When he entered the court, he was surprised to find Arnold Hardcastle sitting alone on the defence counsel's bench. Seb glanced across to see that Mr Carman was already in his place, checking through his closing address. He looked as if he couldn't wait for the starting pistol to fire so he could burst out of the blocks and head for the tape. There are no silver medals for barristers.

'Any sign of our esteemed leader?' asked Seb as he sat down next to Arnold.

'No, but he should be with us at any moment,' said Arnold, checking his watch. 'When I rang earlier, his junior told me he wasn't to be disturbed under any circumstances. Though I must say, he's cutting it fine.'

Seb kept looking towards the doorway, through which court officials, lawyers, journalists and other interested parties were streaming, but Mr Gray was not among them. 9.45 a.m., and still there was no sign of him. 9.50, and Mr Carman began casting the occasional quizzical glance in their direction. 9.55, and Arnold was becoming quite anxious, as the judge would be certain to ask him where defence counsel was, and he didn't know. 10.00.

Mr Justice Urquhart entered, bowed to the court and took his seat on the raised dais. He checked that the defendant was standing in the dock and waited for the twelve jurors to be seated in the jury box. Finally, he looked down at leading counsel's bench to see Mr Carman sitting on the edge of his seat, impatient for proceedings to begin. The judge would have obliged him but he couldn't see any sign of the defence counsel.

'I would call you, Mr Carman, to deliver your closing address, but it appears that Mr Gray is not among us.'

No sooner had Mr Justice Urquhart uttered these words than the door on the far side of the courtroom was flung open and Gilbert Gray came charging in, gown flowing behind him as he readjusted his wig on the move. Once he had settled, the judge said, 'Good morning, Mr Gray. Do you have any objection to my calling Mr Carman to present his closing address?' He made no attempt to hide his sarcasm.

'I do apologize, my lord, but I would beg your indulgence and ask if I can call a witness who has fresh evidence to present to the court.'

Mr Carman sat down and closed his file with a thud. He leant back and waited to find out who this witness could possibly be.

'And who is this new witness, might I ask, Mr Gray?'

'I shall not be calling a new witness, my lord, but recalling Mr Collier to the stand.'

This request clearly took everyone by surprise, including Mr Carman, and it was some time before the chattering subsided enough to allow the judge to ask his next question. He leant forward, peered down at the Crown's silk and said, 'Do you have any objection, Mr Carman, to Mr Collier being recalled at this late juncture?'

Carman wanted to say yes I most certainly do, my lord, but he wasn't sure on what grounds he could possibly object to the Crown's principal witness giving further testimony. 'I have no objection, my lord, although I am curious to know what fresh evidence can have arisen over the weekend.'

'Let's find out, shall we?' said the judge. He nodded to the clerk.

'Call Mr David Collier!'

The senior customs officer entered the room and returned to the witness box. Nothing could be gleaned from the expression on his face. The judge reminded him that he was still under oath.

'Good morning, Mr Collier,' said Gray. 'Can I confirm that you appear on this occasion at your own request and not as a witness for the prosecution?'

Sebastian couldn't help noticing that Mr Gray had put aside his earlier adversarial manner with this witness in favour of a more conciliatory tone.

'That is correct, sir.'

'And why do you wish to reappear?'

'I feared that if I didn't, a grave injustice might be done.'

Once again, loud chattering broke out in the court. Mr Gray made no attempt to continue until silence prevailed.

'Perhaps you would care to elaborate, Mr Collier.'

'On Friday evening I had a call from a senior colleague in Frankfurt to brief me on a recent case in that city, which he felt I should know about. In the course of that conversation I discovered the reason Mrs Aisha Obgabo, the stewardess on flight 207, had only been able to present written evidence to this court.'

'And what was the reason?' asked Mr Gray.

'She's in jail, serving a six-year sentence for a Class A drug offence.'

This time the judge made no attempt to quell the outburst of chattering caused by Collier's revelation.

'And why should that have any bearing on this case?' asked Mr Gray, once order had been restored.

'It seems that a few weeks after Bishara's arrest, Mrs Obgabo was arrested for being in possession of two ounces of marijuana.'

'Is marijuana considered a Class A drug in Germany?' asked the judge incredulously.

'No, my lord. For that offence, the judge gave Mrs Obgabo a six-month suspended sentence and ordered that she be deported back to Nigeria.'

'Then why wasn't she?' demanded the judge.

'Because during the trial it came to light that Mrs Obgabo had been having an affair with the captain of the aircraft on which she was a stewardess. If she had been sent back to Nigeria, my lord, she would have been arrested for adultery and, if found guilty, the punishment in that country is death by stoning. So at the end of the trial, when the judge asked her if she wished for any other offences to be taken into consideration before he passed sentence, she admitted to being paid a large sum of money to place thirteen ounces of heroin in the bag of a first-class passenger on a Nigeria Airways flight from Lagos to London. Mrs Obgabo couldn't recall the name of the passenger, but she did remember that the bag she placed the heroin in was embossed in gold with the initials HB. For this offence, the judge sentenced Mrs Obgabo to six years in prison, which her lawyer assured her was more than enough time for her to apply for asylum as a political refugee.'

This time the judge accepted that he would have to wait a little longer before the court returned to any semblance of order. He sat back in his chair, while several journalists fled the court in search of the nearest telephone.

Sebastian noticed that for the first time the jury were looking at the prisoner in the dock, and several of them were even smiling at Hakim. What he didn't notice was Adrian Sloane slipping quietly out of the gallery. Mr Gray remained standing but made no attempt to speak until order had once again been restored.

'Thank you, Mr Collier, for your integrity and sense of public duty. If I may say so, you bring considerable credit to your profession.' Mr Gray closed his file, looked up at the judge and said, 'I have no more questions, my lord.'

'Do you have any questions for this witness, Mr Carman?' asked the judge.

Carman went into a huddle with the Crown's team before looking up at the judge and saying, 'No, my lord. Although I must confess I find it somewhat ironic that it was I who pointed out to your lordship that this witness's credentials were beyond reproach.'

'Chapeau, Mr Carman,' said the judge, touching his full-bottomed wig.

'And with that in mind, my lord,' continued Carman, 'the Crown withdraws all charges against the defendant.' Mr Carman sat down to a burst of applause from the public gallery.

Journalists continued scribbling furiously. Seasoned court officials tried not to reveal any emotion, while the prisoner in the dock simply looked dazed by what was happening all around him. Mr Justice Urquhart appeared to be the one person in the room who remained totally calm. He turned his attention to the man who was still standing in the dock and said, 'Mr Bishara, the Crown has withdrawn all of the charges against you. You are therefore released from custody and are free to leave the court, and, I must add, without a blemish on your reputation.'

Sebastian leapt in the air and threw his arms around Ross, as the two leading QCs bowed to each other with mock gravity before shaking hands.

'As we appear to have the rest of the day off, George,' said Gilly Gray, 'perhaps you'd care to join me for lunch and a round of golf?'

38

'Welcome back, chairman.'

'Thank you, Ross,' said Hakim, as he took his seat behind the chairman's desk for the first time in five months. 'But in truth, I don't know how to begin to thank you for all you've done, not just for me personally but, more importantly, for the bank.'

'I didn't do it on my own,' said Ross. 'You've got a damned fine team here at Farthings, led by Sebastian, who's been putting in hours that aren't on a clock.'

'Arnold tells me I'm also responsible for messing up his private life.'

'I think you'll find things have thawed a little on that front.'

'Would it help if I wrote to Samantha and explained why Seb had to leave Washington at such short notice?'

'She already knows. But it couldn't do any harm.'

'Is there anyone else in particular I ought to thank?'

'The whole team couldn't have been more supportive, but Giles Barrington deciding to join the board when he did sent a clear message to friend and foe alike.'

'I owe so much to the Barrington family, it will be almost impossible to repay them.'

'They don't think like that, chairman.'

'That's their strength.'

'And your foes' weakness.'

'On a happier note, did you see where our shares opened this morning?'

'Nearly back to where they were the day before—' Ross hesitated.

'—I went to prison. And Jimmy Goldsmith called me earlier this morning to say he'll be releasing his stock slowly on to the market over the next six months.'

'He should make a handsome profit.'

'No one will begrudge him that, bearing in mind the risk he took when most people assumed we were going under.'

'Of whom Adrian Sloane is a prime example. Unfortunately he'll also make a killing, and for all the wrong reasons.'

'Well, at least he won't be able to claim a seat on the board once he's cashed in his shares. Mind you, I would have paid good money to be at the board meeting when Jimmy told Sloane exactly what he thought of him.'

'I think you'll find it's recorded in some detail in the minutes, chairman.'

'It most certainly is, but I wish the conversation had been taped, so I could replay it –' he paused – 'again and again.'

'Sloane wasn't the only person who abandoned what some assumed was a sinking ship. You won't be surprised to hear that one or two old customers are now trying to climb back on board. "I was never in any doubt, old boy."'

'I hope you made those old boys walk the plank, one by one,' said Hakim with feeling.

'I didn't go quite that far, chairman. However, I made it clear that they might not be offered quite the same advantageous terms they'd enjoyed in the past.'

Hakim burst out laughing. 'You know, Ross, there are times when I could do with a modicum of your wisdom and diplomacy.' The chairman's tone of voice changed. 'Dare I ask if we're any nearer to finding out who paid the stewardess to plant the heroin in my bag?'

'Barry Hammond says he's got it down to a shortlist of three.'

'I presume one of them has to be Desmond Mellor.'

'Aided and abetted by Adrian Sloane and Jim Knowles. But Barry's warned me that it won't be easy to prove.'

'It would have been impossible without the help of Mr

Collier, who could so easily have chosen to say nothing, and save face. I'm indebted to him. Perhaps we should send him and his wife on a Barrington's cruise to the Bahamas.'

'I don't think so, chairman. David Collier plays everything by the book. Even when Barry took him to lunch to thank him for all he'd done, he insisted on splitting the bill. No, I suggest a letter of thanks and, as he's a huge Dickens fan, perhaps a complete Nonesuch edition?'

'What a brilliant idea.'

'Not mine. Once again you can thank Barry Hammond for that particular insight. Those two have become thick as thieves and go to watch Wasps together every Saturday afternoon.'

'Wasps?' asked Hakim, looking puzzled.

'A London rugby club they've both supported for years.'

'What do you suggest I do about thanking Barry properly?'

'I've already paid him the bonus you agreed, if you were found innocent, and he's still working on who arranged for the stewardess to plant those drugs in your bag. But he refuses to give me any details until he's nailed the bastard.'

'Typical Barry.'

'He also tells me that you've asked him to make further enquiries about Kristina Bergström, which puzzled me, chairman, because I was convinced she was telling the truth, and I can't see any purpose in—'

'Now that you're no longer chairman, Ross, what are your immediate plans?'

Although the sudden change of subject wasn't subtle, Ross played along. 'Jean and I are going on holiday to Burma, a country we've always wanted to visit. And when we get back to Scotland, we intend to spend the rest of our days in a cottage near Gullane that has stunning views over the Firth of Forth, and just happens to be adjoining Muirfield golf course, where I will spend many happy hours working on my handicap.'

'I'm not following you, Ross.'

'Which is a good thing, chairman, because you'd only end up in the deep rough. Equally importantly, Gullane is on the south shore of the Firth, where the trout are about to discover I'm back with a vengeance.'

'So am I to understand there's nothing I can say to persuade you to stay on the board?'

'Not a hope. You've already had my letter of resignation, and if I'm not on the *Flying Scotsman* this evening I don't know which one of us Jean will kill first.'

'You I can handle, but not Jean. Does that mean you've closed the deal on that idyllic cottage you told me about?'

'Almost,' said Ross. 'I still have to sell my flat in Edinburgh before I can sign the contract.'

'Please give Jean my love and tell her how grateful I am that she allowed you to come out of retirement for five months. Have a wonderful time in Burma, and thank you once again.' Ross was about to shake hands with the chairman when Hakim threw his arms around him and gave him a bear hug, something the Scotsman had never experienced before.

Once Ross had left, Hakim walked across to the window and waited until he saw him leave the building and hail a taxi. He then returned to his desk and asked his secretary to get Mr Vaughan of Savills on the line.

'Mr Bishara, good to hear from you. Can I possibly interest you in a duplex flat in Mayfair, prime location, excellent park views—'

'No, Mr Vaughan, you cannot. But you could sell me a flat in Edinburgh that I know has been on your books for several months.'

'We've already got a bid for Mr Buchanan's property in Argyll Street, but it's still a couple of thousand shy of the asking price.'

'Fine, then take it off the market, sell it to the under-bidder and I'll cover the shortfall.'

'We're talking a couple of thousand pounds, Mr Bishara.'

'Cheap at double the price,' said Hakim.

GILES BARRINGTON

1976–1977

39

THE GOVERNOR'S OFFICE

June 12th, 1976

Dear Lord Barrington

You may not remember me but we met some twelve years ago, on the Buckingham's *maiden voyage to New York. At that time I was a congressman for the eleventh district of Louisiana, better known as Baton Rouge. Since then, I've become State Governor, and have recently been re-elected to serve a second term. May I congratulate you on your own return to the Cabinet as Leader of the Lords.*

I'm writing to let you know that I will be in London for a few days toward the end of July, and wondered if you could spare the time to see me on a private matter, concerning a close friend, constituent and major backer of my party.

My friend had an unfortunate experience with a certain Lady Virginia Fenwick when visiting London some five years ago, who I subsequently discovered is your former wife. The matter I wish to seek your advice on does not reflect well on Lady Virginia, with whom you may still be on

good terms. If that is the case, I will of course understand,
and will seek to resolve the problem in some other way.
I look forward to hearing from you.
Yours sincerely

The Honorable Hayden Rankin

Giles remembered the governor only too well. His shrewd advice and discretion had helped to avert a major catastrophe when the IRA attempted to sink the *Buckingham* on her maiden voyage, and he certainly hadn't forgotten Hayden Rankin's parting words on the subject, 'You owe me one.'

Giles wrote back immediately to say he would be delighted to see Hayden when he was in London. Not least – which he didn't say in his letter – because he couldn't wait to find out how his ex-wife could possibly have come across one of the Governor of Louisiana's closest friends. And it might also finally solve the mystery of little Freddie.

He was delighted that Hayden had been re-elected for a second term but didn't feel as confident about his own party's chances of success at the next election, even though he wasn't willing to admit as much, especially to Emma.

Following the surprise resignation of Harold Wilson in April 1976, the new prime minister, Jim Callaghan, had asked Giles to once again take charge of the marginal seat campaign, and for the past two months he had been visiting constituencies as far-flung as Aberdeen and Plymouth. When Callaghan asked Giles for his realistic assessment of what the next election result would be, he had warned 'Lucky Jim' that they might not be quite as lucky this time.

—◦—

'Can I speak to Sebastian Clifton please?'

'This is Sebastian Clifton.'

'Mr Clifton, I'm ringing from the United States. Will you accept a reverse charge call from a Miss Jessica Clifton?'

'Yes, I will.'

'Hi, Pops.'

'Hi, Jessie, how are you?'

'Great, thanks.'

'And your mother?'

'I'm still working on her, but I was calling to make sure you'll be joining us in Rome next month.'

'I'm already booked into the Albergo del Senato, in the Piazza della Rotonda. It's just opposite the Pantheon. Where will you be staying?'

'With my grandparents at the American Embassy. I can't remember if you've ever met Grandpops, he's super cool.'

'Yes, I have. In fact I visited him when he was the *chef de mission* at the Embassy in Grosvenor Square, and asked his permission to marry your mother.'

'How beautifully old-fashioned of you, Pops, but you needn't bother to ask him again, because I've already got his approval, and I can't think of a more romantic city than Rome in which to propose to Mom.'

'Please don't tell me you phone the ambassador in Rome and reverse the charges!'

'Yes, but only once a week. I can't wait to meet Grandpops Harry and Great-uncle Giles. Then I can add them to my list and let them know you're planning to propose to Mom.'

'Should I presume you've already picked the date, the time and the place?'

'Yes, of course. It will have to be on Thursday, when we have tickets for the Borghese Gallery. I know Mom's looking forward to seeing the Berninis, and Canova's *Paolina Borghese*.'

'Did you know that the gallery is named after Napoleon's sister?'

'I didn't know you'd been to Rome, Pops.'

'It may come as a surprise to you, Jessie, but there were people roaming the earth before 1965.'

'Yes, I knew that. I've read about them in my history books.'

'You wouldn't like to run a bank, by any chance?'

'No thanks, Pops, I just haven't got the time, what with preparing for my next exhibition and trying to organize you two.'

'I can't imagine how we survived before you came along.'

'Not very well, by all accounts. By the way, have you ever come across a man called Maurice Swann, from Shifnal in Shropshire?'

'Yes, but surely he can't still be alive.'

'And kicking, it would seem, because he's invited Mom to open his school theatre. What's that all about?'

'It's a long story,' said Seb.

◄○►

Desmond Mellor was a few minutes late and, once Virginia had poured him a whisky, he got straight to the point.

'I've kept my word, and the time has come for you to keep yours.' Virginia didn't comment. 'I've made a lot of money over the years, Virginia, and I've recently had a serious offer for Mellor Travel, that might even make it possible for me to gain a controlling interest in Farthings Bank.'

Virginia refilled his glass with Glen Fenwick. 'So, what can I do for you?'

'The long and short of it is, I want that knighthood you promised you could fix when you needed my help to convince those American detectives that you were legit.'

Virginia was well aware that the very idea of Desmond Mellor being offered a knighthood was preposterous, but she had already seen a way of turning this to her advantage. 'Frankly, Desmond, I'm surprised you haven't been nominated for an honour already.'

'Is that how it works?' said Mellor. 'Someone has to nominate me?'

'Yes, the honours committee, a select group of the great and the good, receive recommendations and, if they feel it appropriate, give the nod.'

'Do you know anyone on that committee by any chance?'

'No one is meant to know who sits on the honours committee. It's a closely guarded secret. Otherwise they'd never stop being bothered with recommendations from completely unsuitable people.'

'So what hope have I got?' said Mellor.

'Better than most,' said Virginia, 'because the chairman of the committee just happens to be an old family friend.'

'What's his name?'

'If I tell you, you must swear to keep it secret, because if he thought even for a moment you knew, that would scupper your chances of ever being knighted.'

'You have my word, Virginia.'

'The Duke of Hertford – Peregrine to his friends – has been chairman of the committee for the past ten years.'

'How in hell's name will I ever get to meet a duke?'

'As I said, he's a personal friend, so I'll invite him round to a cocktail party, which will be an opportunity for him to get to know you. But we've still got a lot of work to do before that can happen.'

'Like what?'

'First you'll need to mount a major campaign if you want to be taken seriously.'

'What kind of campaign?'

'Articles about your company and how successful it's been over the years, with particular emphasis on your export record, will need to appear regularly in the business sections of the press. The honours committee always respond favourably to the word "exports".'

'That shouldn't be too difficult to arrange. Mellor Travel has branches all over the globe.'

'They also like the word "charity". You'll have to be seen to be supporting a range of worthy local and national causes, with regular photo ops that will attract their attention, so that when your name comes up in front of the committee, someone will say, "Does a lot of charity work, you know."'

'You seem to know an awful lot about this, Virginia.'

'I would hope so. We've been at it for over four hundred years.'

'So will you help me? Obviously I wouldn't be able to put myself up.'

'I would be only too happy to help in normal circumstances,

Desmond, but as you know better than anyone, I am no longer a lady of leisure.'

'But you gave me your word.'

'And indeed I will honour my commitment. But if it is to be done properly, Desmond, I would have to spend a great deal of my time making sure you are invited to all the right society balls, asked to make speeches at the appropriate business conferences, while arranging for you to meet – without anyone knowing, of course – certain members of the honours committee, including the duke.'

'Shall we say five hundred pounds a month, to make it happen?'

'Plus expenses. I'm going to have to wine and dine some very influential people.'

'You've got a deal, Virginia. I'll arrange a standing order for five hundred a month to be transferred to your bank today. And as I've always believed in incentives, you'll get a bonus of ten thousand the day Her Majesty's sword taps me on the shoulder.'

A bonus Virginia accepted she was never going to bank.

When Mellor finally left, Virginia breathed a sigh of relief. It was true that she was an old friend of the Duke of Hertford, but she knew only too well that he wasn't a member of the honours committee. Still, no harm in inviting Peregrine to a cocktail party so she could introduce him to Mellor if it kept his hopes alive, while at the same time ensuring she received a monthly cheque, plus expenses.

Virginia began to think of other suitable candidates for the honours committee she could also introduce to Mellor. It fascinated her that someone who was normally so shrewd and calculating, when taken out of their natural environment could be so naive and gullible. Mind you, Virginia accepted that she couldn't afford to overplay her hand.

40

BY THE TIME THE negotiations had been completed and the contracts signed, Sebastian was both exhilarated and exhausted. The French are never the easiest people to do business with, he considered, not least because they pretend they can't speak English whenever they don't want to reply to an awkward question.

When he got back to his hotel, all he wanted was a light supper, a hot shower and an early night, as he was booked on the first flight out of Charles De Gaulle in the morning. He was studying the room-service menu when the phone rang.

'Concierge desk, sir. We wondered if you would like to take advantage of our massage service?'

'No, thank you.'

'We offer this service to all our premium guests, sir, and there is no extra charge.'

'All right, you've convinced me. Send him up.'

'Actually, it's a woman, sir. She's Chinese and an excellent masseuse, but I'm afraid her English is a little limited.'

Seb got undressed, put on a hotel dressing gown and waited. A few minutes later there was a knock on the door. He opened it, to be greeted by a woman in a white tracksuit, carrying a folded massage table in one hand and a small suitcase in the other.

'Mai Ling,' she said, and bowed low.

'Please come in,' said Seb, but she did not respond. He watched as she set up the massage table in the middle of the room before disappearing into the bathroom and returning a few moments later with two large towels. She then opened her hold-all and extracted several bottles of oils and creams.

She bowed again, and indicated that Seb should lie face down on the table. He took off his dressing gown, feeling a little self-conscious clad only in his boxer shorts, and climbed on to the table.

After a couple of minutes of pummelling, she located an old squash injury in his left calf, and moments later, a recent torn muscle in his shoulder. She dug deep, and Seb soon relaxed, feeling he was in the hands of a professional.

Mai Ling was working on his neck when the phone rang. Seb knew it would be the chairman wanting to find out how the French deal had gone. He was just about to reluctantly climb off the table and answer the call but, before he could move, Mai Ling had picked up the receiver and placed it by his ear. He heard a voice say, 'I'm sorry to disturb you, sir, but there's a Mr Bishara on the line.'

'Please put him through.'

'How did it go?' were the chairman's first words.

'We agreed on a coupon of 3.8 per cent per annum,' said Seb as Mai Ling dug deeper into his shoulder blade and found the exact spot. 'But only on condition that the French franc doesn't fall below its current rate against the pound of 9.42.'

'Well done, Seb, because if I remember correctly, you would have settled at 3.4 per cent and even allowed the franc to be devalued by a further 10 per cent.'

'That's right, but after a bit of negotiating and several bottles of rather good wine, they came round. I've got the contract in French and English.'

'When can we expect you back?'

'I'll be on the first flight to Heathrow tomorrow morning, so I should be in the office before midday.'

'Could you drop in and see me as soon as you're back? There's something I need to discuss with you rather urgently.'

'Yes, of course, chairman.'

'On a lighter note, I've had a charming letter from Samantha to say how pleased she was with the outcome of the trial.'

'How did she find out about that?' asked Seb.

'You evidently told Jessica.'

'Yes, Jessie now calls me two or three times a week, always reverse charges, of course.'

'She's also spoken to me a couple of times.'

'Jessie's been calling you reverse charges?'

'Only when she can't get hold of you.'

'I'll kill her.'

'No, no,' said Hakim. 'Don't do that. She makes a pleasant change from most of my callers, although heaven help the man who marries her.'

'No one will ever be good enough.'

'And Samantha? Are you good enough for her?'

'Of course not, but I haven't given up hope because Jessie tells me they're going to Rome in the summer, when they hope to see all nineteen Caravaggios.'

'I assume you've booked your holiday at the same time?'

'You're worse than Jessie. It wouldn't surprise me if you two were in league together.'

'I'll see you around twelve tomorrow,' said Hakim, before the phone went dead.

Mai Ling returned the phone to the little table in the corner of the room before starting to work on Seb's neck. But he couldn't help wondering why the chairman wanted to see him the moment he got back, and why he wasn't willing to discuss the matter over the phone.

A little buzz on Mai Ling's clock indicated that his hour was up. Seb was so relaxed he'd almost fallen asleep. He climbed off the table, went into the bedroom and extracted a ten-franc note from his wallet. By the time he returned, the massage table had been folded up, the bottles of oils returned to their case and the towels deposited in the laundry basket.

He handed Mai Ling her tip, and she bowed low before quickly leaving the room. Seb sat down next to the phone, but it was some time before he picked it up.

'How can I help you, Mr Clifton?'

'I'd like to place a call to the States.'

41

'ANY IDEA WHY THE chairman wants to see me so urgently?'

'No, Mr Clifton,' replied Rachel. 'But I can tell you that Barry Hammond is in there with him.'

'Right. Send the English copy of the contract down to accounts and remind them that the first payment is due on quarter day, in francs.'

'And the French copy?'

'File it along with the others in the gathering-dust cabinet. I'll catch up with you as soon as I've seen the chairman.'

Sebastian left his office, walked quickly down the corridor and knocked on the chairman's door. He entered to find Hakim deep in conversation with Barry Hammond and someone he thought he recognized.

'Welcome back, Seb. You know Barry Hammond of course, and I think you've recently met his colleague, Mai Ling.'

Sebastian stared at the woman seated next to Barry, but it took him a moment to realize who she was. She rose and shook hands with Seb, no longer deferential, no longer shy.

'How nice to see you again, Mr Clifton.'

Seb decided to sit down in the nearest chair before his legs gave way.

'Congratulations on your triumph, Seb,' said Hakim, 'and the agreement you extracted from the French. Bravo. Just remind me of the details. No, why don't you remind me, Mai Ling?'

'Repayments of 3.8 per cent per annum as long as the exchange rate remains at 9.42 francs to the pound.'

Seb put his head in his hands, not sure whether to laugh or cry.

'And may I add, Mr Clifton, how nice I think it is that your daughter Jessica calls you from the States, twice, sometimes three times a week, and you always allow her to reverse the charges.'

Hakim and Barry burst out laughing. Seb could feel his cheeks burning.

'No harm done,' said Hakim. 'Barry, why don't you explain to Seb why we put him through this charade?'

'Although we're now fairly certain it was either Adrian Sloane or Desmond Mellor, possibly the two of them working together, who were responsible for having the drugs planted in Mr Bishara's bag, we're no nearer to being able to prove it. Sloane, as you probably know, has a flat in Kensington, while Mellor's main residence is in Gloucester, though he also has a pied-à-terre above his office in Bristol. And we recently found out that whenever he comes to London he always books into the same room at the same hotel. The Swan in St James's.'

'The head porter there, who shall remain nameless,' said Mai Ling, picking up the thread, 'is an ex-Met copper, like Barry and myself. He recently suggested to Mellor that he take advantage of the hotel's free massage service, which is available only to regular customers.'

'He clearly enjoys Mai Ling's skills in particular,' continued Hammond, 'because he now always books her well in advance. That's how we know he'll be staying at the Swan next Tuesday night. He's made an appointment to have a massage at 4.30 that afternoon. I've booked his room for the night before, which will give me more than enough time to install the recording device, so we can listen in to what he and Sloane are saying to each other.'

'But what makes you think Sloane will call him at that time?'

'He doesn't have to. Mellor is never off the phone, and the number he calls most frequently is Sloane's.'

'But surely Sloane will be cautious about what he says over the phone?'

'He usually is, but Mellor sometimes goads him, and Sloane

can't resist trying to score the occasional point. And he probably thinks Mellor's calling from his office, so the line's secure.'

'But they may not discuss anything of any use to us,' said Seb.

'You may well be right, Mr Clifton, because this will be Mai Ling's fourth appointment with Mellor, and although certain key words regularly come up whenever he and Sloane talk on the phone – Farthings, Bishara, Clifton, Barrington and occasionally Hardcastle and Kaufman – they haven't yet divulged anything of real significance. But now that I've listened to the three earlier tapes, I'd know Mellor's or Sloane's voice the moment I heard it. That's relevant because David Collier has given me a copy of the tape recording of the anonymous tip-off call. I listened to it again last night and, I can tell you, it was Adrian Sloane.'

'Well done, Barry,' said Hakim. 'But how do we prove that Mellor was also involved?'

'That's where Mai Ling comes in,' said Barry. 'Given time, I'm sure she'll work her magic on him, just as she did on you, Mr Clifton. Unless you have any more questions, we ought to get back to work.'

'Just one.' Seb turned to Mai Ling. 'While I've been sitting here, I've developed a slight crick in my neck, and I wondered . . .'

—◦—

Mai Ling set up the massage table while Desmond Mellor went into the bathroom and got undressed. When he came out, he was wearing only a pair of pants. He patted her backside as he climbed on to the table, pleased to see she'd already put the phone next to his headrest.

Mellor picked it up and began dialling even before she'd begun to work on his feet. He always enjoyed having his feet and head massaged more than any other part of his body. Well, almost. But Mai Ling had made it clear from the outset that wasn't on offer, even if he paid cash.

His first call was to his bank manager, and the only point of interest that emerged was that he agreed the company should pay Lady Virginia Fenwick's latest expenses claim of £92.75, a figure that seemed to increase every month. He would have to speak to her about it. He had also sent a donation of £1,000 to the Bristol Cathedral organ fund, a building he'd never entered.

His second call was to his secretary at Mellor Travel in Bristol. He barked at the poor girl for about twenty minutes, by which time Mai Ling had reached his shoulders. She was beginning to fear that this would be another wasted session until he suddenly slammed the phone down and started dialling again.

'Who's this?'

'Des Mellor.'

'Oh, hi, Des,' said Sloane, his voice changing from bully to sycophant without missing a beat. 'What can I do for you?'

'Have you got rid of all my Farthings shares? I noticed they were at a new high this morning.'

'You're down to the last fifty thousand but you've already covered your original investment, even made a small profit. So you can hold on to them and see if they go any higher, or cash in.'

'Always cash in when you're ahead, Adrian. I thought I'd taught you that.'

'We wouldn't have needed to,' said Sloane, clearly chastened by the barb, 'if that stupid Nigerian bitch had kept her mouth shut. We could be running the bank now. Still, I'll get the bastard next time.'

'There isn't going to be a next time,' said Mellor, 'unless it's a hundred per cent foolproof.'

'It's better than foolproof,' retorted Sloane. 'This time he'll be done for insider trading and lose his banking licence.'

'Bishara would never involve himself in anything that irresponsible.'

'But one of his dealers might. Someone who used to work for me when I was chairman of Farthings.'

'What have you got on him?'

'He has a gambling problem. If you could be paid out for backing the last horse in every race, he'd be a millionaire. Unfortunately his bookies are putting pressure on him to settle his account.'

'So what? The moment Bishara finds out, he'll sack the man, and no one will believe for a minute that he was involved.'

'It would be hard for Bishara to deny his involvement if we had the whole conversation on tape.'

'How's that possible?' barked Mellor.

'Bishara is constantly on the phone to the dealing room from wherever he is in the world, and it's amazing what a skilful electrical engineer can do with the help of the latest equipment. Just listen to these four tapes.' There was a moment's pause, before Mellor heard a click and then the words, *Don't buy Amalgamated Wire, because we're currently in negotiations with them, and that would be insider trading.*

'And now a second,' said Sloane. Another pause. *Buy your secretary something special, Gavin. She's served the bank well over the years. Charge it to me, but don't let anyone know I authorized it.*

'And a third': *You've had an excellent year, Gavin, keep up the good work, and I'm sure it will be reflected in your annual bonus.* An even longer silence followed, when Mellor began to wonder if he'd been cut off.

'Now, after a professional cut-and-paste job,' said Sloane, 'it sounds like this': *Buy Amalgamated Wire, but don't let anyone know I authorized it, because that would be insider trading. Keep up the good work, Gavin, and I'm sure it will be reflected in your annual bonus.*

'That's good,' said Mellor. 'But what happens if the other tapes are discovered?'

'Unlike Richard Nixon, I'll personally destroy them.'

'But your contact could once again be the weak link in the chain.'

'Not this time. The people Gavin deals with don't take kindly to punters who fail to pay their gambling debts. They've already threatened to break his legs.'

'But what's to stop him changing his mind once we've paid them off?'

'I won't be handing over any money until he's delivered the

tape to the Bank of England, along with an *It's with considerable regret that I have to inform you . . .* letter.'

'How much is it going to cost me?'

'Just over a thousand pounds.'

'And there's no chance of anyone knowing I'm involved?'

'Was there last time?' said Sloane.

'No, but there's more at stake this time.'

'What do you mean?'

'Strictly entre nous, Adrian, there's just a possibility that I might be in the New Year's honours list.' He hesitated. 'A knighthood.'

'Many congratulations,' said Sloane. 'I have a feeling the Bank of England would approve of Sir Desmond Mellor taking over as chairman of Farthings.'

'When will your man deliver the tape to the Bank of England?'

'Some time next week.'

The buzzer on Mai Ling's alarm clock starting purring.

'Perfect timing,' said Mellor, as he slammed down the phone, got off the table and disappeared into the bathroom.

Mai Ling agreed. While Mellor was in the shower she unscrewed the mouthpiece on the phone and removed the recording device. She then folded up the massage table, placed the bottles back in the case and threw the soiled towels in the laundry basket.

By the time Mellor came out of the bathroom holding up a ten-pound note, Mai Ling was getting into a car parked outside the Swan Hotel. As she handed the tape to Barry Hammond she said, 'Thank God I'll never have to see that man again.'

—◦—

'Sir Desmond,' said Virginia, as the butler showed her protégé into the drawing room.

'Not yet,' said Mellor.

'But I have a feeling it won't be too long now. Ah,' Virginia said, looking over Mellor's shoulder. 'Miles, good of you to drop by, considering how busy you must be. Have you two met before?

Desmond Mellor is one of the country's leading businessmen. Desmond, Sir Miles Watling, chairman of Watling Brothers.'

'We met at Ascot, Sir Miles,' said Mellor, as the two men shook hands. 'But there's no reason you should remember.' Always be respectful to those who already have a title, was one of Virginia's golden rules.

'How could I forget?' said Sir Miles. 'You were in Virginia's box and you gave me the only winner I backed all afternoon. How are you, old chap?'

'Never better, thank you,' said Desmond, as Virginia re-appeared with a tall, elderly, grey-haired gentleman on her arm.

'So good of you to come, your grace,' she said, emphasizing the last two words.

'Who in their right mind would even consider missing one of your parties, my dear?'

'How kind of you to say so, Peregrine. May I introduce Mr Desmond Mellor, the well-known philanthropist?'

'Good evening, your grace,' said Mellor, following Virginia's lead. 'How nice to meet you.'

'I'm so sorry the duchess isn't with you,' said Virginia.

'I'm afraid she's a bit under the weather, poor gal,' said the duke. 'But I'm sure she'll be as right as rain in no time,' he added, as Bofie Bridgwater walked across to join them, right on cue.

'Good evening, Desmond,' said Bofie, as he was handed a glass of champagne. 'I understand congratulations are in order?'

'You're a little premature, Bofie,' replied Mellor, placing a finger to his lips. 'Although I think I can safely say we're in the home straight.'

The duke and Sir Miles pricked up their ears.

'Should I be picking up a few more shares in Mellor Travel before the news of the takeover becomes public?'

Desmond winked conspiratorially. 'But mum's the word, Bofie.'

'You can rely on me, old chap. I won't tell a soul.'

After he'd had a long chat to the duke, Virginia took Desmond by the arm and guided him around the room to meet her other guests. 'Dame Eleanor, I don't think you've met Desmond Mellor, who—'

'No, I haven't,' said Dame Eleanor, 'but it gives me the opportunity to thank Mr Mellor for his generous donation to the Sick Children's Trust.'

'I'm only too happy to support the amazing work you do,' said Desmond. Virginia's stock answer, when dealing with the president of any charity.

By the time Desmond had spoken to everyone in the room, he was exhausted. Small talk and social etiquette were not his idea of how to spend a Friday evening. He was growing impatient to leave for his dinner with Adrian Sloane, when he would find out if the tape and the letter had been delivered to the Bank of England. But he hung back until the last of Virginia's guests had departed so he could have a private word with her.

'Well done, Desmond,' were Virginia's first words when she returned to the drawing room. 'You certainly impressed a lot of influential people this evening.'

'Yes, but are any of them on the honours committee?' said Mellor, reverting to his old persona.

'No, but I'm confident I can get both Sir Miles and Dame Eleanor to sign your nomination papers, which can't do any harm, remembering they are both friends of the duke.'

'So how much longer will I have to wait before I hear from the Palace?'

'One can't hurry these things,' said Virginia. 'You must appreciate, the committee cannot be rushed.'

'Meanwhile, you're costing me a small fortune, Virginia. You must have wined and dined half the landed gentry.'

'And to good purpose, because they're slowly coming round to my way of thinking,' said Virginia, as the butler helped Mellor on with his overcoat. 'You'll just have to be a little more patient, Desmond,' she added, before allowing him to bend down and kiss her on both cheeks. 'Goodbye, Sir Desmond,' she mocked, but only after the butler had closed the door.

◄○►

Buy Amalgamated Wire, but don't let anyone know I authorized it, because that would be insider trading. Keep up the good work, Gavin, and I'm sure it will be reflected in your annual bonus.

Hakim pressed the stop button. 'What more could we ask for? Once the Ethics Committee hears all four tapes, Mellor and Sloane will be unable to show their faces in the City ever again.'

'But if you were to present those tapes to the Bank of England as evidence,' said Arnold, 'they're bound to ask how you obtained them. And when you tell them, they may think you're no better than those two rogues you want to see behind bars.'

'Why?' said Hakim. 'The tapes prove that Sloane organized the planting of the drugs, and Mellor covered his expenses. And not satisfied with that, they're now trying to set me up a second time using a doctored tape to leave the impression I was involved in insider trading.'

'True, but the committee may feel that by secretly taping them, you've also broken the law. And they certainly wouldn't condone that.'

'Are you suggesting I shouldn't use the tapes to clear my name?'

'Yes, because in this case, the means do not justify the end. Anyone who hears those tapes will know they were acquired without the knowledge of the participants, which would make them inadmissible in a court of law. In fact, it could well be you who ends up being referred to the DPP.'

'But if they're allowed to present their damning fake tape to the committee and I'm not able to show what they've been up to, at best I'll have to spend another year defending myself, and at worst, I'll end up losing my banking licence.'

'That's a risk I'd be willing to take if the alternative is being compared to those two scumbags,' said Arnold. 'And for what it's worth, that's my advice. Of course, you're free to ignore it. But should you decide to go down that road, I fear I won't be able to represent you on this occasion. Now, if you'll excuse me, I'm expected back in court at ten.'

Hakim remained silent until Arnold had closed the door behind him.

'What do I pay that man for?'

'To give you his considered judgement,' said Sebastian. 'Which might not always be what you want to hear.'

'But surely you agree with me, Seb, that I should be able to defend myself?'

'That wasn't the point Arnold was making. He simply feels that the way you went about acquiring the tape leaves you open to being accused of being no better than Sloane and Mellor.'

'And you agree with him?'

'Yes, I do, because I only have to ask myself what Cedric would have done, if he was still sitting in your chair.'

'So I'm expected to suffer another year of humiliation?'

'I've suffered for fifteen years because I didn't listen to Cedric's advice, so I can only recommend you listen to his son.'

Hakim pushed his chair back, stood up and began to pace restlessly around the room. He finally came to a halt in front of Seb. 'If you're both against me—'

'Neither of us is against you. We're on your side, and only want what's in your best interests. You could of course call Ross and get a third opinion.'

'I don't need to call Ross to know what his opinion would be. But what am I expected to do when a member of my own staff delivers that tape to the Bank of England and tells the committee he felt it was no more than his duty to report me?'

'Think like Cedric, be advised by Arnold, and in the end you'll defeat the bastards.'

◄○►

An elderly gentleman shuffled slowly out of the wings, a walking stick in each hand. He came to a halt in the centre of the stage and peered down at the packed audience.

'Mr Mayor, ladies and gentlemen,' he began, 'this is a day I've been looking forward to for over forty years. Forty-two to be precise, and there were times when I didn't think I'd live to see it. Hallelujah!' he shouted, looking up to the skies, which was greeted with laughter and applause. 'But before I ask Samantha Sullivan to open the theatre named after her, can I say how delighted I am that Sebastian Clifton was able to join us today. Because without his unstinting support and encouragement, this theatre would never have been built.'

The audience burst into applause a second time, as Maurice Swann looked down at his benefactor, who was seated in the front row.

'Why didn't you tell me you'd honoured your agreement?' whispered Samantha as she took Seb's hand.

Sebastian had wondered how he would feel about Samantha after the intervening years. Would the memory of things past evaporate into thin air? Or would he . . . He need not have worried because, if anything, he fell more in love with her 'the second time around'. Sam had lost none of her allure, her tenderness, her wit or her beauty. His only fear was that she might not feel the same way. Jessica didn't help with her less-than-subtle hints that it was high time her parents got married.

'I now invite Samantha to join me on stage to perform the opening ceremony.'

Samantha walked up the steps on to the stage and shook hands with the former headmaster. She turned to face the audience, hoping they wouldn't be able to see how nervous she felt.

'I'm so honoured to have a theatre named after me,' she began, 'especially as I've never been a good actress and am terrified of public speaking. But I have to say how proud I am of the man who has made it all possible, Sebastian Clifton.'

When the applause had finally died down, Mr Swann handed Samantha a large pair of scissors. She cut the tape that stretched across the stage and the whole audience rose to their feet and cheered.

For the next hour, Samantha, Sebastian and Jessica were surrounded by teachers, parents and pupils who wanted to thank them for all Mr Clifton had done. Sam looked up at Seb and realized why she had fallen in love with him a second time. Gone were the rough edges of greed, replaced with an understanding of what the other side had the right to expect. Seb kept telling her how lucky he was to have been given a second chance, whereas she felt—

'You can see how much this means to the entire community,' said Mr Swann. 'If there's ever anything I can do to show my appreciation, just—'

'Funny you should mention that,' interrupted Jessica. 'Pops told me you used to be a director.'

'Yes, but that was a long time ago.'

'Then I'm going to have to bring you out of retirement to direct your swan song.'

'That was an awful pun, young lady. What do you have in mind?'

'I want you to put my mom and pops back on stage.'

The old man turned and walked slowly up the steps and on to the stage.

'What's she up to?' whispered Samantha.

'I have no idea,' said Seb. 'But perhaps it would be simpler just to indulge her.' He took Sam's hand and led her up on to the stage.

'Now, I want you centre-stage, Seb,' said Mr Swann. 'Samantha, you stand facing him. Sebastian, you will now fall on one knee, look adoringly up at the woman you love and deliver your opening line.'

Seb immediately fell on one knee. 'Samantha Ethel Sullivan. I adore you and always will,' he said, 'and more than anything on earth I want you to be my wife.'

'Now you reply, Samantha,' said Swann.

'On one condition,' she said firmly.

'No, that's not in the script,' said Jessica. 'You're meant to say, "Get up, you idiot. Everyone is staring at us."'

'This is when you produce the little leather box,' said Swann. 'Samantha, you must look surprised when he opens it.'

Sebastian took out a small red box from his jacket pocket and opened it to reveal an exquisite blue sapphire surrounded by diamonds that Sam hadn't seen for ten years. Her expression was one of genuine surprise.

'And now your final line, Mom, if you can remember it.'

'Of course I'll marry you. I've loved you since the day you got me arrested.'

Seb stood up and placed the ring on the third finger of her left hand. He was about to kiss his fiancée when Samantha took a pace back and said, 'You lot have been rehearsing behind my back, haven't you?'

'True,' admitted Swann. 'But you were always going to be our leading lady.'

Seb took Samantha in his arms and kissed her gently on the lips, which was greeted with a spontaneous burst of applause from an audience who had been sitting on the edges of their seats.

'Curtain!' said Mr Swann.

━◦━

Sir Piers Thornton, the chairman of the court at the Bank of England, wrote to the chairman of Farthings Bank to invite him to appear before the Ethics Committee. He detailed what the bank wished to discuss with him, and enclosed a copy of the tape recording as well as the evidence given by one of the bank's brokers, which had been given *in camera*. The committee offered Mr Bishara four weeks to prepare his case and recommended that he had a legal representative present.

Arnold Hardcastle replied by return of post that his client would prefer to appear before the committee as soon as was convenient. A date was agreed.

━◦━

On the car journey back to London, Sebastian told Samantha about the contents of the damning faked tape and the problem Hakim was facing.

'Cedric would have agreed with your advice,' said Sam, 'just as I do. Sloane and Mellor are obviously both crooks, and Mr Bishara shouldn't need to lower his standards to theirs to prove he's innocent.'

'Let's hope you're right,' said Seb, as he turned on to the new motorway. 'Hakim will be appearing in front of the Ethics Committee next Wednesday and he hasn't got much more to rely on than his good name.'

'That should be more than enough,' said Sam. 'After all, it will be obvious he's telling the truth.'

'I wish it were that easy. Mellor and Sloane nearly got away with it last time, and if Hakim can't prove the tape has been doctored, things could go badly wrong for him. And worse, the four tapes that prove Hakim's innocence have somehow disappeared from the store room.'

'So they've got someone working on the inside.'

'A commodity trader called Gavin Buckland, who's already given evidence to the committee. He told them that—'

'Mom?'

'I thought you were asleep,' said Sam as she looked around to see her daughter curled up on the back seat.

'How could I get any sleep with you two chattering away.' She sat up. 'So let me see if I've fully understood the situation, because it's clear to me, Mom, that you haven't been paying attention.'

'Out of the mouths of babes . . .' said Seb.

'So what is it you think I've missed, Jessie?'

'For a start, why don't you tell Pops about Professor Daniel Horowitz?'

'Who's he?' asked Seb.

'A colleague of mine at the Smithsonian, who . . . of course, how dumb of me.'

'I sometimes wonder if either of you is really my parent,' said Jessica.

42

THE FOUR OF THEM sat facing the committee in a dark, oak-panelled room that no one who worked in the City ever wanted to enter. For most of those who sat on the wrong side of the long oak table, it spelt the end of their career.

On the other side of the table sat the chairman of the committee, Sir Piers Thornton, a former sheriff of the City. On his right, Nigel Foreman of NatWest, and on his left, Sir Bertram Laing of Price Waterhouse. However, perhaps the most important figure present was Henry VIII, whose portrait hung on the red-velvet-covered wall behind the chairman to remind everyone who had originally granted this august body its royal seal of approval.

Sir Piers offered a benign smile before he opened proceedings. 'Good morning, gentlemen. I'd like to begin by thanking you all for attending this enquiry.' What he didn't add was what the consequences would have been had they failed to do so. 'As you know, Mr Gavin Buckland, who has worked as a commodity broker at Farthings for the past eleven years, has levied a serious accusation against Mr Hakim Bishara, the bank's chairman. He claims that Mr Bishara ordered him to purchase a large number of shares in Amalgamated Wire at a time when he knew it was involved in a takeover bid for another company. To compound matters, that company was represented by Farthings Bank.

'Mr Buckland told the committee that he refused to carry out the order as he knew it was against the law and so, to quote him, "with a heavy heart",' said Sir Piers, looking down at the written statement in front of him, 'he decided to report the matter to this committee, and supplied us with a tape of his conversation with Mr Bishara. The purpose of this inquiry, Mr Bishara, is to give you the opportunity to defend yourself against these charges.'

The chairman sat back and produced the same benign smile to show he had completed his opening statement.

Arnold Hardcastle rose from his place on the other side of the table.

'My name is Arnold Hardcastle, and I am the bank's legal advisor, a position I have held for the past twenty-two years. I would like to begin by saying that this is the first occasion anyone from Farthings has been asked to appear before this committee since the bank's foundation in 1866.'

The benign smile returned.

'I am joined today, Sir Piers, by the chairman of Farthings, Mr Hakim Bishara, and his chief executive, Mr Sebastian Clifton, both of whom you will be acquainted with. The other member of our team, with whom you will not be familiar, is Professor Daniel Horowitz of the Smithsonian Institute in Washington, DC. He will explain the presence of the fifth member of our team, Matilda, who also hails from the Smithsonian.

'I will begin by saying a few words about the role Mr Bishara has played since he became chairman of Farthings four years ago. I will not dwell on the countless awards he has received from government institutions and respected organizations from all over the world, but the simple, undisputed fact is that under his leadership, Farthings has opened branches in seven countries, employs 6,412 people, and its share price has tripled. Mr Bishara is well aware that the accusation against him is a serious one because it goes directly to the most important tenet of banking: reputation.

'It will not be me, nor Mr Bishara himself, who defends him against these charges. No, he will leave that to a machine, which must surely be a first for this committee in its five-hundred-year history. The inventor of this machine, Professor Horowitz, may not be known to you, but as he will be our sole advocate on this occasion, perhaps I should tell you a little about his background.

Young Daniel Horowitz escaped from Germany with his parents in 1937. They settled in the borough of Queens in New York, where his father became a pawnbroker. Daniel left New York at the age of seventeen to attend Yale University, where he studied physics.

'He graduated with a BSc before he was old enough to vote. He went on to MIT, where he completed his PhD with a thesis on the impact of sound in an increasingly noisy world. Dr Horowitz then joined the Smithsonian as a lecturer, where nine years later he was appointed as the first Professor of Sound. In 1974 he was awarded the prestigious Congressional Science Medal, only the fourteenth person to be so honoured in the nation's history.' Arnold paused. 'With the committee's permission, Sir Piers, I will ask Professor Horowitz to conduct our defence.'

The professor rose from his chair, although it was not immediately obvious, as he appeared still to be on the same level as the members of the committee who were seated. However, it was not his lack of physical stature that would have struck a casual observer, but the vast bald dome that rested on such tiny shoulders, and made it easy to overlook the fact that his trousers couldn't have seen an iron since the day they were bought, or that his shirt was frayed at the collar. A tie hung loosely around his neck, as if it were an afterthought. It was only when the professor opened his mouth that the committee realized they were in the presence of a giant.

'What a strange, incongruous figure I must appear, Mr Chairman, standing before this august and ancient body to address you on a subject I have spent my whole life studying: sound. I am fascinated by the sound of Big Ben chiming, or a London bus changing gears. Only yesterday I spent a considerable time recording the sound of Bow Bells. You may well ask, how can this have any relevance for the defence of a man accused of insider trading? To answer that, I will need the help of my offspring, Matilda, who like me has never visited London before.'

The professor walked across to a side table on which he had placed a white cube, about two feet square, with what looked like the handset of a telephone attached to one side. On the side facing the committee was a large circular dial with black numbers around its edge that went from 0 to 120. A thick red arrow rested on zero. From the looks on the faces of the committee, Matilda had succeeded in catching their attention.

'Now, with your permission, sir, I shall ask Mr Bishara to deliver the exact words he was accused of saying to Mr Buckland. But please don't look at Mr Bishara, concentrate on Matilda.'

The committee didn't take their eyes off the machine as Hakim rose from his place, picked up the handset and said, *'Buy Amalgamated Wire, but don't let anyone know I authorized it, because that would be insider trading. Keep up the good work, Gavin, and I'm sure that it will be reflected in your annual bonus.'* Hakim replaced the handset and returned to his seat.

'I should now like to ask you gentlemen,' said the professor politely, 'what you observed while you were watching Matilda.'

'While Mr Bishara was speaking,' said Sir Piers, 'the arrow shot up to 76, then fluctuated between 74 and 78 until he put the handset down, when it returned to zero.'

'Thank you, chairman,' said the professor. 'The voice of the average male of Mr Bishara's age will have a volume level somewhere between 74 and 78. A softly spoken woman will average 67 to 71, while a younger man might reach a high of 85, or even 90. But whatever the individual's voice level, it remains constant.

'If I may, I would now like to feed Matilda with the tape on which the allegations against Mr Bishara are based. Once again, I would ask you to watch the arrow carefully.'

By the time the professor had placed the tape into the machine, the committee were leaning forward intently. He pressed play, and everyone in the room listened to the same words a second time, but this time Matilda registered a very different result.

'How is that possible?' asked Sir Piers.

'It is possible,' said the professor, 'because the tape supplied to this committee is a recording not of one conversation, but four, as I shall now demonstrate.' He rewound the tape and once again pressed the play button.

'Buy Amalgamated Wire.' He paused the tape. 'Seventy-six,

Mr Bishara's normal level.' He pressed play. *'But don't let anyone know I authorized it.* Eighty-four. *Because that would be insider trading.* Seventy-six, back to normal. *Keep up the good work, Gavin.* Eighty-one.'

'How do you explain the discrepancy?' asked Mr Foreman.

'Because as I suggested, sir, the tape that was provided to this committee is a compilation drawn from four different conversations. To use a vulgar American expression, the originals have been sliced and diced. I concluded that two of the conversations were conducted on the telephone in Mr Bishara's office as their levels are between 74 and 76; one was from overseas, when people have a tendency to speak up – in this case the level increased to 84; and one from Mr Bishara's home in the country, when the level is 81, and where the sound of birds – blue tits and sparrows, I believe – can be heard faintly in the background.'

'But,' said Mr Foreman, 'he did say "Buy Amalgamated Wire".'

'I accept that,' said the professor. 'But if you listen carefully to that section of the tape, I think you'll come to the same conclusion as I did: that a word has been cut out. I'd stake my reputation and experience on that word being "don't". In doctored tapes, that is the most common word to be deleted. So Mr Bishara's actual words were "Don't buy Amalgamated Wire". You will of course be able to test my theory more fully when you interview Mr Buckland again.'

'With that in mind, professor,' said the chairman, 'may we call on your services when we see Mr Buckland?'

'I would be happy to assist you,' said the professor, 'but my wife and I are only in England for a week conducting further research.'

'Into what?' asked Sir Piers, unable to resist.

'I plan to record the sonic output of London's buses, particularly double-deckers, and to spend some time at Heathrow recording 707 take-offs and landings. We're also going to attend a concert by the Rolling Stones at Wembley, when Matilda's little indicator may hit its maximum level of 120 for the first time.'

The chairman allowed himself a chuckle before saying, 'We

appreciate your giving us your time, professor, and look forward to seeing you and Matilda again in the near future.'

'And I have to confess,' Horowitz said, as he placed a plastic cover over his offspring and zipped her up, 'you only got me just in time.'

'And why is that?' asked Sir Piers.

'Scotland Yard have set me an interesting conundrum that Matilda can't handle on her own. However, I've almost perfected an odious little boyfriend for her, called Harvey, but he's not quite ready to be let loose on the world.'

'And what will Harvey be able to do?' the chairman asked on behalf of everyone in the room.

'He's an equalizer, so it won't be too long before I will be able to take any tape that has been sliced and diced and reproduce it at a constant level of 74 to 76. If whoever tampered with Mr Buckland's tape had been aware of Harvey, Mr Bishara would not have been able to prove his innocence.'

'Now I recall why I know your name,' said Sir Piers. 'Mr Hardcastle told us that you were awarded the Congressional Science Medal, but he didn't tell us what for. Do remind us, Mr Hardcastle.'

Arnold stood up again, opened the Horowitz file and read out the citation. 'At the time of President Nixon's impeachment, Professor Horowitz was invited by Congress to study the Nixon tapes and see if he could show that there had been any deletions or tampering with their content.'

'Which is exactly what I did,' said the professor. 'And as a staunch Republican, it was a sad day for me when the president was impeached. I came to the conclusion that Matilda must be a Democrat.'

They all burst out laughing.

'Mind you, if I had perfected Harvey a little earlier, the president might still have served his full two terms.'

—◦—

Adrian Sloane picked up the phone on his desk, curious to know who was calling him on his private line.

'Is this Adrian Sloane?' said a voice he didn't recognize.

'Depends who's asking.' There was a long pause.

'Chief Inspector Mike Stokes. I'm attached to the drugs squad at Scotland Yard.'

Sloane felt his whole body go cold.

'How can I help you, Mr Stokes?'

'I'd like to make an appointment to see you, sir.'

'Why?' asked Sloane bluntly.

'I can't discuss the matter over the phone, sir. Either I could come to you, or you could visit me at Scotland Yard, whichever is more convenient.'

Sloane hesitated. 'I'll come to you.'

43

THE TOASTMASTER waited for the applause to die down before he banged his gavel several times and announced, 'Your excellency, my lord, ladies and gentlemen, pray silence for the bridegroom, Mr Sebastian Clifton.'

Warm applause greeted Sebastian as he rose from his place at the top table.

'Best-man speeches are almost always appalling,' said Seb, 'and Victor is clearly a man who doesn't believe in breaking with tradition.' He turned to his old friend. 'If I was given a second chance to choose between you and Clive . . .' Laughter and a smattering of applause broke out.

'I want to begin by thanking my father-in-law for so generously allowing Samantha and me to be married in this magnificent embassy with its romantic past. I didn't realize until Jessica told me that the palazzo had its own lady chapel, and I can't think of a more idyllic place to marry the woman I love.

'I would also like to thank my parents, of whom I am inordinately proud. They continue to set standards I could never hope to live up to, so let's be thankful that I've married a woman who can. And of course, I want to thank all of you who have travelled from different parts of the world to be with us in Rome today to celebrate an event that should have taken place ten years ago. I can promise you I intend to spend the rest of my life making up for those lost years.

'My final thanks go to my precocious, adorable and talented menace of a daughter, Jessica, who somehow managed to bring her mother and me back together, for which I will be eternally grateful. I hope all of you will enjoy today, and have a memorable time while you're in Rome.'

Sebastian sat down to prolonged applause, and Jessica, who was seated next to him, handed him the dessert menu. He began to study the different dishes.

'The other side,' she said, trying not to sound exasperated.

Seb turned over the menu to find a charcoal drawing of himself delivering his speech.

'You just get better and better,' he said, placing an arm around her shoulder. 'I wonder if you could do me a favour?'

'Anything, Pops.' Jessica listened to her father's request, grinned and quietly left the table.

◄○►

'What a fascinating job, being an ambassador,' said Emma as an affogato was placed in front of her.

'Especially when they give you Rome,' said Patrick Sullivan. 'But I've often wondered what it must be like to chair a great hospital, with so many different and complex issues every day – not just the patients, doctors, nurses and—'

'The car park,' said Emma. 'I could have done with your diplomatic skills when it came to that particular problem.'

'I've never had a car parking problem,' admitted the ambassador.

'And neither did I, until I decided to charge for parking at the infirmary, when one of the local papers launched a campaign to get me to change my mind and described me as a heartless harridan!'

'And did you change your mind?'

'Certainly not. I'd authorized over a million pounds of public money to be spent building that car park, and I didn't expect the general public to use it for free parking whenever they wanted to go shopping. So I decided to charge the same rate as the nearest municipal car park, with concessions for hospital staff and patients, so it would only be used by the people it had been originally intended for. Result: uproar, protest marches, burning effigies! This, despite a terminally ill patient having to be driven round in circles for over an hour because her husband was unable to find a space. And if that wasn't enough, when I bumped into the paper's editor and explained why it was necessary, all he said was, of course you're right, Emma, but a good campaign always sells newspapers.'

Mr Sullivan laughed. 'On balance, I think I'll stick to being the American ambassador in Rome.'

'Grandma,' said a youthful voice behind her. 'A little memory of today.' Jessica handed her a drawing of Emma making a point to the ambassador.

'Jessica, it's wonderful. I'll definitely show it to the editor of my local paper, and explain why I was wagging my finger.'

◄○►

'How's Giles enjoying the Lords?' asked Harry.

'He isn't,' said Karin. 'He'd rather be back in the Commons.'

'But he's a member of the Cabinet.'

'And he's not sure he will be for much longer. Now the Tories have elected Margaret Thatcher as their leader, Giles feels they will have a good chance of winning the next election. And I confess I could vote for her,' whispered Karin, before she quickly added, 'What's the latest on your campaign to have Anatoly Babakov released from prison?'

'Not a lot of progress, I'm afraid. The Russians won't even let us know if he's still alive.'

'And how's Mrs Babakova bearing up?'

'She's moved to New York and is renting a small apartment on the Lower West Side. I visit her whenever I'm in the States. Yelena remains an eternal optimist and continues to believe that they're just about to release Anatoly. I haven't the heart to tell her it isn't going to happen in the foreseeable future, if ever.'

'Let me give the problem some thought,' said Karin. 'After spending so many years behind the Iron Curtain, I might be able to come up with something that would irritate the Russians enough to reconsider their position.'

'You might also mention my lack of progress to your father.

After all, he hates the communists every bit as much as you do,' said Harry, carefully observing how Karin reacted. But she gave nothing away.

'Good idea. I'll discuss it with him when I next go down to Cornwall,' she said, sounding as if she meant it, although Harry doubted if she would ever raise the subject of Anatoly Babakov with her controller.

'Karin,' said Jessica, handing her a copy of the menu. 'A little gift to mark our first meeting.'

'I'll treasure it,' said Karin, giving her a warm hug.

—◦—

'Do you ever hear from Gwyneth or Virginia?' asked Grace.

'Gwyneth occasionally,' said Giles. 'She's teaching English at Monmouth School, which should please you, and has recently become engaged to one of the house masters.'

'You're right, that does please me,' said Grace. 'She was a fine teacher. And Virginia?'

'Only what I pick up in the gossip columns. You will have seen that her father died a couple of months ago. Funny old stick, but I confess I rather liked him.'

'Did you go to his funeral?'

'No, I didn't feel that was appropriate, but I wrote to Archie Fenwick, who's inherited the title, saying that I hoped he'd play an active role in the Upper House. I received a very courteous reply.'

'But you surely don't approve of the hereditary system?' said Grace.

'No, I don't. But as long as we keep losing votes to the Tories in the Commons, reform of the House of Lords will have to be shelved until after the next election.'

'And if Mrs Thatcher wins that election, reform of the Lords won't be shelved, it will be buried.' Grace drained her glass of champagne before adding, 'Touching on a more sensitive subject, I'm so sorry you and Karin haven't had any children.'

'God knows we've tried everything, even sex.' Grace didn't laugh. 'We both visited a fertility clinic. It seems that Karin has a

348

blood problem and, after two miscarriages, the doctor feels the risk would be too great.'

'How sad,' said Grace. 'No one to follow you into the Lords.'

'Or, more important, open the batting for England.'

'Have you thought about adoption?'

'Yes, but we've put it on hold until after the election.'

'Don't put it on hold for too long. I know you'll find this hard to believe, Giles, but there are some things more important than politics.'

'I apologize for interrupting you, Aunt Grace, but may I give you this small gift?' Jessica said, handing over another portrait.

Grace studied the drawing for some time before she offered an opinion. 'Although I am not an expert, you undoubtedly have promise, my dear. Be sure you don't squander your talent.'

'I'll try not to, Aunt Grace.'

'How old are you?'

'Eleven.'

'Ah, the same age as Picasso when he held his first public exhibition – in which city, young lady?'

'Barcelona.'

Grace awarded her a slight bow. 'I shall have my portrait framed, hang it in my study in Cambridge and tell my fellow dons and pupils alike that you are my great-niece.'

'Praise indeed,' said Giles. 'Where's mine?'

'I can't fit you in today, Uncle Giles. Another time perhaps.'

'I'll certainly hold you to that. How would you like to stay with me at Barrington Hall while your parents are away on honeymoon? In return, you could paint a portrait of Karin and myself. And while you're with us you could visit your grandparents, who are just a couple of miles down the road at the Manor House.'

'They've already invited me to stay. And didn't try to bribe me.'

'Never forget, my dear,' said Grace, 'that your great-uncle is a politician.'

◄○►

'Have you heard anything back from the Bank of England?' asked Hakim.

'Nothing official,' said Arnold Hardcastle. 'But, strictly between ourselves, Sir Piers rang me on Friday afternoon to let me know that Gavin Buckland didn't show up for his second interview, and the committee have decided not to pursue the matter any further.'

'I could have told them he was unlikely to turn up because his letter of resignation was on my desk even before I'd got back from our meeting with the Ethics Committee.'

'He'll never be offered another job in the City,' said Arnold. 'I can only wonder what he'll do next.'

'He's gone to Cyprus,' said Hakim. 'Barry Hammond followed him to Nicosia, where he's taken a job on the commodities desk of a local Turkish bank. He was good at his job, so let's just hope there aren't too many racetracks in Cyprus.'

'Any news of Sloane or Mellor?'

'Gone to ground, according to Barry. But he's pretty sure they'll resurface in the spring like all pond life, when no doubt we'll find out what they've got planned next.'

'I wouldn't be so sure about that,' said Arnold. 'I was at the Bailey last week, and a police sergeant told me that—'

'A little gift for you, Mr Bishara, on behalf of my father.' Hakim swung round nervously, thinking someone might have overheard their conversation.

'What a wonderful surprise,' he said when he saw the portrait. 'I've always admired the drawing of your mother that hangs in your father's office, and I'll certainly put this one in mine.'

'I do hope you'll do one of me,' said Arnold, admiring the drawing.

'I'd be delighted to, Mr Hardcastle, but I must warn you, I charge by the hour.'

◄○►

The loud banging of a gavel could be heard coming from the top table. The guests fell silent as Victor Kaufman stood up once again.

'Not another speech, I promise. I thought you'd want to know that the bride and groom will be leaving in a few minutes' time, so if you would like to make your way to the entrance, we can all see them off.'

The guests began to rise from their places and drift out of the ballroom.

'Where are they going on honeymoon?' Emma asked Harry.

'No idea, but I know someone who will. Jessica!'

'Yes, Grandpops,' she said, running across to join them.

'Where are your mother and father spending their honeymoon?'

'Amsterdam.'

'Such a lovely city,' said Emma. 'Any particular reason?'

'It's where Dad first proposed to Mom, eleven years ago.'

'How romantic,' said Emma. 'Are they staying at the Amstel?'

'No, Pops booked the attic room of the Pension De Kanaal, which is where they stayed last time.'

'Another lesson learnt,' said Harry.

'And have they finally decided which country they are going to live in?' asked Emma.

'I decided,' said Jessica. 'England.'

'And have you let them know?'

'Pops can hardly be expected to run Farthings from Washington, and in any case Mom has been shortlisted for a job at the Tate.'

'I'm so glad you've been able to sort everything out to your satisfaction,' said Emma.

'Got to go,' said Jessica. 'I'm in charge of confetti distribution.'

A few minutes later, Samantha and Sebastian came down the sweeping staircase arm in arm, Seb's limp now almost indiscernible. They walked slowly through a tunnel of well-wishers throwing confetti vaguely in their direction, until they emerged into the evening sun of the courtyard, to be surrounded by friends and family.

Samantha looked at a dozen hopeful young women, then turned and tossed her bouquet of blush-pink roses over her head and high into the air. It landed in Jessica's arms, which was greeted with wild laughter and applause.

'God help the man,' said Sebastian as the chauffeur opened the back door of the waiting car.

The ambassador took his daughter in his arms and seemed reluctant to let her go. When he finally relinquished her, he whispered to Seb, 'Please take care of her.'

'For the rest of my life, sir,' said Seb, before joining his wife in the back seat.

The car drove sedately out of the courtyard through the sculpted gates and on to the main road, with several of the younger guests in pursuit.

Mr and Mrs Clifton looked back and continued to wave until they were all out of sight. Sam rested her head on Seb's shoulder.

'Do you remember the last time we were in Amsterdam, my darling?'

'Could I ever forget?'

'When I forgot to mention I was pregnant.'

44

THE TWO MEN SHOOK hands, which helped Sloane to relax.

'It was good of you to come in at such short notice, Mr Sloane,' said Chief Inspector Stokes. 'When a policeman visits someone like you in their office, it can lead to unnecessary gossip among the staff.'

'I can assure you, chief inspector, that I have nothing to hide from anyone, including my staff,' said Sloane as he sat down, leaving the policeman standing. Sloane stared at the large Grundig tape recorder on the table between them. His mind began working overtime as he tried to anticipate what might be on the tape.

'I wasn't suggesting that you have anything to hide,' said Stokes, sitting down opposite Sloane. 'But you may be able to help me by answering one or two questions concerning a case I'm currently working on.'

Sloane clenched his fists below the table, but didn't respond.

'Perhaps you'd be kind enough to listen to this tape, sir.' Stokes leant forward and pressed the play button on the tape recorder.

'Customs office, Heathrow.'

'Put me through to the senior customs officer.'

'May I ask who's calling?'

'No, you may not.'

'I'll see if he's available.' There was a pause before another voice was heard. *'SCO Collier. How can I help you?'*

'If you're interested, I can tell you about some drugs that a passenger will be trying to smuggle in today.'

'Yes, I'm interested. But first, would you tell me your name?'

'The passenger's name is Hakim Bishara. He's well known in the trade, and is travelling on flight 207 from Lagos. He has thirteen ounces of heroin in his overnight bag.'

Sloane remained silent after the tape had come to an end. The chief inspector removed the spool and replaced it with another one. Once again he pressed the play button. Once again he said nothing.

'Is this Adrian Sloane?'

'Depends who's asking.'

'Chief Inspector Mike Stokes. I'm attached to the drug squad at Scotland Yard.'

'How can I help you, Mr Stokes?'

'I'd like to make an appointment to see you, sir.'

'Why?'

'I can't discuss the matter over the phone, sir. Either I could come to you, or you could visit me at Scotland Yard, whichever is more convenient.'

'I'll come to you.'

Sloane shrugged his shoulders.

'I've had both those tapes analysed by an American voice specialist,' said Stokes, 'and he's confirmed that not only were they made by the same person, but from the same telephone.'

'That's ridiculous.'

'Are you sure?' asked the interrogator, his eyes never leaving Sloane.

'Yes, I am, because the telephone call to the customs officer lasted less than three minutes, and is therefore untraceable.'

'How could you possibly know that, Mr Sloane, if it wasn't you who made the call?'

'Because I attended every day of Hakim Bishara's trial and heard all the evidence first hand.'

'You did indeed, sir. And I confess I'm still puzzled about why you did.'

'Because, Mr Stokes, as I'm sure you know, I was the previous chairman of Farthings Bank, and one of my clients at the time was a substantial shareholder, so I was doing no more than my fiduciary duty. You'll need something a little more convincing than that to prove I was involved.'

'Before we go on to discuss the role you played on behalf of your substantial shareholder, and how you were both involved, perhaps I could play the first tape again. I'm going to ask you to listen more carefully this time.'

Sloane could feel the palms of his hands sweating. He wiped them on his trousers as the tape recorder whirred back into action.

'Customs office, Heathrow.'

'Put me through to the senior customs officer.'

'May I ask who's calling?'

'No, you may not.'

'I'll see if he's available.'

Stokes pressed the stop button. 'Listen carefully, Mr Sloane.' The chief inspector pressed the play button once again, and this time Sloane could hear the faint sound of chimes in the background. Stokes pressed Stop.

'Ten o'clock,' he said, his eyes still fixed on Sloane.

'So what?'

'Now I'd like you to listen to the second tape again,' said Stokes as he swapped the cassettes. 'Because I called you in your office at one minute to ten.'

'Is this Adrian Sloane?'

'Depends who's asking.'

A long pause, and this time Sloane couldn't miss the ten chimes. He felt beads of sweat on his forehead and, despite having a handkerchief in his top pocket, made no attempt to wipe them away.

The detective pressed Stop. 'And I can assure you, Mr Sloane, those chimes came from the same clock, which our American expert has confirmed is St Mary-le-Bow, Cheapside, less than a hundred yards from your office.'

'That proves nothing. There must be thousands of offices in the vicinity, and you know it.'

'You're quite right, which is why I requested a court order to allow me to check your phone records for that particular day.'

'Over a hundred people work in the building,' said Sloane. 'It could have been any one of them.'

'On a Saturday morning, Mr Sloane? I don't think so. In any case, it wasn't the bank's number that I called, but your private line, and you answered it. Don't you get the distinct feeling that these coincidences are beginning to mount up?'

Sloane stared defiantly back at him.

'Perhaps the time has come,' said Stokes, 'for us to consider yet another coincidence.' He opened a file in front of him and studied a long list of phone numbers. 'Just before you phoned the customs office at Heathrow—'

'I never phoned the customs office at Heathrow.'

'You made a call to Bristol 698 337,' Stokes continued, ignoring the outburst, 'which is the office of Mr Desmond Mellor, who I understand is the client you mentioned as having substantial shareholdings in Farthings Bank at the time of the Bishara trial. Yet another coincidence?'

'That proves nothing. I sit on the board of Mellor Travel, of which he's the chairman, so we always have a lot to discuss.'

'I'm sure you do, Mr Sloane. So perhaps you can explain why you made a second call to Mr Mellor the moment you'd put the phone down on Mr Collier.'

'It's possible I couldn't get through to Mellor the first time and I was making a second attempt.'

'If you didn't get through the first time, why did that call last twenty-eight minutes and three seconds?'

'It could have been Mr Mellor's secretary who answered the phone. Yes, now I remember. I had a long chat to Miss Castle that morning.'

Stokes looked down at a page in his notebook. 'Mr Mellor's secretary, Miss Angela Castle, has informed us that she was visiting her mother in Glastonbury on that particular Saturday morning, where they both attended a local antiques fair.'

Sloane licked his lips, which were feeling unusually dry.

'Your second call to Mr Mellor's office lasted six minutes and eighteen seconds.'

'That doesn't prove that I spoke to him.'

'I thought you might say that. Which is why I asked Mr Mellor to drop in and see me earlier today. He admitted that he spoke to you twice that morning, but says that he can't remember the details of either conversation.'

'So this has been nothing more than a fishing expedition,' said Sloane. 'All you've come up with is speculation and coincidence. Because one thing's for certain, Mellor would never have taken the bait.'

'You could be right, Mr Sloane. However, I have a feeling neither of you will want this case to come to court. It might well make your colleagues in the City feel there was just one coincidence too many for them to consider doing business with you again.'

'Are you threatening me, Stokes?'

'Certainly not, sir. In fact, I confess I have a problem.' Sloane smiled for the first time. 'I just can't make up my mind which one of you to arrest, and which one of you to release without charge.'

'You're bluffing.'

'Possibly, but I thought I'd give you the first chance to take up my offer to give evidence on behalf of the Crown. Should you turn me down—'

'Never,' said Sloane defiantly.

'Then I have no choice but to go next door and make the same offer to Mr Mellor.'

The sweat was now pouring down Sloane's fleshy cheeks. The chief inspector paused for a moment before saying, 'Shall I give you a few minutes to think about it, Mr Sloane?'

45

'I'M BEGINNING TO believe that Mrs Thatcher will win the next election,' said Emma after returning from an area group meeting.

'Including Bristol Docklands?'

'Almost certainly. We've chosen an impressive candidate and he's going down well with the electorate.'

'Giles won't be pleased about that.'

'He'd be even less pleased if he could see our canvass returns for the West Country, and if things are the same nationally, Margaret will be taking up residence at No.10 in the not-too-distant future. I'll know more after the national chairman's meeting at Central Office, when she'll be addressing us.'

'That sounds like a whole lot of fun,' said Harry.

'Don't mock or I'll have you thrown in the tower.'

'You'd make a rather good governor of the tower.'

'And you and Giles will be the first on the rack.'

'What about Seb?'

'He always votes Conservative,' said Emma.

'Which reminds me,' said Harry, 'he called last night to say he now has to make an appointment to see you, so heaven knows what it's going to be like after the election – that's assuming Thatcher wins.'

'Actually it will be a lot easier after the election as I'm not eligible to stand for a second term as area chairman. So I'll be able to devote more time to the hospital, and I'm rather hoping that in time Seb will be willing to take over as chairman of Barrington's.'

The company needs a breath of fresh air if we're to compete with the latest luxury liners.' Emma gave her husband a kiss.

'Must dash or I'll be late. I'm chairing a hospital sub-committee in an hour's time.'

'Will you be seeing Giles when you're in London? Because if you are—'

'Certainly not. I shall not be consorting with the enemy until after the election, when he'll be back in Opposition.'

—◦—

'We may have a traitor in our camp,' said Pengelly, once they had left the road and he was sure no one could overhear them.

Karin tried not to show how nervous she felt. She daily lived in fear of Pengelly finding out that it was she who was in fact the traitor. She had often shared these anxieties with Baroness Forbes-Watson, who was no longer just her handler but had become a trusted friend and confidante.

'Am I allowed to know who you suspect, comrade director?'

'Yes, because our masters in Moscow want you to be involved in the plan to flush him out. One of our agents in the Ukraine will pass on a particularly sensitive piece of information to agent Julius Kramer, with instructions to brief you. If he fails to do so, we'll know he's working for the other side.'

'If that turns out to be the case, what happens next?'

'Kramer will be ordered back to Moscow and that'll be the last we'll ever hear of him.'

'And if he doesn't report back?'

'We'll track him down and exact the punishment all traitors can expect if they switch sides.'

They continued to walk for a while before Pengelly spoke again. 'Marshal Koshevoi has another job he wants you to do, comrade. Harold Wilson's unexpected resignation as PM has caused considerable speculation, and the party wants us to take advantage of it.'

'Barrington told me Wilson's doctor detected early signs of Alzheimer's and advised him to resign before it became obvious.'

'But he didn't give that as the reason at the time. No doubt because he was advised against it. So we've come up with our own explanation.'

'Which is?'

'That he was always in the pay of the Russians. MI6 found out and he was told that if he didn't resign they'd expose him.'

'But that's farcical, and Marshal Koshevoi must know it.'

'I'm sure he does, but there are enough people on both sides of the House who would be only too willing to believe it.'

'What do you expect me to do?'

'Tell Barrington you've heard the rumour and ask if there could be any truth in it. He'll dismiss it, of course, but you'll have planted the idea in his mind.'

'But surely the public will never swallow it?'

'As Stalin memorably said, comrade, tell a lie often enough and it becomes the truth.'

—◄◦►—

'Hi Ginny, it's Buck Trend.'

Virginia disliked being addressed as Ginny – so common. But when the person who does so also sends you a cheque for $7,500 every month, you learn to grin and bear it.

'I'm phoning to warn you,' continued Buck, 'that our esteemed Governor of Louisiana, the Honourable Hayden Rankin, is planning a visit to London in July. And, according to my sources, he has an appointment to see your ex-husband, Lord Barrington.'

'What could those two possibly have in common?' said Virginia.

'That's what I was hoping you could tell me.'

'Haven't your sources come up with any ideas?'

'Only that Cyrus T. Grant III is a close friend of the governor, as well as being one of his major campaign contributors. So it might be wise if you and little Freddie were out of town when the governor crosses the Atlantic.'

'Don't worry, Freddie will be spending his hols in Scotland, and I'll be in the Bahamas enjoying a well-earned rest.'

'Fine. But if you do find out why the governor wants to see your ex, call me. Because I need to know if he's trying to find a way of stopping your monthly payments, and we wouldn't want that, would we, Ginny?'

—◄o►—

They never discussed anything serious until tea and two slightly burnt crumpets had been served.

'Giles will be under considerable pressure as we get nearer to an election.'

'He visits a different constituency every week,' said Karin.

'Does he still think it's possible for Labour to win again?'

'He assures me they can over breakfast every morning and I'd believe him if he didn't talk in his sleep.'

The baroness laughed. 'Then we'd better prepare ourselves for a spell of the grocer's daughter.'

'Two teas and two burnt crumpets, my lady.'

'Thank you, Stanley.'

'So what's Pengelly up to?' Her voice changed the moment the waiter left.

'Moscow thinks Julius Kramer might be a double agent.'

'Do they indeed?' said the baroness as she dropped a third sugar lump in her tea. 'And what do they intend to do about it?'

'Kramer will be instructed to pass on some highly sensitive information to me, and if he doesn't they'll call him back to Moscow.'

'But if he does, it means they're not testing Kramer, but you. If he doesn't, it means you're in the clear, in which case his life will be in danger and we'll need to take him out of the front line immediately. You mustn't allow yourself to be compromised, Karin, however sensitive that piece of information might be. So once you've briefed me, you should pass it on to Pengelly as quickly as possible.' The baroness took a bite of her crumpet. 'Did Pengelly say anything else I should know about?'

'All agents are being instructed to spread a rumour that the real reason Harold Wilson resigned as prime minister was because MI6 had discovered he was in the pay of the Russians.'

'Then it's time he bought himself a new Gannex mac with all that extra money he must have been earning.' She took another bite before adding, 'It would be funny, except some fools might actually believe it.'

'He also asked me to tell Giles that I'd heard the rumour and see how he reacted.'

'I'll get Sir John to brief Giles on the real reason for Harold's resignation. Mind you, it would have helped if the PM had been willing to admit he'd got Alzheimer's at the time.'

'Do you have anything you want me to pass on?'

'Yes, I think the time has come for your tiresome "father" to be called back to East Germany. So why don't you tell him . . .'

46

'MY LORD.'

'Governor.'

'Swap?'

'Well, it's funny you should mention that,' said Giles. 'While I've never wanted to be a governor, I've always fancied being a senator.'

'And if you held your equivalent post in the Senate, you'd be Majority Leader Barrington.'

'Majority Leader Barrington. I rather like the sound of that.'

'So how much would I have to raise to become Lord Rankin of Louisiana?'

'Not a penny. It would be a political appointment, made on my recommendation to the Prime Minister.'

'No money involved and you didn't even need to be elected.'

'Certainly not.'

'And Britain still doesn't have a constitution or a bill of rights?'

'What a dreadful idea,' said Giles. 'No, we work on legal precedent.'

'And even your head of state isn't elected!'

'Of course not, she's a hereditary monarch, appointed by the Almighty.'

'And you have the nerve to claim you're a democracy.'

'Yes, we do. And just think how much money we save, and you waste, by electing everyone from dog catcher to president, just to prove how democratic you are.'

'You're trying to get off the hook, Giles.'

'All right, then tell me how much you had to raise before you could even consider running for governor?'

'Five, six million. And it's getting more expensive with every election.'

'What did you spend it on?'

'Mostly negative advertising. Letting the electorate know why they shouldn't be voting for the other guy.'

'That's something else we'll never do. Which is another reason our system is more civilized than yours.'

'You may well have a point, my lord, but let's get back to the real world,' said Hayden. 'Because I need your advice.'

'Fire away, Hayden. I was intrigued by your letter and I can't wait to find out how one of your constituents can possibly have come across my ex-wife.'

'Cyrus T. Grant III is one of my oldest friends, and has also been one of my biggest financial backers over the years, so I'm hugely indebted to him. He's a good, kind and decent man, and although I don't know what the T stands for, it might as well be "trusting".'

'If he's that trusting, how did he make his fortune?'

'He didn't. He owes that piece of luck to his grandfather, who founded the canning business that bears his name. Cyrus's father took the company on to the New York Stock Exchange, and his son now lives comfortably off the dividends.'

'And you have the nerve to criticize the hereditary system. But that doesn't explain how this kind, decent and trusting man crossed swords with Virginia.'

'Some five years ago, Cyrus was visiting London and was invited to lunch by someone with the unlikely name of Bofie Bridgwater.'

'I'm afraid Lord Bridgwater is not a convincing argument for the hereditary system. He makes Bertie Wooster look shrewd and decisive.'

'During lunch, Cyrus sat next to Lady Virginia Fenwick and he was clearly overwhelmed by all her "member of the royal family" and "distant niece of the Queen Mother" rubbish. Afterwards, she went shopping with him in Bond Street to buy an engagement ring for his high school sweetheart, Ellie May Campbell, whom he later married. After Cyrus had bought the ring, he invited Lady Virginia back to his suite at the Ritz for tea, and the next thing he remembers is waking up in bed beside her, and the only thing she was wearing was the engagement ring.'

'That's impressive, even by Virginia's standards,' said Giles. 'So what happened next?'

'That was when Cyrus made his first big mistake. Instead of grabbing the ring and telling her to get lost, he took the next flight back to the States. For a while, all he thought he'd lost was the ring, until Lady Virginia turned up at his wedding looking seven months pregnant.'

'Not the sort of wedding present he was hoping for.'

'Gift-wrapped. The next day, Buck Trend, one of the sharpest and meanest lawyers west of the Mississippi, gave Cyrus's in-house lawyer a call, and once again my friend panicked. He ended up instructing his lawyer to settle before he and Ellie May returned from their honeymoon. Trend extracted more than a pound of flesh, and Cyrus ended up paying a million dollars up front, and a further ten thousand a month until the child has completed his education.'

'That's not a bad return for a one-night stand.'

'If it ever was a one-night stand. What Virginia hadn't bargained for was Ellie May Campbell – now Ellie May Grant – who turns out to be cut from the same Scottish cloth as her ladyship. When Cyrus finally confessed to what had taken place in London, Ellie May didn't believe a word of Virginia's story. She hired a Pinkerton detective and sent him across the Atlantic with instructions not to return until he'd found out the truth.'

'And did he come up with anything?' said Giles.

'He reported back that he wasn't convinced Lady Virginia had ever had a child, and that even if she had, there was no reason to believe Cyrus was the father of the Hon Frederick Archibald Iain Bruce Fenwick.'

'A blood test might narrow down the possibility.'

'And it might not. But in any case, while the boy's at pre-prep in Scotland, Cyrus can hardly drop in and ask the headmaster for a sample.'

'But if he contested a paternity suit in open court the judge would have to call for a blood test.'

'Yes, but even if they turned out to share the same blood group it still wouldn't be absolutely conclusive.'

'As I well know,' said Giles, without explanation. 'So how can I help?'

'As Lady Virginia is your ex-wife, Cyrus and I wondered if you could throw any light on what she was up to during the time he was in London.'

'All I can remember is that she'd been having some financial difficulties and had disappeared off the scene for some time. But when she reappeared, she'd moved into a far larger establishment and was once again employing a butler and a housekeeper as well as a nanny. And as for her son, Freddie, he's rarely seen in London. He even spends the school holidays at Fenwick Hall in Scotland.'

'Well, that at least confirms what our detective has been telling us,' said the governor. 'And according to his report, the nanny, a Mrs Crawford, is five foot one in her stockinged feet and weighs about ninety pounds. Although she looks as if she could be blown away by a puff of wind, the detective said he'd prefer to deal with the Mafia than have to face her again.'

'If she's not proving helpful,' said Giles, 'what about all the other people Virginia's employed over the years? Butlers, chauffeurs, housekeepers? Surely one of them must know something and be willing to talk.'

'Our man has already tracked down several of her ladyship's former employees, but none of them is prepared to say a word against her, either because they're being paid to keep quiet or they're simply terrified of her.'

'I was terrified of her too,' admitted Giles. 'So I can't blame them. But don't give up on that front. She's sacked an awful lot of people in her time and she certainly doesn't believe in handing out farewell presents.'

'Cyrus is also terrified of her. But not Ellie May. She's been trying to convince him to stop the payments and call Virginia's bluff.'

'Virginia is not easily bluffed. She's cunning, manipulative and as stubborn as the Democrats' mascot. A dangerous combination that leads her to believe she's always right.'

'What in God's name ever possessed you to marry the woman?'

'Ah, I forgot to mention. She's stunningly beautiful, and when she wants something, she can be irresistibly charming.'

'How do you think she'll react if the payments suddenly dry up?'

'She'll fight like an alley cat. But if Cyrus isn't Freddie's father, she couldn't risk going to court. She would be well aware she could end up in prison for obtaining money under false pretences.'

'I can't believe the earl would be pleased about that,' said Hayden, 'and what about poor Freddie?'

'I don't know,' admitted Giles. 'But I can tell you, there's been no sighting of the Hon Freddie, or the formidable Mrs Crawford, in London recently.'

'So if Cyrus did cut Virginia off, do you think Freddie would suffer?'

'I wouldn't have thought so. But I have a speaking engagement in Scotland next week so if I pick up anything worthwhile I'll let you know.'

'Thank you, Giles. But if you're in Scotland, why don't you just drive up to Fenwick Hall, bang on the front door and ask the earl for his vote?'

'Earls don't have a vote.'

◄о►

'Why haven't I received this month's payment?' demanded Virginia.

'Because I didn't get mine,' said Trend. 'When I called Cyrus's lawyer he told me you wouldn't be getting another red cent. Then he hung up on me.'

'Then let's sue the bastard!' shrieked Virginia. 'And if he doesn't pay up, you can tell his lawyer that Freddie and I will take up residence in Baton Rouge, and we'll see how they like that.'

'Before you book your flight, Ginny, I ought to tell you that I did call back and threaten them with every kind of legal proceedings. Their response was short and to the point. "Your client had better be able to prove that Cyrus T. Grant is Freddie's father, and that she is even the boy's mother."'

'That will be simple enough to confirm. I have the birth certificate and am still in touch with the doctor who delivered Freddie.'

'I pointed all that out, but I couldn't make head nor tail of their response. However, they assured me that you would understand all too well.'

'What are you talking about?'

'They told me that Ellie May Grant has recently employed a new butler and housekeeper for her home in Louisiana, a Mr and Mrs Morton.'

—◄o►—

Comrade Pengelly was ushered into Marshal Koshevoi's massive oak-panelled office. The KGB chief didn't stand to greet him, just gave a dismissive nod to indicate that he should sit.

Pengelly was understandably nervous. You are only summoned to KGB headquarters when you are about to be sacked or promoted, and he wasn't sure which it was going to be.

'The reason I called for you, comrade commander,' said Koshevoi, looking like a bull about to charge, 'is that we have discovered a traitor among your agents.'

'Julius Kramer?' asked Pengelly.

'No, Kramer was a smokescreen. He is completely reliable and totally committed to our cause. Although the British are still under the impression he's working for them.'

'Then who?' said Pengelly, who thought he knew every one of his thirty-one agents.

'Karin Brandt.'

'But she's been passing on some very useful information recently.'

'And we have now discovered the source of that information. It was a tip-off from a most unlikely quarter that gave her away.' Pengelly didn't interrupt. 'I instructed Agent Kramer to inform Brandt that we wanted you to report back to Moscow.'

'And she delivered that message.'

'But not before she had passed it on to someone else.'

'How can you be sure?'

'Tell me the route you took to Moscow.'

'I drove from my home in Cornwall to Heathrow. I took a plane to Manchester, a coach to Newcastle—'

'And from there you flew to Amsterdam, where you took a barge along the Rhine, the Main and the Danube to Vienna.' Pengelly shifted uneasily in his seat. 'You then travelled from Vienna to Warsaw by train, before finally boarding a plane to Moscow. Shadowed every inch of the way by a succession of British agents, the last of whom accompanied you on your flight to Moscow. He didn't even bother to get off the plane before going back to London because he knew exactly where you were going.'

'But how is that possible?'

'Because Brandt informed her English handler that I had ordered you back to Moscow even before she told you about it. Comrade, they literally saw you coming.'

'Then my whole operation is blown apart and there's no point in my returning to England.'

'Unless we turn the situation to our advantage.'

'How do you plan to do that?'

'You will return to England by an equally circuitous route, so they think we have no idea that Brandt has betrayed us. You will then go back to work as usual but, in future, every message we send through Kramer to Brandt, the British will be confident they have intercepted.'

'It will be interesting to see how long we can get away with that before MI6 begin to wonder which side she's on,' said Pengelly.

'The moment they do, it will be time to dispose of her, and then you can return to Moscow.'

'How did you find out she's switched sides?'

'A piece of luck, comrade commander, that we nearly overlooked. There's a member of the House of Lords called Viscount Slaithwaite. A hereditary peer who would be of no particular interest to us, except that he was a contemporary of Burgess, Maclean and Philby at Cambridge. Once he joined the university's Communist Party, we no longer considered recruiting him as an agent, although he'd like you to believe he's the sixth man. Over the years Slaithwaite has regularly passed on information to our embassy which, at best, was out of date and, at worst, planted to mislead us. But then, without having any idea of its significance, he finally came up with gold-dust. He sent a note to say that Lord Barrington's wife – he has no idea that she is one of our agents – was seen regularly in the House of Lords tea room in the company of Baroness Forbes-Watson.'

'Cynthia Forbes-Watson?'

'No less.'

'But I thought MI6 pensioned her off years ago?'

'So did we. But it seems she's been resuscitated to act as Brandt's handler. And what better cover than tea in the House of Lords, while Lord Barrington toils away on the front bench.'

'Baroness Forbes-Watson must be eighty—'

'Eighty-four.'

'She can't go on for much longer.'

'Agreed, but we'll keep the counter operation running for as long as she does.'

'And when she dies?'

'You'll only have one more job to carry out, comrade commander, before you return to Moscow.'

HARRY AND EMMA
CLIFTON

1978

47

THERE WAS A HESITANT tap on the library door. The second in the past seven years.

Harry put down his pen. As Emma was at the hospital and Jessica had returned to London, he could only wonder who would consider interrupting him while he was writing. He swivelled his chair around to face the intruder.

The door opened slowly. Markham appeared in the doorway but didn't enter the room. 'I'm sorry to disturb you, sir, but it's No.10 on the line and apparently it's urgent.'

Harry rose from his chair immediately. He wasn't quite sure why he remained standing when he picked up the phone.

'Please hold on, sir, I'll put you through to the Cabinet Secretary.'

Harry remained standing.

'Mr Clifton, it's Alan Redmayne.'

'Good afternoon, Sir Alan.'

'I rang because I have some wonderful news and I wanted you to be the first to know.'

'Tell me Anatoly Babakov has been released?'

'Not yet, but it can't be long now. I've just had a call from our ambassador in Stockholm to say that the Swedish Prime Minister will be announcing in an hour's time that Mr Babakov has been awarded the Nobel Prize for Literature.'

—◦—

Within moments of the announcement being made, the phone started to ring, and Harry was made aware for the first time what 'off the hook' really meant.

For the next hour he answered questions thrown at him by journalists calling from all over the world.

'Do you think the Russians will finally release Babakov?'

'They should have released him years ago,' responded Harry, 'but at least this will give Mr Brezhnev an excuse to do so now.'

'Will you be going to Stockholm for the ceremony?'

'I hope to be among the audience when Anatoly is presented with the prize.'

'Will you fly to Russia, so you can accompany your friend to Stockholm?'

'He has to be released from jail before anyone can accompany him anywhere.'

Markham reappeared in the doorway, the same anxious look as before on his face. 'The King of Sweden is on the other line, sir.' Harry put down one phone and picked up another. He was surprised to find it wasn't a private secretary on the line, but the King himself.

'I do hope you and Mrs Clifton will be able to attend the ceremony as my personal guests.'

'We'd be delighted to, Your Majesty,' said Harry, hoping he'd used the correct form of address.

In between repeatedly answering the same questions from yet more journalists, Harry broke off to make a call of his own.

'I've just heard the news,' said Aaron Guinzburg. 'I rang you immediately but your phone has been constantly engaged. But no need to worry, I've already been on to the printers and ordered another million copies of *Uncle Joe*.'

'I wasn't calling to ask how many copies you're having printed, Aaron,' snapped Harry. 'Get yourself over to the Lower West Side and take care of Yelena. She'll have no idea how to handle the press.'

'You're right, Harry. Thoughtless of me, sorry. I'm on my way.'

Harry put the phone down to see Markham once again

hovering in the doorway. 'The BBC is asking if you'll be making a statement.'

'Tell them I'll be out in a few minutes.'

He sat back down at his desk, ignored the ringing phone, pushed Inspector Warwick to one side and began to think about the message he wanted to get across. He was aware that he might never be given an opportunity like this again.

When he picked up his pen, the words flowed easily, but then he'd waited a dozen years to be given this chance. He read through his statement, made a couple of emendations, then checked he knew it by heart. He stood up, took a deep breath, straightened his tie and walked out into the hall. Markham, who was clearly enjoying every moment of the unfolding drama, opened the front door and stood aside.

Harry had expected to face a few local reporters but as he stepped out of the door a mob of journalists and photographers surged towards him, all of them shouting at once. He stood on the top step and waited patiently until they'd all realized he wasn't going to say anything before he had their attention.

'This is not a day for celebration,' he began quietly. 'My friend and colleague, Anatoly Babakov, is still languishing in a Russian prison, for the crime of daring to write the truth. The Nobel Prize committee has honoured him, and rightly so, but I will not rest until he is released and can be reunited with his wife Yelena, so they can spend the rest of their days enjoying the freedom that the rest of us take for granted.'

Harry turned and walked back into the house as the journalists continued to holler their questions. Markham closed the door.

─◦─

It was the first time Virginia had ever visited a prison, although over the years one or two of her chums had been incarcerated, and several others certainly should have been.

In truth, she wasn't looking forward to the experience. Mind you, it had solved one problem. She no longer had to pretend that Desmond Mellor had the slightest chance of being awarded a knighthood. 'Sir Desmond' remained the fantasy it had always been.

Unfortunately, it also meant that a regular source of income had dried up. She wouldn't have considered visiting Mellor in prison if her bank manager hadn't kept reminding her about her overdraft. She could only hope that Mellor was still capable of turning red into black, despite being behind bars.

Virginia wasn't altogether certain what Mellor had been charged with. But she wouldn't have been surprised to learn that Adrian Sloane was involved somehow.

She drove down to Arundel just after breakfast as she didn't want anyone to spot her on the train or taking a taxi to Ford Open Prison. She was a few minutes late by the time she drove into the car park but then she'd never intended to be on time. Spending an hour surrounded by a bunch of villains wasn't her idea of how to spend a Sunday afternoon.

After she'd parked her Morris Minor, Virginia made her way to the gatehouse, where she was met in reception by a prison officer. Once she'd been searched, she was asked for proof of her identity. She handed over her driving licence to show she was the Lady Virginia Fenwick, even if the photograph was out of date. The officer ticked her name off the authorized visitors' list, then handed her a key and asked her to deposit all her valuables in a small locker, before she was politely warned that any attempt to pass cash to a prisoner during a visit was a criminal offence and she could be arrested and end up with a six-month jail sentence. She didn't tell the officer that she was rather hoping it would be the other way round.

Once she had been handed a key and placed her handbag and jewellery in the small grey locker, she accompanied a female officer down a long, fiercely lit corridor before being ushered into a sparsely furnished room with a dozen or so tables, each surrounded by one red and three blue chairs.

Virginia spotted Desmond sitting on a red chair in the far corner of the room. She walked across to join him, her first sentence already prepared.

'I'm sorry it's come to this,' Virginia said, as she took the seat opposite him. 'And I'd just heard from his grace the Duke of Hertford that your knighthood—'

'Cut the crap, Virginia. We've only got forty-three minutes left, so let's dispense with the platitudes and get down to why I needed to see you. How much do you know about why I'm in here?'

'Almost nothing,' replied Virginia, who was just as relieved as Desmond that the case hadn't been reported in the national press.

'I was arrested and charged with perverting the course of justice, but not until Sloane had turned Queen's evidence, leaving me with no choice but to plead guilty to a lesser offence. I ended up with an eighteen-month sentence, which should be reduced to seven on appeal, so I'll be out in a few weeks' time. But I don't intend to sit around waiting until I'm released to get my revenge on that bastard Sloane, which is why I needed to see you.'

Virginia concentrated on what he had to say, as she clearly couldn't take notes.

'This place is not so much an open prison,' continued Mellor, 'as an extension of the Open University, with crime the only subject on the curriculum. And I can tell you, several of my fellow inmates are postgraduates, so Sloane isn't going to get away with it. But I can't do a lot about it while I'm still locked up in here.'

'I'll do whatever I can to help,' said Virginia, scenting another pay day.

'Good, because it won't take much of your time, and you'll be well rewarded.'

Virginia smiled.

'You'll find a small package in . . .'

◄○►

Only Harry seemed surprised by the press coverage the following morning. The newspapers were dominated by the one photograph they had of Babakov, standing next to Stalin. The inside pages reminded readers of the campaign Harry had been conducting on behalf of PEN for the past decade, and the editorials didn't hold back on their demands that Brezhnev should set the Nobel Laureate free.

But Harry feared the Russians would still procrastinate, secure in their belief that, given time, the story would eventually go away, to be replaced by another shooting star that caught the press's fickle attention. But the story didn't go away because the Prime Minister stoked the dying embers until they burst back into flame when he informed the world's press that he would raise the subject of Babakov's incarceration with the Soviet leader when they met at their planned summit in Moscow.

At the same time, Giles put down several written questions to the Foreign Secretary and initiated an opposition day debate in the Lords. But, he warned Harry that when it came to international summits, the mandarins would have arranged the agenda well in advance; the questions that would be asked, the replies that would be forthcoming and even the wording of the final press statement would have been agreed long before the two leaders posed for photographs on the opening day.

However, Giles did get a call from his old friend Walter Scheel, the former West German Foreign Minister, to let him know the Russians had been taken by surprise by the worldwide interest in Babakov, and were beginning to wonder if releasing him wouldn't be the easy way out, as few of their countrymen still had any illusions about how oppressive the Stalin regime had been. And prize or no prize, *Uncle Joe* was never going to be published in the Soviet Union.

When the Prime Minister returned from Moscow four days later, he didn't talk about the new trade agreement between the two countries or the proposed reductions in strategic nuclear missiles, or even the exciting cultural exchanges which included the National Theatre and the Bolshoi Ballet. Instead, Jim Callaghan's first words to the waiting press as he stepped off the aircraft were to announce that the Russian leader had agreed that Anatoly Babakov would be released within a few weeks, well in time for him to attend the prize-giving ceremony in Sweden.

An official from the Foreign Office called Harry at home the following morning to let him know that the Russians had refused to issue him with a visa so he could fly to Moscow and accompany Babakov to Stockholm. Unperturbed, Harry booked a seat on a flight that would arrive at Arlanda airport shortly before the Russian jet landed, so they could meet up as Anatoly stepped off the plane.

Emma revelled in Harry's triumph, and almost forgot to tell him that the *Health Services Journal* had named the Bristol Royal Infirmary as its hospital of the year. In its citation, it highlighted the role played by Mrs Emma Clifton, the chairman of the trustees, and in particular her grasp of the problems facing the NHS and her commitment to both patients and staff. It ended by saying that she would not be easy to replace.

This only served to remind Emma that her time as chairman was drawing to a close, as you were not allowed to serve on a public body for more than five years. She was beginning to wonder what she'd do with her time now that Sebastian had agreed to take over as chairman of Barrington's Shipping.

◄○►

The following morning, Virginia boarded a train to Temple Meads. On arrival in Bristol she hailed a cab, and when the driver pulled up outside Desmond Mellor's office a few minutes later, it was clear she was expected.

Miss Castle, Mellor's long-suffering secretary, showed her into the chairman's office. Once she'd closed the door behind her and Virginia was alone, she carried out Desmond's instructions to the letter. On the wall behind his desk was a large oil painting of stick figures dashing backwards and forwards. She took the picture down to reveal a small safe embedded in the wall, entered the eight-digit code she'd written down within moments of leaving the prison and extracted a small package that was exactly where Desmond had said it would be.

Virginia placed the package in her handbag, locked the safe door, swivelled the dial around several times and hung the painting back on the wall. She then re-joined Angela in her office but turned down the offer of a coffee and asked her to order a taxi. She was back out on the street less than fifteen minutes after she'd entered the building.

The taxi dropped her back at Temple Meads, where she caught the first train to London, so she could keep an appointment in Soho later that evening.

◄◦►

Harry had to abandon William Warwick and any thought of his publisher's deadline as he was now spending every waking hour preparing for his trip to Sweden. Aaron Guinzburg accompanied Yelena when she flew over from the States to stay with Harry and Emma at the Manor House, before travelling on to Sweden.

Harry was delighted to see that Yelena had put on a few pounds, and now even seemed to have more than one dress. He also noticed that every time Anatoly's name was mentioned, her eyes lit up.

During the final week before they were due to fly, Harry spent some considerable time guiding Yelena through what the ceremony would involve. But she only seemed interested in one thing – being reunited with her husband.

When they finally set off from the Manor House to drive to Heathrow, a convoy of press vehicles followed them throughout the entire journey. As Yelena and Harry walked into the terminal, the waiting passengers stood aside and applauded.

After the Nobel ceremony, Anatoly and Yelena would fly to England, where they would spend a few days at the Manor House before Aaron Guinzburg accompanied them back to the States. Aaron had already warned Yelena that the American press corps were just as keen to welcome the new Nobel Laureate, and Mayor Ed Koch was talking about holding a ticker-tape parade in Anatoly's honour.

◄◦►

Virginia didn't care much for Soho, with its crowded bars, noisy betting shops and sleazy striptease joints, but she hadn't chosen the venue. Her contact had offered to come to Onslow Gardens but when she heard the man speak, she thought better of it. The telephone is cruel on class.

She arrived outside the King's Arms in Brewer Street, just before 7.30 p.m., and asked the taxi driver to wait for her, as she had no intention of hanging around any longer than necessary.

When she pulled open the door and stepped inside the noisy, smoke-filled room, she couldn't miss him. A short, squat man who wasn't even wearing a tie. He was standing at the end of the bar, incongruously clutching a Harrods bag. As she walked towards him, several pairs of eyes followed her progress. She wasn't the usual kind of skirt who frequented their pub. Virginia came to a halt in front of the squat man and managed a smile. He returned the compliment, only proving that he hadn't visited a dentist recently. Virginia felt she had not been put on earth to mix with hoi-polloi, let alone the criminal classes, but another letter from her bank manager that morning had helped to convince her that she should carry out Mellor's instructions.

Without a word, she removed the small brown package from her handbag and, as agreed, exchanged it for the Harrods bag. She then turned and left the pub without a word being spoken. She only began to relax when the taxi had re-joined the evening traffic.

Virginia didn't look inside the bag until she had closed and double-locked the front door of her home in Onslow Gardens. She took out a larger package, which she left unopened. After a light supper, she retired to bed early, but didn't sleep.

◄○►

After the plane had taxied to a halt at Arlanda airport, an emissary from the Royal Palace was waiting to greet them at the bottom of the steps, with a personal message from King Carl Gustaf of Sweden. His Majesty hoped that Mrs Babakova and her husband would stay at the palace as his guests.

Harry, Emma and Mrs Babakova were escorted to the airport's Royal Lounge, where the reunion would take place. A television in the corner of the room was showing live coverage of the camera crews, journalists and photographers assembled on the tarmac waiting to greet the new Nobel Laureate.

Although several bottles of champagne were opened during the next hour, Harry limited himself to one glass, while Yelena, who couldn't sit still, didn't touch a drop. Harry explained to Emma that he wanted to be 'stone cold sober' when Anatoly stepped off the plane. He checked his watch every few minutes. The long years of waiting were finally coming to an end.

Suddenly a cheer went up, and Harry looked out of the window to see an Aeroflot 707 approaching through the clouds. They all stood by the window to watch the plane as it landed and taxied to a halt in front of them.

Steps were manoeuvred into place and a red carpet rolled out. Moments later the cabin door swung open. A stewardess appeared on the top step and stood aside to allow the passengers to disembark. Television cameras began to whirr, photographers jostled for a clear view of Anatoly Babakov as he stepped off the plane and journalists had their pens poised.

And then Harry spotted a lone reporter, who had withdrawn from the melee around the steps and turned her back on the aircraft. She was speaking straight to camera, no longer taking any interest in the disembarking passengers. Harry walked across the room to the television and turned up the volume.

'We have just received a news flash from the Russian news agency, Tass. It is reporting that the Nobel Laureate Anatoly Babakov was rushed to hospital earlier this morning after suffering a stroke. He died a few minutes ago. I repeat . . .'

48

YELENA BABAKOVA collapsed, both mentally and physically, when she heard the news of her husband's death. Emma rushed to her side and took the broken woman in her arms.

'I need an ambulance, quickly,' she told an equerry, who picked up the nearest phone.

Harry knelt by his wife's side. 'God help her,' he said, as Emma checked her pulse.

'Her heart is weak, but I suspect the real problem is she no longer has any reason to live.'

The door swung open and two paramedics entered the room carrying a stretcher, on to which they gently lifted Mrs Babakova. The equerry whispered something to one of them.

'I've instructed them to take Mrs Babakova straight to the palace,' he told Harry and Emma. 'It has a private medical wing, with a doctor and two nurses always in attendance.'

'Thank you,' said Emma, as one of the paramedics placed an oxygen mask over Yelena's face before they lifted the stretcher and carried her out of the room. Emma held her hand as they progressed slowly down a corridor and out of the building, where an ambulance, with its back doors already open, awaited them.

'His Majesty wondered if you and Mr Clifton would be willing to stay at the palace, so you can be near Mrs Babakova once she regains consciousness.'

'Of course. Thank you,' said Emma, as she and Harry joined Yelena in the back of the ambulance.

Emma didn't let go of Yelena's hand during the thirty-minute journey, accompanied by police outriders neither even realized were there. The palace gates swung open to allow the ambulance to enter and it came to a halt in a large cobbled courtyard, from where a doctor guided the paramedics to the hospital wing. Yelena was lifted off the stretcher and on to a bed that was normally only occupied by patients who'd spilt blue blood.

'I'd like to stay with her,' said Emma, who still hadn't let go of her hand.

The doctor nodded. 'She's suffering from severe shock and her heart is weak, which is hardly surprising. I'm going to give her an injection so she can at least get some sleep.'

Emma noticed that the equerry had joined them in the room but he said nothing while Yelena was being examined.

'His Majesty hopes you will join him in the drawing room when you're ready,' said the equerry.

'There's not much more you can do here at the moment,' said the doctor once his patient had fallen into a deep sleep.

Emma nodded. 'But once we've seen the King, I'd like to come straight back.'

The silent equerry led Harry and Emma out of the hospital wing and through a dozen gilded rooms, whose walls were covered with paintings both of them would normally have wanted to stop and admire. The equerry finally came to a halt outside a floor-to-ceiling set of Wedgwood-blue sculpted double doors. He knocked, and the doors were pulled open by two liveried footmen. The King stood the moment his guests entered the room.

Emma recalled the occasion when the Queen Mother had visited Bristol to launch the *Buckingham*; wait until you're spoken to, never ask a question. She curtsied while Harry bowed.

'Mr and Mrs Clifton, I'm sorry we have to meet in such unhappy circumstances. But how fortunate Mrs Babakova is to have such good friends by her side.'

'The medical team arrived very quickly,' said Emma, 'and couldn't have done a better job.'

'That is indeed a compliment, coming from you, Mrs Clifton,' said the King, as he ushered them both towards two comfortable chairs. 'And what a cruel blow you have been dealt, Mr Clifton, after spending so many years campaigning for your friend's release, only to have his life snatched away when he was about to receive the ultimate accolade.'

The door opened and a footman appeared carrying a large silver tray laden with tea and cakes.

'I arranged for some tea, which I hope is acceptable.' Emma was surprised when the King picked up the teapot and began to pour. 'Milk and sugar, Mrs Clifton?'

'Just milk, sir.'

'And you, Mr Clifton?'

'The same, sir.'

'Now, I must confess,' said the King once he had poured himself a cup, 'I had an ulterior motive for wanting to see you both privately. I have a problem that frankly only the two of you can solve. The Nobel Prize ceremony is one of the highlights of the Swedish calendar, and I enjoy the privilege of presiding over the awards, as my father and grandfather did before me. Mrs Clifton, we must hope that Mrs Babakova has recovered sufficiently by tomorrow evening to feel able to accept the prize on her husband's behalf. I suspect it will take all your considerable skills to persuade her that she is up to carrying out such a task. But I wouldn't want her to spend the rest of her days unaware of the affection and respect in which her husband is held by the people of Sweden.'

'If it's at all possible, sir, be assured I'll do my damnedest.' Emma regretted the word the moment she'd uttered it.

'I suspect your damnedest is pretty formidable, Mrs Clifton.' They both laughed. 'And Mr Clifton, I need your help with an even more demanding challenge, which if I had to ask you on bended knee I would happily do.' He paused to take a sip of tea. 'The highlight of tomorrow's ceremony would have been Mr Babakov's acceptance speech. I can think of no one better qualified, or more appropriate, to take his place for the occasion, and I have a feeling he would be the first to agree with me. However, I realize such a request would be onerous at the best of times, and I will of course understand if you feel unable to consider it at such short notice.'

Harry didn't reply immediately. Then he recalled the three days he'd spent in a prison cell with Anatoly Babakov, and the twenty years he hadn't.

'I'd be honoured to represent him, sir, although no one could ever take his place.'

'A nice distinction, Mr Clifton, and I'm most grateful because, as a feeble orator myself, who has three speech writers to carry out the task of preparing my words, I am only too aware of the challenge I have set you. With that in mind, I will detain you no longer. I suspect you will need every minute between now and tomorrow evening to prepare.'

Harry rose, not having touched his tea. He bowed again, before accompanying Emma out of the room. When the doors opened, they found the equerry waiting for them. This time he led them in a different direction.

'His Majesty has put this room aside for you, Mr and Mrs Clifton,' he said as they came to a halt outside a door which another footman opened to reveal a large corner suite. They walked in to find a desk and a large pile of paper, as well as a dozen of Harry's favourite pens, a double bed turned down and a second table laid for supper.

'The King can't have been in much doubt that I would agree to his request,' said Harry.

'I wonder how many people turn down a king,' said Emma.

'You will have two secretaries at your disposal, Mr Clifton,' said the equerry, 'and if there is anything else you require, a foot-man will be waiting outside the door with no other purpose than to carry out your slightest wish. And now, if there is nothing else you need, I will accompany Mrs Clifton back to the hospital wing.'

◄○►

During the next twenty-four hours, Harry managed to fill three waste-paper baskets with rejected material, devour several plates of meatballs and far too many freshly baked bread rolls, sleep for a couple of hours and take a cold shower, by which time he had completed the first draft of his speech.

Somewhere in between, the King's personal valet took away his suit, shirt and shoes, and they were returned an hour later, looking even crisper and cleaner than they had on his son's wedding day. For a moment, and only a moment, Harry experienced what it was like to be a king.

Secretaries appeared and disappeared as each new draft was produced and, like his books, every page was worked on for at least an hour, so that by four o'clock that afternoon he was checking through the twelfth draft, changing only the occasional word. After he had turned the last page, he collapsed on to the bed and fell asleep.

◄○►

When Harry woke, he could hear a bath being run. He climbed off the bed, put on a dressing gown and slippers and padded into the bathroom to find Emma testing the water.

'How's Yelena?' were his first words.

'I'm not sure she'll ever fully recover. But I think I finally managed to persuade her to attend the ceremony. What about you? Have you finished your speech?'

'Yes, but I'm not sure it's any good.'

'You never are, darling. I read the most recent draft while you were asleep, and I think it's inspired. I have a feeling it will resonate far beyond these walls.'

As Harry stepped into the bath he wondered if Emma was right, or if he should cross out the final paragraph and replace it with a more traditional ending. He still hadn't made up his mind by the time he finished shaving.

He returned to his desk and checked through the latest draft, but made only one small change, replacing 'magnificent' with 'heroic'. He then underlined the last two words of each paragraph to allow him to look up at the audience, so that when he looked back down, he would immediately find his place. Harry dreaded experiencing the same problem he'd suffered at his mother's funeral. Finally he added the word 'mandate' to the last sentence, but still wondered if the ending was too great a risk and he should scrap it. He walked across to the door, opened it and asked the waiting secretary to type the speech up yet again, but this time double-spaced on A5 cards, in large enough print for him not to have to rely on glasses. She'd run off even before he had time to thank her.

'Perfect timing,' said Emma, turning her back on Harry as he returned to the room. He walked over to her and zipped up a long crimson evening gown he'd never seen before.

'You look stunning,' he said.

'Thank you, my darling. If you don't intend to deliver your speech in a dressing gown, perhaps it's time for you to get dressed too.'

Harry dressed slowly, rehearsing some of the speech's key lines. But when it came to tying his white tie, Emma had to come to his rescue. She stood behind him as they both looked in the mirror and she managed it first time.

'How do I look?' he asked.

'Like a penguin,' she said, giving him a hug. 'But a very handsome penguin.'

'Where's my speech?' said Harry nervously, looking at his watch.

As if they'd heard him, there was a knock at the door and the secretary handed him the final draft.

'The King is downstairs waiting for you, sir.'

—◦—

That same morning, Virginia caught the 8.45 from Paddington to Temple Meads, arriving in Bristol a couple of hours later. She still had no idea what was in either package, and she was impatient to complete her side of the bargain and return to something like normality. Once again, Miss Castle unlocked the chairman's office, and left her alone. Virginia took down the oil painting she didn't much care for, entered the safe's code and placed the large package where the smaller one had previously been.

She had considered opening both packages, and even ignoring Mellor's instructions, but hadn't done so, for three reasons. The thought of what revenge Mellor might exact when he was released in a few weeks' time; the possibility of even more largesse, once Mellor had his feet back under the boardroom table; and, perhaps the most compelling, Virginia hated Sloane even more than she despised Mellor.

She locked the safe, returned the painting to the wall and joined Miss Castle in her office. 'When are you next expecting Mr Sloane?'

'You can never be sure,' said Miss Castle. 'He often turns up unannounced, stays for a few hours, then leaves.'

'Has he ever asked you for the code to Mr Mellor's private safe?'

'Several times.'

'What did you tell him?'

'The truth. I didn't even know Mr Mellor had a private safe.'

'If he should ask you again, tell him that I'm the only other person who knows the code.'

'Certainly, my lady.'

'And I think you have something for me, Miss Castle.'

'Oh, yes.' The secretary unlocked the top drawer of her desk, took out a thick white envelope and handed it to Lady Virginia.

This package she did open, but not until she was locked into a first-class lavatory on the train to Paddington. As promised, it contained a thousand pounds in cash. She only hoped Desmond would ask her to visit him again, and in the not-too-distant future.

49

FOUR OUTRIDERS FROM the royal motor pool led a convoy of vehicles out of the palace gates and made their way towards the city centre. King Carl Gustaf and Queen Silvia travelled in the first car, while Prince Philip and the two princesses were in the second, with Yelena, Harry and Emma in the third.

A large crowd had gathered outside the town hall, and cheers broke out when the King's car came into sight. The royal equerry and a young ADC leapt out of the fourth car even before the first had come to a halt and were standing to attention when the King stepped out on to the pavement. King Carl Gustaf was met on the steps of the town hall by Ulf Adelsohn, the Mayor of Stockholm, who accompanied Their Majesties into the building.

When the King entered the great hall, half a dozen trumpeters nestling in the archways high above them struck up a fanfare, and three hundred guests – the men in white tie and tails, the women in brilliantly coloured gowns – rose to greet the royal party. Yelena, Emma and Harry were guided to three chairs in the middle of the row behind the King.

Once Harry was seated, he began to study the layout of the room. There was a raised platform at the front, with a wooden lectern placed at its centre. Looking down from the lectern, a speaker would see eleven high-backed blue velvet chairs set out in a semi-circle, where that year's Laureates would be seated. But, on this occasion, one of the chairs would be left empty.

Harry glanced up at the packed balcony, where there was no sign of an empty seat. But then, this was not one of those occasions you might decide to miss because you'd received a better offer.

The trumpets sounded a second time to announce the arrival of the Nobel Laureates, who processed into the hall to warm applause and took their places in the semi-circle of seats.

Once everyone was seated, Hans Christiansen, the chairman of the Swedish Academy, made his way up on to the stage and took his place behind the lectern. He looked up at, for him, a familiar scene, before he began his speech, welcoming the prize-winners and guests.

Harry glanced nervously down at the cards resting in his lap. He re-read his opening paragraph and felt the same raw emotion he always experienced just before making a speech: I wish I was anywhere but here.

'Sadly,' continued Christiansen, 'this year's winner of the Nobel Prize for Literature, the poet and essayist Anatoly Baba-kov, cannot be with us this evening. He suffered a severe stroke yesterday morning, and tragically died on his way to hospital. However, we are privileged to have with us Mr Harry Clifton, a close friend and colleague of Mr Babakov's, who has agreed to speak on his behalf. Will you please welcome to the stage, the distinguished author and President of English PEN, Mr Harry Clifton.'

Harry rose from his place and made his way slowly up on to the stage. He placed his speech on the lectern and waited for the generous applause to die down.

'Your Majesties, Your Royal Highnesses, distinguished Nobel Laureates, ladies and gentlemen, you see standing before you a rude mechanical who has no right to be in such august company. But today the paperback has the privilege of representing a limited edition, who has recently joined your ranks.

'Anatoly Babakov was a unique man, who was willing to sacrifice his life to create a masterpiece, which the Swedish Academy has acknowledged by awarding him literature's highest accolade. *Uncle Joe* has been published in thirty-seven languages and in one hundred and twenty-three countries, but it still cannot be read in the author's native tongue, or in his homeland.

'I first heard of Anatoly Babakov's plight when I was an undergraduate at Oxford and was introduced to his lyrical poetry that allowed one's imagination to soar to new heights, and his insightful novella, *Moscow Revisited*, evoked a sense of that great city in a way I have never experienced before or since.

'Some years passed before I once again became acquainted with Anatoly Babakov, as President of English PEN. Anatoly had been arrested and sentenced to twenty years' imprisonment. His crime? Writing a book. PEN mounted a worldwide campaign to have this literary giant released from an out-of-sight – but not out-of-mind – gulag in Siberia, so that he could be reunited with his wife, Yelena, whom I'm delighted to tell you is with us this evening, and will later receive her husband's prize on his behalf.'

A burst of sustained applause allowed Harry to relax, look up and smile at Anatoly's widow.

'When I first visited Yelena in the tiny three-room flat in Pittsburgh in which she was living in exile, she told me she had secreted the only surviving copy of *Uncle Joe* in an antiquarian bookshop on the outskirts of Leningrad. She entrusted me with the responsibility of retrieving the book from its hiding place and bringing it back to the West, so that it could finally be published.

'As soon as I could, I flew to Leningrad and went in search of a bookshop hidden in the backstreets of that beautiful city. I found *Uncle Joe* concealed in the dust jacket of a Portuguese translation of *A Tale of Two Cities*, next to a copy of *Daniel Deronda*. Worthy bedfellows. Having captured my prize I returned to the airport, ready to fly home in triumph.

'But I had underestimated the Soviet regime's determination to stop anyone reading *Uncle Joe*. The book was found in my luggage and I was immediately arrested and thrown in jail. My crime? Attempting to smuggle a seditious and libellous work out of Russia. To convince me of the gravity of my offence, I was placed in the same cell as Anatoly Babakov, who had been ordered to persuade me to sign a confession stating that his book was a work of fiction, and that he had never worked in the Kremlin as Stalin's personal interpreter but had been nothing more than a humble schoolteacher in the suburbs of Moscow. Humble he was, but an apologist for the regime he was not. If he had succeeded in convincing me to repeat this fantasy, the authorities had promised him that a year would be knocked off his sentence.

'The rest of the world now acknowledges that Anatoly Babakov not only worked alongside Stalin for thirteen years, but that every word he wrote in *Uncle Joe* was a true and accurate account of that totalitarian regime.

'Having destroyed the book, the inheritors of that regime then set about attempting to destroy the man who wrote it. The award of the Nobel Prize for Literature to Anatoly Babakov shows how lamentably they failed and ensures that he will never be forgotten.'

During the prolonged applause that followed, Harry looked up to see Emma smiling at him.

'I spent fifteen years attempting to get Anatoly released, and when I finally succeeded it turned out to be a pyrrhic victory. But even when we were locked up in a prison cell together, Anatoly didn't waste a precious second seeking my sympathy, but spent every waking moment reciting the contents of his masterpiece, while I, like a voracious pupil, devoured his every word.

'When we parted, he to return to the squalor of a gulag in Siberia, me to the comfort of a manor house in the English countryside, I once again possessed a copy of the book. But this time it was not locked in a suitcase, but in my mind, from where the authorities could not confiscate it. As soon as the wheels of the plane had lifted off from Russian soil, I began to write down the master's words. First on BOAC headed paper, then on the backs of menus and finally on rolls of toilet paper, which was all that was still available.'

Laughter broke out in the hall, which Harry hadn't anticipated.

'But allow me to tell you a little about the man. When Anatoly Babakov left school, he won the top scholarship to the Moscow Foreign Languages Institute, where he studied English. In his final year, he was awarded the Lenin Medal, which ironically sealed his fate, because it gave Anatoly the opportunity to work in the Kremlin. Not a job offer you turn down unless you wish to spend the rest of your life unemployed, or worse.

'Within a year, he unexpectedly found himself serving as the Russian leader's principal translator. It didn't take him long to realize that the genial image Stalin portrayed to the world was merely a mask concealing the evil reality that the Soviet dictator was a thug and a murderer, who would happily sacrifice the lives of tens of thousands of his people if it prolonged his survival as chairman of the party and President of the Presidium.

'For Anatoly, there was no escape, except when he returned home each night to be with his beloved wife, Yelena. In secret, he began working on a project that was to become a feat of physical endurance and rigorous scholarship, the like of which few of us could begin to comprehend. While he worked in the Kremlin by day, by night he set down his experiences on paper. He learnt the text by heart, then destroyed any proof his words had ever existed. Can you begin to imagine what courage it took to abandon his lifelong ambition to be a published author for an anonymous book that was stored in his head?

'And then Stalin died, a fate that even dictators cannot escape. At last Anatoly believed that the book he had worked on for so many years could be published, and the world would discover the truth. But the truth was not what the Soviet authorities wanted the world to discover, so even before *Uncle Joe* reached the bookshops, every single copy was destroyed. Even the press on which it had been printed was smashed to pieces. A show trial followed, when the author was sentenced to twenty years' hard labour and transported to the depths of Siberia to ensure that never again could he cause the regime any embarrassment. Thank God that Samuel Beckett, John Steinbeck, Hermann Hesse and Rabindranath Tagore, all winners of the Nobel Prize for literature, weren't born in the Soviet Union, or we might never have been able to read their masterpieces.

'How appropriate that the Swedish Academy has chosen Anatoly Babakov to be the recipient of this year's award. Because its founder, Alfred Nobel,' Harry paused for a moment to acknowledge the garlanded statue of Nobel that rested on a plinth behind him, 'wrote in his will that this prize should not be awarded for literary excellence alone, but for work that "embodies an ideal". One wonders if there can ever have been a more appropriate recipient of this award.

'And so we come together this evening to honour a remarkable man, whose death will not diminish his life's achievement, but will only help to ensure that it will endure. Anatoly Babakov possessed a gift that we lesser mortals can only aspire to. An author whose heroism will surely survive the whirligig of time, and who now joins his immortal fellow countrymen Dostoyevsky, Tolstoy, Pasternak and Solzhenitsyn as their equal.'

Harry paused, looked up at the audience, and waited for that moment before he knew the spell would be broken. And then, almost in a whisper, he said, 'It takes an heroic figure to re-write history so that future generations might know the truth and benefit from his sacrifice. Quite simply, Anatoly Babakov fulfilled the ancient prophecy: cometh the hour, cometh the man.'

The whole audience rose as one, assuming that the speech had ended. Although Harry continued to grip the sides of the lectern, it was some time before they realized he had more to say. One by one they resumed their seats, until the acclamation of the throng had been replaced by an expectant silence. Only then did Harry take a fountain pen from an inside pocket, unscrew the cap and hold the pen high in the air. 'Anatoly Yuryevich Babakov, you have proved to every dictator who ever ruled without the people's mandate that the pen is mightier than the sword.'

King Carl Gustaf was the first to rise from his place, take out his fountain pen and hold it high in the air before repeating, 'The pen is mightier than the sword.' Within moments, the rest of the audience followed suit, as Harry left the stage and returned to his seat, almost deafened by the prolonged cheers that accompanied him. He finally had to lean forward and beg the King to sit down.

A second cheer, every bit as tumultuous, followed when Yelena Babakova stepped forward on her husband's behalf to accept the Nobel medal and the citation from the King.

Harry hadn't slept the night before because of the fear of failure. He didn't sleep that night because of the triumph of success.

50

THE FOLLOWING MORNING, Harry, Emma and Yelena joined the King for breakfast.

'Last night was a triumph,' said Carl Gustaf, 'and the Queen and I wondered if you'd like to spend a few days in Stockholm as our guests. I'm assured this is the best hotel in town.'

'That's very kind of you, sir,' said Emma, 'but I'm afraid I have a hospital to run, not to mention the family business.'

'And it's time I got back to William Warwick,' said Harry. 'That is, if I'm still hoping to meet my deadline.'

There was a gentle tap on the door and a moment later the equerry appeared. He bowed before he spoke to the King.

Carl Gustaf raised a hand. 'I think, Rufus, it might save time if you were to speak in English.'

'As you wish, sir.' He turned to Harry. 'I've just had a call from Sir Curtis Keeble, the British Ambassador in Moscow, to say that the Russians have relented and granted you, your wife and Mrs Babakova twenty-four-hour visas so you can attend Laureate Babakov's funeral.'

'That's wonderful news,' said Emma.

'But as always with the Russians, there are caveats,' the equerry added.

'Like what?' said Harry.

'You will be met off the plane by the ambassador and driven directly to St Augustine's church on the outskirts of Moscow, where the funeral will take place. Once the service is over, you must go straight back to the airport and leave the country immediately.'

Yelena, who hadn't spoken until then, simply said, 'We accept their terms.'

'Then you'll need to leave now,' said the equerry, 'because the only flight to Moscow today departs in an hour and a half.'

'Have a car ready to take them to the airport,' said Carl Gustaf. Turning to Yelena, he added, 'Your husband could not have been better represented, Mrs Babakova. Please return to Stockholm as my guest whenever you wish. Mr Clifton, Mrs Clifton, I will be eternally in your debt. I would make a speech, but as you have a plane to catch, it would be neither adequate nor appropriate. *Hang not a thread on protocol, and be gone.*'

Harry smiled and bowed for a different reason.

The three of them returned to their rooms to find their cases already packed, and a few minutes later they were being escorted to a waiting car.

'I could get used to this,' said Emma.

'Don't,' said Harry.

When Yelena walked into the airport on Harry's arm, passengers took out their pens, biros, pencils and held them in the air as she passed by.

During the flight to Moscow, Harry was so exhausted he finally fell asleep.

⊸◦⊷

Virginia wasn't surprised to receive a call from Adrian Sloane. He didn't waste any time getting to the point.

'You probably know that the board have asked me to take over as chairman of Mellor Travel while Desmond is . . . away, if you'll forgive the euphemism.'

Not with his blessing, Virginia was about to say, but she kept her counsel.

'Miss Castle tells me you're the only other person who knows the code to Desmond's safe.'

'That is correct.'

'I need to get hold of some papers for the next board meeting.

When I visited Desmond last week at Ford, he told me that they were in the safe and you could give me the code.'

'Why didn't he give it to you himself?' asked Virginia innocently.

'He didn't want to risk it. Said there were listening devices in his cell that could pick up every word we said.'

Virginia smiled at his simple mistake. 'I'll be happy to give you the code, Adrian, but not until you've paid me the twenty-five thousand pounds you promised to help cover my legal bills when I sued Emma Clifton. A drop in the ocean, if I recall your exact words.'

'Give me the code, and I'll transfer the full amount to your account immediately.'

'That's very considerate of you, Adrian, but I don't think I'll risk it a second time. I'll tell you the code, but only after you've transferred twenty-five thousand pounds to my account at Coutts.'

When the bank confirmed that the money had been transferred, Virginia kept her side of the bargain. After all, it was no more than Desmond Mellor had instructed.

—◦—

How different it all was from the last time Harry had visited the Russian capital, when they didn't want to let him in, and couldn't wait to throw him out.

On this occasion, when he stepped off the plane he was met by the British Ambassador.

'Welcome home, Mrs Babakova,' said Sir Curtis Keeble, as a chauffeur opened the back door of a Rolls-Royce to allow Yelena to get in. Before Harry could join her, the ambassador whispered, 'Congratulations on your speech, Mr Clifton. But be warned, they've only granted you a visa on condition there will be no heroics this time.'

Harry was well aware what Sir Curtis was referring to. 'Then why are they allowing me to attend the funeral?' he asked.

'Because they consider it the lesser of two evils. If they don't let you in, they're afraid you'll say Babakov was never released, but if they do, they can claim that he was never in jail, always a schoolteacher and is being buried at his local church.'

'Who do they expect to fool with such blatant propaganda?'

'They don't care what the West thinks, they're only interested in how it plays out in Russia, where they control the press.'

'How many people are expected to attend the funeral?' asked Emma.

'Only a few friends and relations will have the courage to turn up,' said Yelena. 'I'd be surprised if it was more than half a dozen.'

'I think it may be a few more than that, Mrs Babakova,' said the ambassador. 'All the morning papers are carrying photographs of you receiving the Nobel Prize on your husband's behalf.'

'I'm surprised they allowed that,' said Harry.

'It's all part of a carefully orchestrated campaign known as "overnight history". Anatoly Babakov was never in jail, he lived peacefully in the suburbs of Moscow and the prize was for his poetry and brilliant novella *Moscow Revisited*. Not one paper mentions *Uncle Joe*, or refers to the speech you gave last night.'

'Then how do you know about it?' asked Harry.

'It's all over the wires. There are even photos of you holding up your pen.'

Emma took Yelena's hand. 'Anatoly will defeat the bastards in the end,' she said.

It was Harry who saw them first. To begin with, small pockets of people huddled together on street corners, holding up pens, pencils, biros, as the car swept by. By the time they drew up outside the little church, the crowd had grown – several hundred, a thousand perhaps, all making their silent protest.

Yelena entered the packed church on Harry's arm, and the three of them were shown to reserved places in the front row. The coffin was borne in on the shoulders of a brother, a cousin and two nephews, none of whom Yelena had seen in years. In fact one of her nephews, Boris, hadn't even been born when Yelena had escaped to America.

Harry had never attended a Russian Orthodox funeral before. He translated the priest's words for Emma, although his Russian was a little rusty. When the service came to an end, the congregation filed out of the church to reassemble around a freshly dug grave.

Harry and Emma stood on either side of Yelena as her husband was lowered into the ground. As his next of kin, she was the first to throw a handful of earth on to the coffin. She then knelt beside the open grave. Harry suspected that nothing would have moved her if the ambassador hadn't bent down and whispered, 'We must leave, Mrs Babakova.'

Harry helped her back to her feet. 'I won't be going with you,' she said quietly.

Emma was about to protest, but Harry simply said, 'Are you sure?'

'Oh yes,' she replied. 'I left him once. I'll never leave him again.'

'Where will you live?' asked Emma.

'With my brother and his wife. Now their children have left home, they have a spare room.'

'Are you absolutely certain?' asked the ambassador.

'Tell me, Sir Curtis,' said Yelena, looking up at the ambassador, 'will you be buried in Russia? Or is there some village in your green and pleasant land . . . ?' He didn't reply.

Emma embraced Yelena. 'We'll never forget you.'

'Nor I you. And like me, Emma, you married a remarkable man.'

'We must leave,' said the ambassador a little more firmly.

Harry and Emma gave Yelena one last hug before they reluctantly left her. 'I've never seen her happier,' said Harry as he joined Emma in the back of the ambassador's Rolls-Royce.

Outside the churchyard, the crowd had grown, every one of them holding their pens high in the air. Harry was about to get back out of the car and join them when Emma put a hand on his arm.

'Be careful, my darling. Don't do anything that will harm Yelena's chances of living a peaceful life.'

Harry reluctantly removed his hand from the door handle, but defiantly waved to the crowd as the car sped away.

At the airport, the police were waiting for them. Not this time to arrest Harry and throw him into jail, but to escort him and Emma on to their plane as quickly as possible. Harry was just about to climb the aircraft steps when a distinguished-looking man stepped forward and touched him on the elbow. Harry turned round, but it was a few moments before he recognized the colonel.

'I'm not going to detain you this time,' said Colonel Marinkin. 'But I wanted you to have this.' He handed Harry a small package and hurried away. Harry walked up the steps to the waiting aircraft and took his seat next to Emma, but didn't open the package until the plane had taken off.

'What is it?' she asked.

'It's the only surviving copy of *Uncle Joe* in Russian, the one Yelena hid in the bookshop.'

'How did you get it?'

'An old man gave it to me. He must have decided I ought to have it, even though he told the court it had been destroyed.'

EPILOGUE

1978

'IT IS SATURDAY, isn't it?' said Emma.

'Yes. Why do you ask?' said Harry, not looking up from his morning paper.

'A post office van's just driven through the gates. But Jimmy doesn't usually deliver on a Saturday morning.'

'Unless it's a telegram?'

'I hate telegrams. I always assume the worst,' said Emma, as she jumped up from the table and hurried out of the room. She had opened the front door before Jimmy could ring the bell.

'Mornin', Mrs Clifton,' he said, touching his cap. 'I've been instructed by head office to deliver this letter.'

He handed over a long thin cream envelope addressed to Harry Clifton Esq. The first thing Emma noticed was that it didn't have a stamp, just a royal crest embossed in red above the words BUCKINGHAM PALACE.

'It must be an invitation to the Queen's garden party.'

'December seems a strange time to be inviting someone to a garden party,' said Jimmy, who touched his cap again, returned to his van and drove off.

Emma closed the front door and quickly returned to the breakfast room. 'It's for you, darling,' she said, handing the envelope to Harry. 'From Buck House,' she added nonchalantly, as she hovered behind him.

Harry put down his paper and studied the envelope, before picking up a knife and slowly slitting it open. He pulled out a letter and unfolded it. He read the contents slowly, then looked up.

'Well?'

He handed the letter to Emma, who had read no further than the opening words, *I am commanded by Her Majesty,* before she said, 'Congratulations, my darling. I only wish your mother was still alive. She would have enjoyed accompanying you to the Palace.' Harry didn't respond. 'Well, say something.'

'This letter should have been addressed to you. You deserve the honour so much more than I do.'

—◦—

'Great photograph of Harry on the front page of *The Times*, holding up a pen,' said Giles.

'Yes, and have you read the speech he gave at the Nobel Prize ceremony?' said Karin. 'Hard to believe he wrote it in twenty-four hours.'

'Some of the most memorable speeches ever written were composed at a time of crisis. Churchill's "blood, toil, tears and sweat", for example, and Roosevelt's "day of infamy" address to Congress the day after Pearl Harbor, were both delivered at a moment's notice,' said Giles, as he poured himself another cup of coffee.

'Praise indeed,' said Karin. 'You should phone Harry and congratulate him. He'd be particularly pleased to hear it coming from you.'

'You're right. I'll call him after breakfast,' said Giles, turning the page of his paper. 'Oh, how sad,' he said, his voice suddenly changing when he saw her photograph on the obituaries page.

'Sad?' repeated Karin, putting down her coffee.

'Your friend Cynthia Forbes-Watson has died. I had no idea she used to be the deputy director of MI6. Did she ever mention it to you?'

Karin froze. 'No, no never.'

'I always knew she'd been something in the Foreign Office, and now I know what that something was. Still, eighty-five, not a bad innings. Are you all right, darling?' Giles said, looking up. 'You're as white as a sheet.'

'I'll miss her,' said Karin. 'She was very kind to me. I'd like to attend her funeral.'

'We should both go. I'll find out the details when I'm in the Lords.'

'Please do. Perhaps I should cancel my trip to Cornwall.'

'No, she wouldn't have wanted that. In any case, your father will be looking forward to seeing you.'

'And what are you doing today?' asked Karin, trying to recover.

'I've got a running three-line whip on the education bill, so I don't suppose I'll be back much before midnight. I'll give you a call first thing in the morning.'

◄○►

The last couple of years had been a nightmare for Virginia.

Once Buck Trend had warned her that Ellie May had tracked down Mr and Mrs Morton, she knew the game was up and reluctantly accepted that there was no point in pursuing Cyrus for any more money. And worse, Trend had made it clear he was no longer willing to represent her unless she paid him a monthly retainer in advance. His way of saying she was a lost cause.

If that wasn't enough, the bank manager had reappeared on the scene. While purporting to offer his condolences on the death of her father, in the next breath he suggested it might be wise given the circumstances – his way of reminding her that the earl's monthly allowance had ceased – for her to consider putting Onslow Gardens on the market, withdrawing Freddie from his expensive pre-prep school, and disposing of her butler, housekeeper and nanny.

What the bank manager didn't realize was that her father had promised to leave her the Glen Fenwick Distillery along with its annual profit of over £100,000. Virginia had travelled up to Scotland the night before to attend the reading of the will, and was looking forward to reminding Mr Fairbrother that, in future, he should only ever address her through a third party.

But there still remained the problem of what to do about Freddie. This wasn't the time to tell her brother, the tenth earl, that she wasn't the child's mother and, even worse, the father was from below stairs.

'Are you expecting any surprises?' Virginia asked him as they walked back towards Fenwick Hall.

'Seems unlikely,' said Archie. 'Father disliked surprises almost as much as he disliked taxes, which is why he signed the estate over to me almost twenty years ago.'

'We all benefited,' said Fraser, throwing another stick for his Labrador to retrieve. 'I ended up with Glencarne, and Campbell got the town house in Edinburgh, all thanks to Pa.'

'I think Pa always planned to leave this world as he entered it,' said Archie. 'Naked and penniless.'

'Except for the distillery,' Virginia reminded them, 'which he promised he'd leave to me.'

'And as you're the only one of us who's produced a son, I expect you can look forward to a whole lot more than just the distillery.'

'Does Glen Fenwick still make a profit?' asked Virginia, innocently.

'Just over ninety thousand pounds last year,' said Archie. 'But I've always felt it could do much better. Pa dug his heels in whenever I suggested he should replace Jock Lamont with someone younger. But Jock retires in September and I think I've found the ideal person to take his place – Sandy Macpherson has been in the business for fifteen years and is full of bright ideas about how to improve the turnover. I was rather hoping you might find the time to meet Sandy while you're in Scotland, Virginia.'

'Of course,' said Virginia, as one of the dogs brought a stick back to her, tail wagging hopefully. 'I'd like to get the future of Glen Fenwick sorted out before I return to London.'

'Good. Then I'll call Sandy later and invite him over for a drink.'

'I look forward to meeting him,' said Virginia. She didn't feel this was the moment to tell her brothers that she'd been approached by the chairman of Johnnie Walker, and would be having breakfast with the chief executive of Teacher's tomorrow morning. The figure of a million had already been bandied about, and she was speculating over how much more she could coax out of them.

'What time are we leaving for Edinburgh?' she asked as they crossed the moat and strolled back into the courtyard.

◄○►

Adrian Sloane joined the queue at the ticket booth. He didn't notice the two men who had slipped in behind him. When he reached the window, he asked for a first-class return to Bristol Temple Meads and handed over three five-pound notes. The clerk gave him a ticket and two pounds and seventy pence change. Sloane turned to find two men blocking his path.

'Mr Sloane,' said the older of them, 'I am arresting you for being in possession of counterfeit money, and trading the same while being aware that it was not legal tender.'

The junior officer quickly thrust Sloane's arms behind his back and handcuffed him. They then marched the prisoner out of the station and bundled him into the back of a waiting police car.

◄○►

Emma always took a second look at any vessel that flew the Canadian flag from its stern. She would then check the name on the hull before her heartbeat would return to normal.

When she looked this time, her heartbeat almost doubled and her legs nearly buckled under her. She double-checked; not a name she was ever likely to forget. She stood and watched the two little tugs steaming up the estuary, black smoke billowing from their funnels as they piloted the rusting old cargo ship towards its final destination.

She changed direction, but as she made her way to the breakers' yard, she couldn't help wondering about the possible consequences of trying to find out the truth after all these years. Surely it would be more sensible just to go back to her office rather than rake over the past . . . the distant past.

But she didn't turn back, and when she reached the yard

Emma headed straight for the chief ganger's office, as if she were simply carrying out her usual morning rounds. She stepped into the railway carriage and was relieved to find that Frank wasn't there, just a secretary typing away. She stood the moment she saw the chairman.

'I'm afraid Mr Gibson isn't here, Mrs Clifton. Shall I go and look for him?'

'No, that won't be necessary,' said Emma. She glanced at the large booking chart on the wall, only to have her worst fears confirmed. The SS *Maple Leaf* had been scheduled for breaking up and work was to begin on Tuesday week. At least that gave her a little time to decide whether to alert Harry or, like Nelson, turn a blind eye. But if Harry found out the *Maple Leaf* had returned to its graveyard and asked her if she'd known about it, she wouldn't be able to lie to him.

'I'm sure Mr Gibson will be back in a few minutes, Mrs Clifton.'

'Don't worry, it's not important. But would you ask him to drop in and see me when he's next passing my office?'

'Can I tell him what it's about?'

'He'll know.'

◄○►

Karin looked out of the window at the countryside rushing by as the train continued on its journey to Truro. But her thoughts were elsewhere as she tried to come to terms with the baroness's death.

She hadn't been in touch with Cynthia for several months, and MI6 had made no attempt to replace her as Karin's handler. Had they lost interest in her? Cynthia had given her nothing of any significance to pass on to Pengelly for some time, and their tea-room meetings had become less and less frequent.

Pengelly had hinted that it wouldn't be long before he expected to return to Moscow. It couldn't be soon enough for her. She was sick of deceiving Giles, the only man she'd ever loved, and was tired of travelling down to Cornwall on the pretence of visiting her father. Pengelly wasn't her father but her stepfather. She loathed him, and had only ever intended to use him to help her escape a regime she despised, so she could be with the man she'd fallen in love with. The man who had become her lover, her husband and her closest friend.

Karin hated not being able to tell Giles the real reason she had tea at the House of Lords with the baroness so often. Now that Cynthia was dead, she would no longer have to live a lie. But when Giles discovered the truth, would he believe she'd escaped the tyranny of East Berlin only because she wanted to be with him? Had she lied once too often?

As the train pulled into Truro, she prayed it was for the last time.

◄○►

'So as I understand it,' said Sloane's solicitor, 'your defence is that you had no idea the money was counterfeit. You found it in the company's safe at Mellor Travel's head office in Bristol and naturally assumed it was legal tender.'

'That, Mr Weatherill, is not only my defence, it also happens to be the truth.'

Weatherill looked down at the charge sheet. 'Is it also correct that earlier in the morning on which you were arrested, you purchased three shirts from Hilditch and Key in Jermyn Street, at a cost of eighteen pounds, and paid for them with four five-pound notes, all of which were counterfeit? You then took a taxi to Paddington, another forged five-pound note, where you purchased a first-class return ticket to Bristol, with three more forged five-pound notes.'

'They all came from the same package,' said Sloane. 'The one I found in the company safe in Mellor's office.'

'The second charge,' continued Weatherill calmly, 'concerns the illegal possession of a further seven thousand three hundred and twenty pounds found in a safe in your flat in Mayfair, which you also knew to be counterfeit.'

'That's ridiculous,' said Sloane. 'I had no idea the money was counterfeit when I came across it in Mellor's safe.'

'It's just unfortunate that you transferred the money from Mellor's office in Bristol to your flat in London.'

'I only moved the money there for safekeeping. I can't be expected to travel down to Bristol every time I need some petty cash to carry out Mellor's business.'

'And then there's the problem of the two written statements obtained by the police,' said Weatherill. 'One from a Miss Angela Castle, and the other from Mr Mellor himself.'

'A convicted criminal.'

'Then let's begin with his statement. He says there was never more than a thousand pounds in cash in his Bristol safe.'

'He's a liar.'

'According to Miss Castle's statement, Mellor withdrew one thousand pounds in cash from the company account every quarter, for his personal use.'

'She's obviously covering for him.'

'Mellor's bank, the Nat West in Queen Street, Bristol,' continued Weatherill, 'has supplied the police with copies of all his business and personal accounts over the past five years. They confirm that neither he nor the company ever withdrew more than a thousand pounds a quarter in cash.'

'This is a set-up,' said Sloane.

'There is one further charge,' said Weatherill. 'That you have, for several years, been collaborating with a Mr Ronald Boyle, a well-known counterfeiter. Mr Boyle has signed an affidavit in which he alleges that you regularly met him at the King's Arms, a public house in Soho, where you would exchange one thousand pounds in legal tender for ten thousand pounds in forged notes.'

Sloane smiled for the first time. If only you'd quit while you were ahead, Desmond, you'd have had me banged up for a decade, he said to himself. But you couldn't resist over-egging the pudding, could you?

◄◦►

Giles was dozing when the badged messenger handed him a slip of paper. He unfolded it, read it and was suddenly wide awake: *Please contact the Cabinet Secretary urgently.*

Giles couldn't remember the last time Sir Alan had asked him to call him at No.10, let alone urgently. He didn't move immediately, honouring the House convention that you don't leave the chamber during a colleague's speech. But the moment Lord Barnett had finished explaining his proposed formula for Scotland and resumed his place, Giles slipped out of the chamber and headed for the nearest phone.

'Number Ten Downing Street.'

'Sir Alan Redmayne.'

'Who's calling please?'

'Giles Barrington.'

The next voice he heard couldn't be mistaken.

'Giles' – he'd never called him Giles before – 'are you able to come across to Number Ten immediately?'

◄o►

Sloane's solicitor moved quickly and the police were in no position to turn down his request.

Five other men were selected to take part in the line-up. All of them were roughly the same age as Sloane, and all wore similar City suits, white shirts and striped ties. As Mr Weatherill pointed out to the investigating officer, if his client really had visited the King's Arms on several occasions to exchange real notes for counterfeit ones, it shouldn't be difficult for Mr Boyle to pick out his accomplice in an identity parade.

An hour later, Sloane was released, all the charges against him dropped. Boyle, who had no desire to return to Ford and face Mellor, turned Queen's evidence, confessed to the set-up and was shipped off to HMP Belmarsh to await trial on charges of forgery, giving false evidence and perverting the course of justice.

A month later, Desmond Mellor came up in front of the parole board, with an application to have his sentence halved on the grounds of good behaviour. He was turned down and told that he would not only serve his full sentence, but that further charges against him were being prepared by the DPP.

When Sloane was next interviewed by the police, he was only too happy to supply further evidence to incriminate Mellor.

'Do you wish to add anything else to your statement?' asked the investigating officer.

'Only one thing,' said Sloane. 'You should look into the role Lady Virginia Fenwick played in this whole operation. I have a feeling Mr Boyle might be able to assist you.'

—◄○►—

'Mr Mellor is on line three,' said Rachel.

'Tell him to go to hell,' replied Sebastian.

'He said he's only allowed three minutes.'

'All right, put him through,' said Seb reluctantly, curious to know what the damn man could possibly want.

'Good morning, Mr Clifton. Decent of you to take my call, all things considered. I don't have a lot of time, so I'll get straight to the point. Would you be willing to visit me at Ford on Sunday? There's something I'd like to discuss with you that could be of mutual benefit.'

'What could I possibly want to discuss with you?' said Sebastian, barely able to control his temper. He was just about to slam the phone down, when Mellor said, 'Adrian Sloane.'

Sebastian hesitated for a moment, then opened his diary. 'This Sunday isn't possible as it's my daughter's birthday. But I'm free the following Sunday.'

'It will be too late by then,' said Mellor, without explanation.

Seb hesitated again. 'What time are visiting hours?' he eventually managed, but the line had gone dead.

—◄○►—

'How many years have you worked for the company, Frank?' asked Emma.

'Nigh on forty, ma'am. Served your father, and your grandfather before him.'

'So you'll have heard the story of the *Maple Leaf*?'

'Before my time, ma'am, but everyone in the yard is familiar with the tale, though few ever speak of it.'

'I have a favour to ask, Frank. Could you put together a small gang of men who can be trusted?'

414

'I've two brothers and a cousin who've never worked for anyone else but Barrington's.'

'They'll need to come in on a Sunday, when the yard is closed. I'll pay them double time, in cash, and there will be an incentive bonus of the same amount in twelve months' time, but only if I've heard nothing of the work they carried out that day.'

'Very generous, ma'am,' said Frank, touching the peak of his cap.

'When will they be able to start?'

'Next Sunday afternoon. The yard will be closed until Tuesday, Monday being a bank holiday.'

'You do realize you haven't asked me what it is I want you to do?'

'No need to, ma'am. And if we should find what you're lookin' for in the double bottom, what then?'

'I ask no more than that the remains of Arthur Clifton should be given a Christian burial.'

'And if we find nothing?'

'Then it will be a secret the five of us take to our graves.'

◄o►

Archibald Douglas James Iain Fenwick, the tenth Earl of Fenwick, was among the last to arrive.

When he entered the room, everyone rose, acknowledging that the title had been passed on to the next generation. He joined his two younger brothers, Fraser and Campbell, in the front row, where one chair remained unoccupied.

At that moment Virginia was just leaving the Caledonian Hotel, having enjoyed her breakfast with the chief executive of Teacher's Scotch whisky. A price had been agreed, and all that remained was for the lawyers to draw up a contract.

She decided to walk the short distance to Bute Street, confident that she still had a few minutes to spare. When she arrived outside the offices of Ferguson, Ferguson and Laurie, she found the front door open. She stepped inside to be greeted by an articled clerk, who was glancing at his watch.

'Good morning, my lady. Would you please make your way up to the first floor, as the reading of the will is about to begin.'

'I think you'll find they won't start without me,' Virginia said before she began to climb the stairs to the first floor. The sound of expectant chattering suggested the direction she should be heading for.

When she entered the crowded room, nobody stood. She made her way to the front row and took the empty seat between Archie and Fraser. She had hardly settled when a door in front of her opened and three gentlemen dressed in identical black jackets and pinstriped grey trousers entered the room and took their places behind a long table. Did anyone still wear stiff wing collars in 1978, Virginia wondered. Yes, the partners of Ferguson, Ferguson and Laurie, when reading the last will and testament of a Scottish earl.

Roderick Ferguson, the senior partner, poured himself a glass of water. Virginia thought she recognized him, and then realized he must be the son of the man who had represented her when she had divorced Giles over twenty years ago. The same bald dome with a thin girdle of grey hair, the same beak nose and half-moon glasses. Virginia even wondered if they were the same pair of half-moon glasses.

As the clock behind him struck nine, the senior partner glanced in the direction of the earl and, after receiving a nod, turned his attention to the assembled gathering. He coughed – another affectation inherited from his father.

'Good morning,' he began, in a clear, authoritative voice with a slight Edinburgh burr. 'My name is Roderick Ferguson, and I am the senior partner of Ferguson, Ferguson and Laurie. I am joined today by two other partners of the firm. I had the privilege,' he continued, 'as did my father before me, of representing the late earl as his legal advisor, and it has fallen upon me to administer his last will and testament.' He took a sip of water, followed by another cough.

'The earl's final will was executed some two years ago, and

duly witnessed by the procurator fiscal and the Viscount Younger of Leckie.'

Virginia's mind had been drifting, but she quickly focused her full attention on Mr Ferguson when he turned to the first page of the will and began to distribute what was left of her father's spoils.

Archie, the tenth earl, who had been running the estate for the past twenty years, was touched that the old man left him a pair of Purdey shotguns, his favourite fishing rod and a walking stick that William Gladstone had left behind after spending the night at Fenwick Hall. He had also bequeathed him Logan, his faithful Labrador, but he had died the day after his master had been laid to rest.

The second son, Fraser, a mere lord, had been running the Glencarne estate, with its extensive stalking, fishing and shooting rights, for almost as many years. He received an oil portrait of his grandmother, the Dowager Duchess Katherine, painted by Munnings, and the sword that Collingwood had worn at Trafalgar.

The third son, Campbell, who had lived at 43 Bute Square for the past fifteen years since his days as a houseman at Edinburgh Royal Infirmary, ended up with a clapped-out Austin 30 and a set of ancient golf clubs. Campbell didn't possess a driving licence, and had never played a round of golf in his life. However, none of the brothers were surprised, or displeased, with their lot. The old man had done them proud, as there wouldn't be a lot of inheritance tax to pay on a fishing rod or a 1954 Austin 30.

When Mr Ferguson turned the page, Virginia sat bolt upright. After all, she was the next in line. However, the next recipient to be named was the earl's sister, Morag, who inherited several pieces of the family jewellery and a rent-free cottage on the estate, all of which would revert to the tenth earl on her demise. There then followed several cousins, nephews and nieces, as well as some old friends, before Mr Ferguson moved on to retainers, servants, ghillies and gardeners who had served the earl for a decade or more.

The senior partner then turned to what looked to Virginia like the last page of the will.

'And finally,' he said, 'I leave the five-hundred-acre estate that lies west of the Carley Falls, and includes the Glen Fenwick Distillery –' he couldn't resist pausing to cough – 'to my only grandson, the Hon Frederick Archibald Iain Bruce Fenwick.' An audible gasp went up in the room, but Ferguson ignored it. 'And I ask my eldest son, Archibald, to be responsible for the running of the distillery until Frederick acquires the age of twenty-five.'

The tenth earl looked just as surprised as everyone else in the room, as his father had never mentioned his plans for the distillery. But if that was what the old man wanted, he would make sure his wishes were carried out in keeping with the family motto, "Without fear or favour".

Virginia was about to storm out of the room, but it was clear that Mr Ferguson hadn't finished. A few murmurings could be heard as he refilled his glass with water before returning to his task.

'And last and certainly least,' he said, which created the silence he had intended, 'I come to my only daughter, Virginia. To her I bequeath one bottle of Maker's Mark whisky, in the hope that it will teach her a lesson, although I have my doubts.'

◄◦►

Karin's stepfather opened the front door and welcomed her with an unusually warm smile.

'I have some good news to share with you,' he said as she stepped into the house, 'but it will have to wait until later.'

Could it just be possible, thought Karin, that this nightmare was finally coming to an end? Then she saw a copy of *The Times* lying on the kitchen table, open at the obituaries page. She stared at the familiar photograph of Baroness Forbes-Watson and wondered if it was just a coincidence, or if he had left it open simply to provoke her.

Over coffee, they talked of nothing consequential, but Karin could hardly miss the three suitcases standing by the door, which appeared to herald imminent departure. Even so, she became more anxious by the minute, as Pengelly remained far too relaxed and friendly for her liking. What was the old army expression, 'demob happy'?

'Time for us to talk about more serious matters,' he said, placing a finger to his lips. He went out to the hallway and removed his heavy overcoat from a peg by the door. Karin thought about making a run for it, but if she did, and all he was going to tell her was that he was returning to Moscow, her cover would be blown. He helped her on with her coat and accompanied her outside.

Karin was taken by surprise when he gripped her arm firmly and almost marched her down the deserted street. Usually she linked her arm in his so that any passing stranger would assume they were father and daughter out for a walk, but not today. She decided that if they came across anyone, even the old colonel, she would stop and talk to him, because she knew Pengelly wouldn't dare risk their cover being blown if there was a witness present.

Pengelly continued his jovial banter. This was so out of character Karin became even more apprehensive, her eyes darting warily in every direction, but no one appeared to be taking a constitutional on that bleak, grey day.

Once they reached the edge of the woods, Pengelly looked around, as he always did, to see if anyone was following them. If there was, they would retrace their steps and head back to the cottage. But not this afternoon.

Although it was barely four o'clock, the light was already beginning to fade and it was becoming darker by the minute. He gripped her arm more firmly as they stepped off the road and on to the path that led into the woods. His voice changed to match the cold night air.

'I know you'll be pleased to hear, Karin' – he never called her Karin – 'that I've been promoted and will soon be returning to Moscow.'

'Congratulations, comrade. Well deserved.'

He didn't loosen his grip. 'So this will be our last meeting,' he continued. Could she possibly hope that . . . 'But Marshal

Koshevoi has entrusted me with one final assignment.' Pengelly didn't elaborate, almost as if he wanted her to take her time thinking about it. As they walked deeper into the woods, it was becoming so dark that Karin could hardly see a yard in front of her. Pengelly, however, seemed to know exactly where he was going, as if every pace had been rehearsed.

'The head of counter-surveillance,' he said calmly, 'has finally uncovered the traitor in our ranks, the person who has for years been betraying the motherland. I have been chosen to carry out the appropriate retribution.'

His firm grip finally relaxed and he released her. Her first instinct was to run, but he had chosen the spot well. A clump of trees behind her, to her right the disused tin mine, to her left a narrow path she could barely make out in the darkness, and towering above her, Pengelly, who couldn't have looked calmer or more alert.

He slowly removed a pistol from the pocket of his overcoat, and held it menacingly by his side. Was he hoping she would make a run for it, so it would take more than a single bullet to kill her? But she remained rooted to the spot.

'You're a traitor,' said Pengelly, 'who has done more damage to our cause than any agent in the past. So you must die a traitor's death.' He glanced in the direction of the mine shaft. 'I'll be back in Moscow long before they discover your body, if they ever do.'

He raised the gun slowly until it was level with Karin's eyes. Her last thought before he pulled the trigger was of Giles.

The sound of a single shot echoed through the woods, and a flock of starlings flew high into the air as her body slumped to the ground.

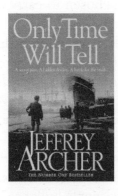
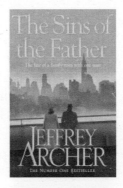
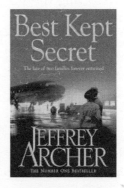
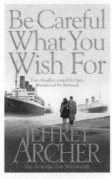
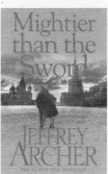
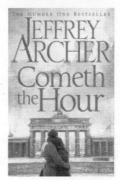